A DUBLIN INK NOVEL

SIENNA BLAKE

DARK INK

A DUBLIN INK NOVEL

SIENNA BLAKE

Dark Ink: a novel / by Sienna Blake. – 1st Ed.
First Edition: January 2023
Published by SB Publishing

Editing services by Proof Positive: http://proofpositivepro.com.

AUTHOR'S NOTE:

This book is darker than the previous novels in my Dublin Ink series.
It deals with violence and drug addiction.
And contains dubious consent, degradation, impact play and breath play.

For anyone who's lived in the dark

And who must forever walk with demons in their shadows

RIAN

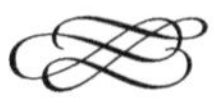

Rian. [Say: REE-an.] Means "King" in Gaelic.

The phone call that changed everything interrupted my song.

It was fate being cruel, of course. If the phone call had never come through, I would have listened to the beautiful lyrics in the warmth of September's last sunny days. I would have closed my eyes as the breeze rustled the brightly coloured leaves of the Dublin Art School campus. I would have sighed deeply, enjoyed my high as I sat on this park bench. Later, crossed the street, passed through those wrought iron gates, visited the dean, agreed to teach another class that semester, returned to the tattoo parlour I ran with my two best friends, continued on in life happy and healthy and sane. I would have had everything.

Except her.

But the phone call came through just then. It came through

and guaranteed that I *would* see her. Guaranteed that the best thing to ever happen to me would appear in my life.

Guaranteed that I would then destroy it.

I was damned either way: happiness, but without her. Misery, but without her. So it didn't matter. Didn't fucking matter at all that the phone call that changed everything interrupted the song that fateful afternoon.

"Who is this?" I answered.

"Raglan Road" was paused on the locked screen of my phone. I could see my reflection in the rest of the black screen. If I'd known it was the last time I would be at peace for a long time, I might have tried to remember it better, my face. To paint it later. To have proof that life could be something other than fucking agonising.

My brother's voice on the other line was like a freight train to the chest.

"Rian. What's the craic?"

Such casualness. Such simple words. My name. Something practically the entire Dublin Art School knew. Thousands of students. And a casual greeting. Something someone on the bus says. Something your weed dealer says. No acknowledgement of blood…of blood *soured*.

"Liam."

At least I had the decency to say his name with spite. To infuse it with something personal: a unique Merrick family blend of hatred and love, anger and understanding, pain and sadness and futile wishing that things had somehow been different. At least I acted like we were still brothers, even if we were estranged (at best).

"Um, are ye alright?" my older brother asked.

I laughed. Maybe because I was a little high. Or maybe because it was funny. That's exactly what he'd say to me after my eldest brother, Alan, or my father beat me. Exactly the words he used when he knelt in front of my trembled huddle with a warm washcloth and an apologetic frown. Exactly all he did: not sticking up for me, not interfering, not taking me away. Just blotting at my bleeding lip and saying, "Um, are ye alright?" Maybe it was funny, how so much time can pass and not a goddamn thing at all changes. Or maybe it was just the weed after all.

"Let's see, Liam," I answered, "not as alright as I was ten seconds ago."

"Rian—"

"Ten seconds ago I still had the chance to get hit by a bus instead of answering the phone. Ten seconds ago a tree limb could have fallen on me and I wouldn't have had to hear whatever you have to say. Ten seconds ago the earth could have literally opened wide and swallowed me whole and I wouldn't have to be here digging my nails into my palms to keep from hanging up on you."

"I don't want to fight."

I already knew that. There was no need at all for him to say that. I'd known that my whole cursed childhood: Liam did not want to fight. Did not want conflict. Did not want to risk a broken cheekbone himself.

"Look," he said, "I don't know how we got off on the wrong foot after I said a handful of words, but—"

"That's a lot for you," I said, unable to keep the bitterness from my voice.

The sunshine was suddenly irritating. The blue of the sky harsh and unnatural. I shifted uncomfortably on the park bench as Liam sighed.

"What is that supposed to mean?" he asked.

I didn't answer. I left it up to him to remember when he ever voiced five whole words to my father. Or to Alan. "Stop" was only one word, and I can't remember him ever uttering even that. I was the runt, the youngest, the one who reminded everyone too much of Ma. *I* was the voiceless. But Liam felt he was the kind brother because he didn't ever hit me. The gentle one because he kept his mouth closed instead of verbally abusing me.

"Rian," Liam eventually said. I could hear him pacing, could hear the familiar creak of old floorboards of the place we'd grown up.

"He's sick."

The urge to throw the phone away from my ear was only slightly less violent than the urge to throw up. I could have imagined Liam anywhere in the world. In the States. In the south of France. In Tahiti. Right across the street from me at the college bus stop. But I never imagined he would be there. That he could ever stand to step foot back onto that godforsaken farm.

I grew claustrophobic despite the expansiveness of the blue dome above me. I sensed those same farmhouse walls moving in on me. I could remember pressing my face against their faded wallpaper to try and hide, wallpaper my da had torn at in the night because she picked it out, because she was gone. I was nowhere near that sagging porch, but my head whipped around like he would appear suddenly behind every big, wide oak tree. I swore he was close. He was coming for me. I strained for any hint of him on the line—a grumbled curse. The shattering of a beer bottle. The crack of a fist against bone. A wet cough.

"Why did you call me?" I asked, my voice hoarse like I'd been screaming.

I wondered if my father was watching Liam now, his red-rimmed eyes narrowing before spitting from the corner of his narrow lips. Was Alan there? In the shadows behind him? Rubbing his knuckles against his palm?

Liam had the decency to sound reluctant at least, to clear his throat in hesitation before daring to say aloud, "I know he wasn't the best father, but..."

I was no longer on that bench, there across from the college. I no longer had good friends who cared for me, cared about my health, my happiness. I no longer worked as an artist, as a professor, as a tattoo parlour owner. I was a kid again. Too scrawny for hard labour. Hands too feminine. Skin too soft. Eyes too much like the sky on the coldest day of winter when the air seems about to snap in two. Eyes too much like *hers*. I was a kid again who was beaten for not being strong. Beaten for not pulling his weight. Beaten for drawing when the others worked. Beaten because it felt good for him. Beaten because he couldn't beat her for leaving. For dying.

The corners of my mouth curled up into a cruel smile. It wasn't a smile fit for a sunny autumn day, but it was no longer a sunny autumn day. Not for me. It wasn't the smile of a healthy man. But I wasn't healthy; I was already circling the drain whether I knew it or not. It wasn't even a natural smile, but I didn't know cruelty naturally. I'd been taught it. Shown it. Had it beaten into me: the wickedness of destroying someone else's life.

"Don't worry," I said, smiling through each and every word. "If I don't see him again in this life—and I won't, God as my witness I will not ever see that man again—I'm sure I'll see him in hell one day. We'll have a big family reunion, us fecking Merricks."

I hung up without waiting for a reply. Nothing Liam could have said or done would have changed my mind. The time for words, the time for action was years ago.

I hung up.

The "Raglan Road" song resumed.

Just as I saw her.

Originally a poem by Patrick Kavanagh, it'd been put to song by Luke Kelly. He sang about a dark haired women who he first saw on Raglan Road and the words slithered into my ears like an omen, wrapped around my throat like a vice grip, intoxicated me like a drug. He knew pursuing her would hurt him but he did it anyway.

She was across the street. Cars passing blocked her from view only for her to reappear, stunning me anew. The wind tugged at her dark hair that she struggled to keep out of her pale heart-shaped face. She looked around her with darting, nervous eyes, like the world was also not as it seemed for her: not blue skies, not warm sunshine, not autumn leaves dancing as they fell. She weaved along the busy sidewalk with a sketchbook clutched tightly to her chest. I imagined it was how you were supposed to hold airline seats when you crash.

I stood. I didn't intend to. I didn't remember telling my legs to move. But I couldn't stop myself. I was drawn to her, my Raglan Road girl, as she disappeared through the wrought iron gate of campus.

I darted across the road. Cars honked and tires screeched and maybe it was me who would be awaiting my father in hell instead of the other way around. But I didn't care. I ran after her. I had to find her. To grab ahold of her. As if touching her would keep her from dissolving into ether.

My eyes skimmed the throngs of students for her as I imagined brushing my fingertips along her pale skin, walking them along the fine bones of her wrists, as delicate as a bird's. I'd slip a single flower between her rigid fingers. *But what kind, what kind?* I thought as I darted down random cobblestone paths, slipping on leaves, bumping into armfuls of textbooks.

A rose?

Never. Not for *her*. Not red. Too overt for the baggy, tattered sweatshirt she huddled beneath like a child.

Lily? No. Not white. Too innocent for those full red lips.

No, for her…a wisp of baby's breath. Gentle as a fine frost. Picked right from the garden.

I spun round.

"Where is she?" I asked a passing student.

He darted away.

"Where is she?" I shouted after him.

I tore at my hair, fumbled in my pocket for a joint. So, my

father was dying, was he? Good. The bastard could rot. He could be buried in a pine box and eaten by the worms.

I wouldn't cry when he died.

I was sure of it. I hadn't cried since my mother's funeral. That earned me an open palm to the back of the head. A hissed, "Man up, you little sissy." I didn't learn many life lessons fast, but I learned that one instantly.

But for my Raglan Road girl, I'd cry. For her I'd take the pain.

The weed did nothing for me. Already I was craving something stronger. I offered my joint half-smoked to a kid on a skateboard. He reached for it and I snatched it out of reach.

"Tell me where she went first."

"Who?"

"My Raglan Road girl."

Me and my smouldering joint were left alone on the sidewalk. It burned down to my fingertips. Burned me. I let it. Let it hurt.

She was gone and my father was dying and if the phone hadn't interrupted the song, I would have been fine. *She* would have been fine.

But now I had to self-destruct.

I needed to find her. I needed to catch her like she caught me.

A snare weaved for me. A snare weaved for her. My Raglan Road girl.

A funeral for us all.

EITHNE

Eithne: [say: EN-ya]. Means "little fire" in Gaelic.

The figure taking form on the easel in front of me was that of a man walking toward me along the beach from a long way away. I tried to capture the assuredness of his gait with the charcoal in my fingers. His head was down, bent severely, like he was trying to keep out the wind or sleep while walking. I sketched the broadness of his shoulders, the narrowness of his hips. But his face was elusive. My strokes were steady, but he was not. He was coming closer and closer and I was trying to capture more of him, all of him, but it was so warm and the charcoal was melting and—

"Not even close to a likeness, Ms Brady."

I jolted from my daze to just catch the unimpressed frown of my professor before he continued on to the next student. I wiped at my eyes only to realise my fingers were covered in charcoal. I bunched up the sleeve of my old sweatshirt to clean myself. Though I probably just added to the dark circles under my eyes.

"Turn," the professor called out to the nude model on the pedestal in the ring of drawing students as I tore the man on the beach from my pad.

It felt like I'd barely focused on the middle-aged woman on the pedestal before the professor was thanking her for her time. My sketchpad remained mere scribbles and lonely hesitant lines. I couldn't seem to grab ahold of any of her. Not her full hips. Not her breasts that sagged against her top of her stomach. Not her pigeon-toed stance that drew everything inward, as if to hide, as if to show as little of herself as possible. Nothing of *her* made it onto my page. But I don't think she was the problem. It was me.

I was too tired to take on anyone else. That's what drawing someone required: to let them in. To give them room within my soul. To find myself within them, and allow them to do the same within me.

In that moment it was just too much. I wondered if that would change any time soon.

The sad part was it didn't have to. I'd already decided I would put my frivolous dreams on the back burner. I'd already switched my degree toward more practical pursuits, art in commercial advertising, art in communication, digital art for branding. I'd already circled entry-level job opportunities for after I graduated in a semester: steady, solid jobs. Jobs with deadlines. Jobs with cubicles. Jobs with a guaranteed income stream. Jobs that did not require of me what art that stirred my passions required of me.

It was frightening to think that I'd never get that back, that room within in, that space within me to create, to make something beautiful.

But it was more frightening that I wouldn't be able to be there for Stewart if he needed me. And he would, I knew. Need me. It was only a matter of time.

I was startled out of my daze by a commotion at the door of the studio. Whispers travelled to me from both sides of the circle as if it had been lit on fire. I leaned to the side of my easel to see, just as all the other students were doing. When I saw *him*, I understood. *He* had lit us on fire.

Tall, wide shoulders, narrow tapered waist like he'd stepped off my paper and into real life, tattoos covering both forearms from under the pushed-up charcoal cable-knit sweater. He stood all harsh stern lines, hard jaw, sharp cheekbones, intensity rolling off his every move.

"Professor Merrick," my professor protested. "Really this is quite improper."

Rian Merrick—*the* Rian Merrick—patted the man who *should* have been the next nude model on the shoulder and leaned against him heavily. His grin looked almost wicked and it didn't reach his eyes, hooded under thick dark brows.

"No bother, mate," he said to my professor. His deep melodic voice reaching in to touch the depths of me. "I'm not teaching this semester. It's grand."

I watched, stunned like all the rest, as Rian told the scheduled model that he could go before Rian climbed up onto the pedestal and pulled off his sweater and the ripped black t-shirt underneath. That disappeared too. Then he unbuttoned his black ripped denim…

We shouldn't have been surprised. But we were. Or at least, I was.

Everyone knew Rian Merrick. He was sort of infamous on campus. The bad boy professor. Known for…well, known for shite like this: barging into classrooms unannounced, taking over, and stripping down to nothing in front of his students. Or *not*-students apparently. During my first two years I'd tried so hard to land a class with him. But so had everyone else. Just to be in the same room as genius. To let some of his sparkle rub off on us. To see what crazy shite he'd do next. It didn't matter now. He wasn't teaching anymore; I wouldn't have needed it for my degree anyway.

But *I* knew Rian Merrick because he won the National Gallery of Ireland's Young Portrait Prize for his haunting likeness of Ireland's beloved poet, Patrick Kavanagh. Then he'd won the RTE, This is Art! Competition for a disturbing metal sculpture of this man-creature who seemed to be eating himself from the inside. Rian Merrick had been Ireland's brightest young artistic star, a genius who refused to stick to one mode of art, to one form, to one style.

Then to piss the fine art world off, he'd taken to tattooing and picked up the grand prize at Dublin's Tattoo Convention years ago. I just so happened to have a poster of him I used to hide from my father in my closet. I was just a young dreamer at the time and he was my idol: daring, bold, talented as fuck...and beautiful. If my father knew the thoughts I had about Rian as a fifteen-year-old girl with my ma's gold cross between my teeth and my fingers cresting the edges of my panties...

Rian removed the last remaining piece of clothing he had on: his boxers. He straightened in the nip without a lick of hesitation.

The room erupted into a small roar.

"Enough, enough!" my professor chastised the class. "What have I told you of maintaining professionalism? We are to respect the human form in all its myriad of shapes and sizes, now aren't we?"

"Yes, Professor," came the red-cheeked mumbles from the class.

I sucked in a heavy breath as my gaze travelled down Rian's naked form, over the rippling muscles of his back beneath his tattoos, like him, a jumble of styles, a refusal to be categorised, to be confined. I swallowed down the lump in my throat before I dared to look over the swell of his muscled ass, down his tattooed thighs, long and lean, before whispering to myself, "Yes, Professor."

"Draw, draw, draw!" my professor snapped, clapping his hands as he circled the room.

I dropped the charcoal. It fell right from between my fingertips.

"Clumsy, clumsy, Ms Brady," my professor grumbled. "You're wasting valuable time!"

I scrambled for it and stood. But the second I had the piece of charcoal back between my fingers, the second I felt its silkiness, the second I let my eyes fall on Rian's still form, I needed no time at all.

His form fell onto the page as if he had landed there, the muscled lines, the sharpness, the intensity. My heart raced in my chest. I hadn't drawn so effortlessly, so confidently, lost completely in the art itself, for so long. It felt like riding a bike again: the thrill of the wind in your hair, the wonderful strain of your pumping thighs, the fear of going just a little too fast down the grassy hill.

"Turn!" my professor shouted. Rian shifted, angling more toward me. "Draw!"

The studio was filled with the noise of pages being torn from sketchpads, pages dropping to the floor, stools screeching as student scooted closer.

I was barely aware of it and I lost myself in the way my charcoal dashed across the page.

"Turn!" my professor called out. Pages tearing. Pages falling. Fingers flying. "Draw, draw!"

My eyes did not leave Rian as my charcoal moved across the page. I had his profile now. I felt the severity of his strong jaw in the angular strikes of my charcoal. It was as if I was drawing my own hand over his skin. The stubble of a few days prickly. The heat of his skin searing me, trickling down my spine, rushing through my blood like a drug.

I could almost feel the bones his of cheek as I pressed the charcoal in harder, deeper. There was the sharpness of his nose.

The deep sockets of his eyes staring out over the easels. The brooding brow. I no longer drew with the light touch, half lost in dream. I practically tore at the page, my breath going ragged. Gouged it like my little piece of charcoal had turned into a flashing claw.

"Turn!" my professor shouted. And Rian was turning even further toward me. "Draw, draw, draw!"

I could almost taste him as I shaped his mouth, the plumpness of his bottom lip, the pronounced Cupid's bow. I could almost lean in and lick the hollow of his throat. Could imagine his scent —musky and masculine—in my nose.

I could *feel* the heat of him as I shaped his body onto my page. The roundness of his shoulders. The ridges of his six-pack. The tattoos that moved over him as naturally as wind over the emerald hills, wave after wave. Shivers ran up and down my spine as I fleshed out each defined muscle, revelling at the contrast between the curves of his stomach to the sharpness of that hip bone, the V down to…

His cock. Thick and perfect. My mouth watered.

I did not flinch from drawing that, from drawing all of him. From *feeling* the weight of his cock in my hand, blood surging in my veins as he hardened.

"Whore," his voice called out in my mind, *"just like your mother."*

I kept drawing even as I squeezed my thighs together, even as the shame of arousal threatened to stop me.

"Look at you. Drawing a naked man. Drawing his cock. *Enjoying it. Wanting it. Disgusting, Eithne."*

But I didn't stop. Not even as my knees trembled, as my lungs tightened around every withheld groan, as my nipples pebbled to painful points against my bra. Not even as lust and shame burned me with its poisonous cocktail.

This was beauty. Rian was beauty.

And he was turning even more toward me. One more rotation and he would be facing me head-on.

"Welcome back, Ms Brady," my professor said as he walked behind me, hands clasped behind his back. "Lovely, very lovely."

I tore Rian off my pad, unable to take it anymore. Needing a fresh blank sheet. Needing relief.

I looked down only for a moment. Only long enough to grab a fresh piece of charcoal.

"Turn!" my professor shouted. "Draw!"

I looked up to Rian.

Our eyes met. And he and I sucked in a collective breath.

My charcoal remained suspended just above the page. I did not dive into his drawing like the others. Despite him being all there for me. Facing me. All of him exposed. All of him ready for me to claim.

Rian looked at me like he knew me. Like he'd recognised me from somewhere. Like he was stunned to see me once more. And it confused me. Because we hadn't met, despite the nights I'd dreamed of him in my bed, pressing my thighs together to try to ease the ache and hating myself for it. He couldn't possibly know me.

So why was he looking at me like he did?

My professor called for Rian to turn, but he did not move. He shouted it again and still the same.

"Professor Merrick, please," he tried.

Rian turned, but his face stayed on me. He smiled. He laughed. He shook his head and looked away. That one moment was all it took. My phone buzzed. Rian had released me enough that I thought to check it.

It was Stewart.

It was urgent.

RIAN

The auditorium of third-year students all blinked at me like baby owls.

I stood behind the lectern. Drummed my pencil against its edge. Tapped my toe impatiently beneath it. I sucked in an irritated breath. I exhaled noisily.

One student cleared his throat. Another coughed a tiny little cough hidden behind cupped hands. Still another one shifted the tiniest bit in her chair and blushed bright red as her chair creaked in the eerily silent classroom.

I wished one of them would have the fucking nerve to say something. To do something. To get up and leave. To yawn rudely. To turn to his neighbour and mutter with a flicked thumb toward me, "What the fuck is up with this guy?"

They'd never make great artists. The whole fucking lot of them. Wasted. Ruined. Spoiled. They'd had the talent trained out of them. The rawness polished. The gifts wrapped up in bureaucratic bullshite.

They'd all been on time. Worse than that, they'd all been to class early. I had to watch them all, one by one, filing in. One by one, smiling so fucking politely at me. One by one, committing the greatest sin of all: *not. being. her.*

"How'd you all find out I was teaching a class this semester?" I demanded.

One of the students raised his hand and I threw my pencil at him.

"You're not in kindergarten," I shouted at him. "I'm not going to fecking call on you. Just tell me."

"We received an email," the kid said.

Poor thing, I'd scared him shiteless. Maybe I'd make an artist out of him after all. Pass on the favour my dear old man did for me.

"An email," I said. "And this went out to all third-year students? It said I was teaching. And to come?"

The kid almost raised his hand again before nodding and answering with a croak, "That's right."

I drummed my fingers on the lectern. I'd only agreed to take on this class in order to find my Raglan Road girl. I'd almost been convinced she'd just been a figment of my imagination, a mirage, an LSD-induced siren, when I'd turned on that pedestal to find her right in front of me. Staring back at me. As real as my demons. I'd been shocked, then a rush like the first hit of a crack pipe. She was real. And she was mine.

Imagine my shock, my fury, when I looked away for one fecking second, one bleedin' second to catch my breath, to calm the pounding of my heart in my ears and found her gone.

I'd barely had the sense to put my pants back on before I'd stormed into the dean's office.

"You want to teach?" the dean asked, raising his white eyebrows up over his drooping eyelids. "Professor Merrick, you told me you wouldn't, and I'm quoting you here, 'Dublin Art School can shove it.' That you'd teach here again over your dead body."

I dismissed his words with a wave of my hand. "Yes, yes," I said. "But aren't we all just decomposing flesh, Dean?"

He stared at me in continued shock.

I sat down, carded my fingers under my chin. "I need to teach something all third-year students are required to take."

He'd asked if I was high.

I said "quite".

That's how I ended up here, in front of a lecture hall of third years at the start of term.

"Would she have gotten these emails?" I asked, glaring at the clock. Fifteen minutes past the start of class. And counting. Each second reducing the chance she would show up.

"She?" my star student asked.

"Yes, *her*," I said.

I received nothing but confused looks. I scooped up the chalk from the board and sketched her. My Raglan Road girl. It was easy enough. I'd already practiced dozens of times. I stepped away from the board and smacked the point of the chalk against it.

"Her!" I said loudly. "Did *she* get the email about this class?"

They were all just as clueless as before. All just hunks of clay with unblinking glass beads wedged deep inside. Clueless about love. Clueless about passion. Clueless about pain.

I jabbed the piece of chalk at the boy in the front row. The one with all the answers. The one who knew fucking nothing. Nothing at all.

"Listen, kid, your grade in my class depends on telling me. Your future in the art world itself depends on you telling me. Tell me and I'll connect you with every black-turtlenecked asshole in Dublin. Don't tell me and you'll be lucky to paint a spare piece of cardboard with a McDonald's ketchup packet, okay?"

He'd gone white.

"Did *she* get the email?!"

I jammed the piece of chalk so hard against the board that it snapped in two. The kid stammered. I glared at him, which only made it worse.

"Professor M—Me—Merrick," he tried. "I—I—I mean, I'm, I'm sorry. I—I don't know her."

I sucked in a shaky breath and leaned with my elbows against the lectern. My head fell between my shoulder blades and I let it hang there. Maybe I shouldn't have gotten so high before class. But I didn't sleep the night before. It was either thinking of my father and the phone call with Liam or thinking of the girl.

The phone call was something real, tangible. It was a pit in my stomach, a wound through the heart, a black eye that would only get blacker. I could touch it, feel it inside of me. I knew its shape, even in the dark.

But the girl was elusive. She was mere shadows. Mere light. The flicker of sunlight and shadow on the grass beneath a tree. I tried to grab ahold of her, but she always darted away. Always just out of reach.

She was exhausting me. And so it was the weed to calm down. It was speed to wake up, to keep going.

"It's okay," I said, holding up a hand as I tried to shake my head clear. "It's fine."

When I looked up, my classroom of little owls were clearly concerned. I had a well-earned reputation for being a little… eccentric on campus. My art was experimental, my drug propensity common knowledge, and my behaviour erratic. This was perhaps a step too far.

This was a little too close to the real me. The tattered, torn, falling apart me. The "can't keep doing this" me. The "something has to give" me.

"It's fine," I repeated as I began to gather my things into my bag. "It's fine. Really. I'm fine. I'm totally fine."

The girl wasn't coming. I'd made a wrong conclusion somewhere along the line. She either wasn't a third-year art student.

Or she was the one student at Dublin Art School uninterested in taking my class.

Or she never existed at all and I was just way too high out of my mind yesterday. I told Conor and Mason as I drew her obsessively last night, trying to grab ahold of something solid that wasn't pain, that she was real. But maybe she wasn't.

Maybe I was just chasing a ghost. My mother maybe. A woman to love me. To heal me. To protect me.

My hands shook as I fumbled with the clasp on my old leather satchel.

"I'm not going to go there again," I muttered, remembering that familiar cliff face, that sensation of falling, that peculiar feeling of not caring at all about hitting the bottom. The drug den. The indiscernible passing of time. The pain of clawing my way back out… "I'm not going to go there again."

I needed to find Mason or Conor or Aurnia. I needed to talk to someone. To get help. To stop obsessing over some girl who I was becoming less and less convinced was really real. I needed to get fucking high again. *That's* what I really needed.

A student, a girl with a shrill voice stopped me.

"Aren't you going to like, assign anything for us?" she asked.

"Draw her!" I shouted, pointing at the chalkboard. "Draw her and see if any of you can forget her!"

Because I couldn't. But I had to. But I couldn't. I didn't want to. I wouldn't. I would not forget her.

I'd find her.

Whether she was real or not.

EITHNE

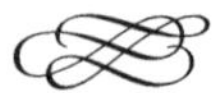

What frightened me the most was just how calm I actually was.

My big brother had just overdosed. He'd been rushed to the hospital. He'd been "this close to dying". "This close" again. My big brother, the only family in the world that I had left. My big brother, the one who practically raised me. My big brother, who I cared about and loved and cherished and worried over more than anyone else. More than even myself.

I'd almost lost him. Almost lost him again. My big brother had a problem and it was going to kill him one day. It had nearly killed him this time. But I guess it had nearly killed him too many times.

Because what I felt wasn't fear, it was numbness. It was emptiness. It was exhaustion.

The sight of him alive and smiling at me from the made-up couch in my living room that morning hadn't filled me with relief like it used to. The smile I returned before hurrying out the door wasn't natural anymore, wasn't from a place deep within me anymore. The breath of fresh air I inhaled into my lungs as I ran to class made me want to cry. Because *that* was relief. *That* was happiness. Escaping. Running away. Leaving my brother behind.

That's what frightened me. *That's* what scared the living shite out of me.

I was late to Rian's class because I'd been tending to Stewart non-stop after getting him back from the hospital. The taxi ride home was busy spent comforting a distraught Stewart and counting pennies in my purse. Then there was the usual post-overdose routine: making Guinness stew, Stewart's favourite, to help him feel better, listening and nodding along as he went on and on about how he was doing better this time, how he really felt like he was on the right track, how if it hadn't been for this or that he would have stayed on the straight and narrow. There was the checking his bags for drugs, checking the apartment for drugs, rummaging through the medicine cabinets and kitchen drawers and beside tables for anything he could use as drugs. Anything he could use to harm himself. There was more cooking, more cleaning. There was the taking of his temperature, the waking up in the middle of the night to make sure he was still alive, the rolling out of bed before the alarm because he was already going through withdrawal and needed the trash bin.

Sometime amongst all of that I happened to check my phone. Happened to see that Professor Merrick was teaching a third-years-only fine arts course. Happened to be feeling reckless enough to sign up for it, despite knowing it wouldn't help me get a job after graduating, wouldn't do me a damn bit of good.

It wasn't exactly the best foot to get off on for a new class with a demanding professor: reluctance and tardiness. But neither was to be helped. Stewart needed me. And I wasn't feeling much of anything those days. No anger, no joy. Just flatlining with no one around to revive me.

I arrived at the big lecture hall at the centre of campus breathless. Late. Very late. Cheeks flushed. My second-hand satchel was falling from my shoulder, my sketchpad slipping from my fingertips, my hair tumbling over my bargain-bin sunglasses.

But the lecture hall was completely empty.

I dumped my stuff on the closest chair with a sigh. Pencils rolled out of my satchel and my sketchpad slipped to the row in front of me. I ignored all that as I stared at row after row of empty seats, bathed in warm afternoon sunlight. I checked the big clock on the wall. I checked my email. I ducked outside and checked the room number.

"What the hell?" I muttered as I stepped back inside, hands on hips.

Then my gaze fell to the chalkboard at the very front of the hall. I squinted my eyes, squinted a little more and then said much more loudly, "What the hell?"

I hurried down the shallow steps, shoving my sunglasses atop my head, holding back my long black hair. I went straight to the chalkboard. Stopped right in front of it. Crossed my arms and stared at the image drawn there, taking up the full height of the board. I leaned my head back. Tilted it from side to side. Scratched at my neck. Moved back. Moved closer. I scoffed indignantly. I laughed in disbelief.

"What the hell?!"

It was me. It was fucking me. I was sure of it. Or at least as sure of it as I could be. It was my face. *My* face. Strands of hair were lashed as if by the wind across my cheek, concealing half my distant gaze. But it was me. I reached out and traced the line of the lips drawn in chalk as I mirrored the movement on my own lips. The chalk came off on my fingertips and I gazed down on it like there should be the red of my favourite lipstick.

But it was just chalk, fluttering like dust as I rubbed my fingertips together. I stared back at the image.

Strange. I recognised myself more in the hastily sketched drawing, lines rough, more like an outline than a finished product, than I did in the mirror. Recently it was like I was gazing at myself through a fog. Like the steam from the shower never quite evaporated.

But there on the chalkboard I was so clear. So present. So vivid.

I was there, captured on the chalkboard. All of me. Everything of me. For what felt like years I'd been trying to hold onto me, hold onto the girl I'd been, grasp at the fading image of the woman I'd wanted to be. But she'd been slipping through my fingertips like sand. I grabbed and grabbed and always came up empty. And yet there she was. There *I* was.

"What the hell?" I said, laughing this time. Laughing even as my eyes shimmered.

I spun around and shouted into the empty auditorium, relishing the sound of my voice loud, devouring my own echo, "What the hell?"

My heart was racing in a way that frightened me. Really frightened me. My cheeks were warm and it had nothing to do with running across the cobblestoned paths of campus to get to class. I dragged my fingers through my hair, breathless yet again, and was about to turn around to look once more when I noticed the haphazard stack of big sketchpad papers on the edge of the professor's desk.

This time it was not with giddiness or excitement or the budding of happiness that I whispered, "What the hell?"

I leafed through the stack, eyes moving quickly from one page to the next. I could move quickly because they were all the same, more or less. They were all the same girl from the chalkboard. They were all, in effect, me. Me, me, me again. I riffled through them like a child's flipbook, watching my features move, shifting slightly, contorting strangely.

I reached the end and I let go of the whole stack. They slipped off the edge of the desk and with a whoosh like a flight of startled birds spread in all directions.

The whole of the lower portion of the lecture hall was

covered with the sketch pages, covered with imitations of my face. No, imitations of the *drawing* of my face. The one on the chalkboard. The girl I could hardly recognise in my own mirror.

They were not as expertly done as the one on the board. But they were all clearly me. None of them captured me like the one that first transfixed me, delighted me, made me wonder for the first time in years. Maybe that was what made them especially frightening.

They all were a tiny piece of me, giving the floor the appearance of a shattered mirror.

Perhaps I should have known then that I was being drawn into something I should be wary of. Something, or someone, that was dangerous.

Something that could destroy me.

RIAN

The sign read in big, bold letters, visible from all the way across the leafy quad:

FREE TATTOO.

Free, because I'd snuck into Dublin Ink that morning to grab some supplies—Mason still asleep, Conor not yet in, and Aurnia already on campus for class. And tattoo, because I was only offering one. Singular. One option. No more. No fucking less.

I'd bullied some timid first years out of their canopy where they'd been trying to get other first years to come to some sort of social. Probably with fruit punch. And no drugs. They'd left with threats to go tell on me, but they'd left, and that was all I cared about in that moment.

I'd set up my tools, laid out all the different inks, and taped the drawing I was offering for free to permanently inject into any taker's skin. I quickly had a line across the cobblestone square in the centre of campus. Students with their hoods up against the blustery wind laughed nervously as they waited, craning their necks to see how much longer they had to wait. An industrious third year had seen the chaos and brought a twenty-four pack of cans to hawk for five euro a pop. It had the air of Temple Bar on a Saturday night. Merriment and craic. Someone played upbeat Beoga, a modern Trad band, on a little portable Bluetooth speaker.

Well, good for fucking them.

Because beneath the shade of the canopy I was sweating like a pig, antsy as hell, and raging to boot. I hadn't smoked that morning like usual. I'd wanted to be clear-headed, focused. I didn't want to get the tattoo wrong. A wanted poster with a botched face wasn't worth a damn. And I had a lot of wanted posters to ink.

I don't know which one I was on. It could have been the first. It could have been the twentieth. Hell, for all I really knew I'd tattooed through the night and the girl with squirming hips and a ring through her septum was my lucky hundredth customer. But out of the noise of the ever-growing crowd, which now included plenty just come to watch me work, came a familiar voice.

"Rian?"

I was almost convinced it was her. The girl. My Raglan Road girl. Such a sweet voice. I was certain that I would know it when I heard it. As if from a dream. Or a past life. Or from somewhere deep inside my soul. I looked up with swelling hope.

My face fell and I grumbled, "Oh, it's you."

Aurnia laughed, slightly nervously, as she ducked under the canopy, glancing down the length of the bustling line.

"Yeah," she said, fingers grazing the edge of the taped-down image I'd drawn for the tattoo on the table, "nice to see you too, boyo."

I bent back over my work, moving as quickly as I dared without compromising the perfection of the features. I sensed Aurnia hovering over me. I bristled at her closeness. At her nervous tapping of her fingers against her thighs.

"Um, so, what's the craic, Rian?" she finally asked.

"Aurnia, I'm up to ninety," I answered brusquely. "Do you see the length of this line?"

I glanced up to see that Aurnia was not looking at the line. Not looking at the beachball someone had brought to entertain the masses. Not at the general atmosphere of fun that was wrong, all wrong. This was serious. We were finding someone. We all needed to find someone.

Aurnia was looking at me. "Rian, can I talk to you?"

I dipped the tattoo gun into the ink and shrugged. "Sure look, you can talk. No sayin' if I'll hear much. I have to crack on."

Aurnia cleared her throat. "I think you should take a break and have a little chat with me."

I sighed and ignored her. She'd go away.

She didn't. She moved closer.

"It's just..." Aurnia said in a softer voice, "it's just this is a little concerning is all."

The girl I was tattooing dismissed Aurnia with a wave.

"Oh, no, it's grand," she said, "my skin is pure sensitive, like. If anyone even touches me, I go all red. If anyone brushes their fingers against my skin, I go red. If anyone..." I felt the girl's eyes on me even as I worked on her, "anyone at all kisses me, anywhere, anywhere they want to kiss me, I go red."

I stopped my work long enough to point at the girl, give Aurnia a look, and say, "See? She's grand. Not concerning at all."

I swatted the girl's hand away from my inner thigh and turned the gun back on. Aurnia, like a persistent fly, circled around so she was on the opposite side of the girl.

"Look," she whispered, "I know you're a bit out there sometime, but... someone keeps calling the Dublin Ink line for you. And Mason and Conor—"

"Mason and Conor can go mind their own fecking business," I said to Aurnia's face before smiling and bending once more over the girl's arm.

My friends thought I was selling again. Getting dragged under again. Using the hard stuff again. The bags under my eyes. The strange phone calls I wouldn't tell them were Liam. The obsessive drawing of a girl they couldn't believe was real. I admit it didn't look good. But I had more important things to focus on than their needling worry.

Aurnia's fingertips on my shoulder were meant to be comforting, I know. I know. I know they were meant to be kind. Since coming into our lives, little A had become like a kid sister to me. I loved her. Cared for her. She was a part of our family. But I shrugged her off of me like her touch was fire ants.

"I just want to help," she said.

"You want to help?" I asked, throwing down the tattoo gun. I felt bad that Aurnia and the girl both jumped in fright. I knew well enough what it was like to fear a man. But I hadn't slept and I'd been tattooing for hours and I wasn't exactly in complete control. I jammed my finger against the drawing and yelled at Aurnia, "If you want to help me, tell me who this girl is. That's how you can help me. Tell me who she is. Tell me where I can find her. God, where can I just fucking *find* her?"

I grabbed at my hair and tugged as Aurnia's wide eyes darted between the drawing of the girl, the half-tattooed face on the red arm, and me.

"I—I don't know, I guess she kind of looks familiar. Maybe I've seen her around, but—Rian, why are you doing this?"

I calmed myself, picked back up the tattoo gun and went back to work.

"Kop on, Aurnia. It's pretty obvious," I said. "It's the best way to find her. Nobody looks at lamp posts these days. The second you put up a poster some poser in a garage band smacks his flyer up over yours. And besides, lamp posts don't move, you know?"

The girl I was tattooing craned her head around to look at me and said, "Wait, is that what I am to you? A lamp post?"

I pushed her head back around and said, "Yes."

She shrugged and then looked back around after a second thought.

"How about you be a lamp post to me, Professor?"

All this time Aurnia just stared at me with those big deer eyes. I was about to reassure her that I was grand. No bother. This was all normal. At least normal for me. I wasn't a mentaller, at least not more than usual. I wasn't any more off my nut than usual. Before I could speak, a kid with a backwards baseball cap and an oversized Tipperary GAA jersey ducked his head under the canopy.

"Professor M, 'bout ye?" Tipperary said, "Your sign doesn't have an 's', like."

"What an astute artistic eye," I said, deadpan, not bothering to give him a second look. "You'll go far. I can tell."

"He's just doing the one tattoo, eejit," the girl told him as she stretched to poke at the girl's taped-down face.

Her movement made the gun jolt. I was about eat the head off her for ruining my work when Tipperary said, "You're tattooing Eithne's face?"

I dropped the gun. Looked across the table. I almost didn't dare to speak.

"Rian, please—" Aurnia started, but I held up a finger to her.

"Repeat what you just said," I told Tipperary.

He looked at Aurnia.

"You! You, you bollocks!" I said to him, "What did you say?"

He shrugged. "Your sign don't have no s?"

I was going to murder him. "After that. What did you say *after that?*"

"I don't know," he said. "Something like, 'How come you're not doing any tattoos except Eithne's face?"

"Eithne," I whispered.

I felt like a guilty man proved innocent as the sinking exhaustion of *relief* came over me. I was right. She had a name. She was real. She existed. I could hold her. Eithne. My Raglan Road girl. *Eithne.*

"Rian," Aurnia tried once more, but I couldn't hear anything except *Eithne* now.

"You know her?" I demanded of Tipperary.

"I mean, not really," he said with a shrug. "I tried asking her out once, but she turned me down and, I don't know, I think she's touched, ye know?"

I reached across the table and grabbed the little shite by the collar of his jersey.

"Take me to her," I said, shaking him.

I wasn't the scrawny little runt any longer. And I wasn't the kind little kid either.

I was strong, thanks to years of daily gym workouts. I was fuming.

And I was this close to getting what I wanted.

Eithne.

EITHNE

I felt like I was stuck between two dead ends.

The first was the drone of my Commercial Advertising Design professor at the front of the lecture hall. The second was the seemingly endless amounts of Google hit results for: how to fix a drug addiction. The first led to an office in town, a stretch of grey carpet, and a cubicle a fifth the size of a jail cell. The second led to site after site that said the same feckin' thing: you can't do anything. A person has to want to seek help. A person has to do it for themselves first and foremost.

They both drained me. They both left my life colourless and beauty-less and hopeless. They both made me want to stand up and scream and slash a paintbrush across a canvas. Again and again and again till I was so exhausted that I couldn't lift my arms.

I sank down into my chair and stared up at the ceiling.

The professor said, in a voice that indicated he was just as bored as the rest of us, "Sure look, just because your goal is increasing a firm's profit, doesn't make you any less of an artist. An artist is one who elicits something from someone. Some elicit joy or rage or frustration. Some elicit positive quarterly earnings.

Some stir hearts, some stir pennies from pockets. See? We're all artists here."

I sighed as I returned to searching the internet for a new way to try to help Stewart. I wondered if my professor believed his own bullshite. I wondered if one day I would too. A solid, steady paycheque would probably help. Like a dose of anaesthesia helps. Like a fucking Vicodin helps. Like unconsciousness always helps. For as long as it lasts.

It wasn't like I could do any real art now anyway. Not with the stress of rent. Of Stewart's medical bills. Of the creditors calling from the last place Stewart trashed on a bender. Of the university calling for tuition. Of everyone wanting money. Wanting a piece of me. Wanting more and more of me. Fuck. There was nothing left of me. Nothing left of me *for* me, let alone for my art.

I was reading through ways to talk to loved ones suffering through addictions, ways to be honest and open about how they hurt you. I closed out of that quickly. I didn't want to put that on Stewart. Didn't want to make him feel any more guilt than he already did. That I was pretty sure he already did. I wanted to *help* him. Why couldn't any of these online resources get that?

I was scrolling, eyes glazing over from tiredness and probably something deeper than tiredness, when I overheard two girls whispering back and forth in the row of desks just in front of me. I had no qualms about eavesdropping. Most people went to the movies for a bit of escapism; I didn't have the cash for that so I had to take it where I could get it. They were talking about a guy, an older guy. My love life had been non-existent all throughout school. There was always class. Work. Always an extra shift here, an extra shift there. There was always Stewart.

"I swear, he was into me," the one girl said. "I mean, the way he looked at me with those pale blue eyes. They're like endless, you know? Like depthless."

"Did he get your number?" the other asked.

"Well, I mean, no, but like he was just so focused on my body, ye know?"

I raised a curious eyebrow. I liked the way this was going. I didn't get off much these days. There wasn't much time and when there was, I had a hard time touching myself without feeling like I was doing something wrong, something dirty. When this just served to turn me on even more, I got so scarlet with guilt that I had to take a long shower. Long and hot enough to get clean. Long and hot enough that I could barely drag myself to the bed and flop over it before passing out.

The one girl continued, "Yeah, he was draped all over me, like. And there was this…intensity to the way he moved. Like I can't even describe it."

Describe it, an urgent voice murmured in the back of my head. I squeezed my folded thighs. I willed myself not to feel the building heat; it didn't work.

"Like there was sweat on his brow he was exerting himself so much for me, ye know?" the one girl continued in a frantic whisper to her friend. "Like I could feel his hot breath on my neck. It sent such tingles down my spine you have no fucking clue."

"Oh my God," the other girl replied.

The same words echoed through my head. *"Oh my God." "Oh my God, yes." "Oh my God, this is wrong."* I tried to refocus on what Professor Levine was explaining, because it was wrong. Listening in. Getting aroused in class. My oversized hoodie, washed so many times it was as soft as down, suddenly felt rough against my hard nipples. The friction as I shifted made me bite my lip.

What was wrong with me? Why did my body react this way? Why did I hate it so much, that my body reacted this way?

"And it hurt," the girl went on as I stifled a moan. "Like I'm not going to tell you it didn't hurt. It was like way bigger than I thought it was going to be. And it just kept going in and in and in. And at this pace that I was, like, shite, this is mental. Like how can you sustain this? And like how can I not scream my fecking head off, ye know?"

I wanted to watch. I wanted to watch this girl get stripped naked by this man. I wanted to see his big cock drive into her as she struggled not to scream. God, I wanted to get off on them. I wanted the sight of them to drive me mad, to send me over the edge, to give me some fucking relief.

My mouth was dry. I licked my lips and tried to remember when last I had water. Had I ever had water? I could lick him, when they were spent. I could lick her. I could lap up their pleasure. I could get by on just a drop. Of sweat. Of cum. Of just a lick of the very tip of his tongue.

My fingers flinched toward my clenched inner thighs and I hated myself. I could hear his words. *Slut. Whore.* I could see me. *Slut. Whore.* Getting off in public.

"But when he was finished," the girl whispered, her voice thready, almost desperate. I was desperate, too. Desperate and ashamed. "When he was finished, it was so fucking beautiful. Like I'd never seen anything like it. Just like, I don't think anything could have been more perfect."

I imagined his back arching. His fingers digging into her skin, needing something to hold onto. Needing *me* to hold onto. I imagined his teeth sinking into the crook of her neck to stifle his own screams. I imagined his teeth sinking into the crook of *my* neck. I imagined him filling me. Collapsing on me. Melting into me. Me. *Me.*

"And now I'll have a part of him forever," the girl whispered.

"Yes," I whispered to myself.

"Do you want to see?"

"Yes, yes," I whispered again.

I couldn't help myself. I leaned forward to spy on the two girls. I wanted to see scratches so deep they'd leave an everlasting scar. I wanted to see a bruise from his digging thumbs that would never heal. I wanted to see the indentation of teeth at the swell of her breast that would never go away, so ferocious was his bite.

When I saw the girl's arm, when I saw the peeling back of the bandage, when I saw the tattoo, I was at first disappointed. Then ashamed at my disappointment. Then fucking livid.

Call it emotional whiplash. Call it whatever you bleedin' want. But you try seeing your fucking *face* tattooed on some random bird and tell me how keeping your emotions in check went, okay?

"Where the fuck did you get that?" I hissed, leaning over the top of my laptop.

The two girls looked up at me, clearly startled.

"Mind your own business," the girl with my fucking *face* on her arm told me.

I jabbed my thumb into my nose, yes, *my* fucking nose, there on some stranger's arm and she yelped in pain. She pushed away at me, but I had the advantage of the higher position.

"Where did you get that?" I hissed again.

The girl's friend was the first to notice. Her annoyed look switched to confusion and then surprise and then excitement.

"Oh shite," she said, knee bouncing as she patted her friend's leg. "*Look.*"

Perhaps given different circumstances I might have had more of a chance to be jealous of their obvious friendship. I might have longed for that kind of easy communication that comes from time spent drinking pints at the local together and between over-stuffed vintage racks and sprawled out on the Mallorca beach together.

But the fact that I was staring at my face permanently inked onto someone I didn't know *by* someone I didn't know kind of took precedence.

The girl with the tattoo seemed to at last recognise me as the person from her own limb. Somehow that pissed me off even more. When did I become a fashion accessory? Adornment for an arm? A piece of art to be gazed at every now and then and forgotten?

When did I become so little? Why had I let myself become so small?

"I'll ask one more time," I said through clenched teeth as I squeezed the edge of the desk so hard I thought it might splinter, "who in God's name did that to you?"

Did that to me, I thought, but did not dare say aloud.

Before the girl could answer, the door at the bottom of the lecture hall banged open. Necks all around me snapped in that direction as Rian Merrick barged in without warning, dragging along with him some random student. He began to look over the class row by row with a sort of manic thoroughness. I stared in shock and confusion with everyone else.

The girl with the tattoo giggled, covering her mouth, and elbowed her friend, having completely forgotten about me, the girl who was forever inked into her skin. "Speak of the devil!" she said. "The sexy, sexy devil!"

And then, "Do you think he's here for me?"

RIAN

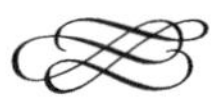

I'm not sure which drew the most attention: the sudden noise of the auditorium door banging against the wall, Tipperary, squirming and swatting at my fist the back of his collar, or me, panting like I'd been running for miles. Whichever it was, we had everyone's full attention.

My eyes darted wildly around the lecture hall as Tipperary grumbled, "Mate, let go of me," and drywall tumbled to the floor from the hole the doorknob had punched through.

Where was she? Where was she? My heart was racing. I could feel her pulsing through my veins, burning me from the inside, and I hadn't even shot her up yet. I hadn't run my nose along her thighs, heated her lips with my flickering finger, tasted her nipple on my tongue. I hadn't breathed her, smoked her, injected her and yet I pulsed with her, throbbed with her, fought to not go under with her.

"Professor Merrick."

I vaguely heard my name. It was like the snap of someone's fingers in front of your face. The pat of their hand against your cheek. Annoying at best. Dream-destroying at worst.

"Professor Merrick, can I help you?"

A girl in one of the back rows was pointing down at me. Laughing. The girl next to her was giggling. The girl behind her was not.

I let go of Tipperary as my arms fell limply to my sides. He cursed me out, called me a freak and left. The class's professor asked again if he could be of any assistance. I answered him this time.

"No," I said, not daring to take my eyes off her in case she disappeared again. "I'm afraid there is no assisting me at all."

"I'm sorry?"

Sunbeams from the windows cast her face into light and shadow. She was partly hidden behind her laptop, but I wanted her naked at her desk. I wanted to see her whole body bathed in light and dark. To trace the line where light met dark all the way from the top of her head to her toes. I wanted to fist my hand into her raven hair to see how long her strands held onto the warmth of the sun.

I wanted to tease the vein along her pale, elegant neck with my tongue, down to the valley between her breasts. To dive to her soft valleys and explore the delicate skin of her inner thighs from the folds of her pussy to the pucker skin behind.

"I'm afraid there's no help for me," I said, answering the professor.

My Raglan Road girl looked away when she noticed the other students turning in their chairs, searching my eyeline to find what had so transfixed me. She ducked her gaze as her beautiful cheeks reddened. A colour for my palette: white and black and red. As murmurs began to circulate, the rising of cicadae in the summer, my Raglan Road girl slipped down further in her chair. Her eyes darted to me over the top of her laptop. I could see red there, too.

"Alright class," I shouted, clapping my hands. "Let's put away those useless laptops of yours."

"Professor Merrick?" came the rather confused, rather timid protest from the professor of this class.

"You'll need pencil and paper," I announced as I turned to the chalkboard.

I frowned at the scribbles of useless information: design standards, discussing the client's needs, putting the client's artistic sensibilities above your own. I searched for the eraser. If I could have torn the whole board down and just written on the wall, I would have.

"If you do not have pencil and paper," I continued as I snatched up the eraser. "A pen and the outside of your laptop will do just fine. Or the top of your desk. Or your neighbour's back. Or your very own skin, ladies and gentlemen."

I was halfway through erasing the board with big, wide sweeps of my arm before the professor (really, why the fuck was he even still here?) tapped my shoulder.

"Can I help you?" I asked.

The professor glanced toward the auditorium of what used to be his students and leaned forward after nervously licking his lips to say with a slight laugh, "I don't quite understand what's going on here."

The students were shifting in their chairs, waking up from their sunny snoozes, leaning forward, chairs screeching on the old wood floors.

Something was happening.

I was happening.

"That's quite alright," I said. "You *were* teaching this course before, but not anymore. I'm teaching it. So you're free to go."

The old professor blustered.

"Free to— No one said anything to— Professor Merrick, does the dean know about—"

Whatever words the dear, sweet professor intended after that caught in his throat like a hunk of meat.

I hadn't meant to scare him. Really all I did was sigh, set

down the eraser, and turn fully toward him. It wasn't my fault I was taller. Obviously stronger. Probably looked a little terrifying with my sweater pushed up showing off the dark ink—dark as my glare—all over my forearms and neck. It was probably my fault that I had a certain…reputation around campus. For erratic behaviour. For instability. But even that wasn't *really* my fault given the role society had cast for the troubled artist, was it?

They liked me a little high. A little mad. A little violent for the sake of my art, should I be pushed too far…

The professor swallowed heavily and to save face turned to the eagerly awaiting auditorium and said, "Class, today—" He stopped to clear his throat. "We have a guest lecturer—"

"Get out," I said, pointing toward the door. I hadn't wanted to get angry. "Get out now."

The professor blubbered something about needing to collect his things. I swept up what was on the desk into my arms, stalked to the door still wedged into the wall, and threw everything outside. Before he had even sulked away, I wrote in big, sloping letters across the board as I said, "This class is now *Seducing Out Your Artist's Voice*."

The piece of chalk snapped in half when I finished by jamming the end against the board.

"Forget everything you learned about suppressing yourself for some corporate ego," I said as I turned around. My eyes found hers like they were true north, me a helpless needle. "We're going to strip everything away till all that's left is you."

My Raglan Road girl, my Eithne, shifted uncomfortably in her desk. Students around her whispered, cupped their gossiping lips and crowed at one another. But I didn't care.

"We're going to strip away everything outside of our true artistic selves," I continued, my hands flinching as I imagined tearing clothes off her. "We're going to expect and settle for nothing less than perfect, vulnerable nakedness."

The thought of Eithne naked and before me made me let out a low groan.

I was going too far. I was losing control. If I wasn't careful I was going to get an erection right there in front of a hundred students. I was going to get carted off to prison. Or a loony bin.

But I couldn't stop myself.

The sight of her was driving me mad with lust, with need, with irrepressible desire.

"I want nothing between us," I said, throat raw and rough, my stare burning into her, promising her everything I would do to her. "Just skin against skin. Soul against soul. Nothing around us but art. Nothing between us but wet...paint."

I'd looked at her too long. I'd kept my gaze fixed on her too long. Everyone knew I was looking at her. Everyone knew I couldn't turn my gaze from her. So they were looking, too. All of them.

And still I couldn't stop.

The only sounds in the auditorium were my ragged breathing and then the sudden screech of a chair as she pushed up from her seat. Everyone turned to me, but I had my eyes on her as she fled, arms full of her books, head lowered.

The door hadn't even closed behind her at the top of the lecture hall and I was already moving toward the exit.

"Is there homework?" a girl shouted.

"Get a life," I shouted back.

Get a love, I thought as I hurried after my Raglan Road girl.

Get an obsession, I thought as I took the stairs two, three at a time.

Get a drug, I thought as I followed Eithne out into the sunlight.

Get a poison, I thought as I caught sight of her and didn't let go. Get a blissful, beautiful poison.

And don't let go.

EITHNE

Somehow I knew he would come after me.

I wanted to get away. But I also wanted him to catch me.

The light in the auditorium had been so soft, almost hazy. So seeing Rian had almost felt like a dream. He'd fixed his glaze on me like he'd done in so many of my fantasies and didn't look away. His attention, his focus was so powerful it caused everything, everything else in that lecture hall to blur out of focus.

And then he'd spoken to me—to *me*.

"I want nothing between us. Just skin against skin. Soul against soul."

His words had cut through my armour, shredded my defences, and plunged themselves into the core of me. An ache radiated from the depths of me. A delicious sinful ache.

And I couldn't take it anymore.

So I ran.

Outside the hall I shielded my eyes from the direct sun with my forearm and struggled to keep my portfolio tucked against my chest as I stumbled across the cobblestones.

I felt him before he touched me. The hairs on the back of my neck standing to attention even before he grabbed my elbow. And tugged.

I spun and crashed into the hard wide plain of his chest.

Dear God.

I could smell his scent, dark and masculine, musky and thick with spice. Only the hint of hidden sweetness. I could feel the heat radiating off him, could feel it already sinking into my muscles making me pliant, making me melt against him, give in to hi—

No!

I wrenched myself from his grip and staggered back, my chest heaving as I struggled for air. As I struggled to clear his intoxicating smell from my nose, from burning in my lungs.

It wasn't enough. His draw was still there, his hooded eyes still pulling me back into his violent gravity.

"Class isn't over yet, *Eithne*."

I sucked in a breath, my name sounding like he'd growled it between my legs. I tried to clench my thighs without making it obvious.

I swallowed. "How— How do you know my n—?"

"I typically don't give good grades to students who make a habit of ditching class early."

This was bullshite. Everyone knew Rian's grading was as arbitrary as his own attendance at class lectures. The student who showed up every day on time, turned in assignments by the due date, and actively participated in class discussion was more likely to be at the bottom of the class than the top. He wanted "true artists". Who the hell knew what the fuck that meant.

"I'm not taking 'Seducing Your Students'. I don't need it for my major."

"Seducing Out Your Artist's Voice," he corrected as he took a step toward me.

I cowered back and bumped into the building's rough stone wall. "I— I don't need that either."

"What do you need?"

It startled me. The way he asked it. Like I was in unbearable pain and he really did want to give me whatever I needed. A drug. A swift release. A little dose of mercy in this fucking world.

"Eithne?" He closed the gap between us with one long step, closing me in.

His eyes were startling up this close. The striations of varying blues and greens tossed and turned like a rough sea. I was drowning in them, my lungs filling with the scent of him again.

I barely registered how inappropriate this was, him this close. If someone were to exit the class, to turn a corner, to spot us...

I could lose my scholarship.

Shite. My scholarship.

My future. My job prospects. Safety. Security.

What the fuck was I doing risking all that?

"What do you need, Eithne?" he whispered, his breath, sweet from spearmint and marijuana, caressing my forehead.

"I—I need what Professor Levine was teaching. Advertising Design. That's what I need."

"Why?"

His question was like a prickly thorn in my side. I wanted to pull it out and throw it far, far away. I knew that discomfort well, though. I'd asked myself the very same question during a million sleepless hours.

"Because I'd like some stability in my life," I answered irritably as I pushed past him. "I want a well-paying job with a reliable paycheque," I rambled—to him, to myself—as he chased me down the stone path. "I want to know I can pay rent and buy groceries and care for— I just want some stability. Is that so fucking wrong?"

"Yes," he said, and blocked my path with his wide frame. Damn his long legs. Damn his rounded shoulders and his eyes and the "black hole" of him sucking me in.

I stepped back because I didn't want to collide with him.

Couldn't risk the brush of skin against skin. I was afraid he was contagious. His madness. His craze. His devotion to beauty and love and all things impractical in this world.

"It's the worst fucking thing I think I've ever heard," he said.

I wanted to punch him square in the face. He didn't know me. Didn't know my life. The burdens I shouldered. He couldn't know how heavy they were for me. How much I wanted to set them down. And couldn't.

At the same time, I wanted to throw myself into his arms and moan, "I know. It is fucking wrong. It is. Please show me. Open me up. Strip me down. Tear me in two. I want to create art with you. Make love with you. Leave some sort of impression on the world with you."

But I couldn't admit that. Could I?

"Worse than tattooing a random student's face onto another random student's arm?" I challenged.

"You're not some random student."

He sounded so sure. I didn't know why.

"We don't even know each other."

"I know you."

Rian looked at me with arms crossed. A challenge in his eyes. A dare in the drum of his tattooed fingers along his sweater pushed up his muscled forearms. An urgency in the unblinking of his eyes.

"You don't—"

"I saw you across the street the other day."

We were alone on the stone walkway. It was cooler than the hazy auditorium, high arching columns shading the path, the stone remembering winter in its depths.

"I heard you," he said. "Your body, your soul. Singing to me. Calling to me."

"You're insane," I told him. "And I don't need insane right now."

But I did, my soul moaned. I needed stupid and crazy and

reckless and *him*. I needed him to tear responsibility and real life from my shoulders. I needed a mad man—this mad man —inside me.

I needed to get ahold of myself. *Kop on, Eithne.*

"And I think you know me."

"I don't even know your name," I said. "I wouldn't even know who to report to the Garda for stalking me and tattooing my face onto everyone."

"Everyone knows who I am," Rian said.

"Well, I don't," I insisted. "All I know is that you've crossed a line. A really fucking big one. You've violated me, you know?"

"That's all you know?"

"Yes."

"You know nothing more of me?"

"Nothing."

"Liar." He smiled and leaned in. "I think I speak to you. I think my soul calls to yours the same way yours calls to mine."

I laughed even as shivers went down my spine. "No."

"You haven't dreamed of me?"

I couldn't help the gasp. How did he—?

"Just leave me alone!" I shoved past him, aiming blindly for escape. Anywhere.

I didn't take two steps when Rian's hand grabbed my arm.

My portfolio tumbled from my grip and spilled across the stone. My heart dropped as I watched the papers slide loose and scatter like autumn leaves. I could have fallen to my knees to lunge for the drawings. To sweep them against my chest. To try to hide them.

But it was too late. My fate was sealed.

I stood there. Looking down as he looked down. Frozen as he stood frozen.

Nothing moved except the edges of the pages, rustling at the edges.

There were the nude drawings I'd done of Rian when he'd

appeared like a tornado without warning into the centre of my class. There was his bare ass, drawn without embarrassment, sculpted with charcoal. I saw each variation there across the marble floor. Rian turning, turning, turning. Rotating toward me. The reveal of his muscular chest. Tattoos unveiled as the shadows receded turn by turn. His cock coming into view. His eyes about to find mine. His gaze about to startle me, confuse me, doom me.

They were all there, the hasty, frantic, desperate drawings from the studio, but there were more. Many more. Rian had been drawing me. Ordering others to draw me. Tattooing me onto flesh, mixing me with blood. But I had been feeding off of him, too. Drawing him into my veins like a drug just the same. I had been yearning to find him as well. Searching for him in pencils and paint. Digging for him on thick pulped paper. Pinning him down on my desk above my clenched thighs.

He was naked. He was clothed. He was turned away. He was looking head-on. He had his eyes closed. He had his eyes open. Wide open. Staring. Seeing. He was curled in on himself. He was beating his chest. He was flinging his arms wide and screaming at the world, at himself, at me. He was in black and white. He was in every shadow of coloured pencil I owned. He was everywhere and everything.

My deepest desires laid bare.

I'd wanted to claim him. To make him mine. To open my very chest for him, crack out my bleeding heart and offer it to him.

I lifted my eyes as Rian did the same. Our gaze met. His pupils were wide. Mine wider. I should have run. But now there was nowhere at all to run to.

When he closed the gap this time, I didn't move back, I fell into him. His lips crashed onto mine and the world—my problems, my responsibilities—vanished into dust.

I should have known his kiss would be just like him: intense and consuming. Totally unrelenting. His lips were warm and bruising, his tongue insistent as he licked at the seam of my lips, demanding, without preamble, for me to open up for him. I did as he wanted. As I wanted. I opened up. He buried his tongue into my mouth and his fingers into the flesh of my hips and my back and I felt his growl rumble all the way down my spine. The resulting ache pulsing between my legs left my legs trembling. I might have fallen if he wasn't holding me up, crushing me to him so hard I no longer knew where I ended and he began.

I threaded my fingers through his hair. He walked me backwards as if he were pushing me off the edge of a cliff. We fell together against a door. If he had given me a moment to pause, I might have stopped him. If he had given me a millimetre of breath, I might have said stop.

But he didn't.

So I didn't.

The door gave way behind me. And we stumbled back.

RIAN

We crashed into desks of the empty classroom. Sent them falling over. Crashing noisily. Tripped over metal chair legs, caught our hips on sharp, hard edges, hit open space like being thrown from a plane and gasped against each other's mouths. My back collided with the blackboard.

We flipped over each other, over and over like rolling together down a grassy hill. Chalk covered our clothes, our hair, imprinting us as she stole my breath and I stole hers.

She was everything I'd thought she'd be. And more.

She ran in through my blood like heroin. Hot and sweet. Every little noise she made, every little moan I elicited from her as I pushed my hands under her clothes, every gasp as I pressed my hardened cock against her yielding flesh, was like another hit. More, more. Until I destroyed us both.

"You'll be the death of me," I whispered into her mouth, as my fingers found her soft breast underneath her bra cup.

"Fuck," she said on a hiss.

I rolled her nipple between my fingers. Nothing had ever delighted me more than feeling it pebble to stone.

Except for maybe my name on her lips.

"Rian."

"Yes. You're going to say my name over and over again, just like that, as I strip you, then I feast on you, then as I fuck you."

"You're…what?"

I pressed her against the chalkboard with my body, holding her still as I gathered her wrists and bound them above her head. Thin strips of light streaked her flushed cheeks as she stared up at me, panting. "Wait…"

"Not. Waiting." I pressed my lips back to hers, crushing her further into the blackboard. I was going to consume her. To own her.

She wrenched her mouth free. "Wait! We can't…"

I buried my mouth into her neck. Fuck, she smelled better than I imagined. Like a cool autumn day, fresh and sweet. "Let me show you how much we *can*—"

"No, I mean, we *shouldn't*."

I pulled back to look into her eyes. Her pupils were blown wide open, her eyes wide. She was warring with something in her head. I could see it.

"Why not?" I asked softly.

"You're my professor."

"I quit. I'm not your professor anymore." I lunged for her mouth, kissing her hard as I travelled my free hand down her stomach to her skirt.

She tore away from me again, chest heaving so that I could feel her diamond-tipped nipples pressing into me. "No. It's wrong."

"It's always better when it's wrong." I slid my hand up her skirt. She gasped and made a weak attempt to free her hands from my grip above her head.

"No, Professor Merrick, we…can't."

"Stop playing games, Eithne, you and I both know—" I

pushed aside her panties, "you want this as much as I do." I slid my fingers down her soft wet slit.

She moaned and sagged against me, already giving up the fight.

"See, soaked as fuck."

"I—"

Before she could protest any further, I pushed two fingers into her. She let out a noise that sounded halfway between a sharp intake of breath and a sob.

Fuckkkkkk. Her wet heat felt incredible. My tongue ached to lap at her and circle her clit until she came, my dick ached to feel her wrapped around me until she shuddered her release.

But first…I'd make her come with my fingers.

"If you really want me to stop, I will," I said gently as I slid my fingers in to the hilt. "All you have to do is say so."

Her head fell onto my shoulder and she let out a long low groan that sent vibrations through my body. I worked my fingers slowly in and out of her, relishing the coating of her juices that made them slide without resistance.

"Go on, Eithne. Tell me you don't want this."

"I…" She breathed.

"Tell me to stop."

I slid my fingers all the way out.

"No!" she cried.

I chuckled as I circled her clit with the tips of my fingers. "Good girl." Before plunging them back inside her.

I curled my fingers around, finding those precious ridges. Then I began to massage that spot.

"Oh God," she whispered as she shuddered. "What—what are you *doing* to me?"

I grinned to myself. "I'm not done yet." I'd barely started.

"That—that spot. What are you touching?"

I froze and she whimpered. "You've never had anyone work your g-spot?"

"My what-spot?"

"Fucking eejits," I growled under my breath, "the men who came before me should be castrated."

She blinked. "There've been no *men* before you."

"Boys then."

"There've been no boys either."

I froze. Shite. A virgin. A fucking virgin.

Eithne just oozed so much sexual energy that I just assumed…

Okay. We could go slow. *I* could go slow. I gritted my teeth.

"Then I can't wait to show you what you've been missing."

I began to massage her g-spot again with my fingertips, stroking her in a "come here" motion. Her moans became louder, more unrestrained.

Her hips bucked against me, her muscles tightening around my fingers. I let go of her wrists still above her head and her arms collapsed around my shoulders. She held onto me, her nails digging into my back as I pressed her into the blackboard, as I worked my fingers inside her.

"Still want me to stop?"

"No, God, no. Fuck. More."

My little Ragland Road girl was so fucking responsive. So fucking needy. How she'd managed to go this long without sex was beyond me.

I wrapped my other hand around her neck and pushed her head against the board so she faced me.

For a second, she looked almost scared. "What are you—?"

"You're going to look at me when you come."

Oh little Raglan Road girl. You have no idea what pleasures and pains I'm going to teach you.

I circled my thumb around her clit and the look dissolved into one of pure pleasure. I felt her tighten, heard her breath coming in short pants, felt the wildness to her bucking.

"Oh God oh God oh God," she whispered.

She was so close. But she hung there, right on the edge of pleasure. She just had to let go. She just had to accept it.

"Oh God, no, no, God, no..." her cries of pleasure turned to panic, her eyes snapped open as if she'd just realised where she was. "Stop!"

She shoved at my hands. I was so shocked I stumbled back.

The door of the classroom swung open.

I turned, blocking Eithne from view as a student looked up in surprise from his cell phone.

"Get the fuck out!" I shouted, as I pressed Eithne back against the board, protecting her from sight.

The student was unable to move for a moment. His eyes focused on me. On the more than obvious erection in my pants. On my panting chest. He looked past me to the body half hidden behind me. A devastated sob broke from hidden lips.

I threw my arm out and shouted even louder, "I said, 'Get the fuck out!'"

This broke the student free of his trance and he mumbled an apology before slamming the door shut. I heard the echo of running footsteps down the hall and then there was silence again. Silence and Eithne's broken sobs.

"It's fine," I said, shifting around. "He didn't see you."

Eithne flinched away from me and wouldn't make eye contact.

"Don't touch me!" She ran for the door.

"Hey, just wait a second," I tried calling after her.

"I can't do this," she said as she tugged open the door. "It's wrong. It's *wrong*. *I'm* wrong."

The door slammed shut. I dragged my fingers through my hair.

That should have been the end of things. I should have moved on. It wasn't meant to be.

If it had been anyone else, I probably would have. But my little Raglan Road girl had left me with a mystery. With a curiosity. With a piece of the puzzle missing. And I had to know more. She hadn't said "this" was wrong, but that "she" was wrong.

I'd found a flower that hadn't bloomed in the sun. One that'd been kept in the dark, out of the sun. I was determined to be her moon. I'd rise above her. Peel her back, velvety petal by velvety petal. Smell her scent. Own her body. Steal her soul.

And have her secrets. All of them.

EITHNE

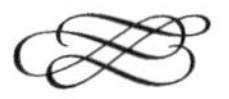

The mug shattered above my head.

All the glasses I owned were already shattered, in a half-swept pile on the dirty tiles of the small kitchenette.

I should have been thinking how to get out of this violent situation. I should have been thinking about where my phone was in case I needed to contact the police. I should have been knocking on the neighbour's door for help (before they came knocking on mine).

Instead I was thinking: what is Stewart going to drink water out of now? Where could I find a place to buy cups that was open this late at night? How am I going to leave him alone? How can I possibly leave him alone? How can I possibly ever leave him?

Stewart was rocking back and forth on the couch, fingers gripping the hair that wasn't already plastered to his pale forehead. The old cushions had plenty of stains already. It had been given to me by the previous tenant and I think the only reason they didn't ask for money was because I'd saved them the effort of dragging it out to the dumpster. But still, his sweat stains were obvious amongst the rest. A crumpled pillow half fallen off the headrest was practically soaked through. The living room was a mess of half-drunk Gatorade bottles, trash bags that needed taking out after Stewart threw up in them, and pamphlets I'd picked up from a local clinic on ways to seek help; these were all either balled up, torn up, or thrown up upon.

My place needed cleaning. Desperately. But there were more pressing matters. Like Stewart standing shakily from the couch. Sobbing. Stumbling unsteadily toward me.

"Eithne," he sniffled, eyes struggling to keep ahold of mine. "Eithne, Eithne."

He backed me up till my shoe heel crunched on a piece of the broken mug. Till my shoulder blades collided with the cracked drywall. Till his weight was pressed up against me, his arms encompassing my head, his fingers stroking my hair as I clenched my eyes shut.

"Eithne," he cooed, his breath hot and foul against the crown of my head. "Eithne, I'm so sorry. I'm so sorry."

I tried not to flinch away from my brother. Tried not to gag at the stench of his body odour or squeeze away from the dampness of his dirty shirt. I tried not to sob myself as his tears travelled down my scalp.

Stewart mumbled on and on, repeating my name, repeating his apologies, repeating that he was committed *this time,* no matter how hard it got *for him.* Not for me. *Him.* Stewart went on, but I lost focus. My mind went back to being pressed up against a different wall. By a different body.

I couldn't help but think of Rian. Of the way he crushed me to the blackboard. Of the weight of him. Of the presence of him invading my air. He'd wanted to give to me. To make me feel pleasure, to feel pain. To lavish on me. In taking from me, he was giving to me. He pulled me against him not because he needed to be held. But because he wanted to hold me.

My lips trembled as I remembered and I hoped Stewart hadn't noticed.

It took every ounce of will inside of me to lift my arms. To place my hands gently against his slick back. To comfort him as his fingers caught painfully in my hair.

"It's okay, Stewart," I whispered. Whispered because we were so close. Whispered because I didn't trust my voice not to crack if I spoke any louder. "It's okay. You're going to be alright. We're going to be alright."

I'd given in to temptation, in to Rian's siren call, but I'd been thankfully spared. I'd seen the light. I wouldn't make the same mistake again. I'd again devote myself to helping my brother. I'd refocus on classes. We'd get through it. We'd be okay. We'd maybe even be happy. One day.

This was right. Yes, this was right. This was what I was supposed to be doing. This was right.

Stewart pressed even tighter, almost too tightly. I could feel his ribs against mine. My lungs didn't have enough room to expand. I gasped for little, shallow breaths.

"I'm going to get better," Stewart said, and I felt his lips move against my hair, felt his teeth scrape against my skull. "For you. I love you. I'm going to get better for you. I love you, Eithne. I love you. I love you. And for you, it's for you that I—it's for you. For you. I just need a little money."

I'd dreaded this moment. They say that fear is just the unknown. But that's bullshit. Because I knew this moment was coming. Knew it like the back of my hand. Knew it like the sun rising in the morning. Knew it like a cold pit in my stomach. And yet it scared me each and every time. And it scared me again. Scared me to death.

I knew it wasn't best to let the silence stretch on too long. It built hope in Stewart's scattered, frenzied brain. It made it worse. And yet I had to build courage. Like a car gaining speed before a jump over a canyon always too wide. You had to gain speed, you know? Before plummeting into a fiery crash.

I sucked in what little breath my caged ribs would let me and said, with manufactured firmness, "Stewart, I can't."

All of Stewart's movements stilled. As if he'd just been switched off. His clammy fingers stopped stroking my hair, stopped tearing it when they got caught. He stopped squeezing my head tighter to his chest like a child drawing a blanket closer and closer beneath their chin to stave off nightmares. He stopped speaking and seemed to even stop breathing.

We went back to silence. We went back to that frozenness. Neither of us moving, neither of us breathing. Then Stewart's ribs scraped against mine as he began to laugh. Bone against bone, I thought I could even hear it, that horrible scraping. Like nails on a chalkboard.

"Stewart, I'm only trying to help you," I insisted futility as he pressed himself away from me.

He shook his head. His neck was bent like a doll's, toppled over with his chin against his chest. And he shook his head back and forth, back and forth. It was almost like an animal shaking himself dry after bathing. But Stewart was not clean. He shook his head back and forth and chuckled darkly and I braced myself.

We were still plummeting, the two of us. Falling…falling… falling… There was no escaping the burning. It was just a matter of different flames.

"You really get off on this, don't you?" Stewart said. "You really fucking get off on this?"

I pressed my palms against the wall behind me to steady myself as Stewart finally lifted his head. He was both too far and too close to me all at the same time. Out of reach, but within a tight enough space that I'd never get a head start. Too far to see the flicker of pain in his eyes as his detoxing body rebelled against him, but plenty close to see his cruel smile. Too far to shove him away from me. And too close to hope to block out his words with my fingers shoved deep into my ears.

"Stewart, please," I pled.

It was of no use. But what else was I to say?

"Does it get you wet?" Stewart said with a twisted snarl. "Putting me down like this? Putting me in my place? Lording yourself over me?"

There was no use in arguing. No point in trying to be reasonable. Fighting back only made him more vicious.

Stewart laughed again and said, "Like mother, like daughter, eh, Eithne?"

I'd heard the words before. I even knew what was coming next. It was like a record that just kept playing and playing. And yet it cut to the bone without fail. I never seemed to grow numb to it. Everything else in my life, everything good and loving and hopeful had dulled, gone grey, lost volume as if I were going deaf. And yet Stewart's tirade when he was in pain never did. It was him and Rian. Pain and pleasure. And nothing in between.

"You're a whore, Eithne," Stewart said. He was no longer laughing. I'd never been. "Just like her. Just like dad always said. A *whore*."

Maybe I said, "Stop." Maybe I said nothing at all. It didn't matter.

"Sleeping around. Fucking other men whenever, wherever. Making yourself cheap. Getting on your knees for a stranger's dick because you *like* it," he ranted, gaining momentum. "Because you can't help yourself. Just like her."

My mother didn't do anything of those things as far as I knew. Her greatest crime, her only crime, was dying too soon. But that didn't matter to a wounded, pained heart like my father's. Nothing mattered. Nothing but hurting someone. Lashing out. Striving to make the pain go away by any means necessary.

"Is that why you won't give me the money, Eithne?" Stewart

shouted, now pacing back and forth, fingers fidgeting, twisting in his damp shirt. "Because you only *take* money? Is that it? That stream only flows one way, eh? Money in, dicks in, cum in. But nothing fucking out! Not even for your own flesh and blood!"

He upended the coffee table and I flinched even though I knew he would do it. He'd done it to a dozen different coffee tables in a dozen different apartments.

"I bet that's what you're doing," he said, looking more and more like my father with each passing word. "When you say you're off taking classes. I bet you're just finding easy cock to suck. I bet I'm right."

I shrank back against the wall the way I'd done that terrible night years ago. It had been my father then. My father huffing and puffing. My father red-cheeked and wild-eyed. My father breaking things. It was Stewart now. But the words were all the same. I felt just as small, if not smaller. Just as timid, if not more. And just as shamed, if not more.

Because back then my father's empty accusations were only true in theory. In the confines of my mind I'd done the things he was accusing me of. In my dreams, too. In the hesitant, fluttering, and then retreating fingers between my legs beneath the sheets. But never in real life. Never truly. But now I had. Now it was true. Now there was tar for Stewart's, for my father's hurled words to stick on.

I didn't even know Rian. Not really. I'd only ever exchanged a few words with him. He hadn't ever taken me on date. Hadn't ever even asked. He stalked me. Stepped over a million boundaries. He was not only much older than me but a college professor. It was wrong. It was *wrong*.

And yet with hardly any hesitation I'd let him drag him into a classroom. I'd let him push his fingers inside me. I'd almost *come* around those fingers with his hand around my throat.

I'd risked my scholarship, my place at the college, my future.

For an orgasm with an older man I didn't even know. *Shouldn't* even know.

"Look at you," Stewart said, laughing again. "You know I'm fucking right. You know it. You know you're a slut like Ma. You know you're a whore. You know there's something nasty inside of you. Dirty and rotten and perverted. She spoiled you. Ruined you. You, whore!"

My face was hot. My skin seemed to burn as I remembered Rian's fingers curling around to press at that spot inside me. I wanted to curl in on myself. To ball up on the floor. To run to Rian's arms and let him do it again. If I was doomed, I wanted to be doomed with him.

"And now you won't even help your own brother," Stewart said, collapsing once more onto the couch. "Because the one thing you want, I, as your flesh and fucking blood, can't give. Or is that your price, Eithne? Is that how demented you are? Is that what you've wanted this whole time?"

Silence came again at last. I couldn't stop thinking of Rian. Waves of shame rolled over me. I needed a shower. I needed to run away. I needed to run to Rian. I was exactly who my father said I was when everything went to shit, when Stewart and I ran away. I was who I told myself all these years that I wasn't. I was a whore. I was a slut.

"I'll just get it somewhere else," Stewart said in a softened voice.

He'd lost his fire. Detoxing takes it out of you, I guess. Small fucking mercies.

"The money," he said. "I'll just go get it somewhere else if you don't give it to me." He added, "Whore" as a last blind swing.

I watched as shivers wracked his rounded spine. He moaned softly as his eyes searched the living room in caged panic. His body needed a fix. And there was none. My brother was in agony. And I was all he had. That was it, plain and simple.

"Come on," I said, pushing myself away from the wall. "Let's get you comfortable."

I helped Stewart lie back down. I arranged a blanket he immediately kicked off and then immediately whined for. I pushed his hair back from his forehead. It was going to be another long night.

"Rest," I whispered as a tear ran down my still burning cheek. "I'm going to go find something to hold your water."

EITHNE

Perhaps Rian wouldn't come to class today.

My eyes twitched constantly toward the clock on the wall as the minutes, seconds ticked away. He'd not show. He'd not come. He was leaving me alone. I'd not seen him since he'd fingered me against the blackboard last week. I'd avoided the campus for days until I'd not been called to the dean's office, not been expelled. The student who walked in on us mustn't have seen me. I'd been given a second chance. A reprieve. I would not screw up again.

And it looked like Professor Merrick was making sure he wasn't going to screw up again.

I thought I might cry when the door at the base of the auditorium opened. To cry in relief, to cry in frustration? I don't know. Both.

I gripped the edge of my desk as Rian stepped into the class. I hated how my lungs constricted at the sight of him, gasping for air already like I was close to climax. My heart thudding erratically in my chest as I drank in the tousled hair falling over those hooded eyes, followed the dark lines along his bare forearms to where they disappeared under his cable knit grey jumper, knowing where they led underneath his clothes.

His gaze found mine and I was trapped underneath the weight of his stare.

"I'd like everyone to leave," Rian said.

There was a seriousness to his voice that wasn't quite like him. Rian was passionate, intense, probably a little crazy. But here was a man set on a straight and determined path. No wandering, no musing, no stops along the way. Here was a man not searching for what he wanted, but going after it with blinders set against everything else. Here was a man that had nothing left but a singular goal.

At first nobody moved. Was this another of Professor Merrick's unconventional lectures? Another strange start to some profound end thanks to "Professor Merrick"? Hearing my mind muse on this enigmatic "Professor Merrick" almost made me laugh. "Professor Merrick". It was funny. It was fucking funny. Because his tongue had been in my mouth, his fingers had been inside my pussy. And he was always inside my head.

Students began to look around at one another. He'd said to leave, but no one wanted to be the first to stand. To be the proverbial lightning rod, should this still be some sort of disguised lesson about the stubbornness or tenacity of art itself. No one wants to be the first gopher to pop out of its hole when the blue-eyed hawk is circling.

I didn't engage in this social anxiety. This twisting in chairs. This spreading of whispered questioning. This licking of lips and slow book gathering and checking once more if anyone had dared to actually leave. I kept my focus on Rian. I could see the tired slope of his shoulders, the slight tremble of his hands. He was just as tired as me. Just as exhausted. We were parasites to one another. So why did we persist? Why couldn't we just stop? Admit we were no good for one another and part ways? Why did I have a pit in my stomach, fearing, no, *knowing* that this would never be the case?

"Leave. Now."

It was easier now for a handful of students to risk standing halfway in their chairs. Glancing at Rian. Hesitating but a moment. Seeing that the coast was clear and stuffing books and paper and laptops into bags. Heading toward the exits. And once those daring few made the jump, others invariably followed. The auditorium filled with the sound of scraping chairs, hushed conversations about early dinners or extra library studio sessions, and shoes shuffling across wood floors.

I'd love a nap in this spare time. But I knew I wouldn't sleep. Not when there was more to do. Always more to do, and wasn't that what I was always begging for? More time? I'd call Noah for an extra shift at The Jar. I'd get started on assignments for next week. I'd tackle a few more post-graduation job applications. I'd call that free clinic about Stewart. I'd grocery shop, cook, scrub the toilet. I'd maybe even shower. Probably not. If I went home, I'd probably have to let Stewart talk through what was a very traumatic experience for him. I'd have to make him tea, switch out his bandages. I'd get *him* to sleep again. I'd—

"Everyone but Ms Brady."

The backpack slinging, the line shuffling, the low conversation humming all stopped. Most of the class was congregated around the two exit doors. Myself included. I stood in a crowd of forty, pushing for the gift of a free period. Rian's words sliced through them all like a knife. Eyes turned to me. I could feel them. Shifting in their sockets. Scanning face to face. Landing on me. Settling on me. Weighing on me.

Professor Merrick spoke again. "Out. Everyone. Ms Brady... you stay."

There was no need for uncertain restraint this time. The first snicker came fast. The anonymity of the throng of students gave the culprit courage. The first nasty look followed quickly on its heels. A girl I didn't know with a snarl. Her eyes trailed up and down my body as I clutched my books timidly. The disapproving click of a tongue. It sounded like the first shifting pebble of a landslide. It was the first shifting pebble of a landslide.

My classmates filed past me and every jammed shoulder was sharp as stone. Every gaze was cold as marble. Whispers twisted and turned round me, filled my ears, my eyes, my nose like rising dust. I stood in the midst of it all like I was pinned down. Like I couldn't move.

Why her? Did she suck his cock? Was her pussy that tight? Was it for a grade? Would he share, dirty, filthy Professor Merrick? I could hear their thoughts as easily as if they were saying them, spitting them in my face. *I would never lower myself like that. What kind of nasty things do you do with the ole prof, sweetie? Why hide under that big, baggy sweatshirt if you give it all away to a teacher?*

I thought my imagined thoughts couldn't hurt worse than anything actually said aloud, but the last girl out whispered to her friend, "Whore."

I knew then why I hadn't moved. I was tied down by my past, bound by the cruelty of a man who never loved me, the insensitive repetition of a brother who used me. I didn't move because I'd been told all my life that they were right. I was a whore. I was a slut. I tried to do good, stick up for my brother, love my father in his eternal grief, but my nature was rotten. Wicked. Debauched. So where did I have to go? Who did I have to turn to?

When the door clicked shut behind the last student, silence seeped in from the crack like water. It pooled round my petrified ankles. It rose too quickly. I couldn't breathe.

Rian climbed the shallow steps toward me with the careful movements of a man approaching a wild animal. It took too long for me to mentally pry the cold ghostly hands off my feet rooting me to the spot.

I had to run. To stop this. To break the cycle. Rian wasn't going to do it for me.

I lunged for the door. But I was too slow, too transparent with my intentions, too fucking hesitant to actually run from him.

I was his obsession.

But he'd also become mine.

He caught the door first. He slipped between me and it and my way out was gone. Would I have actually left? Had I been faster? Had I not hesitated? Would I have proved my father wrong? Could I have?

Or was it all just pretence? All just show? Something to help me sleep at night: I tried. I tried to escape. I tried to run. I tried to be better. More chaste. Sweeter. More innocent. Was it my intention all along to wait to be caught? Linger just a little too long. Allow Rian to climb one stair too many.

Did I ever really have a chance at freedom? Did I ever really want it?

Was I serious when I said in a whisper, "Let me go"?

Or did I really mean, "*Never* let me go."

RIAN

"Let me go."

I knew she meant more than just out of the auditorium. She wasn't just asking me to step away from the door I blocked, stay back as she walked into the hallway. Eithne, my little Raglan Road girl, wanted free of me. Free of the binds I was weaving around her, free of the snare I was trapping her in, the dark and toxic world I was dragging her into.

Didn't she know? I was far from free myself. She was asking me to unlock her chains, but I never had the key. She could scream against me, rail against, fight and buck and kick, but our ankles, wrists, and necks were bound with the same rope, weighed by the same anchor. We were sinking together. I could no more let her go than she could me.

Despite the fire in her eyes, the tremble in her white knuckles gripped over the edges of her books, the unwavering strength of her voice, I think she knew this.

It wasn't a demand. It was a plea. One I could never ever grant.

"I'll give you an A."

It felt crass. On equal grounds with offering cash. It wasn't what I wanted for the beautiful girl I first saw in sunlight. When the autumn trees, vibrant and full and lovely, seemed to dance just for her. The wind moved just to feel the softness of her hair. Fate itself worked so that I would see her. She came with poetry. She came with music. She came with something pure and gentle and sacred.

But I was tired of our dance. Tired of the steps forward, the steps backwards. Tired of the distance maintained between us like opposing magnets.

The crossroad devil offers deals. Anything for the price of a soul. The world for one little signature. I thought myself better than the devil, serving a silver platter to my minx in the form of the good grade she thought she so desired. I thought myself better, but not by much.

Eithne stared at me with the expected shock. I'd degraded her. She needed to act that way, at least to justify her standing there, with me, just a little bit longer. But she didn't move for the door. She didn't repeat her command, her secret plea. The fire in her eyes dimmed, the whites of her knuckles receded, and she still was silent.

"You don't even have to come the rest of the semester," I added. "Guaranteed A and all you have to do is spend the rest of the period with me. Here."

I'd sweetened the pot irresistibly. All Eithne claimed to want was to graduate with honours so she could get a good, soulless, mindless job. I knew this. She knew this.

But I believe Eithne was tired of the dance, too, because she didn't bother with any false act of deciding, this way or that. She sighed through her nose noisily. Glanced once at the door over my shoulder. Drew her lips into a straight line as she glared at me.

"I'm all yours, Professor."

It was not said with playfulness. Nor alluringness. There was no sweetness, no tease, no twinkle at the corner of her unnarrowed eyes. She would go to the fiery stake. But she was determined to show no eagerness for its blaze. I couldn't really say I blamed her.

She followed me back down the stairs willingly enough. I checked a few times that she hadn't darted back up the stairs to the door and each time she hadn't. She merely assessed me with an arched eyebrow that seemed to say, *"Something wrong, Professor?"*

At the front of the auditorium, Eithne stood at a distance as I pulled a stack of heavy paper and several charcoal pencils from my satchel. I held them out for her. She remained where she was. Stubborn as a mule. I cursed. I walked over to her. She stared down at the blank pages unimpressed as I nudged them closer toward her. Finally I let them all drop. The stack of paper carded out like I was going to select a tarot card. The pencils spun like the arrows of a wayward compass.

"Draw an orchid," I instructed and then without another word, returned to the desk behind the lectern.

Out of the corner of my eye I saw Eithne hesitate. Again a little glance toward the locked lower door, shade pulled tight. Was it for my sake? Or hers? I busied myself with essays I wasn't really reading (never did, never would) as she lowered herself slowly to the floor.

"Is this what you want?" she asked, breaking the silence that had threatened to crush the two of us alive in that empty auditorium. "Me on my knees, Professor Merrick?"

She was mocking me. I ignored her taunts and replied calmly, "If you just took the paper, you wouldn't be on the floor, Ms Brady."

"But how would you get hard then?" she shot back.

I didn't like this flippant side of her. It aroused in me too easily a desire to put her in her place. To punish her. To take her over my knee. Turn her ass cheeks red. If she wanted me so badly to be Professor Merrick, I'd more than gladly make of her

Pupil Brady. But these were distractions, fun as they were, that I didn't need for the time being. I had other aims in mind for that late afternoon than *my* pleasure.

"An orchid, Ms Brady," I told her. "Is the problem that you don't know how to draw one?"

Eithne glared and fumed as she took up her charcoal pencil and began to scratch it across the page. She worked quickly. I kept my focus on the blurred words of the essay in front of me, but it was difficult with the way her long dark hair curtained her pursed lips and hard-set eyes. I longed to sketch the indentation the heel of her boots made in her ass or the tops of her breasts hanging like forbidden fruits I could just make out from the limp collar of her sweatshirt.

When Eithne was finished she looked up at me like a child seeking release from the time-out corner. I held out my open palm and she rolled her eyes. Her steps were petulant: slow, loud, drawing attention to herself. The paper crumpled where she jammed it at me with her thumb.

She stood a little too close as I examined it. Her scent was too present and it was far too easy to imagine the smell of sweat, of dried paint, of her desire. It threatened to make me hard. It guaranteed to make me hate myself even more than I already did. I told myself I was making amends. I told myself I was making things better. I told myself this was for her.

The orchid was lovely. Stunning really. It showed true talent. A unique perspective. She grasped not for the thing itself, but the thing it stirred inside of me. It was good. Very good. I tore it up in front of her and didn't wait for her foot stomping to speak.

"Now draw your pussy."

"*What?*"

"Your pussy, Ms Brady."

Eithne glared down at me. I stared calmly back up at her. I could see the resistance in her. The unwillingness. But there was also that stubbornness. She didn't want to draw her pussy like I'd told her, but she didn't want me to know she didn't want to. *Why?*

Eithne returned to the floor and again picked up the charcoal pencil. Again the curtain of hair, the swelling of her ass around the heels of her boots, the forbidden fruit, hanging, eager to be licked, bitten. Again she looked up when she was finished like I should go to her. Again I held out my open palm, barely feigning to glance in her direction.

Her drawing of her pussy was everything her orchid wasn't. I wasn't disappointed, only because I suspected this would be the case.

"It looks like it belongs in a medical journal," I told her.

"Then we're done here?" she asked, rocking like a schoolgirl back and forth on her heels, hands clasped behind her back. "I suppose the commission on a drawing like that would pay my rent for a month."

I balled up the piece of paper. Threw it toward the waste basket. Eithne was already glaring when I said, "I want you to draw your pussy."

The second attempt was even more than the first, mostly because the lines were thicker, rougher. Drawn with the untrained fist of a caveman. She was angry and she was taking it out on the page. Good. I might make a professor of myself after all.

"I want you to draw your pussy," I said.

"I did."

This time I did look up at her. It felt almost like a weapon, my eyes on hers. Our standoff lasted several tense seconds where I thought she was either going to hit me or tear off my clothes.

"No," I said finally. "You did not."

Several more attempts all resulted in failures. In balled-up pages. In increasingly frustrated huffs of breaths. Once she added so much artistic flare, trying to please me, I'm sure, that it was unrecognisable as a pussy. Another was, amusingly, I admit, done in a cubist style. Still another was an abstract mess of scribbles she had to inform me was a "pussy, feck ye."

It was growing increasingly harder for me to maintain my composure as the period wore on, the disappearing stack of paper marking out the time like an hourglass. Eithne gripped the charcoal pencil with a fist, pumped it hard across the page as her breathing grew louder, more frantic. As her body grew slick with sweat even after she pulled off her sweatshirt to reveal a skin-tight white shirt underneath.

I imagined she was gripping my cock instead of that damn charcoal, her moving over me like she moved over her drawings, hearing her grunts of effort as if she were pouring them into my mouth or against the wiry hair of my groin. It was impossible to not get hard, so I just hid behind the lectern, gripping the edges of it to keep myself from slipping my hand inside my pants.

"No," I repeated for what felt like the hundredth time when Eithne again came to me, childlike with her cherry-red cheeks and flustered hair.

My little Raglan Road girl also seemed to feel the same frustration, because she parroted me, jabbing the page at me. "No? No? What the feck is wrong with it?"

I refused to take the page. What she'd drawn was vacuous, clinical, passionless. I shook my head. Eithne balled up the page and threw it to the floor.

"Will any of them be right?" she asked angrily. "Or is this just another fucked-up, twisted, demented point you're trying to make?"

The throbbing of my dick was distracting. It made my tongue heavy, my words hard to find.

"Draw it like you drew the orchid, Ms Brady. Then it will be right."

Eithne threw up her hands. "What in God's name does that mean? I drew the orchid, I drew the pussy. What's the difference?"

"You'll see the difference when you see the difference. Now draw your pussy."

Eithne let out a quick scream before stomping back and collapsing to her place on the floor. My imagination ran wild with her frantic sounds. I could see her between my legs. I could see her digging her nails into my chest as she bucked her hips harder. I could see everything, anything. I could see my arm careening back, I could see the rippling of my muscles as I held nothing back, I could see the violence of the brush-turned-whip, the fury as I covered her with paint-streaked cum.

Another rejection would threaten to send her over the edge, but I would not accept anything less than what I was looking for. I wanted Eithne to see the beauty of her pussy in the way she'd so clearly seen the beauty in the orchid. Once recognised, I wanted her to do more than just that: I wanted her to claim it as she had the flower. To draw it with power and self-assurance. To see it as her own. To not be afraid to soften the edges of its petals with her tongue-wetted thumb. To smudge the lines that were too perfect, to embrace imperfections with a gentle gaze. To see a part of herself in it. To see herself lovely and delicate and sensual in it. I wanted most of all for it to stir something inside of her, as I knew it could, as I was damned determined it would.

It wasn't a surprise, the failure Eithne brought me. Nor was it a surprise the tantrum she threw upon hearing this, though I suspect it was also not a surprise for her. She seemed ready to throttle my neck. To shove at my chest. To tear my clothes from my body.

Anger boiled inside of her as she paced back and forth in front of me as I remained as calm as possible. Not watching the bouncing of her tits behind that thin, buttery-soft material. Not yearning to be the cause of the red flush across her throat. Not letting myself rut my erection against the side of the lectern. No, definitely not that.

When I considered it mostly safe to speak, I said, a broken record if ever there was one, "Draw your pussy, Ms Brady."

"I am!" she shouted, whirling on me.

Up until this point I'd managed to maintain control. But this sent me over an edge I hadn't realised I was so close to. Eithne's self-denial. Her throwing away her God-given talent to sit in some cubicle for a meagre salary. Her walking across the street at exactly the wrong moment to throw her into my self-destructive path. Her pushing me away as I tried to make her cum. Her terror at her own pleasure. Her refusal to accept that her need for pleasure was *normal*. All of it. All of it came rushing up in my throat like bile.

"You are not," I shouted at her, startling her. She walked back as I approached like a summer thunderstorm, fists at my sides. "You're not being honest. An artist has to be completely honest with herself. Or else how is she supposed to know what she wants in this godforsaken fucking world?"

It wasn't about art. It never was. I knew this. Eithne knew this. Rage clouded her face as she jerked her chin up at me, suddenly defiant.

"Why don't you draw me then?" she said in a low, threatening voice. "If you see me so clearly, *Professor Merrick*."

My name was a snarl on her curled lips. I panted as she fell to her knees. The thud echoed round us, too loud, too violent. Eithne shoved at the charcoal pencil and it rolled across the wood floor, coming to a stop at my toes. She was breathing heavily herself as she glared across at me, hard nipples clearly visible.

I licked my lips. My cock twitched. I knelt to pick up the pencil.

Class had begun.

EITHNE

Rian came to stand just before me where I knelt on the wood floor, the toe of his boots just a hair's breadth away from my knees. For a moment I kept my gaze down. I felt like a schoolgirl about to be punished. A daughter who failed to obey her father. A sinner at the altar, my priest backlit by the rain-streaked stained glass high above. With my eyes hidden from him, with my chin tucked against my chest, hair shadowing my face, I thought that I might be able to hide that my heart was racing, that my palms were growing slick where they rested against my thighs, that I wanted this. If there was a way to hide this obvious desire from myself, I would have done whatever it took.

Slowly I raised my chin up. It took craning my neck back, stretching the skin along my throat to see him; the motion compressed my arteries and I could feel every strained pump of my heart. Rian's gaze was cool as he looked down at me. Already he'd taken the role of the artist. In his head I could see him assessing colour, perspective, form, style. And I hadn't even spread my legs yet.

Rian's fingers moved to my hair with a distant professionalism, and yet it took everything inside of me not to lean into his touch. To flutter my weary eyes closed. To rest against the warmth and strength of his palm. The shifting of my hair sent goose bumps down my spine. When Rian lifted my chin a little higher, drawing my eyes to his, I squeezed my kneeling thighs tighter when he gave a soft little sigh. To please him, pleased me. I wished it was different. But it wasn't.

I remained as a doll would, still, silent, ready to be moved this way and that, *made* to move this way and that, as Rian let my chin fall, stepped back, and then circled me. I kept my gaze forward as the echo of his footprints bound me as surely as a rope around my chest would have. He squatted just a foot or two in front of me. Moved with the grace of a panther a little to the left. Then the right. On all fours he crawled to me. I shivered at the intensity of his pale blue eyes trailing over my body, looking for what, I wasn't sure. But I craved the attention. I longed to be adored, wanted, lusted over. Even if I'd never really allowed myself to admit it.

Rian was gentle as he took one boot in hand and slowly guided one leg and then the other untucked. For a second I really did feel like a doll: legs extended out in front of me, hands limp at my sides, not moving them from where they'd fallen. But I was sure dolls didn't feel lightning when a man brushed his fingers over their legs.

I was pliant, body feeling suddenly warm and loose, as Rian lifted my arms over my head, lifted my shirt from my body. I sucked in a breath as he leaned into me, his arms going around me so he could undo my bra. He set my clothes down carefully, unlike the sweatshirt I'd previously flung aside, placing it amongst the torn-up shreds of the pussies I'd drawn and seen rejected. He didn't touch me, though I saw it took a considerable amount of self-control not to as he pulled back and gazed upon me. My breasts were exposed, the soft skin over my clavicle there to skim his fingertip over. But he kept himself back.

The outline of his erection pressed needily against the front of his pants. A sweat glistened on his brow. His lips seemed to be dry as he kept licking them. From time to time he would bite down on his lower lip, or, maybe thinking I couldn't tell, chew at the inside of his mouth. The white cotton of his shirt clung to his shoulders as if he'd been working in the hot sun and there was an unsteadiness to his breathing. But he kept himself back.

When his fingers began to work on the button of my jeans, it was with the impersonality of opening a tub of acrylic paint. Pulling down the zipper seemed to have little difference from pulling a new brush clear of its plastic encasing. The only weakness Rian revealed was a quick hitch of his breath when his hands skimmed across my hips as he moved to help me out of my jeans. I watched him as I lifted my hips just enough for him to pull the thick material down. He kept his gaze on the blue folds always, but I saw the temptation of my milky flesh; it was like trying to watch the ocean without noticing the sky, big and expansive and calling above it.

My boots joined my shirt on the floor. Then my socks. My jeans. My panties. I expected the wood floor beneath me to have the cold sterility of a doctor's examination chair. But I found it warm beneath my palms, like sand that holds its heat for the moon. Was I running a fever? Had I given in to madness at last? Allowing my professor to undress me on the floor of his lecture hall? Praying for him to touch me, move me, mould me? Getting wet at the idea of him taking up a pencil and his eyes falling on me, on my pussy, for inspiration? Or was it just the friction of my angry feet that had warmed it? Was it pleasure or rage that kept away the cold? Did it even matter?

Rian came in close enough that I could make out the distinct colours of his irises. The palest of blues speckled through the deepest of blues like light through leaves. The contrast was subtle, nearly not there. And it was the trying to find it that drew me in like a labyrinth.

I kept my eyes on his as he carefully arranged my hair. I shivered when a silky strand came to cover one peaked nipple. My eyes fluttered closed when Rian adjusted that lock further, making it meander across the swell of my breast like a stream down a mountain. I noticed the stubble across his strong jaw as he worked.

The purple beneath his eyes seemed more pronounced, up this close. It made me wonder if real art really did require something of oneself, some sort of sacrifice. And was it really worth it? Art feeding on Rian like a succubus, *me* feeding on Rian like his very blood alone could sustain me.

Rian gave soft instructions even as he lifted my hands himself, beckoned my shoulders this way, my chin that way.

I was wet by the time his hands moved to my knees. I found myself more turned on than I could ever really remember. The close attention. The softness of his voice. The pampering, almost; time just for me, touch just for me.

Of course he had to move my legs apart. It was after all, my pussy that I'd dared him to draw. To show me what I apparently could not see. It was bound to be the final piece of the puzzle. What was all this for without it? And yet as Rian began to part my thighs a panic took over.

Whereas his touch on every other part of my body had been a pleasure, a tingling delight, I found his manoeuvring of my legs caused pain. Everything inside of me tensed to the point of snapping. I relented only because I was frozen with a sudden onset of terror. It was the very human fear of being awake for a surgery and not being able to tell the intent, huddled over, nameless doctors.

And the worst part was I didn't understand why. Why was it that the same girl who let her professor thrust his fingers into her soaking cunt in an art classroom now tremble at the thought of the same man simply looking at her, there on the floor?

"Relax, Eithne."

In my muddle of fear, I just...obeyed. Eased into his command. It felt so easy. It took all responsibility away from me. I was sinless. I was merely a puppet, I could tell myself, forced to submit.

Rian eased my knees apart until they could fall out no farther. He leaned back on his heels and sucked in a breath as he stared. He'd been able to hide his emotions before, but not anymore.

He picked up his charcoal pencil and began to work.

Fuck, it was too intimate. Too close. There on the floor I felt defenceless. Fear seized me. I was just a little girl with her legs spread for an older man. Never had I been so certain that my father was right about me. This was how my professor would remember me: the girl who barely fought when he pulled her thighs apart. When he took his token for later use. When he left her like that for whoever came next.

The sound of Rian sketching became the sound of claws on a cage. Out in the hall I heard movement, voices, a class dismissed, and I was sure they were all talking about Eithne Brady, Professor Merrick's toy, pet, slut. Easy, they whispered. Pathetic, they laughed. I hear she can't even come, they said. I hear she doesn't even care because she's a whore.

It all became too much. The scratching, the eyes, the murmuring voices just past the door, so thin, so insufficient. I tried to stay where Rian had put me, tried to remember the pleasure of this. There had been pleasure, hadn't there? But I was overwhelmed.

My heartbroken sob was masked by the hollow knocking of my knees together as I snapped my legs shut.

RIAN

The snapping together of Eithne's knees sounded like the jaws of a wounded animal. I set down my charcoal pencil as if to show her I meant her no harm. For I didn't. I was certain, at that point, that I couldn't.

Eithne flinched slightly as I moved to pick up the page. I paused. Glanced over at her. She met my eyes with shimmering ones of her own. Her bottom lip trembled. The first tear fell down her cheek and when I tried to get closer, she shut down completely. Forearms covering her face, elbows over breasts, fingers tearing at the crown of her head as she bent over herself. A doll folded back into its box. Playtime over.

Distraught moans came muffled from behind Eithne's cocoon. I touched her ankle; she wrenched it away. I brushed the soft skin of her thigh and she drew her knees up like a scared child. I sank back onto my heels for a moment and considered whether I was doing something good here. Whether it would have been better to do as Eithne commanded, pled, to let her go. Maybe a better man would have. A man with more control. A man who didn't love the edge like I did. A man who didn't miss the falling.

I was not that better man.

"Ms Brady," I said softly. I repeated her name, "I'd like to show you what I've drawn."

Eithne's shoulders shook and tears ran down her forearms, collected on her elbows like dewdrops on two blades of grass, fell silently as she sniffled.

"I believe it might help," I told her.

The formality. The distance. The foolish roleplay of a normal professor and student relationship. As if I wasn't, at that very moment, longing for the heat of her around me. As if she wasn't naked on the floor of the auditorium, her clothes spread artfully around her failed attempts to capture the most intimate part of her. As if we could ever be anything like that, anything close to Professor Merrick and Ms Brady.

"I'd like you to learn," I said when Eithne remained hidden, upset. "Ms Brady? Ms Brady!"

My strict tone echoed off the whitewashed walls, bounced off the high, murky ceiling. Eithne's sobs ceased. She parted her forearms to blink warily at me. Eyes puffy and red, eyelashes sparkling like iced branches on deadly cold winter mornings. She responded to my strictness. It was something she was comfortable with. Obeying. Following duty. Doing as she was told no matter what.

"Come here," I told her.

Eithne dragged a hand under her nose. Wiped at her eyes with her arm like a little girl. I wanted her to nestle against me as she scooted obediently toward me. I wanted her cheek on my chest, her still stuttering lungs beneath my palm, her fingertips a little too close to my still hard cock. But Eithne folded her legs beside me like this was indeed class, me the teacher, she the student. Intimacy remained foreign, rules and politeness and being a good pupil well understood.

Her knuckles rested against the wood planks of the floor. There was an innocence to her nakedness now, the exposure of her breasts, the long expanse of her spine, the little patch of dark hair stained wet between her pale thighs. I focused on my drawing to keep myself from reaching over and claiming her with my fingers, with my mouth, with my cock.

"Do you see the difference between what I drew of you and what you drew of you?" I asked in that same professional, restricted tone.

I watched as Eithne drew her eyes to the page. It filled me with pleasure when I saw her pupils widen, heard her breath catch. "It's…beautiful."

"Indeed."

I felt pride in my art that I hadn't felt for some time. The power to communicate. To reach someone. To bond.

She shook her head. "That's not me."

How could she not see? What was it that had blinded her to her beauty, to her sweetness, to herself? It made me mad once more. I wanted to shake Eithne. Slap her. Choke her. Knock sense into her. Peel whatever blinders she had taped across her eyes away without mercy. I sucked in a shaky breath, held it, and exhaled evenly.

"Ms Brady," I said softly, gently. "I'd like you to touch yourself as I guide you through this piece."

The revulsion was immediate. She tried to mask it. Tried to hide from me what was so obviously natural, impulsive.

Her voice was small as she replied, "I don't think that's necessary, Professor Merrick."

I took her hand. Warily she watched me from the corner of her eye. I raised her hand to my lips. Pressed the warmth of her fingers against mine. I trailed kisses along each one, soft, fluttering kisses. Eithne watched every press of my lips. She did not stop me as I guided her hand in between her crossed legs, pressed her fingers lightly against her lips as I had mine.

"Good girl," I murmured even as I felt her stiffen beside me.

I rested the paper across her knee and mine, her pussy

spanned the short distance. My fingertip brushed against the rough charcoal.

"Follow along," I commanded.

I got no response.

"Ms Brady?"

Her eyes were wide, a little frightened, a little excited, as she looked up at me, slightly startled from some reverie. She nodded curtly.

"Yes, Professor Merrick."

I traced the lines I'd drawn as I explained why I'd drawn them like that, as I explained what I'd seen. I instructed Eithne to find the place on herself, to touch it, to feel it, really *feel* it as I spoke. At first her fingertips barely skimmed across her lips. I wasn't even sure that if I were to take her fingers into my mouth that I would be able to taste her wetness. But as I spoke, clearly and calmly, I saw her move without being prompted.

I'd never much enjoyed teaching, never gotten much out of it. I mostly did it for an income to supplement what Mason, Conor and I paid ourselves from Dublin Ink. Also, to give myself a little more of a chance at that old straight and narrow: deadlines, structure, schedules, busy work, people who counted on me. But watching Eithne begin to connect herself with the drawing I'd done of her made me see what joy could be accomplished from teaching. The problem was I was always asked to teach about shite I didn't care about. I cared about Eithne. I cared deeply about Eithne. I was going to find out that I cared far, far, *far* too deeply for my little Raglan Road girl.

"Do you see the difference now?" I asked with a strained, tense voice because the need was becoming too much. My charcoal fingers longed for the real thing to trace, to plunge inside of. "Do you see the difference in what I drew of you?"

My breath caught in my throat when I noticed Eithne's finger moving, just a little, in and out of her pussy.

"You saw the beauty."

Such a simple answer. But never one more perfect.

I couldn't tear my eyes away as Eithne slipped a second finger inside of her. It turned me on more than I could say to know that she was watching me. That she was getting off on me watching her. Caring for her. Loving her.

"You deserve to see that beauty, too, Eithne," I said, my voice a haunting whisper. "You deserve to care for yourself. To love yourself. To pleasure yourself."

I swallowed heavily and added, "You deserve to be pleasured. And not just as a lucky happenstance of *me* being pleasured."

Eithne tucked her dark hair behind her sweet little ear so I could see all of her features, her swollen bottom lip as she moved her finger to circle her clit, the way it made her pupils dilate, her cheeks redden, the blinking of her eyelids go heavy, intoxicated, intoxicating. Eithne licked her lips, her mouth curling at the edges as she watched me watch her.

"I," I dared to say, "I want to teach you that, too."

EITHNE

Rian crawled on his knees toward me, his gaze on my pussy. I kept waiting for the tension, the fear, the shame. I knew it was there. Lurking just out of sight.

He paused before me, kneeling like in prayer as he exhaled deeply.

"Fuck, you are perfect."

My chest hitched as Rian lowered himself down between my legs. In that tiny gap of space before he touched me, where I was just a girl naked and exposed on the floor, instead of a grown woman about to be pleasured, I imagined alarm bells clanging out.

I tore my eyes away from him, sinking back on my elbows, staring up to the ceiling like I was in a dentist's chair trying to distract myself, trying to pretend this wasn't happening.

He traced the edges of me with the tip of his tongue, tentatively at first. My heart was racing faster and I waited for the panic to set in.

But Rian's tongue was like a drug of its own. Instead of stiffening, I melted into the wooden floor. I thought I could almost feel the charcoal on the crumpled pages beneath me, feel it sinking into me, entering my bloodstream, making me high as I began to writhe.

A little moan escaped my lips when Rian circled his tongue around my clit. The skin there was so sensitive, so electrified by any touch. I could feel an almost sort of buzzing in Rian's tongue. A longing for more. And I almost cried when I realised I wanted that, too. My body buzzed in time with his licks, reaching, yearning for a higher and higher pitch. A fever pitch. A burning, aching, throbbing fever pitch.

"Please," I moaned softly, the word drawn out of me as natural as breath while sleeping.

Rian circled my entrance with his finger. "Good, Eithne. Good."

Gone was Ms Brady. Gone was the pretext that I was his student, he my professor. There on the floor we were lovers. We were something natural, pure, beautiful. He wanted me to feel pleasure, and I, hardly daring to trust myself as I thought this, wanted to feel it.

I lifted my head and gazed down the length of my chest. It was something I'd never seen before. My tits rising like two snowy hills. The fine hair along my lower stomach raised as if a lightning storm were gathering on the horizon. A pair of piercing, pale blue eyes, hovering just above the juncture between my legs, somehow both natural and devastatingly unnatural. From another world. From a far-off heaven. It was a sight untouched by convention and morals and expectation: wild, pure, untouchable.

Then he slid his finger inside and curled it around to that spot—that fucking spot. At the same time his licks became firmer, more insistent.

My cries of pleasure were almost immediate as well. It was all so overwhelming that I had no mind for the closeness of the door, nor its thinness, nor the students passing beyond it like wraiths. Rian didn't stop me either. Rather he seemed spurred on by the involuntarily noises coming from my gasping lips as I clung to handfuls of his hair.

I screamed and rolled my hips against Rian's mouth like a madwoman.

Like a *whore*.

Panic came at me like a knife to the heart. Oh God, what was I doing? What was I letting him do? What was I risking? Pleasure seeping away like there was a hole in my gut.

"Stop!" I cried, panic clawing at my throat.

But as Rian held me tighter, as his tongue found my clit again, as he added a second finger. Pleasure and panic warred in me, the natural rightness of a body being pleasured fought with a lifetime of being taught this was *wrong*.

"Stop," I gasped as I stopped trying to tug Rian closer and began to push him away.

But he was too strong. Too consumed by me. Too desperate to throw us both off the edge. He growled against my pussy, "Come."

That single command. That was enough to free me from sin.

My back arched off the floor, crumpled pages sticking to it, as I came. I'd never felt such an intense pleasure, such an all-encompassing bliss. My vision flashed white and I lost myself completely as Rian licked me through wave after wave of intoxicating heat.

I barely realised that my own hands were travelling all up and down my body. Palms skimming over my achingly hard nipples. Fingers tightening and releasing and tightening again around my throat. I pressed my hands down my stomach, ran my fingertips along my thighs, sucked at my pointer finger with wet pops. I didn't realise I was doing any of this, lost in the pleasure that my body could give me, till I heard the frantic scratch of a charcoal pencil on paper.

I opened heavily lidded eyes to find Rian sketching me. It was different from last time, though he worked quickly for both.

Now he had a strange urgency, like I was a sunset quickly sinking. It was different, too, this time, because I could see what he saw. I was beautiful, stunning, worthy of being captured on the page. The pleasure I'd received was something transcendent.

And I lay there, watching him, letting him capture me on paper.

So he could keep me.

So at least in one way, I could be his.

RIAN

I showed up to class a full ten minutes late.

I opened the door and the quiet chatter immediately stopped. A few chairs screeched on the old wood floors. There were a few coughs, the opening of a notebook or two, a whisper here, a whisper there and then silence. I kept my chin against my chest as I crossed the short distance to the lectern. I kept my gaze away from the eager students all staring at me as I arranged my papers across the smooth panel of well-worn wood. I adjusted my pens. Made sure they were side by side. Perfectly straight. Caps all facing the same direction.

Only then did I look for her.

The dozens of faces blurred from one to the next as I searched row after row for her. She'd been all I could think about the past two days since she ran off after we got caught in the classroom across campus. She'd given me more of herself to draw. More of herself to obsess over. I'd anguished over the curve of her mouth as she came, over the exact shade of her pussy lips for hours upon hours. I'd missed work. Avoided calls from Mason, from Conor, from Aurnia. All I thought about was how to get Eithne to let me in. How to open her up. How to get close enough to her.

My only connection to her was still just the class. The one place I knew she would be. Had to be, if what she said about her major, about her goals was true. It felt like she was a vault with one door. And this class was that one door. What I said to her during this hour lecture would gain me entrance. Or lock me out forever.

The rest of the students didn't matter. The boys and girls that my eyes moved over faster and faster as they each one after the other proved not to be her, didn't matter. Nothing that I was about to say would be for them. It would all be for her. My Raglan Road girl. She alone would have my focus. If the others complained, then fine. I'd take a termination. I'd never teach at the university ever again in my life if it meant getting just one hour, just thirty, just fifteen minutes to speak to her without her pushing me away, without her running from me.

I scanned the top room of the lecture hall and reached the very last student there by the rear exit and it wasn't her. I scanned the class again just to be sure, but I knew…

She hadn't come.

She'd snag my gaze like a nail on an old sweater: tearing me in two, ripping me apart, ruining me forever like she already had. I looked once more, but it was as I suspected.

Eithne was not there.

I cleared my throat and said something like, "Today's lesson is that sometimes life doesn't turn out the way you thought it would."

I stacked my papers again as a dissatisfied murmur went through the lecture hall. Fuck them. Fuck them all. They knew nothing. And they never would, no matter what I said or didn't say.

"Oh, don't be such fucking ba—"

I was cut off by a hand on my groin. Whatever I was saying trailed off as I looked down between me and the lectern. I immediately recognised the milky-white skin poking out from the end of a scrunched-up old grey hoodie. It was all I could see of her, the rest hidden, lost in shadow. But it was all I needed to see. Her fingers brushing against my rapidly engorging cock was all I needed to feel.

Eithne had come.

I cleared my throat and looked up to see a lot of rather confused faces watching me intently. Half the students had already begun packing up as well, seemingly having given up on me. Those were the smart ones. If I ever had any intention of actually doing my professorly duties and passing out grades, I might have noted which ones were already halfway to the door. But I hadn't. It was hard to think when the zipper of my pants was inching down prong by painful prong.

"Is everything alright, Professor Merrick?" someone asked.

I struggled to maintain composure as I stepped a little closer to the lectern and said, "What I meant by that was that a lot of you probably thought I wouldn't just come in here and teach a lesson, but that's exactly what I'm going to do so..."

Everyone who had been heading toward the door nearly tripped over themselves trying to get back to their seats. The ones who hadn't yet moved gave the others self-satisfied smirks. If they only knew I had nothing at all to say to them.

I tightened my grip on the sides of the lectern as Eithne finally reached the very bottom of the zipper. I stared up at the high auditorium ceiling as Eithne tortured me with slipping the button through the hole so carefully and so slowly you'd think she was disarming a bomb. I wasn't exactly sure how I was supposed to put together coherent sentences while she did what I was sure she intended to do. I refocused on the words I'd written for her. But just when I got ahold of them, the button came loose and the relief of pressure in my groin made the words blur and swim away.

"Um," I said as the awkward silence in the auditorium grew more awkward. I had to say something. Anything. Before someone came over to check me for a stroke and found a student hidden beneath the lectern with my cock headed toward her outstretched tongue. "Um..."

The hollowed centre of Eithne's tongue touched the swollen head of my dick. My nails dug into the wood grain of the lectern and I cleared my throat, desperately trying to buy myself more time.

I clenched my eyes shut, chin fallen against my chest. How was I going to string words together when all I could think about was my little Raglan Road girl's warm knees against the cool floors? How was I supposed to make any thought coherent when I was already struggling to keep myself from panting like a dog? And how was it not completely obvious to anyone sitting in the deadly silent auditorium that I was lost in bliss and getting more lost by the second? How were the boys not all achingly hard like me? The girls all slipping their mouth-wetted fingers between their soaking thighs?

Eithne guided my cock fully into her mouth. I trembled as she wrapped her lips around my shaft. I felt the fullness, the velvety softness of her lips. I saw them in my mind, rolling over me like she was moving a red lipstick across her lips, back and forth, back and forth. I thought my knees would buckle when she circled her tongue round me, experimenting like she would with a brush.

"Professor Merrick?" a brave, or perhaps stupid, student asked, leaning forward to prop his elbows against the edge of his desk. "Do you need a glass of water or something?"

My shoulders were shaking from the pressure in my tensed arms. I shook my head. I gripped the lectern tighter. I raised my face to the class like David facing Goliath.

"I wanted to talk today about pleasure," I said, each word more difficult to force out than the last as Eithne began to bob her head slowly up and down the length of my dick. "Because art is nothing but pleasure."

It was a welcome reprieve to hear the scrape of pens on paper, the click of keys on a keyboard as the whole auditorium began to take notes. It allowed me the mercy of a quick, quiet groan. Hidden beneath the lectern I felt Eithne pause when she heard me.

Yes, I wanted to say to her—to whisper, to growl—*it feels good. Yes, it feels so fucking good. Yes, it's you, it's your tongue, it's your timid little knees bent beneath me that elicited that sound from deep in my chest. Keep going. Don't fucking stop.*

"If our art is not in the pursuit of pleasure, of toe-curling, mind-fucking, white light-flashing *pleasure,* then our art is a waste of time, an exercise in futility, in absurdity, in—" I clutched at the lectern as Eithne gagged on me, having pulled me as far as I could go into her mouth, "in straight-up fucking masochism."

The sound of notetaking filled the air of the too hot, too unmoving, almost unbearable auditorium. I wanted to strip off my clothes, in front of every single one of my students if needed. I wanted to buck my hips into Eithne's mouth. I wanted to be so damn rough that the sound of her gagging, choking, moaning for more filled every corner of the auditorium. I wanted more. More of her. More of her tight little mouth. More of that heat in my stomach that was threatening to take off like a wildfire.

"I'm not talking about some lofty fucking ideal," I continued as Eithne found a steady pace, my head colliding deliciously with the back of her throat on each deep thrust. "Fuck the pleasure of high society. Of improving oneself. Of raising humanity to some arbitrarily defined artistic height. Fuck all of that."

Fuck Eithne's mouth. Fuck her lips, red and swollen by now. Wet with her saliva, with my pre-cum that dripped down her chin, ran along the hollow of her delicate, pale throat, staining that hoodie I was going to tear in two right down the front of her fuckable tits. Fuck her little pussy that was wet for me, there in the shadows of the lectern. Fuck her till she screamed and showed everyone exactly what the fuck I was going on about, half out of my fucking mind.

"I'm talking about carnal pleasure," I said even as I stopped myself from doing exactly what I wanted, stopped myself from fucking Eithne's eager mouth. "I'm talking about the pleasure of the body. Of the naked, exposed, ravaged body. I'm talking about pleasure that leaves you breathless and sends shock waves through you, minutes, even hours later like little drops of LSD in your spinal cord. I'm talking about pleasure that drives you mad because you want it so…fucking…bad…"

I pounded the lectern and everyone in the hall jumped. Pencils lifted from smeared paper. Fingers bounced from keyboards. I startled everyone. Everyone but Eithne, down beneath me. I could almost feel her smiling round my seeping cock. She rolled my balls again in her damp palm like she'd just done and I gritted my teeth.

"Art," I said in a lowered voice as sweat broke out along my brow like I was feverish, like I was getting clean after years of using, like every nerve in my body was on fire, "art is giving that kind of pleasure. Art is receiving that kind of pleasure. Art is opening yourself wide to it. Spreading your fucking legs for it. Guiding it in deeper and deeper and, oh my God, *deeper*."

I was going to lose it. There was no way I could keep going like this. My legs were shaking. My nails stung from digging them so deeply into the sides of the lectern. I wasn't going to last much longer. I *couldn't* last much longer.

The class was in complete awe. Everyone hung on my every word. They thought I was taken over by some hypnotic passion for my craft. That I was imparting wisdom on them from the very depths of my soul.

I was, I supposed. But it wasn't just me. It was Eithne, too. Our joining together. Our becoming one. My cock. Her mouth. My precum mixing with her saliva. My hips rocking in time with her mouth. Her tits hard, my dick harder. Her tongue quivering, my thighs shaking so badly I thought I'd rattle the lectern.

Eithne gripped my shaft and twisted as her mouth pulled off of me, twisted as she sank her dripping wet, hot mouth back over me. Her other hand rolled my tightening balls like dice. A lucky roll. A pair of sixes. Everything going right. Everything going so goddamn perfectly.

I wanted to hold on just a few seconds longer. I wanted to say this to Eithne. Because it was all for her. All for fucking her. I needed to hold on. I tasted blood in the side of my mouth where I'd bitten it before I started speaking again in a voice as tight as a bow string about to snap.

"You'll never know art if you never open yourself to pleasure," I practically gasped. "Because art is pleasure. That's all it is. All it will ever be."

Eithne was choking on me with every thrust. Only my voice masked her frantic movements, the slick twist of her palm, the pleasured gag at the back of her throat. It was as if we were in a race with one another. A competition. She wanted to get me off before I could finish. I wanted to finish only when I was finished. Maybe she didn't want to hear what I had to say. Maybe she liked my cock so much she couldn't help herself. Either way I felt I was losing.

"You need to let me give you pleasure, show you pleasure, show you what this feels like," I said, staring out in front of me without seeing. I don't know what the reaction in the auditorium to these words were.

I'm sure most just wrote it down. Something to show their friends, look what Professor Merrick said. Something to jack off to in the middle of the night, yes, Professor Merrick, show me, show me pleasure. I couldn't be bothered to notice regardless. My vision was going blurry at the edges. Everything took on a white-hot glow. I wasn't even in the lecture hall anymore. It wasn't even the wood grain that my nails were digging into. I was in Eithne. It was her skin that I was digging into, causing to bleed.

Eithne squeezed tighter, sucked harder, brushed her fingertips along my drawn-up balls with such a shiver-inducing touch that I had only seconds left.

"Let me in," I said. "Let me have—"

I collapsed against the top of the lectern as I came. I buried my face within the confines of my arms and sank my teeth into my lower lip to try and muffle my uncontrollable groan. I would have sunk farther against the lectern, probably even until it fell over, revealing Eithne and her lips shimmering in the late afternoon sunlight, if it hadn't been for the jolts her lapping tongue sent through me. She was not only swallowing all of me, but she was doing it hungrily, greedily, eager for each and every last drop.

I was about to beg her to stop. Plead with her to give me mercy. Pull myself from the intense heat of her mouth. But it wasn't possible. I couldn't. I was a slave to her. In bondage to the whims of her perfect little tongue.

"Let me have you," I groaned into the cocoon of my arms that hung around my head limply, as if they too had been sucked dry. "You," I repeated, babbling like a tired child. "You, you, you."

My cock slipped from Eithne's mouth and everything was silent. I couldn't hear her over the continued pounding of my heart. I also couldn't hear a single student in the completely full auditorium. Coming to my senses slightly, I raised my head just enough to spy over the tops of my stacked forearms.

Every pair of eyes was on me, wide, shocked, aroused. They'd witnessed something that they couldn't understand. That they couldn't possibly ever know. I looked over the poor bastards and then sighed.

"Class dismissed."

EITHNE

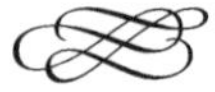

The floor beneath me rattled as the class began to file out of the auditorium.

I wiped my mouth in the dim light beneath the lectern and licked my lips. I could still taste the saltiness of Rian's cum. I savoured it. Held it on my tongue. Still, I wanted more.

My mouth watered. My nipples ached against the fabric of my sweatshirt, and my slick thighs were squeezed together as I sat on my kneeling knees. Rian's cock still hung free from his pants. Still long and thick. Still glistening with my saliva. Still alluring as I slipped my hands beneath my butt to keep myself from reaching out for it. Guiding it toward my pussy. Taking my own pleasure.

My cheeks flared hot and uncomfortable. It had nothing to do with the voices of students just beyond a thin panel of wood behind me. They were trying to ask questions to Professor Merrick; Professor Merrick was trying to get them to leave.

"No, I have some pressing business to attend to," I heard him tell them.

It must have been slightly confusing to them. When he said this and then remained frozen at the spot. Not gathering up his bag that was limp beside the lectern. Not heading toward the door. I alone knew why. And it turned me on. I bit my lower lip and told myself to stop.

"Not now," Rian tried again.

He shifted in tighter toward the empty space beneath the lectern, shifted in tighter toward me. I knew it was just to hide his spent erection from his students. But I liked it, nonetheless. Him close. Him closer. His body within reach. His cock meant just for me. My stomach clenched. My chin fell to my chest like I was praying, kneeling before a pew in a dusty, sunlit church.

"Pray. Go on and pray. Pray for your damned soul. Pray for your whore mouth. No one's listening, Eithne. Not a goddamn one."

Rian called toward the door, "Yes, yes, next class. Yes, no, really, get the fuck out now!"

I'd told myself that I'd just been here to pay him back. That now that I'd made him come, tasted him, we were even and we didn't have to keep going.

But I was lying to myself.

I wasn't just here for him. I was here for me. I wanted him to carry out everything he'd promised me. Pain. Pleasure. I wanted to know everything about sinful sex. I wanted Rian.

The truth was I hadn't been able to *stop* thinking about him. I'd been walking around in an agitated jittery state, desperate for release, desperate for him.

Later I'd have to live with myself, live with the truth that my father was right all along. Right now, I didn't care if he was.

The door clicked shut. For a moment there was nothing. Just the panting of my own breath in that hot dark. Just the ticking of the clock on the wall. Just the beating of my ashamed heart in time. Slow and anguished and devastated.

Rian slipped his spent cock back into his pants. Zippered. Buttoned. His legs moved away from the lectern and I froze.

Oh God, what had I done? Oh God, what I had *done?*

I heard a lock switch on the door, footsteps coming back.

Rian again stood before the lectern. But this time he lowered himself in front of me, reached under the desk for me. His strong hands closed around my upper arms. I barely had time to resist before he was pulling me out to my feet and I was blinking at the light.

I thought I'd see amusement on his face; what a joy it must have been, to not even ask for a too-young student to suck him off during class, to swallow every last drop as he lectured. I thought there would be a look in Rian's eyes that resembled my father's, that resembled Stewart's, fevered and disgusted.

But that wasn't the way Rian looked at me at all.

He looked at me like he'd just woken up starving. Like I was his next meal.

"You…" his voice, dark and husky, slid down my body in shivers, "have been a very naughty girl."

His hands slid down my body, causing heat to pulse in my core. He grabbed my ass, he lifted me to sit at the edge of the lectern. Before I could close my legs, he stepped between them, forcing me to stay open. His gaze dropped to my skirt riding up my thighs. Fuck. My pussy clenched.

I swear he could see, he could tell, that I wasn't wearing any panties.

"Fuck, I can *smell* you. So sweet. Can't wait to sink inside you…" He reached for my skirt.

Before I could stop myself, I pushed his hands away.

"I… I need to go," I said, my voice sounding like I hadn't used it for years.

"You need to come…" Rian's hands slid onto my thighs and held me down, held me in place like nails to a cross, his touch sending another wave of need through me, "…all over my face…" his eyes not once flinched from mine, "with your thighs over my shoulders. With my fingers deep in your cunt and your ass. Your taste on my tongue."

I tried not to squirm, I really did. Tried not to let my body react the way it did to his filthy words. But I was leaking all over this lectern. If I moved now, I'd leave a wet streak of my shame.

This was all my fault, getting myself into this mess. I couldn't control myself. I was entangled now. I was caught in his snare and fighting was only making it worse.

Still, I fought. "I—we shouldn't."

I tried to pull his fingers off my thighs, but instead of freeing myself, my fingers became entangled with his.

Rian just looking at me with that burrow-deep-into-my-soul stare. Like he saw me—*all* of me—and desperately wanted what he saw.

"Fuck 'shouldn't'," he said. "Your job as an artist, is to say 'I can' and 'I will.'"

"I...can't." My words sounded weak even to me.

"Then why did you come..." he chuckled, "why did you make me come down your throat in front of all those students?"

"I...I just wanted to repay you. We're even now. It's done."

I went to hop off but all I did was move closer to him. I gasped as my core pressed against his hips.

The hunger behind Rian's blue eyes illuminated them like he wasn't quite human. All dazzling, refracted light. All sharp jewel edges. All angry seas.

"Just a repayment, huh?"

"Yes, sir."

"So if I reach under this skirt, I won't find you wet?"

I swallowed a moan.

I didn't dare more—dare breathe—as his fingers slid up my thigh, until his fingers slid in the sinful shame that coated my inner thighs.

He groaned low in his throat and I felt it vibrate all through my body. "Eithne...you are soaking."

His fingers climbed farther, brushed the creases where my thigh met my pussy.

"Fuck," he hissed, he choked, he cursed, "you didn't wear any…"

His other hand released my thigh, only to grab my neck, my chin, my face and hold it inches from his. He forced me to face him, forced me to stare right back into his eyes.

"Mark my words, Eithne, I'm going to fuck you. I'm going to mark your ass with my palm. I bet you'd love it. I bet you'd beg like a whore."

Heat flooded the space between my legs and I repressed a moan. I *was* a whore. I was *his* whore but for some reason I liked it.

"I bet you'd even let me lick your ass. I bet I'd have to hold your hips down to the ground as you tried to fuck my face because you wanted *more*."

I let out a groan as his words seared my insides like flames, as the wicked thing inside me took over.

"Yes—"

"Yes, what?" he demanded. His fingers traced me, my slick folds yielding to him as he found my clit.

My chest was stuttering. I was racked with guilt, with shame, with desire. I opened my mouth, but my lips floundered. Rian's fingers never moved, never circled me as he promised he'd do with his tongue. He wouldn't give me the satisfaction until I gave him his.

"Yes, I want to fuck your face."

He grinned. "Good girl."

He slid three fingers inside me all the way to the hilt, filling me. I was so wet all resistance had disappeared.

"Oh sweet Raglan Road girl, you're going to get fucked so hard."

The rattle of the doorknob jolted us both from our trance, shattered the bubble that had formed around us. It shocked me like ice water thrown over me. The wicked thing retreated inside me until cold fear was all I felt.

I shook my head and tried to pull away from Rian's hand. "Professor Merrick—"

"Ignore them."

"We can't."

I shoved myself to my feet, my legs shaking as I brushed down my skirt, and hurried toward the door that rattled again. Behind the frosted glass a voice called, "Hello? Is there someone there?"

Rian caught me with an arm around my waist halfway to the door and he crushed my side to him. "This isn't over."

The intensity of his gaze frightened me. The urgency of his cock against my thigh, hard already again for me, shook my resolve. God, I wanted him. Wanted his fingers, his tongue, his cock, in all the ways he promised me and more. In every single needy hole.

If it weren't for the voice outside the door, things would have been different. I didn't know whether to be grateful or angry at the interruption.

"You need to leave me alone," I said weakly, trying one more time to "do the right thing". After all, I was a good girl. I had to be a good girl.

He gave me a dark smile. "You don't actually want that."

"I'll…I'll leave the school—" I said weakly.

"I'll find you." The muscles in Rian's arms trembled. "Wherever you go…"

I believed him. It should scare me, what he just said. This obsession. Instead it lit something inside me. A fire I never knew I had. An ache, a burning. I felt *alive*.

"Then…later," I whispered, aware of the shadowy outline just past the panel of glass. "Maybe later you can…help me with my art."

"Your art?"

I nodded, hoping he'd understand that I needed this flimsy excuse. Needed another reason to see him other than because I wanted to get fucked. Other than he brought out something wicked in me and I wanted to be wicked.

"Okay, I'll help you with your…art."

"Okay."

"Tonight," he said without question.

I swallowed, then thinking of Stewart, said, "It has to be your place, though."

Rian nodded again. "Do you know the Dolphins Barn area?"

I shook my head.

"Then meet me nearby at a place called Dublin Ink."

RIAN

The problem with the good things is...if one is good, why isn't two better? If two is better, why not three? And if you make it to three, how the fuck are you supposed to ever stop since it's that fucking good?

There were lots of good things in life. Friends. A pint of beer. Sunshine. A new tattoo. Weed. Drugs.

Eithne.

How was I supposed to know which one to stop at one? And which one to never stop. How was I supposed to tell when more would heal me? Or when more would kill me. If it was all good, if it was all so fucking good, then why stop? Why not just keep going till you couldn't. Till you just fucking couldn't.

"Maybe we can just chill for a second, eh?"

The joint unleashed curling tendrils of smoke between Conor and me in the faint pink neon glow of Dublin Ink. I held it extended toward him. My arm felt heavy on the armrest of the couch. Felt good. Felt like I could sink into the faded floral cushions and just keep sinking. I looked with hooded eyes at Conor. Looked at the joint and its alluring red smoulder. Looked back at Conor. Squinted. Groaned.

Great. Fucking great. I was getting "concerned" Conor. The Conor who held his thick arms crossed a little too high on his mammoth chest. The Conor who smiled even less than usual. The Conor who would in a moment or two clear his throat and say we really should have a good chat. "Concerned" Conor fucking sucked.

Rolling my eyes felt like looping over the bar on the swings as a kid, aka impossible. I got halfway, tired, and let my eyes fall back down. This probably did not manage to make "concerned" Conor any less "concerned". I didn't give a fuck. I shrugged my shoulders, drew the joint slowly back to my mouth, and inhaled deeply before saying, "I don't have a clue what you could possibly be talking about."

It was midnight. Or maybe it was two a.m. Hell, maybe time didn't even exist anymore. All I knew was that it was past eight. And Eithne hadn't come.

She hadn't fucking come.

"Look," Conor said, wriggling his folded arms even higher up his chest till they practically skimmed his bearded chin, "we've had a fun night. Talked a bit. Let's call it a day I think."

I snorted smoke from my nose. My night was shite. I'd jumped at every person passing down the sidewalk like a skittish alley cat. I stood by the window for what felt like hours, staring down at the rickety old bus stop. I stalked outside in the rain from corner to corner in case she'd gotten lost and was just out of sight.

The whole night I felt like my heart was racing, my skin was burning, my mind was diving off a deep and endless cliff. The whole night I sucked at joint after joint like it was Eithne's nipple, like it was Eithne's bottom lip, like it was Eithne's clit. The whole night Conor said two fucking things: "pot?" and "sure, I guess".

Conor glanced up toward the stairs. He was hoping Mason would come down from fucking Miss Last Night (wait, I guess she was Mrs What Happened In Vegas). Conor was hoping Mason had worked up a thirst, an appetite, an urge for whipped cream. For anything. Conor was hoping he'd get some "backup". Someone who was better at this whole "talking" thing.

I guess I should have been grateful that it was Conor who decided to hang out with me as I waited for Eithne to not fucking show. He was totally out of his depths. I inhaled again and relished the burn in my lungs.

Conor dragged a hand through his hair to his bun. "Erm, Rian, well, look, I don't want to say this, but..."

Then don't. Then fucking don't.

"...Aurnia told me about the, um, tattoos."

I flicked some ash from my knee. The silence became as heavy as my eyelids. I thought I could sink in it, too. Sink deeper and deeper into the silence till I couldn't even hear her name repeated like a broken record: Eithne, Eithne, my little Raglan Road girl...

"Rian?"

I'm not sure how many times Conor had to say my name. Hers was all I heard.

"Rian!" Conor snapped. He was actually angry when I lolled my head over to the side to look at him. "You can't just disappear like that when I'm trying to talk to you."

I mumbled around the joint which was already burning my lips, "So you've finally discovered that I'm a tattoo artist. All you needed was a junior sleuth by your side to crack the case."

Conor was not amused.

"What do you want?" I asked. "A fucking medal? The keys to the city?"

"You know what I mean," Conor grumbled.

"I don't," I said. "I'm a tattoo artist who owns a tattoo parlour who does tattoos. I don't see what big mystery you've unearthed here."

The soft buzzing of the neon light cut into the silence.

"Aurnia said it was a girl's face," Conor finally said. "Again and again, Rian."

I cherished the smouldering paper against my lips. If Eithne couldn't bite me, wouldn't bite me, I'd let my drugs do it. I shrugged after a moment or two.

"It's a good face."

"She said you were looking for *her*," Conor said.

"Aren't we all just looking for someone?"

Conor adjusted himself in the armchair.

I avoided his gaze and stared up at the ceiling through an exhale of smoke.

"Is this girl even real?" Conor asked.

I snorted. "Is any of this even real?"

"Rian…"

I clenched my fists. Wasn't it just my luck that Aurnia came into Conor's life and went about this nasty business of making him a better man and all that bullshite just when I needed the old Conor? The distant, moody, impersonal Conor? The Conor who let another someone else handle it when things got…sensitive? The Conor who shared nothing except the occasional angry scowl? Why couldn't he just drop this? Why couldn't he just leave this the fuck alone?

Damn, and now my joint was burned down.

I lifted my hips to reach the papers and the little baggy of weed in my back pocket. Conor let out a low grunt of discontent. I rolled another joint on the little coffee table in front of the couch, nestled like an island amongst the black leather tattoo chairs. I drew my tongue slowly along the thin paper, aware the whole time of Conor's eyes on me. My fingers began to tremble when I remembered what I could have been drawing my tongue across instead, what I *should* have been attending to with my tongue. I masked the shaking with the flicker of a match's flame. Smoke rose between Conor and me, another divider amongst many, as I waved the spent match.

Conor waited till I'd taken my first long drag, waited till I'd held it deep in my lungs, waited till I exhaled and sank back, completely unarmed, completely at his mercy, before attacking.

"Rian..."

It wasn't his voice I wanted to hear say my name. It was hers. As the pot made everything hazy, it was all I could think about. My name on her tongue, the tongue that had held my cockhead, hollowed out for the length of my shaft. My name from her lips, wet or trembling or moaning, it didn't matter. My name from the back of her throat, from the depths of her lungs, from where smoke swirled in mine making my head light and my heart heavy.

"What?"

"Is she real?"

I attempted to pass Conor the joint, but he shook his head. I guess his concern had just intensified; to me that's exactly when you need a good hit, but to each their own.

"Yes. No..." I said, words twisting in the air above me just like the smoke had as I watched. "Every time I try to reach for her, she slips away. Every time I try to get closer, she disappears. Every time I see her in my dreams, I wake and I'm alone, terribly alone."

I inhaled and the end of the joint flared red.

"Maybe I'm just making her up to torment myself," I went on, vision hazy, words growing vague, distant even as I spoke them aloud. "She'll always be almost real. I'll always want her, but I'll never be able to have her. She'll consume me and I'll die insisting that it was real. That she was mine. That we had something. But it won't be true. It'll all be in my head."

Conor had gone silent. I might have worried if I'd been sober. But I was far from that.

"I don't even care if she's real," I said in a half whisper. "I'll chase her to the ends of the earth. I'll lose my sanity for her even if she's the thing that's driving me insane."

A car passed. Its lights illuminated the unmoving interior of Dublin Ink. Conor and I squinted against its light before we were plunged back into darkness. A darkness that seemed deeper now, having seen for just a moment something brighter.

"So to answer your question," I said with a wry smile. "She's real. Or not. I don't fucking care."

I pushed myself to standing. Conor flinched when I rocked unsteadily.

"I'm fine," I said, laughing. "Really, I just need some air."

"Who keeps calling?" Conor said.

I shrugged again. "Not her."

I moved toward the door. Conor stood and blocked my path. At his full height he had nearly a head on me. And I'd say fifty pounds. Of muscle. I reminded myself to politely ask Aurnia to stop whatever voodoo she was doing on my friend. I really didn't have time for his newfound sincerity. This new caring-ness.

"Rian, I'm worried about you," he said.

"This will help," I said, offering again the joint.

"I'm serious."

Conor met my gaze and I could see he was remembering a time…a dark time. I sighed and patted his arm.

"Listen, it's not like before," I told him. "It's not going to be like before."

Conor's eyes went to the joint.

"I'm in control," I reassured him. "I know what it's like not to be. To lose yourself. And I'm not going there again. I know what that cliff face looks like."

"Yeah, well, so does everybody who's already falling from it," Conor replied. "When it's already too late."

I reached for the door and Conor did not stop me.

"I'll never go back there," I told him, hesitating in the doorway. "It's hell. Nobody seeks out hell."

The night breeze was icy. It signalled the end of autumn. It meant a shift was occurring. A change coming.

But my change had already come. Swept in early on the wind. My Raglan Road girl. She'd found her way inside of me and I would never be the same. I had as little control over it, over her as the trees had of losing their leaves, the grass of withering beneath the frost, the air of turning cold, brittle, cruel. I could tell myself she wouldn't destroy me, but wouldn't it be foolish? A rose never expects to last the winter. Why should I?

"It's not empty, you know?"

I glanced back over my shoulder, collar turned up against the increasing wind. Conor had his head out the door of Dublin Ink. I stared back at him, joint between my lips, hands stuffed into my pockets.

"Hell," Conor called out, his voice unattainable in the silence of the night. "Maybe nobody seeks it out, but that doesn't mean people don't end up there anyway."

I stared at him without speaking.

"You'll tell us if you need help, won't you?"

I felt bad for Conor for a minute. For Aurnia. For Mason. They wanted to help. But I knew they couldn't.

"Of course."

EITHNE

All it took was one phone call.

I could have ignored it. If the bus had arrived twenty seconds earlier, I could have been so preoccupied with squeezing myself through the crowded rows of seats that I could have missed it entirely. It would have gone to voicemail. I would have checked it only once I left Dublin Ink. I would have still had Rian's ink-stained fingers on my art, his ink-stained fingers on me.

But I didn't ignore it.

"This is Eithne," I said over the frazzled noise of evening traffic, students tramping the sidewalks toward the nearest bar, and my own breathless excitement as I rose onto tiptoes to see if my bus had at last rounded the busy intersection.

"Ms Brady?"

"Yes, that's me. Who is this?"

I fumbled with my portfolio, wedged it under one arm so that I could plug one ear to hear better.

"This is your very pissed off landlord, Ms Brady."

My stomach dropped. I'd gotten calls like this one before.

More times than I could count. But I'd never been so devastated to get one of those calls.

The bus I had intended to get on pulled up with a cough of smoke. The door screeched open and people piled in. The doors closed and I remained there on the sidewalk.

I sank onto the gum-speckled bench and watched the bus I was supposed to be on disappear around the corner. I could almost see myself on that bus, the *me* that just wasn't to be: lower lip held anxiously between my teeth, a grin I couldn't quite contain curling the corners of my mouth, my eyes bouncing from building to building, eager to spy the first glimpse of Dublin Ink.

"Ms Brady?"

The image of *me* on that bus disappeared.

"Early this afternoon we received several complaints about noise coming from your apartment. When we tried to reach you with no luck, I entered the apartment to find a man who was out of his mind, and not on the lease, I might add, destroying the place in some kind of wild frenzy."

I glanced at the old lady seated beside me, clutching her groceries to her narrow chest. I cleared my throat.

"He's my brother," I said in a small, embarrassed voice.

"Is that supposed to explain why you allowed him to come into the place and destroy it?"

"No," I said pitifully. "It just—I—he was probably just looking for his medication. He gets quite distressed when he can't find it, and listen, I'm terribly sorry for the mess and the noise and I'll of course clean everything up and—"

"Ms Brady," the landlord interrupted and then once more when I kept rambling on, "I'm sorry if I didn't relay the seriousness of the matter, but there are holes in the walls and cabinets torn down. You should be worrying less about fixing the mess and worry more about me calling the police and having your brother arrested. I can't have you staying there anymore."

I begged for a second chance. Tried to offer more money. An additional security deposit. An extra month's rent. Tried to argue that my brother was sick and I couldn't afford the time or money to find a new place when I needed to spend my time tending to him. None of it worked.

I was being evicted. Again.

This was my punishment, for thinking I could just *take* pleasure. That I could meet my professor after school with the flimsy excuse of looking at my art. I had responsibilities. Bills. Work. Study.

Rian was the snake offering me the apple. I was so weak that I yearned to take it. That I let him give it to me on the floor of the lecture hall.

"I will offer you this piece of advice," the landlord said as I fought back tears there on that bus bench—as another bus that could have been going to Dublin Ink closed its doors in front of me. "You seem like a nice young lady. I'd question whether your brother really wants to get better, Ms Brady. Because there will always be more walls to tear down in search of his 'medication'."

It was too far. Too far.

"You don't know my brother," I said, lifting my sunken chin.

"No, I don't," the landlord said. "But I'm suggesting you might not either."

She hung up and I stared at the screen—7:32 blinked in red. Seven minutes and thirty-two seconds. That's how long it took to destroy what I'd built over the last six months. Seven minutes and thirty-two seconds. Long enough for the tides to come in, as they always did, and sweep away the little castle of sand I'd stacked with my little bucket. Seven minutes and thirty-two seconds. I wondered if the Eithne that got on the bus would be at Dublin Ink in seven minutes and thirty-two seconds. I wondered how fast I'd have to run to catch up with her.

To catch up with the life I'd never have.

~

My legs shook like I'd been running as I stood in front of the desk at the college registrar's office.

"I'll be wit' ye in just a moment," the woman working the desk called to me.

She had an armful of manila folders and was wrangling them without much success into an old filing drawer. I sighed. Drew my fingers through my hair and propped my elbows on the desk littered with pamphlets for all kinds of other opportunities I'd never take.

"No rush," I said.

My heart no longer beat wildly like it had last night at the bus stop. I no longer felt that urgency in my tapping toes, that excitement in my bloodstream. I no longer craned my neck to see if it was coming, finally coming, the bus to take me to Rian and the opportunity to escape it all, if just for one night.

Now there was a heaviness in my feet, a stiffness in my neck, a weariness in my bones.

"Sorry about the wait, dear." She dusted off her hands and arranged herself in the office chair behind the big desk.

"I'd like to switch out of this class, please," I said, handing across a form. "It's no longer in line with the degree I need. A waste of time at this point."

The woman lowered her glasses to the bridge of her nose and typed some information from the form into her computer.

"Now," she said as she scrolled the page. "Now..."

I fought the heaviness of my eyelids as I waited. I was already exhausted and I hadn't even begun all the work before me: packing, finding a new place, settling Stewart down, nursing him if he was sick again, finding him if he tried to run off. Then there was studying, working, eating. It was all too much. But Stewart had to be my priority. Getting him better. That was number one. I saw that now.

It had been silly, this fantasy with Rian. This alternate life where we pored over art in a tattoo parlour late into the early hours of the morning. Fingers brushing. Then knees touching. A spark of electricity. Then everything. All at once. His body. Mine. Art and clothes and us on the floor. This alternate life where I wasn't just a whore who hid beneath lecterns. Because Rian loved me. Because with his love I was cleansed.

"Now..." the registrar said once more before slipping the form back across the desk toward my fingers. I hadn't realised how tightly I'd been squeezing the edge, knuckles white.

"All done?" I asked.

A pen tapped a signature box at the bottom of the page.

"This course requires the professor's signature to switch out of," she said. "So just get that for us and we'll get you all sorted."

My heart seized.

"The professor's signature?"

The registrar turned to me with a smile that I did not share. "Professor Merrick."

RIAN

She was cool to the touch.

My palms cupped her and she was soft, supple, wet. She responded to the slightest pressure. Just a little too much and she would squirm away. Just a little too soft and she would try to take control. She felt like butter beneath me. Like silk. I worked her till she was to the point of breaking. I pushed her further. She could take it; I was sure she could take it. She moved with me like we were partners in a dance. Like we were holding each other in a lake, bobbing with its rhythm. Like we were fucking.

She relented to my pressure. She was mine. She was all mine.

The door to the college's pottery studio slammed open. It was all the distraction I needed to lose control. The clay I'd been spinning whipped from the stand and landed with a wet splatter a few feet away. Before me stood Eithne. Darkness in her eyes, hair uncombed and tangled. Old collegiate sweatshirt crumpled and limp on her shoulders as if situated haphazardly on a spare hanger. In her hands she gripped a piece of paper.

She glared at me from across the pottery wheel that kept spinning between my thighs.

"You're supposed to be at your office hours," she said, pointing indignantly at the clock. I did not follow her finger, did not take my eyes off her in case she disappeared again.

"You were supposed to be at Dublin Ink yesterday." I tried not to let bitterness cloud my voice, but her rejection still stung.

"I've searched all over campus for you and frankly I have a million better things to do," she added with a huff, ignoring my statement.

She remained half a room away, but I could feel her desire to step closer. It was as if a tether was wrapped around the spinning pottery wheel and with each rotation it was tightening. I knew soon she would have no choice but to step closer. Or get dragged.

"Come here," I commanded.

My hands were still wet from the clay. I wanted to drag them across her skin before they dried. I wanted to see my handprints against her pale chest. I wanted to draw lines across her naked back like a map, in case I couldn't find her again. In case I doubted once more that she was real, like Conor and Mason and Aurnia.

"No," Eithne said.

I stopped the wheel. The pottery room suddenly felt hollow. Deadly silent. Not even the clock on the wall seemed to be ticking.

"What did you say?"

Eithne swallowed. Gripped the piece of paper clutched in her hand even tighter.

"I need your signature to switch out of your class," she said. "That's all I need from you. It's the reason I came here, the reason I found you. The only reason. Once you sign this form, I'm leaving. And I'd really much prefer that you come to me."

Eithne said these sentences like they were rehearsed. Like a little girl in a school play with a handful of lines she committed to memory each night before bed. Like if she didn't say them all, and just right, she would turn into clay right there at the door and let me have my way with her, form her as I willed. Do with her supple, relenting body as I willed.

"You need my signature," I repeated slowly.

Eithne nodded. Was she afraid to speak? Afraid to say she needed more than just that? Much more? Was she afraid to say she was like me? Hungry? Helpless?

"And if you don't have my signature..."

Eithne set her jaw. She extended the form toward me. She didn't move any closer. But she stretched out her arm. A little girl feeding the strange dog. The dog that might lick her hand. The dog that might bite.

"I need to get going," she said.

"I thought you needed my signature."

Eithne kept her gaze steady on me and she kept the bunched-up form steady in her extended arm. With a sigh, I pushed up from my knees. I noticed a slight exhale of relief from my little Raglan Road girl. Her arm sank an inch or two. She thought she was getting what she wanted. Or rather what she thought she wanted.

It was a pity I didn't see her reaction when I bent down to retrieve the tossed clay. I liked her angry. Liked the way the burning red emotion made her freckled nostrils flare. Darkened the pupils of her eyes. Brought colour to her pale cheeks.

My back turned to her as I walked back to my stool. My gaze was fixed downward as I repositioned the clay between my palms and began the wheel turning once more.

If I couldn't have her in the flesh, I could have her this way. I could mould the narrow curve of her waist. I could grip her thigh with both hands like I was pulling myself up it to her wet pussy. I could imagine her heartbeat under my mouth in the steady rhythm of the wheel round and round and round.

"Are you punishing me for not coming over?" Eithne asked after several terse minutes.

I pressed my thumbs into the clay like I would the swell of Eithne's hips and relished the cool clay absorbing me, coming around my fingers like waves.

"Are you?" Eithne pressed, anger flaring in her voice. "Because I wouldn't let you fuck me? Your *twenty-one*-year-old student?"

I ignored this. "I have a lot to teach you, Ms Brady."

I let her mind spin like the wheel. What could I possibly mean? What could I teach her? What could her body learn from mine? What new pleasure could I engrain in her head? In her heart?

"I already told you what I'm majoring in," Eithne replied. "It has nothing to do with whatever grand speech about pleasure you gave last class."

I looked up, an eyebrow lifted.

"You were listening?" I asked. "I thought you might be a little preoccupied."

This drew even more colour to Eithne's face. She waved the form at me. Was it already going damp in her palm? Was it soon to go limp, limp like she would be atop me, after I sated her, gave her what she needed, what I needed?

"I'm asking you to sign the fucking form, Professor Merrick," she said.

I shrugged.

"And I'm saying no."

I could sense her anger rising. Sense it like you could in a bull who snorts and kicks in his pen. Eager to be released. Eager *for* release.

"You'll take my class," I said. "And you'll be glad you did."

Her teeth were surely clenched as she said, "I don't want to learn anything you have to teach me."

"I disagree."

"Are we still talking about college?"

I raised my gaze again as the smooth clay twisted and writhed between my fingers.

"What else would we be talking about?"

She glared at me.

"Wasn't it art that you wanted to show me?" I said, squeezing the clay a little tighter as it threatened to buck. "Wasn't that all you wanted? Wasn't that all you wanted of me? My...eyes? My appreciation. My appraisal?"

Eithne's arm with the unsigned form fell to her side. She either no longer had the strength to hold it up or she'd given in. Realised I wasn't going to give her what she wanted. Because I knew it wasn't what she wanted.

"You don't know me," she said. "You think you do. You think that's me between your hands right now. But it's not. You think that just because I sucked your cock that you understand who I am. You don't."

Her voice was rising steadily and the fire in it turned me on. The clay I was still squeezing too hard covered my growing erection. Because she was right: I didn't know her. I didn't understand her. But it was all I fucking wanted in the world.

"You think if you just keep moving your thumbs like that that I'll forget all about this form, strip off my clothes, and take that hunk of clay's place beneath you," she went on, face flushed with colour. "You think I won't be able to resist because I'm a slut, and what slut doesn't want to be manipulated like clay? You think all I can think of when I see you there is me in your hands."

The pressure of my cock against my pants was growing uncomfortable. She'd gotten me fully hard, whether she'd intended to or not.

"Come here," I said.

"Sign my fucking form," she shot back.

"Come here, Eithne."

"Why won't you just let me go?"

I looked up from the pottery wheel as it slowed. Our eyes met across the light-stripped room as it came to a stop. I felt the clay unmoving beneath my fingers.

In the silence I wondered if she could see. See that I wouldn't let her go. That I couldn't. It was the last thing in the world she wanted, to *be* let go.

I could hold her like that un-beating clay loose in my hands. I could be gentle, smooth my palms against her curves like she was made of water. But I knew she didn't actually want me to be gentle. She wanted my violent need, my furious desire. Screw, slow. Fuck, gentle. Slow and gentle were for ghosts pretending to be alive. There was too much life inside her, too much unlit fire, a bed of kindling in her soul that was just waiting for a spark.

I wondered if she could see herself reflected in my eyes. See her desire. See her need. See that her body was calling for mine. See that it was entirely outside of our control now.

"I'm not signing that form."

With a growl she balled the paper in her fist. "Why can't just one person in my life try to make things easier on me? Why can't just one fucking man *help* me?"

"You'll thank me."

"Thank you? *Thank* you?"

She dug her nails into a block of clay on the nearest table and threw the torn piece at me. It collided with my chest like a fist at the boxing gym.

"Fuck you!" she shouted, panting as her chest heaved.

I retrieved the clay from where it had fallen and added it to my clay on the wheel. Eithne's breathing got more frantic when I turned on the wheel again. A second chunk of clay hit me on the shoulder. I collected this one much the same.

Her footsteps were fast and erratic. A little crazy. Just the way I liked them.

I turned and Eithne was standing before me. Before I could say a word, she jammed her hands into the clay, destroying my work. Our fingers touched amongst the cool wetness. Our eyes locked. There was frustration there. Fury even. But there…in the depths of all that hatred, was a spark.

Eyes not leaving mine, she pulled her hands free and dragged them, covered to the wrist in wet clay, down my chest.

She was on fire now. There was no going back. No extinguishing it.

She knew that now.

Me? I'd always known.

EITHNE

I'd wanted to hurt him.

Whether I realised it in the moment or not, I'd wanted him to feel pain. The clay was heavy. Solid. Dense. I heard the smack of it against his chest. I hadn't held back as I drew back my arm. I hadn't hesitated as I whipped it forward. There was no regret as I watched it sail, sent with the force of all my frustration, all my hurt, all my anger. It was what I wanted. The look of surprise. The look of discomfort. The look of betrayal and desire and magnetism.

I'd wanted to hurt him, because I was sure he was going to hurt me. I was never more sure of anything in my life. And I was sure I was going to let him. I was sure I was going to yearn for him to hurt me. Beg for him to hurt me. Dream of him hurting me, awake to him hurting me, come back as he hurt me time and time again.

When I dragged my hands down his chest, fingers catching in the thin material of his t-shirt, I felt like I'd lost. The battle was already over. Rian, the victor. Me, the vanquished. I was fully clothed, and yet it felt like he was already inside of me. Already thrusting his cock as I clutched for purchase on his sweat-slick skin. Already gasping for more as he claimed me. Made me his. His little slut. His little whore.

I stared at the clay marks I'd left on him as Rian stared at me. I could feel his gaze on me. Steady, but not for long. The storm cloud inside them threatened thunder and lightning and total devastation.

My fingers trailed away at Rian's lower stomach, brushing against the outline of his erection. His hard cock.

I flinched back. Fuck, what was I doing? I stumbled back. "I… I have to go."

I made to leave but he stopped me with his hand around my upper arm then my neck, forcing me to look at him, not hard, just enough pressure to let me know that I wasn't going anywhere.

My skin felt electrified, my nipples straining against my shirt, desperate to be touched by him. God, why was I responding this way?

Fear flashed through my needy hunger as he tugged me closer, tracing my cheek with his nose. "You're not going anywhere."

"Professor Merrick—"

I cut off with a moan as he ground his cock against me, sending sparks through my body.

"You loved it when I choked you before."

I whimpered.

"I bet you're going to love it when I punish that innocent little ass. When I take that pussy rough, when I push you to your knees and fuck your throat until you gag."

"Oh God," I panted, his words were so filthy. So wrong. But they set my body alight. Made my knees tremble.

He grinned. Then sank to his knees in front of me, hands gripping my ass and pushed his face into my skirt-covered pussy, inhaling me.

"Rian, what are you doing?"

He let out a groan. "Fuck, you smell amazing." He flipped up my skirt and pressed his nose to my panties.

I pushed at the top of his head. "No…we…shouldn't."

"I know." He tugged down my white cotton panties and let them drop to the floor.

Before I could protest any further, he licked my clit.

If I had any hesitation before, any fight left, it evaporated.

I carded my fingers into his hair. "Oh fuck."

He used his fingers to spread me open wider so he could lick deeper. "You…" he said between long languid licks, "are my dirty greedy little slut."

I choked.

"Say it."

"I…can't."

He stopped licking.

I let out a whimper. "Don't stop."

"Then. Say. It."

"I'm…I'm your…"

He growled against my pussy, his breath a form of torture on my sensitive folds. "Own it, Eithne."

"I'm your greedy little s-slut."

"Good girl." He rewarded me by plunging two fingers into my pussy and ravishing me with his tongue. All I could do was grab onto his hair and try not to let my legs give out.

I soared, my body hurtling to the edge at the feel of his talented fingers and tongue, at the nasty wet unapologetic noises that my pussy made as he worked it, the audible proof of my wickedness.

But I was too far gone to care.

Before I could shatter, he pulled his fingers and hands from me. I let out a long moan, frustration coating my pleasure like a sheen.

"Rian, what are you…?"

He stood licking his fingers, I stared at him in horror.

"You ready to admit you want this?" he said.

Before I could stop myself, my hand lashed out and cracked against his cheek.

Shit. I just hit my professor.

For a moment I thought I'd gone too far. Rian's pupils were blown wide, his irises nearly gone. He tried to breathe out steadily but it shook, trembled.

I winced when his hand shot out like the strike of a viper's. He gripped me by the back of the neck, damp fingers digging in, and pulled my lips to his. My knees collided with the pottery wheel as I fell into him. We crashed to the floor together, me atop him, smears of wet clay between us. I tasted it on his mouth as our lips collided, as our tongues twisted. Bitter. Cold. Like wet earth. Like life itself.

Rian tore at my clothes and ended up with half a handful of clay, half a handful of my sweater. I dug my clay-covered fingers through his hair. My hips rocked against Rian's hard cock as the clay smeared between our chests. I flinched as the cold clay on his hands came in contact with my bare stomach as he pushed my sweater up.

It was like plunging into an icy lake the colour of slate, of concrete. My stomach muscles contracted at the first contact, cold and harsh and inescapable. It rose with Rian's probing fingers along the centre of my trembling ribcage. It covered my breasts, stung against my peaked nipples. It constricted around my throat, made it hard to breath, made it hard to even want to.

"Get this thing fucking off," Rian muttered against my lip, nipping at me from word to word, biting a little harder each time.

I rose above him, knees straddled across his hips. He already looked out of his mind as he watched me hook my fingers under the hem of my sweater and pull it over my head, bra and all. I felt Rian's cock twitch needily against my pussy as my hair fell across my bare shoulders. My chest was coated in clay, traced with his fingers, smeared with his sweating palms.

He slapped the nipple that hadn't already been painted with clay. I gave an involuntary moan, soft and pitiful. I didn't need to tell Rian to do it again. The sting of his open hand was immediately chilled by the clay. I leaned back and thrust my tits out. Rian slapped me again with more clay.

"No," I groaned, hands trembling on Rian's thighs.

Rian's fingernails dug deeply as he scraped them over my tits. I shook all over.

"Just look at you, dirty girl," he groaned himself. "Just fucking look at you, Eithne."

The words sent heat between my legs and then ice at the base of my spine. I imagined someone catching us like this. Spine arched atop my professor. Clay smeared over me like I was a wall, a canvas, an object. Nipples so hard I was sure they would break like glass. Filthy sounds coming from my mouth. Revelling in it all. Ready for more. *Desperate* for more.

Rian grabbed my calves and flipped me over on all fours before shoving my skirt up around my waist.

Cold air rushed around my slick thighs, around my soaking bare pussy. Rian groaned behind me at the sight of me.

Slap! His palm came down on my ass. I let out a cry.

"Dirty fucking girl, you're going to beg for me to fuck you."

His hand came down on me again, the coolness of the clay on his hands not masking the fire crackling through me at the impact.

"No," I moaned even as my hips pushed back, begging for more.

Smack!

His hand came down on the other cheek and I flinched, pain ebbing through me then pleasure rushing in after. "Such a fucking liar."

I heard Rian shifting behind me as I clenched my eyes shut,

my thighs shaking with need. I heard his own shirt, wet with clay, come off. I heard the clatter of his jean button hit the linoleum floor. I clutched at the floor slippery with clay and tried to keep my arms from shaking. I hated myself for the groan that Rian elicited when he ran his hands greedily over my body, smearing cold, wet clay around my waist and across my breasts, up my inner thighs and around my ass.

I felt his cockhead at my soaked pussy. I needed it really. I needed his thrusts, his fucking, his release. I needed my pleasure, his pleasure. Then maybe we could stop this ridiculous obsession with each other.

But he didn't thrust into me. I moaned and pushed my ass up even higher for him.

"Whores beg. So beg," he commanded.

"What?" It felt like icy water splashed on the back of my neck.

He rubbed his end of his cock along my slit, teasing me, dipping just the tip in. I moaned and pushed back, wanting more and whimpered when he pulled back just out of reach.

"Rian, please…" I panted. My pussy was so swollen, so needy from him cruelly leaving me on the edge.

"Beg."

"Oh God, fuck me," I moaned.

I cried out when Rian thrust into me. There was no preamble. No circling of the precum slick head around my folds. No gentle easing inside of my pussy. No whisper against the sensitive lobe of my ear, "Are you ready, Eithne?" Just a flare of painful pressure. A wave of apprehension and excitement. A low, drawn-out groan from deep inside of me that I was at a complete loss to control. Exactly how I wanted it. Exactly how I needed it.

"Yes. More," I begged.

He chuckled, his hands caressing my back like penance. "Such a perfect little slut."

"Yes," I moaned. Why did I fucking love it when he called me that? Why was that word so terrible coming from anyone else's mouth except for his?

Why did I want to be *his* perfect little slut? His greedy whore.

"Fuck me like a whore," I begged. I wanted it. All of it. I wanted him to tear me apart.

I heard a growl from behind me, felt another smack on my ass, before he began to thrust. His balls slapped against my ass as he fucked me. My tits bounced roughly as his brutal pace only seemed to quicken, drying clay crackling off me onto the floor.

He bent over me, pinning me down to the floor with his body, reaching around to wrap one hand around my throat, clay and skin slapping between us. I felt degraded and wild and so fucking close.

"You like that?" he asked with a squeeze of my throat.

"God, yes." I gasped as I struggled to keep my arms from buckling.

"Such a good little whore."

I grunted as he squeezed my throat just a little tighter. Sparks danced in front of my eyes, my lips tingling.

His cock driving into me was rough and brutal and I bucked back against him.

"Oh God, I'm so close."

His hand squeezed around my neck as my insides tightened. I felt myself hurtle over the edge. I let out a scream as I came, as his hand released, that rush of blood through my body like a second wave meeting the first. I had been too loud, but I didn't care. The entire school could walk in through that door and I'd just keep right on coming.

Rian pulled out and let out a long growl. I felt his hot streams of cum against my thigh. He collapsed against me and we fell onto the floor, a puddle of limbs, wet clay and cum.

I trembled in Rian's arms as he ran his hands over me softly, over my neck, my breasts, my ass, over the places that he'd smacked.

"Shit," he mumbled. "Are you okay?

"It's fine," I said turning toward him.

Worry laced his beautiful features. "You make me…so fucking crazy."

I grabbed his hand and laced my fingers through them, stopping him from tracing the places on my body where he'd marked me.

"Rian, honestly. I liked it. More than liked it. But…"

Surprised flashed in his eyes. "But?"

I pulled myself from his embrace. "But now we've got each other out of our systems. It's…over." I stood and began dressing without looking back at him. I ignored the urge to taste his cum as I pulled my skirt. I tugged my dirty sweater back over my bare chest when I heard Rian say, "This will never be over."

I peeked over my shoulder. He was beautiful. On his side. Thick cock still semi-hard on his thigh. Tattoos flashing in the streaks of sunlight. Clay deepening in the streaks of shadow. He was art himself. But wasn't that what I had to give up…art?

"Sign the paper, Professor Merrick," I told him, my voice as cold as the hardening clay.

I picked up the crumbled registrar's form and placed it on his pottery wheel on my way out. Maybe he'd have mercy on me after all.

But as the door closed behind me, closed on him, I knew he wouldn't.

He couldn't.

And I didn't want him to.

RIAN

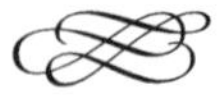

It was easy enough. Too easy. Really I should have been scared how easy it was to do. How easy it was to justify.

I lit a joint in the hallway outside the college's administration office. I let it burn for a minute or two, resisting the urge to draw in a quick smoke. I balanced it on the lip of the old peeling white wainscotting. I entered the administration office under the guise of updating my information. The stern elderly woman behind the desk gave me a suspicious look that told me I'd picked the perfect person to dupe. I smiled kindly as she opened the system. I sniffed. I sniffed louder when it was clear that she hadn't heard me. I turned my head toward the hallway. I frowned.

I asked, "Do you smell something?"

The woman looked up from her half-moon glasses perched at the end of her long nose. She sniffed when I sniffed.

"Smells kind of funny, doesn't it?" I said. "I mean, I have no idea *what* it is, but—"

The woman pushed her chair back with a scowl.

"*I* have an idea," she grumbled as she hobbled around the corner of the desk, past me and into the hallway.

All it took was a whistle, a quick mosey, a click or two, and there it was: Eithne's address.

"Marijuana!" the woman snapped when I came up to her in the hall. "A menace! An absolute menace! The culprit must have run when he heard me coming, the little bastard."

"The little bastard indeed," I agreed.

"This has to be reported, Professor," she said, glaring distrustfully at the smouldering joint held suspended between her pointer finger and thumb like a murder weapon.

"You know," I said, rocking back and forth on my heels, "I was on my way to the dean's office. I'd be happy to report it. Unless you wanted to walk all the way across campus yourself?"

She beamed at me. "You're such a dear."

I hardly waited till the old woman's back was turned to me before drawing in deeply and exhaling merrily through my nose as I pushed open the doors into the waning sunlight.

It wasn't that I was stalking Eithne. Or at least it was fairly easy to convince myself that I wasn't stalking my student. It's just that she hadn't been to class since we fucked in the pottery studio. I was worried. Or obsessed. Hell, why not both?

I knew from the direction of the bus that she lived in a bad part of town. But it wasn't until I was walking up the stairs that I realised my little Raglan Road girl lived in the bad part of the bad part of town. It made Dublin Ink's neighbourhood look like it was gated. The sound of shattered glass seemed to come from all around me as I slowed my step, nearing the shabby door. A child would cry, a woman would shout, and somehow the silence that flooded back in was more menacing than either. A car alarm always seemed to be going off with no one to turn it off despite the fact that the cars parked along the pothole-littered road appeared undriveable.

A fierce desire came over me to take Eithne away from this place. Abduction isn't abduction if it's for the best, is it? If it's done with love? Right, Judge?

A quiet knock to the front door caused the door to swing in. The revealed two inches was enough to peek inside. I checked over my shoulder to make sure no one was watching. It was a silly thing to do. There were no nosy neighbours tugging down blinds to squint between in this part of town. People had their own shite to deal with. And your shite wasn't theirs. Ever. No matter what. People were on their own here. Eithne was on her own here.

Blinking into the dim light through the cracked door was enough to make my stomach drop. The place was trashed. I pushed inside without a second thought.

"Eithne!" I called, fearing the worst.

A burglary gone wrong. A home invasion. A man that followed her home. Forced himself on her. Laughed as she fought back. An actual stalker.

"Eithne!"

I ran through the overturned furniture, the drywall scattered across the dirty carpet, the broken pieces of dishware everywhere, ready to cut, to slice, to kill. Blinds were torn down and light from the streetlamps spilled out across the destruction like garish yellow paint. In the small dingy kitchen, every cabinet door was ripped from its rusted hinges. It made the dark space look cavernous, tunnels extending in every direction.

"Eithne!" I shouted, spinning around.

When the door down the end of the narrow hallway opened, I grabbed a cabinet door, ready to swing. If the man who stumbled toward me holding his head hadn't looked so pathetic, I would have attacked him. But it was clear that, whoever he was, he would have been no match for Eithne.

"What the hell, man," the stranger grumbled, his voice rough. "What's with all the shouting?"

A peculiar thing for an inhabitant of a place to say. Perhaps something more like, "Who the hell are you and why are you in my place?" would have been more appropriate. I narrowed my eyes suspiciously at the haggard man as his torso disappeared behind the fridge door. No light came from the interior and he cursed. He didn't bother closing the door as he turned around to riffle through the exposed cabinets.

"Got anything to drink?" he asked me.

I lowered the cabinet door, rested it against the beaten-in kitchen island.

"Where's Eithne?" I asked, ignoring his question.

"Eithne?" he asked distractedly as his search continued, shaking fingers trailing over spilled bags of flour and rice.

I tried to get a good look at him. He was unshaven. Hollows had formed beneath his too sharp cheekbones. His neck was scrawny, his clothes baggy. I couldn't guess his age, but I was fairly sure that any guess I gave would far exceed his actual years. He reminded me of someone I used to know. Someone I promised never to see again. Especially when he turned to me and I saw the vague sense of panic in his eyes, like a river just beneath the surface that never stops running.

"Do you really not have anything, boyo?" he said.

"Are you fucking her?" I asked.

A silly flare of pride. But I really couldn't help myself. The stranger laughed.

"Gods no," he said and turning away added, "I'm her brother."

He rounded the corner into the living room. I heard him rummaging around. Always in search of something. I recognised that, too.

"Is Eithne alright?" I called out to him.

"Eithne's always alright," he called back.

"What happened here?"

"We're moving," was his only reply.

I lingered in the kitchen. Unsure of myself. It was a particular shadow from the bedroom down the narrow hallway that caught my attention. It was as familiar as the back of my hand, as that man I used to see all the time in the mirror. I went down the hallway as if in a trance.

It was the shadow of an easel. It somehow escaped the destruction of the rest of the place. The sheets were crumpled. The rod from the closet had been chopped in two, the clothes a mess on the floor. And everywhere you stepped it seemed there was another drawer from the toppled armoire. But the easel remained upright, sending its skeletal shadow across me as I stood amongst the chaos.

Eithne's easel? I tried to imagine her painting there. But there was so much destruction. She didn't seem to fit. There was a portfolio leaning against the base. Eithne's portfolio.

The springs of the tired mattress moaned in protest as I sank into them with the portfolio across my knees. The stranger, Eithne's brother as he called himself, was still out in the living room moving things here and there, but I could hardly hear him anymore. I was far too absorbed with Eithne's work. From the very moment I opened the portfolio.

The potential was there. As obvious as a rising sun. Sketches drawn with such a light, natural touch that you might mistake them for the rapid blur of a hummingbird's wings from a distance. Paintings in colours so subtle you had to lean in closer, as if to hear a whisper, in order to make them out from one another. Emotion that slipped under your collar like a cruel wind, passion that surprised you like a landmine, honesty that made you squirm, then still, then weep. It was all there. A rising sun, a rising artist.

Eithne could be anything, anyone she wanted. That much was obvious.

I found myself lighting a joint as I flipped from page to page. It seemed natural to me: whiskey and rain, Guinness and music, weed and art. I breathed deeply the smoke as I breathed in just as easily the images before me into my eyes, into my soul. It was good, too, the joint, to ease a nagging trouble that only seemed to grow with each turn of the thick, heavily pulped pages.

Because Eithne had talent, but Eithne also had bridles. Blinders. Ropes wrapped round her ankles and wrists. It was as if her art was screaming through a gag. It gave me shivers to imagine what she could sound like if the gag were removed. If *I* were to slip it from between her bruised lips.

The drug must have hit me fast because I suddenly gained this grandiose assurance that I could be the one to unleash Eithne's full potential, to release whatever block she was struggling against, to break her loose so she could fly. I saw her with a gallery of her own. I saw her in a sleek black dress, open at the back, only the tiny hairs fallen free from her bun tickling the back of her pale neck. I saw her out a place like this, a shite hole like this, a fucking death sentence like this.

The weed burned on my lips, burned in my lungs. I would save Eithne. I *had* to save Eithne.

Movement at the door caught my eye. The brother leaned against the doorframe. His haggard eyes bright. A grin of yellow teeth. He wasn't looking at me, but instead what was smouldering between my long fingers.

"Care to share?"

EITHNE

The unassembled moving boxes shifted in my hands like kittens. No matter how I arranged them, no matter how tightly I pressed my arm to my side, no matter how firmly I squeezed them from underneath where they cut into my already scraped palm, they just kept squirming.

When I did manage, for just a moment, to get them calm, a stranger inevitably bumped me on the sidewalk, the bus hit a pothole, or a sudden gust of foul wind came upon me like a homeless man begging for change. I was already exhausted from the effort of finding a new place, putting in application after application, getting rejection after rejection. "I'm sorry…given your past rental history…too much of a risk." Exhausted from schoolwork, or the stress of not being able to do schoolwork. Exhausted from an extra shift at my new gig at The Jar. I was already exhausted from trying to resist Rian in my dreams, resist Rian in my thoughts and in the flutter of my fingers against my clit before I dragged myself out of bed.

I really didn't need to be even more exhausted from a fucking armful of flattened boxes, but wasn't that just life?

I climbed the stairs to my apartment (ex-apartment) and

caught the edges of the boxes on the final post in the railing. I stumbled, let go of everything to catch my fall, and watched as the boxes went sliding all the way down. For a moment I was saddened, remembering fashioning such slides with Stewart as kids. Screaming gleefully as we bounced down the stairs in the rare times when my father left the house.

But Stewart wasn't my big brother anymore, my protector, my comfort in the night, always there with a flashlight and a story for beneath the covers.

He was an addict. He was in need of help. And *I* was all he had.

I let out a tired sigh. Noah, the owner of The Jar, had been kind enough to give me the boxes, unused after deliveries of liquor and limes. I needed them. Before I could take my first step, I heard a strange noise from inside the apartment. I paused. Fingertips light on the railing. Ready to run. Ready to call for help. I listened more closely. I frowned.

It was singing.

The words came to me faintly through the blare of a car alarm down the street. It was like reading a poem with half the words blacked out. I grasped at meaning I was sure was there. I struggled to find it, the message. I picked up words like petals from a dying flower; I held them in my palm, small and fragile.

Raglan Road... and knew... dark hair... snare that... rue...

I mounted the stairs slowly this time. A strip of flickering yellow light extended over the top two stairs. The front door was cracked open. Candlelight inside. How strange, I thought, unsure if I was truly awake. Candlelight and music. It sounded like the scene from a distant story, a life that wasn't mine. Not in time. And not in place.

I pressed my fingertips against the peeling paint of the front door. I closed one eye and aligned the other with the crack.

I saw Rian. Rian at an easel. Rian painting. Rian singing. The sight of it filled me with a sense of belonging. A sense of place. A sense of comfort. I imagined coming home to this every night. Music, art, a tomato sauce simmering gently on the stove. Two glasses of wine. Two sets of toes pressed against one another as the candlelight shimmered in our eyes.

I couldn't see the destruction of the apartment. Not in that soft, forgiving light. The punches through the wall were out of sight. The carpet, stained and torn, appeared as lush as a meadow in the dew of the morning. The cardboard boxes I was supposed to be packing were out of mind.

Rian filled my vision. He had pushed his sleeves up to above his elbow. I could see him doing it; eyes fixed on a blank canvas, lips set in a determined frown, long pale fingers pushing up the charcoal cable-knit of his sleeve to reveal the muscled ink-stained canvas of his tattooed forearms.

It was an art form, painting, but it was hard work, too, drawing something from deep inside of you. My one open eye drifted down his body. I watched the flick of his brush even though he was blocking the canvas from view. His singing was relaxed, but there was a strain in his biceps, his thighs. A tension. A need almost, driving him forward. A compulsion. He dominated the canvas the way I imagined he might dominate a woman, the length of his body over the length of hers.

I could see myself as that woman, face to face with his intoxicating blue eyes. My pleasure there for him to see, to drink in, to amplify with a flick of his hips. I could see myself with those lean, muscular arms on either side of me, could see myself prone beneath him as his hips pressed against mine. I could see myself laid so bare before him, so unrelenting and eager to receive as that canvas. But that woman could never be me.

I could see Rian.

But where was Stewart?

A tightness clenched my chest as I pushed the creaking door open. Rian didn't turn at my presence. He was too lost in his painting. Gone somewhere far away, unreachable, incapable of even wanting to be reached. The sight of him which just moments before had made me sink into a warm fantasy, an impossible future, now made my stomach turn. It filled me with more rage than I could ever remember feeling.

Stewart was on the couch, or what was left of it. His fingers tore impulsively at the white fluff on the shredded armrest. There was an urgency that scared me, a compulsion, much like Rian's, that made my heart stop. It was the only thing about Stewart that moved. The only thing at all. His open eyes stared blankly ahead of him. At the drywall he'd kicked through. At the cheap bookshelf he'd knocked over. At the little life I'd built for years and he'd destroyed in minutes. I wasn't even sure he was breathing. His chest fluttered like a hummingbird's, but I saw no contraction of his ribs, no exhale of breath. His lips hung open, chapped and pale. His other arm hung limply beside him, the skin clammy, the bones prominent. A joint was burning a hole in the fabric of the couch cushion.

I ran to Stewart, because it was what I always did. It was my duty. My responsibility. He'd taken care of me and now it was my turn. I ran to him because it never crossed my mind to run the other way. To run out the door. Down the stairs. Across the street. Across the city. Across the world. I ran to my older brother because I was frightened for him and that was a much easier thing to be than angry. Bitter. Tired.

"Stewart," I called to him as I huddled beside him on the couch and slapped his cheek. Gently at first. Then not so gently. "Stewart!"

Rian still didn't turn to me. I don't think he even flinched. He kept singing that damned song. Kept painting with a sweat-inducing intensity. Stayed in his own fucking world with no idea about the realities of mine.

Stewart responded dimly when I shook his shoulders. A low groan. A curling of his lips, more of the natural curling of a dead spider's legs than a smile. My fingers felt for his pulse at his wrist. His skin was hot. Wet. I gathered the fingers that were impulsively tearing at the couch's fluff into my hands. I smelled the joint, afraid it was more than just weed.

I'd never felt more alone. Stewart, gone. Rian, gone. Both of them there. And not. And wasn't that even worse? Worse than being truly alone. I felt my whole world collapsing around me. It was all there: a brother I loved, a degree in art I cared about, a man who wanted me. And yet I had none of that. My brother was in shambles. My heart was hollow for the art I was pursuing. And the man who wanted me couldn't even bother to realise I was in the bleedin' room, that he'd done me harm, that he was making things harder when they were already so fucking hard.

It was with clenched teeth that I threw a disembowelled cushion at Rian's back. It caught Rian between the shoulder blades and he startled like he'd been deep asleep, lost in a dream. Well, he could fucking wake up. I knew I had. His gaze was unfocused, distant even as he turned around, even as he saw me.

So he was high, too. He was somewhere else. No one was here with me. I tried to remember this. It was supposed to be a lesson I learned a long time ago. No one sticks around for the slut. They're there for a night and then gone. That's how it worked.

"What have you done?" I asked in a trembling voice, tears in my eyes and heat in my cheeks.

"Eithne," Rian gasped like *I* was the dream he was awaking to. "come. Come and look at this."

He didn't even seem to notice Stewart. Not his shallow breathing. Not his sickly skin. Not the joint smouldering on the couch that could have easily burned the whole fecking place down.

"Did you give my brother drugs?" I asked, already knowing the answer.

There were a million questions I didn't know the answer to: What are you doing here? How did you know where I live? What in God's name gave you the right to come here? To stalk me? To invade my privacy?

"Eithne," Rian repeated, urgent and excited. Had he really not seen the state Stewart was in? "Come here. Come look."

Rian's hand extended toward me though he hadn't stepped away from the easel. Hadn't replaced the brush on the little ledge. Hadn't focused his gaze. I reached out blindly for whatever was closest at hand. This time it was an ashtray. I hurled it at Rian and it caught him on the shoulder before continuing on to knock the wet canvas to the floor.

"Get out!" I shouted.

Rian stared at me, an incredulous look on his face. Like he didn't understand what I was saying or why I was saying it.

Stewart coughed weakly beside me, sending another rush of fury through my veins.

I pointed at the front door. "Get out of here, Rian! Get the fuck out!"

"What? Eithne..." Rian said.

He didn't have a goddamn clue. He was too busy fighting against whatever drug was coursing through his veins, burning in his lungs. Fighting to think clearly. To see. But he would never see. He couldn't see me.

"Get. Out."

"Eithne, I don't underst—"

"He's an addict!"

Stewart moaned softly and I realised how terribly tightly I had been gripping his hand. I willed myself to loosen my grip.

"You never should have given him drugs," I said bitterly, fighting back tears.

Rian's eyes seemed to clear. He looked at Stewart. He looked at me. He looked at how I was holding his hand. How tightly. How I couldn't seem to let go.

"Eithne," he said slowly, paintbrush still in hand, though loosely and at his side, "your brother is an adult."

"He's an addict," I hissed. "And he was doing better before you came here."

"Eithne—"

"I want you out."

"Eith—"

"Get the fuck out!"

I released Stewart's hand and stood. I grabbed ahold of Rian's charcoal sweater. The one I'd imagined as softer. The one I'd imagined as warmer as I slid it from his shoulders. The one I'd imagined could be on the floor beside my bed one day, stained with paint.

Rian didn't protest as I dragged him across the ruined carpet to the door. I shoved him out and he went. I caught just the flash of his face before I slammed the door shut; he had the audacity to be angry. To be fucking angry.

I bent over and screamed against my knuckles. Stewart didn't stir. I punched the wall myself because there was nothing left to protect, nothing left to preserve. The sight of the canvas overturned on the ground sent my blood boiling. I stalked over to it. I almost resisted the urge not to look at it as I carried it to the back stairs to throw out over the filthy, stinking dumpster. Almost resisted.

As it sailed from my fingers into the ugly yellow glare of the one working light in the alley, I saw a woman in a backless black dress. She was at some sort of art gallery. She was looking at a piece of art unseen. Everyone else in the room was looking at her. She was beautiful, but she was smeared. The wet paint rippled and distorted from the fall.

She was me, I knew.

But I left her there in the dumpster. I left her behind.

There was Stewart to watch. A long night ahead. And the fantasy was nothing short of laughable.

RIAN

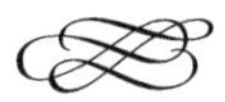

"Everyone shut yer gobs!"

I shouted into the bustling auditorium before the door had even begun to close behind me.

A startled silence fell over the room darkened by a late afternoon storm as I stalked to the podium. There was the rustling of papers, the scooting in of a chair or two, a last whisper here and there. Then there was only the sound of barren tree limbs scraping against the windows.

I managed to keep my breathing under control as I slung my satchel to the floor. As I arranged my lecture, three pieces of loose paper covered in gouging, frantic scribbles. I looked up to find the class with pens poised, fingers waiting on keys.

I managed to keep my rage under control up until the moment that I laid eyes on her.

Again in the back row, farthest from me, hidden in shadows. She sat in the desk nearest the rear exit door. Ready to escape. Ready to run. Ready to disappear from sight again. Her eyes were hidden in shadows, but I imagined the glare in them, I felt it. Her lips painted in a deep purple line. From this distance I couldn't tell whether she was breathing or not. Whether she was panting like me, ready to fight, ready to win. She was out of my reach. But I knew she could hear me. And I was determined that she *would* fucking hear me.

Eithne thought she had a stranglehold on angry. On indignant. On "right". She had another feckin' thing coming.

"Today I want to discuss the people in an artist's life," I began, no longer needing the reminder of my notes. "The people in *your* life."

My gaze was fixed on her. No one in the class seemed to notice as chins tucked to chests, eyes trailed across their lined notepads, fingers found the letters on the keyboard: P - E - O - P - L - E.

"Why put care into the brush you select for a painting? Why anguish over the quality of a gouache? Why spend a month's rent on a set of watercolours? Or worry over how perfectly a canvas is stretched over a frame?" I said as I gripped the edges of the lectern, as I leaned forward, speaking to her—speaking *just* to her. "Why do any of that if you don't use any of that discernment, that high standard, that obsessive selecting for the people in your life?"

The sounds of frantic note taking faded. I had the sense that Eithne and I were alone in the lecture hall growing darker and darker by the minute.

"Because if you think a cheap brush will ruin your work, you have no fucking clue what a blood sucker, time sucker, money, heart and soul sucker will do," I said, voice rising in volume as I grew madder. More indignant. More sure that I was fucking right.

And she was fucking wrong.

"An artist," I said to her, to her and no one else, "an artist must be very careful of the influences she lets into her life. Of the artists she emulates. Of the styles she takes to heart. Of the professors she listens to. Or doesn't listen to. Yes, I know, you'll argue that it only applies to the 'art world'? That this ends at the gates of the college?"

Everyone jumped when I suddenly banged my fist against the lectern.

"You're wrong," I said. And I was talking to Eithne. The subtle narrowing of her eyes told me she knew it. Knew it was for her.

"If your roommate is interfering with your art, move out. If your friend is interfering with your art, find a different friend. Go friendless, if you have to. If your brother is interfering with your art, drowning you, tying rocks to your ankles and pulling you under, let…him…*go*."

Eithne was the only student that wasn't taking notes. Her arms were crossed over her chest. Her body was as still as a marble statue in her sweatshirt, cleaned and scrubbed of all clay memories. Her eyes were daggers.

"If your brother has an addiction, then he needs to help himself," I continued. "If he won't help himself, you certainly can't help him. If your brother is sucking up your time and your money and your passion, then you need to cut him out of your life. Immediately. Fucking yesterday."

Perhaps the specificity of this portion of the lecture caused a few students to pause, hesitate. A couple heads lifted. A few looked around them like coming out of a trance. Why was it suddenly so dark? Why was the professor breathing so heavily? With sweat on his brow? With knuckles white on the edge of the lectern? Why wasn't he looking at anyone else except for a paralysed girl in the back row right by the exit door? What the fuck was going on?

"He's no good for you," I said. "I mean your art. He's no fucking good for your art. Do you hear me?"

Eithne called out, "Professor Merrick?"

I think everyone in the auditorium was just as surprised as I was. Heads whipped around. Pencils dropped, rolled off the corners of desks. Fingers stilled over keys.

I gritted my teeth, tensed my jaw. I'd worked myself into a sort of frenzy. A dictator imposing my will. A tyrant before his masses. Now here was a dissident. A thorn in my side. An opposition voice. I didn't want to hear it. I didn't want to hear her. I wanted her to listen. To do as I said. To come to me. To be with me. Just being with me.

"Yes, in the back," I said begrudgingly.

Eithne scooted to the edge of her seat. She rested her elbows on the end of her desk. Her hands hammocked her chin, almost sweetly. She smiled and her eyes flashed in the dim light of the storm. Just above us. About to let loose.

"Professor Merrick," she said, just loud enough for me to hear, just loud enough for the whole auditorium to hear, "I think what you're suggesting we do might kill an artist's work just as efficiently as keeping around a source of inconvenience."

She spoke naturally. Completely at ease. Confident. Completely fucking confident.

"Say with your example of the brother," Eithne continued, "say you cut him off. Abandon him, leave him to his addiction, as was the case in your totally random example, no?"

My little Raglan Road girl had the class as transfixed as I had. Eyes darted to me as Eithne spoke. Could they sense too that she was disrupting something? Ruining something? Could they feel the tension? The frustration in my every bone at her not just *listening*? At her not rolling over for me?

"What does that do to the soul, I wonder," Eithne said, closing the trap she'd so effortlessly laid out. "Because wouldn't you agree that art, great art, comes from the soul? What kind of soul would abandon flesh and blood? What kind of art could possibly come from something so black? Pearls are made under pressure, Professor Merrick. No pearl ever came from a pit of tar."

It was clear that she was finished as she leaned back in her chair, a satisfied smug smile toying at her mouth. She was confident that she had emerged the victor.

The class's attention came back to me. They were no longer the flock of loyal sheep. They were spectators of a sport. I'd been levelled with my student; opponent against opponent. I hated Eithne in that moment. Hated her defiance. Her stubbornness. Her foolishness she called "a soul", the masochism she called love.

"Is that what you're trying to create, Ms…?"

I paused. Her voice came through clenched teeth. She knew damned well I knew her name.

"Brady."

"Is that what you're trying to create, Ms Brady? A pearl? A pretty little thing rich women wear at the perfumed hollows of their throats and then store away for days, weeks, years on end? Hidden in dark velvet? Kept from the sun? Kept from life? Devoid of life?" I hadn't realised how furious she'd made me till I was gasping for air. "Is that what you suggest the ideal of art is, Ms Brady?"

The faces watching me in the dim light were pale, drained of blood from the anger in my voice. Every face was a frightened child's, except hers.

"What are *you* suggesting the ideal of art is, Professor Merrick?" Eithne shot back a little too comfortably, a little too quickly. It wasn't the rebuttal of a student. It was the counterattack of a lover. I suspected some of the students sensed this. I didn't give a fuck.

Apparently neither did Eithne. "Are you suggesting art should be a weapon?" Her voice rose in volume. "A dagger to cut down anything and anyone in one's way? A bludgeon to keep people away?"

"You know that's not what I'm fucking saying, Eithne."

The shock on the class was great. The shock on Eithne was even greater. I'd used her name. I'd revealed an intimacy. I'd uncovered us as surely as pulling a sheet off our naked, intertwined bodies.

The stunned silence hung over the auditorium as low as those slate-grey clouds that churned and rolled and rattled the branches against the windows. I stared at her, she stared at me. There was horror on her face. She slunk back into more shadow as heads began to turn, whispers began to circulate.

I slammed my fist against the lectern. Partially to take everyone's attention off of her. Partially because I wanted to. It felt good. And because I was that goddamn mad at myself.

I made a show of crumpling up the rest of my lecture notes. A show of shoving them into my satchel. A show of cursing low under my breath as I stormed toward the door. It was enough to allow Eithne to slip out unnoticed. To escape once more. To run. Maybe for good this time.

There was no point in telling the class they were dismissed as I slammed the door to the auditorium shut behind me. It was more than obvious. Maybe it was already clear that there was no class; that there was never any class. That there was only ever Eithne and me.

And now I'd driven a wedge between us. Cleaved us in two. Sentenced us to opposite sides of a canyon. She wasn't going to listen to me. She certainly wasn't going to jeopardize her place at the college *for me*. Her graduating for me. Her soulless, well-paying job for me. Her brother for me.

I'd still risk it all for her.

EITHNE

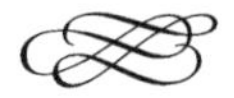

I should have just let it go.

Things had calmed down. Gone back to normal or whatever you want to call it. Life was as it was before I met Rian. Or rather, before he saw me.

I had a new place that looked much like the other before Stewart destroyed it: yellow linoleum in the kitchen, bathroom tiles that never looked clean no matter how hard I scrubbed, worn-down carpet, thin walls, scratch marks on the keyhole at the front door.

Classes were as they were before: boring, uninspiring, steady as a dripping tap that wouldn't turn off. I worked my shifts at The Jar. I checked in on Stewart who was one day, then one week, then one month clean. I studied. I slept when I could. I saved. I rode the bus and hardly ever daydreamed of Rian.

Hardly ever…except at night when I'd stopped running, when the noise of my day faded and there was just his voice in my ear, telling me all the bad things he was going to do to me, to my desperate body, to my greedy pussy.

Things were good. Okay, not good exactly but not bad. Not violent. Not turbulent. Not wrong. No fucking older professors.

No inappropriate relationships. No touching myself in lectures. Or sneaking underneath lecterns. No art either. But it was the right choice. If a sacrifice was to be made, I'd made the right one. Art wouldn't pay the bills. Art wouldn't support me, protect me.

So I should have let it go.

I should have pulled up the calculator on my shitty phone, crunched the numbers, and assured myself that it wasn't going to jeopardise my graduating, convinced myself it didn't matter one tiny bit. I should have at least slept on it. Seen how I felt in the morning. Taken a step back. Given myself some distance.

I most certainly should not have boarded a late-night bus to Dublin Ink with the intention of confronting Rian over a B- on a recent art assignment. That was the last thing in the fucking world I should have done. But I did it anyway.

My heart pounded the whole way there over the thought of seeing Rian up close again. Not from thirty rows of desks away. Not from across a crowded campus, a passing glimpse here and there, gone so quickly I couldn't be sure it was even him.

I feared the clamminess of my palms as I gripped the page he'd attached to my work. At his scrawled note:

A pearl. Pretty, but no more. B-

He'd written this and signed it, not Rian. But Professor Merrick. PM.

I feared his name on my tongue once more. Rian. Rian. Rian. I feared it hanging between us. A curtain of intimacy to fling open. A barrier torn down. An invitation I was sure I would regret. I feared what I would do once the yelling stopped. Once what I'd said about him jeopardising my future was all said. Once there was nothing but silence between us. The pretext dropped. The excuse revealed as flimsy. The grade dropped and forgotten at our feet.

It was almost enough to make me stay on the bus, to ride it round, all the way back home. To congratulate Stewart on another day clean. To make dinner. To pass out across my books.

But I was suddenly on the sidewalk, the bus doors closing behind me with a hiss and a clatter and that was really what I feared most of all: that I never had any bleedin' choice. I was always going to find a reason to go to him. I was never going to be able to stay away. I would always be a whore. A slut.

The street that housed Dublin Ink was silent. No cars. No pedestrians out for a late-night stroll. No television sets from open windows. It was a step up from the neighbourhood I lived in. Though really more of a baby step.

I gripped the crumpled page with my grade and assessment more tightly in my fist as my footsteps echoed on the pavement. It was as if I thought I could protect myself with that flimsy little page. It was my weapon against an attacker from the darkened alley. It was my weapon against Rian. *"See, I have a reason to be here. It has nothing at all to do with you. I still want absolutely nothing to do with you and the pussy-aching, thigh-tightening desire you bring. See!"*

Music came as a subtle rumbling through the silent night. At first, I assumed that it couldn't be Dublin Ink. It was late. The place would be closed or closing at least. But light shown through the thin gaps on either side of the curtains. And there it was, the sign on the little stained-glass window of the front door of the red brick townhouse. Dublin Ink.

I knocked. But I doubted they'd hear me over the damn music inside. I shoved at the door and after a beat of resistance, it swung open. Jaysus, I'd made some sort of mistake. The place was unrecognisable as a tattoo parlour save a chair or two pushed to the side of the room like forgotten wallflowers. If anything I would have said the place looked like one of those cheap chapels they have in Vegas for people too drunk to realise what a horrible mistake they're making as they slur vows of eternity. There was an Eiffel Tower painted on the big wall of the atrium. There was champagne in red solo cups being passed by girls with bunny tails. Standing near the door was a bride with her tits out and a groom with nothing but a bow tie and pants. It was a shiteshow.

I would have bailed if I hadn't seen Rian, a one in a million glance. The room was packed so tightly the windows dripped with condensation. It was only the perfect timing of a dozen or more heads turning, moving, ducking, leaning back to laugh, that allowed me to spy him across the room before he was swallowed whole once more.

I gritted my teeth, set my jaw, and ploughed inside, elbowing past what looked like the bride and groom. Rude, I know. But it wasn't like I was on the guest list. On the way to Rian I had a beer spilled on me, an explosion of confetti sprinkled on me, and more laughter than I could bear hurled on me. It was horrible. Horrible because it was wonderful. And I'd never been all that well acquainted with wonderful.

Rian, to my extreme frustration, seemed entirely unsurprised to see me. I told myself he hadn't been expecting this, expecting me; he was just high. It dulled his responses, numbed him. This wasn't some trap he'd laid for me. And I certainly hadn't just walked into it like some fool.

I held up the grade up and shouted over the music and noise. "This is bullshite!"

Rian was lounged on one of the tattoo chairs. Stretched out across it like an alley cat in the sun. His long fingers splayed across the leather of the armrests like he was floating on water. He seemed to not have a care in the world. This was simply unacceptable.

"You gave me this grade as a punishment," I shouted, fighting the wave of anger that was cresting in my chest. "I demand you change it."

I hated how young I sounded. How immature. How naive. Here was a wedding going on, adults socialising with friends and family, real life pulsing around me in time with the rhythm of the music and I was moaning about a B-. But there was no other option. It had to be the reason I was there out of the blue. It had to.

"You received the grade your work deserved, Ms Brady," Rian said as he hauled himself out of the chair. "Now, can I get you a drink?"

Rian's arm came to rest across my shoulders. I squirmed away petulantly.

"I met all the criteria you set out," I shouted even as people around us began to stare. "I followed the syllabus. I turned it in on time."

Rian's lips brushed against my ear, his breath hot. He had no need to shout like a child with her tantrum.

"Which is why you didn't receive a C, Ms Brady."

This time Rian slipped his arm around my back, his hand coming to rest against my hip. He took the grade from my clenched fist. I was so stunned by his easy dismissal that I let it go with hardly any protest. Rian balled it up even further and stuffed it into someone's cup as we passed. The disco lights flashed across his face as I stared up at him in astonishment.

"You can't do that," I said, feeling utterly pathetic.

Rian's eyes did not come to meet mine as he guided me toward a makeshift bar in a crowded little kitchen.

"Why did you come here tonight?" he asked.

"Because of my grade. I need to graduate with honours to—"

"A B- won't do a damned thing," he said. "Why are you really here?"

I tried to wrench myself free of him, but he gripped me, dug his fingers into my flesh through my sweatshirt and old thrifted trench.

"You're ruining my life," I growled in frustration as I tried to pierce the skin of his hand with my fingernails.

Rian had me spun around, my back pinned to the wall, and his body pressed up tight against mine before I could hardly even gasp. His eyes were on mine now. Intense. Penetrating. Frightening. I would have trembled if I could have breathed. I would have breathed if I could have thought to. I would have thought to if I had any space left inside my head except an alarm screaming, *"This is a mistake! A mistake! A huge mistake!"*

"Would you like a drink?" Rian asked after several tense moments where the crowds moved around us, where the music beat against us.

"I have homework to finish," I said, feeling years younger than twenty-one with my thirty-something-year-old professor's groin against my hip in this foreign place.

I wasn't sure whether Rian wanted to brush his lips against my lips or wrap his fist around my throat as he stared down at me in the ensuing silence. I felt like a mouse who'd walked into the open jaws of a snake. I felt like a mouse who liked to be stung. Who *wanted* to be stung.

"Rian?"

Both our heads whipped at the same moment to see a girl my age beside us. She looked vaguely familiar: the sleek black hair always falling over one eye, the tiny bones like a little bird, the big, waifish eyes. She held a drink with both hands like it was a cup of milk. Her eyes travelled between the two of us, between the very, *very* short distance. She smiled hesitantly at me.

"It's Eithne, right?"

She stuck out her hand. I had to snake mine between Rian and my chest to shake it.

"We know each other from school," the girl said cheerfully. A little too cheerfully for my liking. "Well, I mean, know of each other at least. I'm Aurnia."

I grumbled a "hello" and then said I was just about to leave. Homework to do. She'd understand. With a quick flicker of her eyes to Rian, Aurnia put her hand on my arm to stop me.

"One little drink wouldn't hurt, would it?"

One moment's hesitation was all it took for Aurnia to have her hand in mine, dragging me quickly behind her toward the kitchen table. I glanced over my shoulder at Rian. His face was unreadable in the flashing lights. Then he was gone. Disappeared around the corner.

"Bottom's up!" Aurnia shouted.

I hadn't even realised that a shot was in my hand. Nor that I was lifting it numbly to my lips and pouring the burning liquid down my throat as I stared at the empty space where Rian had just been. Aurnia laughed as I coughed. Tears came to my eyes as I pounded my chest.

"What was that?!"

"Tequila!" Aurnia replied, passing over a beer she'd already popped open for me. "Where have you been?"

I sipped at the lukewarm beer to cut the sting of the liquor. I didn't tell her I'd been far, far away from anything like this. Parties. Gatherings. Drinks. Music. Dancing. Friends. Laughing. Unwinding. I'd been at work. I'd been on the bus. I'd been passed out across my bed with my shoes still on and study books across my chest.

I fiddled with the beer can's tab. She scooted closer as we leaned against the kitchen counter.

"You're a third year, right?" she asked.

When I just stared at her warily, she continued, "I'm a first year."

I nodded. Sipped a little more beer. Prepared an easy excuse to get out of there.

"What's your major?" she asked a little too loudly in my ear.

"Listen," I started to say, "thanks for the beer and the tequila and all, but—"

"Eithne."

I froze because Aurnia's hand was on mine again. Not to drag me somewhere like before. Just resting there. Just holding my hand. I stared at it like it was a foreign bug just landed on me. Like something I couldn't understand. Like something I wasn't quite sure what to do with.

Aurnia squeezed my hand and whispered confidentially, "It's just that I kind of know a thing or two about...unconventional relationships."

My eyes darted to hers. I began to pull my hand from hers.

"I just want to make sure you're okay," Aurnia insisted.

"Okay?" I laughed.

She licked her lips as I watched. She hesitated. But only for a second.

"I know Rian can be...strange at times," she said. "And God knows he can come off as unhinged. I mean, I love him, too, but—"

"I don't love Rian," I interrupted.

Aurnia seemed surprised. "No, I mean, well, maybe it's not there yet... I didn't mean to assume or anything, but—"

"We're not even in a relationship."

The beer was at my lips again. It was tumbling down my tight throat faster than it should have been. Why was the can suddenly empty? Were they supposed to be empty so fast?

"Oh, um, okay," Aurnia muttered awkwardly. "It's just that...I mean, I thought."

"Is there more of this?" I asked, holding up the beer can.

Aurnia looked surprised. "Yeah, sure."

"Wait," I said, my hand on hers this time. "Is there more of that other stuff?"

"Tequila?"

I nodded. "Yeah, tequila."

Aurnia and I did another round of shots. Then another. It was easier then. To talk about art. To talk about school. I'd never done that. I knew almost none of my classmates. I'd hardly ever been invited to anything. And on those rare occasions I'd never really considered going. It was always school. Grades. Work to pay rent, bills, debt left over from the places Stewart had trashed. Stewart. Each was more than enough on its own.

She introduced me to her boyfriend, Conor, one of Rian's

best friends. I barely repressed the look of surprise on my face as I glanced between the two of them. He must be at least a decade older, probably more. Not that there was much less of an age gap between Rian and me.

Then she dragged me over to meet Rachel, the bride, married to another one of Rian's best friends, Mason.

Aurnia and I exchanged numbers somewhere during the night. Sometime before the numbers blurred too much to see. Sometime after I'd danced on the kitchen table with Rachel. After Mason winked at me before picking his wife up off the table and throwing her over his shoulder. She screamed with glee as he carried her off, probably to finish off what I'd interrupted by barging between them at the front door.

I vaguely remembered Aurnia whispering, "Call me if you need anything. Please, Eithne. If you need *anything*."

I vaguely remembered her eyeing Rian.

I vaguely remembered Conor and Rian arguing, Aurnia jamming her finger against Rian's chest, Aurnia glancing back once more at me, all as my eyelids got heavy as I lay on the couch.

The memory of Rian coming to me, however, was all crystal clear. The heat of his arm beneath my knees. The wrapping of his fingers around my shoulder. The ease with which he pulled me up into his arms. I remembered perfectly how nice it felt to rest my cheek against his chest as he climbed the stairs. The peaceful feeling as the music grew softer, his breathing louder. The way my fingers curled in his shirt as we made our way through total darkness.

Rian lowered me onto a mattress which was so cool it made me shiver. I wrapped his arm around me as he came beside me.

"I don't get it," I said drunkenly, slurring probably, maybe already even getting ridiculously emotional.

"Get what?" Rian whispered into the crook of my ear.

I was silent for a moment. Rian probably thought I'd passed

out, fallen asleep. He was probably just about to slip his hand from mine. Leave.

"Who were all those people?" I asked finally, sleep indeed pulling at me.

It hurt to ask that. The alcohol surely didn't make it any better. I'd kind of thought that Rian was like me. Alone. Distant from other people like an island is distant from the main shore. Not because it necessarily wants to be. But because it is. Because it has to be. Because that's the way things are.

There I was, closer to him than I'd ever been despite the clothes, his and mine, between us. And yet I'd never felt so far away. Never felt so lonely.

"They're my family," Rian replied.

It was the answer I feared most. It meant there was something wrong with me. If someone as eccentric and independent and difficult as Rian could have a family, then there had to be something wrong with me. My father was right. I was perverted. Wrong. Fucked up.

I started to cry. I cried because I was too drunk. I cried because I'd never had the chance before to get too drunk. I cried because I wanted Rian but I was so tired. But mostly because…

"I'm alone," I admitted on a broken sob.

I was alone. And I always would be.

"Shh, now," Rian whispered softly as he pulled me tighter. "You're not alone. You have me."

My tears fell onto his hand as I tugged it up beneath my chin like a child with her blanket.

"Shh, my little Raglan Road girl."

RIAN

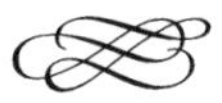

My dream girl was finally in my arms. And it was perfection.

Or at least it was until she started thrashing and pounding against my chest.

It wasn't exactly the way I'd imagined waking up beside my little Raglan Road girl: the rage-filled eyes on the verge of tears, the quivering snarl, the angry flush on her cheeks. It was louder than I expected. More painful. And certainly more clothed.

"I was supposed to go home, you dipshite!" Eithne kicked at my shins, shoved at my arms that had just seconds before been wrapped tightly around her as she slept against my chest. "This is all your fault!"

I rolled on top of her and grabbed ahold of her wrists, pinning her legs down with mine. She thrashed to get loose, but soon collapsed when it was clear I would not let her up. Her angry breathing fluttered the dark strands covering her face, falling across her pink lips.

"What's the problem?" I said as calmly as possible. "I can drop you off home now if you like, no bother."

Eithne cursed me out. I would have let her keep going, wear

herself out again, but there was Mason and Rachel and God knows who else leftover from the wedding downstairs. I already had enough people keeping a mistrustful eye out on me; I didn't need more.

I corralled Eithne's wrists into one hand and clasped my other hand over her mouth. Her eyes flashed daggers.

"Eithne," I said, staring down at her as I tried not to get hard at the feel of her soft warm body underneath mine, "what's wrong? You're fine. Nothing happened last night."

She growled something incomprehensible against my hand. I lifted it to let her speak.

"Exactly!" Eithne repeated. "Nothing happened! I was supposed to go home and paint something for class today which is in one fucking hour and because of you I have nothing! Nothing! You fucker! You—"

I muffled her again with my palm. I considered the dilemma as I tried to keep other things from my mind. Like how much I liked the fiery red of her cheeks and the feel of her vibrating with rage under me. How my palm was wet from her lips, from her mouth. Blood rushed to my groin.

I stood and heaved her over my shoulder. She screamed and pounded her fists against my back as I carried her across the little peaked attic room on the very top floor of Dublin Ink with nothing but its spare mattress and dust motes. She thrashed against my back and threatened to send us crashing back down to the dusty floorboards as I hoisted her up the ladder to the roof.

The blast of icy morning air was like a slap to the face for both of us. Eithne stilled as I set her down. She shivered in silence as she watched me spread the old canvas tarp across the small rooftop patio, little more than a few square feet of cracked concrete between four rusted fences. I knelt beside the forgotten tins of paint we stored up there, excess from when we redid the downstairs before opening the tattoo parlour. My fingers went numb prying them open with a nearby crowbar.

Eithne glared at me as I set the tins of paint in front of her and stepped to the centre of the canvas tarp.

"What the fuck is this?" she asked.

Her voice was a snarl, but she hadn't left. Hadn't stalked past me. Hadn't run for the bus. I knew she wouldn't.

"Do your homework, Eithne," I told her as I opened my arms out at my sides.

She arched a dark eyebrow at me before glancing around her. We were at least a floor above all the surrounding buildings of the neighbourhood. Beneath the clouds above twisting with slate and gold, we were entirely alone. The wind nipped at our exposed cheeks and the tips of our noses.

"I'm leaving," Eithne threatened, though she did not move from her spot.

"You'll fail your class," I told her. "How will that look on job applications?"

"Because of you," she snapped. "Because you can't let me go. Because you keep dragging me back into your life. You didn't have to give me that B-. You didn't have to force me to come here last night."

"I didn't force you. You *chose* to come here," I told her.

Her chest began to rise and fall more rapidly now. I was stoking the flames the cold had momentarily extinguished.

Eithne said through gritted teeth, "I'm not playing this game."

"What game?"

"This," she waved her hand between us, "us. We're never going to be together."

"We're together right now."

"No, we're not," she said, stepping forward and knocking over an open tin of paint.

She didn't glance down, like she wanted me to believe that it was accident. She didn't seem to notice as it spilled across the canvas, advancing toward me as she did the same. But I knew. I knew and I think this made her furious.

Good.

"'Together' is not stalking the other," she said, her eyes fixed on mine. "Or showing up uninvited at the other's home. 'Together' is not sabotaging the other's brother like a sociopath. 'Together' is not bringing the other up to a rooftop instead of home where she can try to piece something together for class."

Her footsteps smacked wetly on the canvas as she stomped toward me.

"'Together' means that we can just show up at each other's homes." I matched her steps until we met in the centre of the canvas. "'Together' is not letting leaches like your brother take advantage of you. 'Together' is bringing you up to this rooftop so you *can* piece something together for class." I leaned in, growling into her face. "Supporting one another is not letting your talent go to waste."

She flinched. "I have responsibilities, Professor Merrick."

"Like your homework?"

"Like my homework."

I lowered my gaze to her mouth, her pink lips parted as she sucked in air. Fuck, all I wanted was to taste them. To trace the edges of her lips with my tongue.

"Then do your fucking homework, Ms Brady."

I could see the tension in her jaw. The fire in her eyes. The hatred in the tightness of her lower lip, the desire in the indentation as she bit down on it.

I'm not sure who moved first, her or me. But the next moment our lips were crushed together, our arms winding round each other, fingering hair, fisting in clothing. I hissed when she sank her teeth into my lower lip.

"I hate you," she said as she tore off my shirt over my head.

"Fine line between love and hate." I grunted as I tugged her top off. Tit for tat. Blow for blow.

She groaned as my hand reached up her skirt, finding her soaked panties. "It's not love."

I smiled as I bit along her neck, leaving bruises as I pushed her bra strap off her shoulder. "Sure, it's not."

Eithne made a noise of frustration before she shoved my pants down to my ankles.

Our movements were rough and ungraceful. I tripped or perhaps she tripped. We fell to the ground and I rolled our bodies so I took the brunt of the fall. Paint cans clanked as they were tipped over, as we pulled the rest of each other's clothes off.

Neither of us gave a shite about the paint running across the canvas, under our bodies as my hard cock slid along her wetness.

"What do you call this?" I asked before I took her nipple into my mouth and sucked hard.

She whimpered and moaned, grinding her pussy against me, just enough to drive us both crazy, but not *enough*. "Temporary insanity."

I grabbed her roughly by the hair at the base of her neck and forced her to look at me. "Stop denying yourself."

"I don't—"

"You deny your talent. You deny what you truly want. Even your own fucking pleasure."

Her features broke in front of me. But I did not let her go, did not let her get relief.

"Take it. Just fucking take it, Eithne." *Take* me.

She glared at me. She hated me for calling her out. But I would not be another person in her life that let her get away with repressing herself. She deserved more.

She lifted her hips off me and her knees slid in the slickness of the paint. She caught herself roughly with her palms against my chest. Then she dropped down onto me, let me sheath her in one go.

It stole the air from my lungs. Then our twin groans echoed across the Dublin rooftops, caught in the wind.

Eithne wasted no time in rocking her hips back and forth atop me. Her movements were angry, jerky, echoing her frustrated grunts.

The back of my head knocked painfully against the canvas, against the concrete. I felt cold wet paint against my cheek. The wind didn't seem so cold anymore, a heat was spreading through me, travelling out of me into the paint like flames licking at wild grasses.

I clutched at the canvas on either side of me, trying so hard to just let her take over completely. Paint went under my fingernails, traced the lines of my palms. But she felt too good, her wet slick heat too much like that first hit. I tore at the canvas before I grabbed for her, pulling her mouth to mine.

"Such a greedy slut." I rolled her to her back, ignoring the paint streaking the canvas, coating our skin. Ignoring the rest of the cans that tipped over.

"Yes," she breathed, her chest hitching at my words, as I pushed her knees up so I could fuck her deeper. Her hips bucked up to meet mine.

I groaned as I glanced down between us. "Look. Look at this greedy pussy taking me so fucking well."

She looked down toward where my cock was disappearing into her and she let out a long moan. "No."

"Yes. You love it, my dirty Raglan Road girl. Don't ever deny it."

"No, I—"

I cut her off with my hand across her mouth as I quickened my pace. "Shut up and take it." I could feel her muscles squeezing me, telling me the truth even if she kept trying to deny it.

She loved being fucked hard and rough.

"Take it like the perfect little slut you are."

Her eyes rolled into her head as the orgasm took over her, as her muscles milked my cock so tightly my own eyelids fluttered shut.

She screamed under my palm, screamed out to the wind, as her head thrashed from side to side, flicking paint across the canvas like a snow angel.

Her body sagged.

I pulled out as I fell over the edge, coming across her stomach and the canvas. Then I collapsed half on her, half on the canvas.

We rolled until we were on our side, her back tucked against my front. I let myself come back down to earth like this, let my heart steady against her spine. Only then did I realise she was tracing her fingers through my come on her, on the canvas, mixing my seed with the paint.

I brushed paint from her cheek, my breath stilling as it always did when she glanced back at me.

"Any ideas about how to dry this in fifteen minutes?"

EITHNE

The canvas hung from two tacks pinned into the long strip of cork above the blackboard. No carefully measured frame. No perfectly guided in nails. No measuring or adjusting or fine tuning. Nothing was stretched, smoothed, trimmed, or bound. The edges were raw from the dull scissors, from tearing more than cutting. From hurried fingers in the cold.

I wasn't even sure that all that paint was dry. There was certainly no way it hadn't been smeared during the trip on the bus, the canvas rolled up beside me, fitted to the curve of my hip, the lingering warmth from Rian's body most likely imagined. Any other artist with any other piece would declare it ruined. Wrecked. Its integrity destroyed. But not me.

I believed that this was the best art I'd ever produced, if that's even what you could call it. Best art I'd ever created, perhaps. Best art I'd ever had a hand in, a bruised knee in, a curling toe, a trembling finger, a muffled scream in.

Amongst the erect easels and hardened canvas stiff with glue, amongst the daintily added signatures and finely printed placards, amongst the proper art and conventional standards, I stood proud with my tattered flag of surrender, messy from battle.

"Alright now..." Professor Sauer droned on as his finger ran down the class list. "Ms...Brady."

Before that moment he had his face cast down. Presentation after presentation, he scrolled not so subtly through his phone. He would nod here and there, make a noncommittal "emm" from deep in his throat, and thank the student an awkward fifteen seconds or so after they had finished speaking. When he glanced up to find me, to skim across all the beautiful paintings all beautifully displayed, his chin jerked up. I watched as his eyebrows knitted together, a grin crawling across my lips. Professor Sauer adjusted himself in his desk, sank his chin into his palm, and nudged his round gold-rimmed glasses back up his nose.

"Yes," he said, "alright, Ms Brady. Please tell us about what you've done."

I couldn't exactly do that now, could I? I hid a blush as the memory of my fisted hands crumpling sections of the canvas, as my knees made insistent marks on either side of the outline of Rian's body. Perhaps I should have considered this on the bus ride over to campus instead of running over the moment of my climax again and again in my head: that intoxicating heat, that irresistible need, that sensation of being carried over the rushing edge of a waterfall, white noise in your ears, dazzling sparkles behind your eyelids, stomach clenched, heart in your throat.

I looked at the canvas hanging beside me with a growing sense of panic as the class joined Professor Sauer in leaning forward to see. I had the attention of the entire studio. And yet all I could think of was Rian's cock inside of me, my hips rocking back against his groin, the taste of his throat against my mouth. That's all I could see on my canvas, the outline of bodies and lust and swirls of cum drying in the paint.

"Um," I said, clearing my throat, shifting from foot to foot, "with this piece I wanted to...I, um, I wanted to..."

I closed my eyes briefly. I shivered as I went back to the biting wind, to cold paint against naked skin. I smoothed my clammy hands down my thighs as I remembered the goosebumps that spread across my bare thighs like a wildfire. I pressed my toes against the soles of my boots as I tried to go back there: tiptoeing across the canvas, careful not to touch the paint, careful not to leave a mark…

"What I wanted to do here," I finally said as I opened my eyes to fill my gaze with the canvas, Professor Sauer forgotten, the awaiting class ignored, "was to show passion."

I heard Professor Sauer murmur a low, "Interesting."

I traced the lines that Rian's fingernails had clawed through the still wet paint as I rode his cock.

"We see their movement," I said as my eyes trailed over the outline I'd poured around Rian. "We see them there, on the canvas. Their thighs, their shoulders, their hips. We see their desire, their yearning, their… burning for something. There's no restraint. They take what they want. They move how they will through the piece, through his world. They will claim what they want."

I swallowed heavily. I couldn't stop the memory of Rian beneath me from invading my thoughts. It coloured all I said about the art. Because he was the art. *We* were. It was his words that enraged me, his body that aroused me, his taunting that drew me nearer. But on that canvas, I took what I wanted as much as he did. I claimed as much as I was claimed.

The art was us and we were the art.

I found my breath fluttery, weak inside my chest. "As first I wanted him to dominate the piece, this mystery man, this enigma that we fully see but cannot even begin to understand," I continued, my fingers tracing the dominant paint outline of Rian's back. "It would be easier to pretend that she didn't also want to dominate. To take. To claim."

I rubbed the half-dried paint between my fingers, remembering how my knees had slid, how it was inevitable, the paint, the art drawing me closer to Rian, drawing me down onto Rian.

My eyes darted to Professor Sauer. He was at the edge of his seat. His eyes fixed on the canvas. I was in uncharted waters, finding the meaning that was always there, but hidden. Unearthing bones buried long ago. I wasn't sure what I would find. I wasn't sure whether I even wanted to find anything at all. I was suddenly frightened. Suddenly very, very excited.

"Go on," Professor Sauer said, and I realised I'd stopped speaking for too long.

I sucked in a shuddering breath, licked my lips which I hadn't remembered as being quite so dry, and let my gaze fall again on the art I'd created with Rian.

Because of Rian.

It was just like that, falling. Letting go of who I thought I could be, letting go of who I thought I *should* be. Seeing nothing but what was right there. Seeing nothing but myself, my true self.

"At first glance, there's hardly a trace of her on the canvas itself," I said, my voice almost haunted, sounding much farther away.

My fingertips brushed against the smears my knees had made. It didn't look like much. Just streaks of paint on the right and the left of the outlined figure. A minor discrepancy. An error even, if you wanted to see it that way. A tiny imperfection that caught the eye like a splinter.

"When you look without much thought, just a passing glance, you don't even see her. Maybe you have to want to see her. Maybe you have to stop. Search. Grab hold of her. Grab hold of her even when she tries to hide. Tries to deny. Tries to not be seen...here on the canvas."

"But then here..." I said as I moved my fingers across the canvas in the same direction we had rolled and I traced the angel I'd made on the canvas, the strands of hair fanning out from my head, the fingers streaking to fists on either side of my hips.

"Here I…" I caught myself and reminded myself to be careful. I almost revealed the truth of the painting's conception. "*She* appears. She…accepts. Here she *arrives*."

I was gaining confidence as I spoke. It seemed the meaning of the painting was rising up like a bubble of air from dark depths. I could see it. Its shape, its form. I could touch it. If I dared.

"She embraces her passion just as fiercely," I said, feet shifting excitedly as I forgot Professor Sauer once more, forgot my classmates, turned to face the canvas fully. "And then you realise that she is everywhere. Because every mark made by him is dictated by her. Is a response to her. Is in effort to please her, to pleasure her, to give her control. Every movement by *him* is a reaction to *her*. Like simple physics. Even when we can't see her, we 'see' her because of him, through him, in opposition to him, in union with him. Them. Their desire. Their craze. Their curse."

I'd lost myself. Lost myself in finding myself. I wasn't in the art studio at college. I was back on that roof. I wasn't looking at the canvas. I was watching myself. Thighs covered in goosebumps from the cold. Knees astride Rian's cock. Nipples hard beneath my sweatshirt. I watched myself seek out pleasure for myself and take it. I watched myself move not with shame or disgust, but pride and fury. I heard him call her "his dirty little slut, his perfect greedy whore," and she claimed it. Reclaimed it.

I watched the girl I'd never thought I could be, be.

My chest was heaving. My breathing was loud in the sudden silence of the room. I came back into awareness and my cheeks flared red from embarrassment. I was sure I had gone too far. Lost myself too much. I was afraid to face my professor, my classmates. They knew; surely they knew how this painting was made. Surely they would see me as my father saw me. Surely I would turn to find judgement and scorn. Worst of all, even pity. The poor little slut.

But when I turned, I found Professor Sauer smiling. I circled my gaze and none of my classmates were even looking at me, but instead at my art, heads tilted, chins held between thumb and forefinger.

Professor Sauer nodded and said, "I'd like to see more of this, Ms Brady."

A blush fell over my whole face and neck like a shadow as I remembered exactly *how* the piece had come together.

"Well, um," I said, flustered, "well, recreating this…and the, um, situation that, um, made it all come— I mean not *come* but come together. I'm saying come a lot, I'm sorry."

Snickers filtered amongst the art studio and I resisted the urge to hide my face.

"While I find the artwork rather stupendous, Ms Brady," Professor Sauer said, taking back control of the class, "what I really mean is more of *this*."

I frowned slightly as he waved his hand vaguely at me.

"More of this kind of *you*, Ms Brady," he clarified.

I made a noncommittal noise in the back of my throat.

"I want this passionate, engaged, talented student who has something to say and knows how to say it," Professor Sauer continued. "If this is a lovely little butterfly emerging from her cocoon, please don't retreat back inside. Forgive the cliché metaphor, Ms Brady, but spread your wings. Or I fear I may be gravely disappointed. And reflect that disappointment in your term's final grade."

With that, Professor Sauer moved on to the next student. He retreated into his bored, half-paying-attention slump. I grinned once more at my art. It didn't even bother me that I'd just set myself up to receive a lower grade, should I not perform. It just felt too good to have created art, real art. Art that people looked at. Wondered at. Art that made people feel something. Art that raised expectations, even if that was, given my present situation, highly impractical.

After class was dismissed, I checked my phone to find several missed calls from Stewart. They were the kind of missed calls that stacked up like Jenga bricks. Within seconds of one another. Desperation and panic obvious in the long, long call log I scrolled through as I walked out of the studio.

Before I would have called Stewart back immediately. I probably would have dropped my artwork, already running toward the bus so that I could get to Stewart faster. If I'd received this many missed calls just days earlier, my whole world would already be Stewart: his needs, his emergency, his care afterwards, his bail, his medicine, his weak stomach, his high fever, his cruel words as I tried futility to keep him from using again.

But the rain outside felt like it could wash anything away. Clean me of anything, everything. I let it fall over me. Tilted my head up toward it. Breathed deeply.

And remained in my world. Art. Success. Rian. *Me.*

RIAN

I was hoping she would come.

No matter how many sternly worded emails I received from college's dean, no matter how many distressed students I had running up to me on the lawn as I struggled to light a joint, no matter how enticingly they accommodated the small, cosy space with its big windows overlooking a sea of trembling red oaks, I never quite saw the appeal of "office hours". It was too much waiting. Too much small talk. Too much nodding and bridging my fingers under my chin and trying not to yawn.

I had no interest in grades. No desire to clarify things I couldn't remember saying from lecture. No patience for the stuffy leather chair that smelled like old men and stuffy art history books.

But I checked the schedule I'd deleted from the registrar's office, hunted down the little brass key from my underwear drawer, and kept the door to my office cracked just enough to hear footsteps creaking down the old hall.

I waited. Toes impatient on the oriental rug. Eyes unfocused as rain pattered gently against the peaked windows. Chin jerking at every moan of a floorboard.

For a long time no one came. I suspected many had, earlier in the term. I could easily see a line down the wainscoted hallway. Books clutched too tightly to chests. Skirts bouncing a little too eagerly against freshly shaved legs. Bottom lips held between teeth as the seconds ticked by and Professor Merrick failed to show up again. At the very least, I'd taught my class that: I was not available for them. I was not here for them. I had absolutely no interest in them.

I was here for one thing. For one person. For *her* and her alone.

When Eithne hesitated outside my door, I thought I must be dreaming. It was too perfect. Me being there. Her coming as I'd hoped. I couldn't quite believe I hadn't accidentally gotten too high while searching for the little brass key. Stumbled upon something stronger than I remembered. Smoked it a little too quickly in my excitement. Passed out with my arms hanging limp over the edge of the bed as I stared at the ceiling and sought out her face in the dancing shadows of the leaves from the tree outside.

I still wasn't sure this was all entirely real as Eithne pressed her delicate fingers against the door. Stuck her head inside. Asked in a soft, sweet voice, "Is it alright if I come in, Professor Merrick?"

I spoke mostly to see whether I'd hear myself. "Close the door behind you, Ms Brady."

Eithne did as I told her. She handled the door so carefully that neither of us heard the click of the metal tab slide into place. It was as if she had walked straight through the wood itself. It was as if the real world had no limits on her. It was as if she had always been there, fidgeting with the hem of her sweatshirt, and I was just now seeing her. She was just now *letting* me see her.

The two of us were silent for a moment as the rain drummed

on what was left of the vivid red leaves of the oak. There was plenty left unsaid between us. Why she'd come to Dublin Ink the night before. Why she'd drawn me closer there in bed, falling asleep as her tears dried on my hand. Why she'd ridden me on top of that canvas. Why she seemed unwilling now to speak first when there was so much to be said.

"Would you like to take a seat?" I asked.

It seemed like something a professor would say to a student who came to his office hours one rainy afternoon. I knew it would never be us, my little Raglan Road girl and me. The innocent student. The uninterested professor. Detachment would never be ours. We could never discuss her midterm project without stolen glances or hastily locked doors. I would never let her go from my mind when she left. There was no next student for me.

But it seemed to calm her, this role playing. She thanked me with a timid politeness. With the awkwardness of a young girl who didn't know this adult, casually, intimately, especially not carnally.

She sat, knees together, toes tucked primly beneath her as if she wasn't the same girl who fucked me like a savage there on the roof. She placed her fingertips on her knees and cleared her throat.

"I don't want to take up too much of your time." Eithne's gaze remained fixed on her fingertips. She'd cleaned the paint from beneath her nails. I hadn't. "It's just…well, I found your…guidance this morning very beneficial for my assignment."

Lifting her eyes, she assessed me shyly from across the office. We could pretend there was nothing more than this, professor, student. Young girl, adult. Passing ship, passing ship. We could pretend. But not for long.

"I just wanted to say thank you, is all," Eithne said, fingertips tightening on her knees as doubt drew her dark eyebrows together. She added, more softly this time, less sure, "I think that's all I wanted, Professor Merrick."

The rain was steady on the windows. The hum of the radiator, newly turned on for the coming months of cold, was steady. The ticking of the wall clock was steady, too. But all that served to do was prove how unsteady I was: my heart, my mind, my hold on my self-control.

"No," I said.

Maybe the words were rash. Maybe they were all too soon. I should have let our little role play go on a little longer. It was all bound to come crashing down eventually, as inevitable as our clothes hitting the floor.

Eithne looked almost frightened as she whispered, "No, what?"

I stood from my chair. It felt good to be free of that stiff leather. Those cold brass buttons. The straight back that was too unyielding, that refused to arch beneath me. The height of me made Eithne shrink back.

"I don't want your thanks," I told her.

I slipped my hands into my pockets. Looked down at her. Her next line was obvious. The question she was supposed to ask was right there at the tip of her tongue. All she had to do was open her mouth. Or she could leave. Nod. Smile. Accept that what she had to give was not what I wanted. Disappear once more.

I waited. Hid the fact that beneath the cool demeanour of my casual posture I was pinching at my skin, piercing my flesh.

Eithne leaned forward slightly. Blinked at me through long, sweeping eyelashes. She said the words I had wanted to hear, the words I thought I would lose myself over if I didn't hear.

"What do you want?"

No more than a whisper. No more than the brush of a fingertip over goosebumps. But enough.

"I want something with you, Eithne," I said before quickly shaking my head. "No, I want everything with you."

I pulled my hands from my pockets. The release of pain was hardly a relief. My chest burned like I was struggling to remove a boulder from crushing it. I advanced on Eithne. She did not flinch away as I stood above her.

"I want everything," I repeated. "I want all of you. All of your body. All of your mind. All of your soul."

I leaned down and put my hands on the armrests of her chair. She remained seated so properly, so ladylike. Stiff back like that goddamn chair. Fingertips frozen like a line of those tufting brass buttons. Lips stiff and unrevealing as my face came closer and closer to hers.

"I want too much," I whispered. "I want more than I can ask. More than I should ask. I want a reckless amount of you, Eithne, a dangerous amount of you. I want to drown in you. Choke on you. Smother myself with you."

Eithne listened with eyes wide with fear, darkened with arousal. I scared her, I know. She scared me, too. But the fear was cut with attraction, magnetism, desire, lime for tequila, orange peel for whiskey.

"And yet it's what I want. What I'll ask for. What I'll demand."

Eithne shuddered. It drove me mad. I could no longer contain myself.

I grabbed her shoulders and yanked her out of her chair. "What I'll take."

She gasped and I swallowed her fear, her lust, her hesitation, her impulsive abandon. I crushed her to me as I kissed her deeply. Her lips relented to my tongue with a soft moan that only served to spur me on.

I was vaguely aware of the back of her coming into contact with the wall as I pushed her against it. It seemed as unimportant as a boat knocking against a dock; all that mattered was that Eithne and I were intertwined in the hull, sweating beneath the high noon sun. I hardly felt at all Eithne's fingers come to the collar of my shirt, hardly noticed at all as she tugged me closer; I was a planet in her orbit and it was as natural as gravity to crash into her. There was the scuffing of shoes, the knocking of knees as I widened her stance with my leg, but none of it was as present, as pressing as the simplicity of Eithne's lips against mine.

I breathed what she breathed: musty office air, expectations, fears, a pervading sense of wrongness, a deep conviction that this was *right*. I inhaled when she inhaled, exhaled when she told me with panting little groans. My fingers burned with the warmth of her neck, twisted with the tendrils of her dark hair. I tugged her head back, loomed over her, darkened her heaving chest like a solar eclipse. Claimed her even as she claimed me.

A creak of the door interrupted us. I looked with irritation at the disturbance. A glare in my eyes. A snarl of my lips. Whoever was there was an obstacle to clear, a hurdle to get around. I had nastiness forming on my tongue. I had Eithne to get back to.

But for Eithne, the shocked face of a fellow student peeking hesitantly inside was something far different. It was a splash of cold water. An alarm that screamed her awake because she was drifting out of her lane in the dark. An excuse to pull away, hide her face in the crook of her neck, and whisper, "Oh my God."

I shooed away the student. Crossed the short distance across the oriental rug. Closed the door after saying politely more for Eithne's sake, "I'll be right with you." But when I turned around, I found Eithne with her bookbag over her shoulder. Her sweatshirt tidied. The back of her hand drawing across her lips. Wiping away us. Wiping away me.

"Don't go," I told her.

I hadn't meant it to sound like a command, like an order. But emotions were boiling up in me, boiling over in me. I couldn't keep doing this. Couldn't keep watching her leave. Letting her disappear. I couldn't continue without her in my arms, without her in my life. Every time she pulled away, she was taking a piece of me with her. I was being shredded. Destroyed. Torn apart. I'd snap eventually. I'd lose it.

I hadn't meant it to sound like a command, like an order. But it was. Because it had to be. Because I couldn't help myself. Because only Eithne could help me now.

"I'm sorry," Eithne said, slipping by me without meeting my eyes. "I don't have everything to give."

She opened the door roughly. Not bothering to hide the creaking this time. Not caring that the noise was nails on a chalkboard to my ears. Eithne left the door open behind her and that was almost somehow worse. There was nothing to close the door on, it seemed. We'd never been anything so there was nothing to end. We'd never truly been together so no final separation was even needed. I dug my fingernails into my palms as I heard her outside.

"You can go in now," she said to the faceless student I'd soon have to face. "I'm finished."

Her footsteps retreated quickly. Each one filled me with anger. With frustration. With fear. I'd become obsessed with her, my little Raglan Road girl. And I couldn't have her. Couldn't get my hands around her. Couldn't get her inside of me.

The student, a girl, freckles, eager eyes, poked her head back inside.

"Professor Merrick," she said as if I was listening, "you're here."

But I wasn't. I was with Eithne in the rain.

I was still haunting her. She might have walked away but…

I would never ever let her go.

EITHNE

The rain was loud against my umbrella, but it couldn't quite drown out the noise of my thoughts, as relentless as the stream of cars that kicked up muddy waves onto the sidewalk, battering me like the wind that buckled my umbrella.

I could have stayed. I could have met that girl's shocked gaze and kept it as I flicked the tip of my tongue across Rian's lower lip. I could have drawn Rian closer instead of pushing him away.

I fought against these thoughts. They flooded in like the tide, drowning me and there was no help in sight. My only salvation was Rian. But I'd turned away from him once more.

My status at the college was more important. My graduating was not a luxury, but an absolute necessity. I had responsibilities, I had bills, I had Stewart.

These were the thoughts I grappled for like a lifeline in the choppy waves. But they slipped through my fingers every time I brushed against them. These thoughts were no longer the sturdy, reliable safehold they once were. Rian had eroded the rock as effectively as time itself. I was losing control. Control over my actions. Over what I thought I once believed, over what I thought was important. Control over myself.

I climbed the stairs to my new apartment. What was Rian doing? Was he still thinking of me? Did he regret letting me leave? Had I pushed him too far away this time? Had he decided that I just wasn't worth it? The trouble. The effort. The instability.

As I pushed open the door, I considered calling him. Inviting him over. Continuing where we left over. Continuing what I shouldn't have stopped. Continuing what I was increasingly wishing I hadn't stopped.

But the idea of calling Rian fell from my head the very second I flipped on the lights. I don't know what it says about me that my first thought was that the blood on the carpet wouldn't come up easily. That I'd be scrubbing at it all night long. That yet again I would be not getting my security deposit, my hard-earned money, back because of my older brother.

I don't think it says anything good considering that Stewart's hands were bound behind his back, blood dripped from his busted cheek, and a man with crazed eyes sat perched on the back of the couch next to him with a baseball bat slapping in rhythm against his open palm.

"This must be the sister then," the man said, grinning maniacally.

A black hoodie covered a shaved head. It was damp from the rain so it clung to the shape of his skull.

"The sister who would surely answer the phone. The sister who *always* answered," the man continued, smacking Stewart's cheek with the baseball bat, making him wince. "The sister who had to answer, just *had* to answer if you let me call one more time, Nick. Just one more time. Just one more time!"

I let out an involuntary scream as the intruder, Nick it seemed, brought the bat down on Stewart's knee with a sickening crunch of bone. I tried to run to my brother's side, but

Nick stopped me with the bat pointed at my chest. He clicked his tongue as he wagged it back and forth.

"Don't hurt him," I said, voice little more than a pathetic squeak.

I heard the words, my words, but it was as if my ears were stuffed with cotton. They sounded muted. Distant. Unreal. It didn't sound like anything I would ever say. *"Don't hurt him."* Too much like a nightmare. Too much like something that happened in the movies. Too ridiculous.

But it was all I knew to do. Because I hadn't done what I was supposed to do, what I should have done: pick up the phone. Call Stewart back. Be there for my brother.

I saw it all before me as I stood there in the harsh glare of the yellow bulb (I hadn't even bought a lampshade yet. There was already blood on the couch, on the floor, and I hadn't even bought a lampshade yet). I saw Stewart's fingers fumbling over the numbers as he tried dialling again. I saw him hunched over as the rings continued uninterrupted, his bony spine already preparing for the impact of this stranger's bat. I even heard his whimper of despair as my pre-recorded voice announced that I was unable to come to the phone. That I was too busy obsessing over my professor. That I had better things to do like trace my fingers over the place where my knees, straddled across Rian's naked groin, had smeared the paint across the canvas. That I had seen Stewart's call and ignored it, because I wanted to see Rian again. Run my tongue along his lips again. Take his cock inside of me right there in his office.

Guilt flooded through me as I imagined Stewart not understanding why I wasn't answering, why I chose this very moment to abandon him. Not understanding that I chose bodily pleasures over familial bonds.

I couldn't explain any of it. Not just because Nick was there with his baseball bat and dangerous flint in his black eyes. I hardly understood it myself. Who had I become? When had the decision become so easy: Rian over Stewart, my professor over my own brother, my pleasure over my responsibilities? I couldn't explain it. Other than to say I was sorry. Other than to vow that I would never make the mistake again. Other than to whisper, whimper, *beg*, "Don't hurt him."

A voice laughed inside my head. Maybe it was my father's. Maybe it was Stewart's. Maybe a chuckle or two was already there, behind the saliva-soaked gag tugging back the corners of his lips. *You've already hurt him, can't you see? The damage is already done.*

"Stewart," I tried to say, reaching out, fingers grasping at air. "Stewart, I—"

I would have preferred to see anger in his pain-hazed eyes. He had a right to be angry. To be upset. I'd failed him. I'd promised to be there for him, like he'd been there for me when our father had been cruel. I'd failed. Anger would be right. I could take anger. But it wasn't anger. It was fear. Terror. A man lost at sea. A boy who couldn't find his way home.

My heart broke and yet I still couldn't run to him, still couldn't wrap my arms around him, nurse him, comfort him, love him. The end of a baseball bat pressed harder against my ribcage. A pair of pupils narrowed at the other side. My skin crawled. He was smiling. Corners creased in merriment. Almost fucking twinkling with delight.

"Seems Stewart here was right about something after all," Nick said, gaze darting between the two of us siblings, "you do love him."

I could imagine Stewart on his knees. Snot and blood streaming from his busted nose. Hands clasped at his chest like he was kneeling before a priest instead of a madman as he said those very words, "She loves me." I was sure that mental image hurt worse than anything Nick could have done to me with his bat.

Nick added more, "That you would never abandon him."

"She would never abandon me," I heard Stewart sob as he crawled backwards, shielding his face as the bat rose over Nick's head, water droplets from his wet hood springing loose like spittle from a mad pit bull.

My stomach clenched painfully.

"That you would do anything for him," Nick said, eyes gleaming as he studied me, trembling there a few feet away from him like a deer too stupid to run at the first sign of danger.

Something flinched inside of me when I heard this. It was a thought I wanted to push away, to hide from. I saw Stewart once more. I heard those same words in my head repeated. This time there was something more than fear. More than faith in a loved one. There was entitlement. Smugness. A circus performer sure that his lion would jump through any hoop, ringed with fire or not. I didn't want to see my brother that way. The way Rian saw him, as using me, manipulating me, controlling me.

It was a relief when Nick spoke again. A relief when he said with a twisted smile and flashing eyes, "Is he right, too, when he says that you're quite the artist, pet?"

It was a relief because it was a chance to go back to the easier image: my brother as someone I loved, who loved me, and who I failed. Let down. Disappointed. It was a relief because Nick was offering me a chance to fix the easier of the two problems: Stewart's debt to him versus Stewart's hold on me. It was a relief because working with my hands was easy.

Struggling with heart was not.

"Yes," I said, sagging with relief. "Yes, I am."

Nick smiled.

RIAN

I suppose that's what friends are for. For dragging you out when you want to stay in and sulk. For shoving a bottle of beer into your hand when you want to reach for something stronger. For shouting in your ear over the pounding music when your thoughts are almost too loud to handle.

For pulling you back from the edge when the edge feels so fucking good.

The Jar was packed that night. Though wasn't it always. Band stickers smacked all over the windows and doors, the heavy beads of condensation on the glass, the general smell of stale beer and cheap perfume. All that was left to alert you to its presence was a sign outside. It was one of those places that you knew if you knew. And if you didn't, well, that was rather a shame, now wasn't it?

Normally I loved the place. Plenty of people to watch. Plenty of smoky corners to get lost in. Plenty of good drink and good friends. But that night I was a reluctant participant to say the least. As Noah and Aubrey moved expertly behind the crowded bar, I caught glimpses of myself in the long back mirror, the liquor bottles lining in front of it like stalagmites. And me, the lurking creature. The dark thing. The bat.

I certainly didn't appear as something used to the light. My skin was paler than usual making the tattoos down my forearms seem even darker. A hollowness to my eyes. Even I couldn't seem to maintain my gaze. I'd tried to catch sight of myself but my shifty eyes were hard to catch. I looked like I was on something, fingers twitchy on the sticky edge of the bar top, lips dry as I licked them too often. I was unsettled. Uncomfortable.

Conor pretended not to notice this as he sat on one side of me, elbows propped on the bar as he watched Rachel and Aurnia dancing. It was Mason's turn, apparently, to be Bad Cop.

"You haven't touched your beer," Mason shouted in my ear.

I leaned the bottle back, noticed the brown liquid shift up the long, narrow neck.

"Do you want me to drink my beer?" I asked, glancing at him out of the corner of my eye.

Mason narrowed his eyes. Considered. Looked to Conor for help. Conor ducked his head. He'd be no help. Before Mason could decide on an answer, I tipped the bottle back and drained it in one go. I put it back down too roughly and it toppled over, rolled, and shattered where it fell behind the bar.

"What would you like for me to drink next?" I asked Mason, fingers carded in front of me.

I was being an asshole. I was in no mood to be out. I'd gone along because my friends made the fair point that I'd been rather distant. Or more distant than usual. And because I still had a vague sense of self-preservation. Still had a sliver of hope that I wouldn't go careening over the edge. Still thought I'd try to try, at least for a little while longer.

But the music was too loud. The beer too weak. And Mason was too in love with Rachel to be of any help. I needed misery, not happiness. But speak of the devil and the devil shall appear, right?

"Did you know about this?" I asked Mason angrily, eyes darting between him and the man making his way from the door.

Mason turned in confusion. Confusion I didn't quite believe. Or was too unwillingly to believe.

"Know about what?" he asked.

"Did you tell him I'd be here?" I heard the paranoia in my voice, the flitting with craziness; I didn't care. "Did you bring me here because of him?"

Mason was looking in bewilderment at the throng of people behind him. Maybe he thought I was seeing things like he thought I was seeing my mystery girl. Maybe he was too drunk to remember that Eithne was real. Or maybe I'd made up that memory, too, Eithne at Dublin Ink. Eithne being real. Maybe this was a nightmare and he wasn't really walking toward me.

I'd prefer that. Insanity over this. Insanity over *him*.

"My brother," I snarled. "Liam."

Vehemence dripped from my lips as surely as if I had spilled my beer; I could feel it, cold, wet, unnatural. Mason was trying to deny his guilt, but I was certain he was in on it. Like a caged animal my head whipped around the too packed bar. I was certain Aurnia and Rachel were over there laughing at me: a plan gone perfectly. I was certain Conor was ready to grab me with those bear arms the second I attempted to escape. Even Noah and Aubrey and little, crazy Candace collecting empty beer bottles, even all of them, I was certain had played a part. I was outnumbered, cornered. Everyone was against me. My friends had turned. My family had not only abandoned me, but actively worked against me. If it was paranoia from the drugs I'd been taking with too much regularity, I was way too far away from sober to realise it. All I knew was that I had to get out of there. And fast.

I shoved Conor away without warning and he growled like a beast, beer bottle shattering on the floor as he stood for a fight.

Mason hollered something as eyes turned to the disturbance. Aurnia and Rachel had stopped dancing. I shoved past Mason as he shouted, "Rian, what the fuck?!"

"Fuck you," I said to Mason first. Then to Conor who was still smouldering mad and ready to fight. "And fuck you, too," I shouted at the girls who stared in shock as they got jostled about by people on the dance floor.

The gust of chilled air outside The Jar was no relief. It just brought me back to the wind that somehow slipped through the boards of the barn, somehow found its way beneath the burlap I huddled under, somehow always howled the second I managed to fall asleep. The emptiness of the street was the same emptiness I found when I stumbled dead tired off a bus in Dublin for the first time, nothing on my back but my own shirt.

The hand suddenly on my shoulder brought back baseball bats, lengths of rough rope, and frying pans still searing hot from the stove.

I shirked off Liam's grip, but he circled round me like I was nothing more than a frightened calf who knew no better, who needed protecting, who needed being told where to go. I wanted to hit him, my own flesh and blood. It ran in the family, after all.

But there he was. Blocking my path. Standing right in front of me. Taller than me by a good two inches. Broader in the shoulders. Hands big and meaty. A "real" man, my father would have said. A "true" man, he would have sneered as he looked me up and down and found me always lacking. Easy to push around. Easy to beat. Easy to take his anger out on because I looked like her. It was the only way I recognised my brother after years apart: he had Mom's eyes, too. Pale in the pulsing lights. Like a cloudless sky. Something I knew little of.

"Rian," Liam said, holding up his hands like he didn't want to fight.

I snickered. Liam never did. I'd heard my name spoken softly like that a million times. Always kind. Always gentle. Always with a pack of frozen peas at the ready. But never when I really needed him. Never when our father's knuckles were finding their way between my ribs. Never when Alan laughed and tripped me as I tried to run away. Never when they locked the doors of the barn on howling winter nights to "toughen me up", to "make me a man", to "prove whether I was a sissy or not". Never then. In those moments I never heard my name. Never saw Liam's face. Never had anyone but myself, the blooming bruises, and the quiet hope that one day I'd run away from it all. Escape it all.

Escape. That's exactly what I was going to do.

"He's getting worse," Liam said, blocking me as I tried desperately to get around him.

I was being flippant when I asked, "Who?" Of course I remembered my goddamn father; how could I forget the bastard who haunted my nightmares?

Liam tried placing his hands on my shoulders. Couldn't he see this just made me angrier? Being alone to fight your demons was one thing. But expecting someone to come and fight with you, and then them not showing up, was something entirely else. There was a difference between loneliness and abandonment. And my brother had abandoned me.

"Get your *fucking* hands off of me," I said, voice trembling with rage.

I wouldn't be comforted by him. I wouldn't be soothed or calmed or talked down off my self-righteous little edge. I wouldn't be the sweet little brother any longer. I was ruined. Broken. Fucking angry. And I liked it that way.

Liam hesitated, but only for a moment before pulling his hands off of my shoulders. He frowned and leaned in a little closer. "Are you alright?"

He followed me as I backed up from the glare of the streetlamp, hid in the circling shadows.

I wiped at my sweating forehead. "That's none of your business."

In truth, I didn't feel alright. Far from it really. A clamminess clung to my skin like morning mist. My fingertips wouldn't stop trembling. My heartbeat felt fast and faint, like hooves galloping away with no way to stop them. My vision wouldn't focus on anything. And a pounding in my head was growing louder.

"I tried calling you on the phone, but you wouldn't answer," Liam said softly in that fucking tone of his I hated so much. He started to reach out but thought better of it. "I—I had to talk to you."

"So you got my friends to set me up?" I asked bitterly. "Couldn't let me have anyone for myself?"

Liam acted surprised. Mocked innocence just like the rest of them. I was shaking more, there on the sidewalk. It was easy enough to convince myself that it was the cold. The wind against sweat. The frozen concrete against shoes too thin.

"I don't even know your friends," Liam said. "I don't know anything about your life here. I mean, I hardly recognise you. You have tattoos. Your face is…more severe. And you've gained what seems like fifty pounds of muscle."

It was an attempt at brevity. At brotherhood. At reconnection. I wanted to spit it from my mouth like poison.

"No longer the scrawny runt to scapegoat for Mom's death," I muttered under my breath.

Liam sighed, dragged his fingers through his hair that belonged to Alan, belonged to my father. It was easier like that, with his pale blue eyes fixed on the cracked concrete. I could hate him more. When I didn't see myself. When I didn't see Mom.

"We can still heal," Liam said, lifting his eyes to me.

I had to turn away. I couldn't keep that fuel of anger burning if I imagined the request coming from beyond the grave. I never really knew my mother, but it seemed like something she would say. Something she might even want. Healing. Restoration. *Family*.

I pushed the image of her away with a snort of derision and a tightening of my hands into fists.

"Heal?" I laughed. "You want me to go heal the man who made my life a living hell? You want me to mend fences in what was to me a literal prison? You want me to ease the guilt of a monster? I thought I'd said it already, but I'll say it again, dear brother, 'Fuck him. And fuck *you*.'"

This time Liam didn't try to stop me as I went around him. Nobody tried to stop me. Not even the little voice in my head that wanted to be healthy, happy, *good*.

There was just me and my old faithful friend, self-destruction. He walked beside me into the dark like a dutiful dog, wagging his tail, tongue lolling from his too sharp teeth, eager for the chaos that was to come.

In that moment, he felt like my only *real* friend.

EITHNE

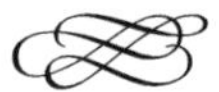

I only allowed myself to cry once Stewart was asleep in my bed.

After Nick had left with a malicious whistle on his chapped lips. After I'd run to my brother, cut his bindings, blood-smeared zip ties, wiped his burning cheeks still wet from tears with frantic strokes. Only once I'd cleaned him up, made him tea, spooned him soup as he whimpered again and again till he finally passed out, tearing me in two all anew with each repetition, *"Where were you, Eithne? Where were you? Where were you? Where were you, Eithne?"*

Even then, after all that, did I only allow myself two minutes of grief. Guilt. Shame. Terror. Despair. Two minutes and two minutes only. I would have even set an alarm if I hadn't heard every second passing like a ticking clock in my pounding chest. I couldn't have escaped that two minutes, even if I had wanted to. And I hadn't wanted to. Nor felt I deserved to.

I kept the lights turned off as I settled in at my old, slow computer. No tea for me. No little shot of whiskey for the pain. No blissful nothingness of sleep. I had work to do. Penance, maybe. Atonement, perhaps. I had failed my brother when he needed me the most. All those years of looking after him, picking up after him, providing for him, all those years off my life no longer counted in my mind. I had wiped the slate clean with one swipe of my thumb across my phone: Ignore. All the good will, good karma, good whatever the fuck you want to call it that I'd accumulated through literal blood, sweat, and tears all came crashing down the second I chose Rian over Stewart, chose myself over family, chose pleasure over duty.

I didn't allow myself to glance at the little display of the time in the illuminated corner of the screen. It didn't matter how long it would take. I would work till it was finished. Till I made sure Stewart was safe. Till his debt had been paid. And mine.

I chastised every yawn, slapped my cheeks every time my eyelids began to droop, straightened by back against the hard chair every time I found myself slumping over, the temptation of my cheek against the desk for just a second or two so, so, *so* alluring. The clicks of my mouse became my lullaby, the dragging of the arrow back and forth my gently swaying mobile. It was soothing, I told myself as my thoughts grew fuzzier and fuzzier, making up for my mistakes. It was like a dream, I could almost convince myself, feeling no more shame. Earning my way to no more shame.

Stewart slept behind me without a sound. Without moving. I, too, was motionless. Just the twitching of my hand from left to right across the mousepad to tell that I was still awake. The heat of my coat enveloped me; I hadn't taken it off yet, I dimly realised. The rhythm of my work, easy and monotonous, lulled me into a strange trance. I wasn't even sure I was fully awake at that point.

When Rian appeared at the doorway, he was little more than a silhouette. A looming shape in the dark. He lurched backward and forward, unsteady. But I knew it was him. Sensed, maybe, that it was him. Or perhaps I was dreaming at that point and simply wished it was him. Either way he did not frighten me. Not until he switched on the light.

It was very much like waking up, Rian turning on the light. It was nothing more than a bare bulb hung above the mattress on the floor, but it was harsh nevertheless to my eyes. It drew me out of my work as if from under warm, cosy sheets. I blinked like I was trying to remember where I was, who I was. Then it all came back. Unwanted. Cruel. Painful. And I was very much afraid.

My gaze went first to Stewart, to see if he woke up. Thankfully he remained a motionless heap under the blanket.

Next, I looked at Rian. His skin was deadly pale. A sickly gleam covered his face and neck, coat turned open despite the early winter chill of the night. The collar of his thin grey t-shirt looked clawed at as if by some wild animal. His pupils were dilated in a way I recognised all too easily. The pale blue of his irises had been chased away, almost nothing of it remained at the rim.

I should have moved faster. Perhaps things would have been different. But I was tired, exhausted really. The hard, uncomfortable chair had become a bed of my own; I didn't want to leave it. Wasn't sure I could. So instead I sat there. Sat there dumbly as I watched Rian piece it all together in his head: Stewart with his swollen eye and red-marked wrists, me at the computer with fake IDs half edited up on the screen, the baseball bat left leaning against the couch as a warning, as a threat, as a reminder that even without this weapon Nick could hurt us. *Would* hurt us.

I was up before Rian managed his first word. Pushing him back out of the room. Closing the door behind him. Placing a finger to his lips.

"What are you doing here?" I hissed. "You need to leave."

"Who was it?" Rian demanded, not bothering at all to keep his voice low.

I shoved him toward the door.

"You can't just hunt me down whenever you want, Rian."

"It seems I'm not the first," he shot back.

I glared up at him. "I have things under control."

"What's his name?"

Rian had stopped in the centre of the living room, halfway toward the door. I pushed at him, but he was immobile. As immovable as a stubborn bull.

"You stink like alcohol," I told him, diverting. "And you're high as a fucking kite. There's nothing you can do for me."

Rian was staring past my shoulder. Staring at the baseball bat just a few feet behind me against the couch. My hands were flat against his chest. I could feel the unhealthy heat of his body. The burning. There was the temptation to believe he'd come to save me, to help me. But I could see it was again the other way around: *I* would be the one to save *him*. To keep him from doing something he'd regret. To prevent him from harming himself. To make sure he made it to dawn alive.

No one was coming for me. The calvary was fucking here and they were a goddamn liability.

"Rian," I said softly as I watched his gaze try to focus. "Rian, why don't you just sit down. I'll get you a cup of tea. Did something happen?"

Rian was too far gone for me to reach him, his too bright eyes unblinking. I tugged at his wrist, but he didn't react. I wasn't strong enough to push him around.

"Rian," I tried again. "I'm fine. We're fine. I'm just…doing someone a little favour. Just some editing work really. No different from what I do for school."

My tone was soft, gentle. I thought if I couldn't get in with a hammer, I'd try a feather. My thumb circled the bone of his wrist. I checked over my shoulder to see if there was something else he was looking at. There was only the baseball bat and its anarchy stickers and smashed-in nails. I drew my attention back to Rian when his breathing went ragged. I was sure

I'd felt his pulse jump in his wrist, his heart leap beneath my palm.

I spoke more quickly now. "I'm not hurt, okay? He didn't touch me. And he won't. Because I'm fixing everything. Rian?"

"That bat..." Anger contorted Rian's face, colour flooding his pale cheeks. If there was any of the pale blue left in Rian's eyes it was gone now, burned away at his fury.

I saw only my own reflection when he looked down at me: a frightened girl who couldn't fix a goddamn thing.

"It was Nick, wasn't it?" Rian asked in a hoarse voice as if he'd been shouting all night.

"How do you know Nick?" I blurted out without thinking.

It was a stupid mistake. Stupid. But it was as good as an admission.

Before I could correct my mistake, Rian stormed out, muttering, "I'll kill him. I'll fucking kill him."

RIAN

The black wrought iron gates of campus rose up in the dark like a mouth to swallow me. I plunged inside without a second thought. I hardly knew where I was going. Across Dublin. Across campus. I wasn't certain I was taking the shortest path to one of Nick's drug dens, but I knew with an unwavering conviction that if I just kept walking I'd find one. I'd find him. Then I'd kill him.

Eithne screamed out for me to stop, but I barely heard her. I was too far gone. She tugged at my arm, trying to get me to slow; instead I dragged her with me.

Nick had put his hands on her. He had *hurt* her. I would tear him limb from limb.

"Stay with me."

That made me freeze and cock my head toward Eithne. "What do you mean?"

"Don't find Nick." She pressed her body up against mine, her breasts into my chest, her hot pussy against my thigh. "Be *with me* tonight." She grabbed my hand and pulled it to her breast, her nipple like a pebble under my palm.

"Take it out on me. Punish me."

I knew she was doing this to try to stop me. Using my desire for her, my need for her to stop me. The larger part of me didn't care.

"Don't offer something you don't really—"

"I want it. I fucking want it so bad."

I wrapped my hand around her throat firmly. "What do you want. Say it."

She whimpered. "Please… I *need* you to do bad things to me, to hurt me a little. Need you to call me your little whore."

I pulled her into the nearest darkened building and kicked open the closest door.

I pushed her into one of the art studios. Ironic that it happened to be the very studio where I'd stood there naked on the pedestal and spotted her among the canvases.

"Take your clothes off like a good little slut."

I stood there breathing like a wild bull through my nostrils, as Eithne locked eyes with me. She gripped the hem of her sweatshirt and pulled it off. Then she pushed down her jeans and panties too. She shivered in the dim light filtering in through the opaque windows from the corridor. I let my eyes travel over her beautiful naked body.

"Turn around and bend over the desk. Show me that pussy."

Fear reached her eyes before she turned her back on me. She'd do whatever I told her to tonight just to stop me from committing murder. I wasn't a good enough man not to take advantage of this.

Her hands trembled as she found the edge of the desk, her knees wobbled as she bent over.

I stalked over to her. Her breath hitched as I neared, my footsteps echoing in the silent art room.

I kicked her feet out wide so that her thighs were forced to part. "Whores don't close their legs. Don't you dare close them again. Understand?"

She let out a small moan. Fuck, I could smell her pussy, ripe and juicy and I hadn't even touched her yet. I bet she was already wet just at my words.

I grabbed her hair and pulled back, just enough to cause her to whimper. I bent over to growl in her ear. "Do you understand?"

"Y-yes…sir."

My cock swelled.

I let go of her hair and she sagged against the desk.

"Good girl."

I straightened and reached down between her legs to touch her pussy—*my* pussy. Fuck, she wasn't just wet, she was dripping like paint all over the floor. I rumbled with approval. "You little whore. Your greedy little cunt is already soaked for me."

I ran my fingers along her slit, eliciting moans from her, her hips arching back toward me, begging for more. I rubbed her juices back and forth bringing more of it back toward her asshole. She didn't know it yet, but I was going to fill both her holes. And she was going to love it.

When I touched her puckered hole, she flinched, her thighs threatening to snap together if it weren't for the boot I had between them.

I brought my palm down on her ass with a loud crack.

She yelped then let out a moan.

"What did I say about closing your legs?"

She widened her legs, but not as wide as they were before.

"Wider." I punctuated my admonishment with another smack, this time just a little too hard.

She hissed. But she did what I demanded.

I brushed my fingers lightly over the red mark I'd made on her ass, a reward. Before running them along her crack again and circling her asshole. She tensed.

"Breathe, Eithne. I promise, you'll fucking love this."

I felt her inhale then as she relaxed, giving herself to me, her complete trust rushing through my veins like cocaine.

I massaged her asshole with the fingers of one hand, circling her clit with the fingers of the other, until she was pushing back and moaning. I grinned to myself. "Such a good little whore."

I pulled my hands off her only to strip myself of clothes.

She moaned. "Rian, please… I need…"

"I'm right here, baby."

I snatched a paintbrush from a pot hanging on an easel, the smooth handle was about the width of a thumb. Perfect.

I kneeled behind her and rubbed the handle end along her pussy, coating it until it was wet enough to slide inside her. She moaned and bucked back.

"Fuck, yes. More."

"Such a greedy slut," I breathed against her folds before I licked a long line all the way back and up.

She shuddered. "God, yes."

She was more than ready for it. I plunged my tongue into her sensitive back hole as I fucked her with the paintbrush, angling it so it hit her g-spot.

"Oh fuck, oh fuck," she chanted as I worked her holes. As I brought her all the way to the edge.

And pulled away.

She let out a cry. "Rian, please—"

"Only whores get to come."

"W-what?"

I straightened and brushed the soft end of the brush along her pussy and her back hole. Her body shook as I teased her. The touch wasn't enough.

"Own it, Eithne."

I circled the handle end of the brush around her asshole rim before pulling away as she bucked back, trying to get it inside her.

"Own it."

"I'm a whore."

"A beautiful little whore."

"Your little whore."

"Yes," I hissed, circling her back hole with the handle end again as I ran the finger of my other hand against her clit, another reward.

"I'm a whore and I need to come, oh God Rian, I need to come so bad."

I grabbed my cock and positioned at her entrance. "And you deserve to come." I pushed the end of the brush into her ass, her body just accepting it, tightening around it. At the same time, I thrust my cock inside her pussy.

I groaned feeling her body tighten around me, feeling the pressure of the brush in her ass against my cock.

I timed the thrusts in a wave from the brush in her ass to my cock in her pussy, in, in, out, out. Over and over until she was screaming. "Fuck me. Fuck me like a dirty little whore."

Until my timing was forgotten. Until I left the brush in her ass and grabbed her hips, driving myself deep inside her over and over.

I felt when she peaked, when her whole body tightened around me so hard I thought I might explode. Then she came, hard. Her body vibrating against the desk, milking the come out of my cock, her screams echoing around the empty art room.

I could barely pull out before I came all over the backs of her thighs, the orgasm roaring through me like a thunderous wave. I gripped the desk as we panted together in the dark.

Carefully, I slid the paintbrush out of her. I found a discarded but clean paint rag and used it to wipe her up.

Then I pulled my clothes on and helped her into hers. I picked her up like a baby and she snuggled into my arms as I carried her out of the art room, out of campus.

"Where are we going?" she mumbled against my chest.

I said, simply.

"Home."

~

I slipped Eithne into my bed and pulled off her shoes before sliding in behind her, both of us still fully clothed. I tucked her against my chest and she nestled even further against me, sighing happily, the sound warming my insides more than a hit of cocaine ever did. She looked like a sleeping angel in this dim moonlight filtering through my window.

I brushed the hair out of her face and prayed that I wouldn't fuck this up.

"Rian," she mumbled.

"Shh...go to sleep, baby."

"Thank you."

I blinked. "What for?"

She shrugged, her eyes still closed. Then sighed. "For... making it okay. For making...*me* okay."

My arms tightened reflexively around her. "You're more than okay. You're perfect."

She smiled. "I'm not perfect." Her features darkened. "I just... my father always told me there was something wrong with me. With who I was. With what I wanted...sexually, you know?"

I gritted my teeth. He was the reason why Eithne had been so unable to accept pleasure, unable to see the beauty in her own body. "I'll cut out his tongue for saying those things to you."

Her mouth twitched in a half-smile. "That's the nicest thing anyone's ever said to me."

She thought I was joking. I wasn't fucking joking. "Tell me where he is." When she didn't reply, I added, "I'll find out regardless."

Her eyes opened, her gaze pinning me to the mattress. From

the pain and relief in her eyes, I knew it before she spoke. "He's dead."

I fell silent, intrusive thoughts of my own asshole father and his own nearing demise twisting up my insides.

She nudged me. "Rian?"

"When did he die?"

"A few years ago. Heart attack. Right before I…I applied for art school."

I nodded. His death had been a release for her. It'd given her the courage to reach for what she wanted. What she loved. Art.

"I thought I would feel sad that he was gone." Guilt flashed across her face, a feeling I knew all too well. "I mean, I did kinda feel sad. But…"

"You felt relief," I said for her.

She nodded. "You get it."

"My father's dying," I said before I could censor myself.

It'd been the first time I'd actually said those words out loud. She was the first person I'd told. To my utter surprise, I felt the weight on my chest lessen.

Her stricken face turned to mine and her fingers came up toward my cheek. "I'm so sorry."

"Don't be." I weaved my fingers into hers and clasped them to my chest, against the beating heart that she owned. "He's an asshole. Broke several of my ribs and my collarbone before I was even twelve."

Eithne's eyes filled with tears as she watched me in the dark. "I'll chop off his hands for hurting you."

I let out a half laugh, half choke. "That's the nicest thing—"

She cut me off with a kiss, soft and intense, her tears making her lips salty. A kiss that absolved me. That called me back from the abyss.

She sat up and tugged at my shirt, pulling it up over my head. I let her push me back to the sheets with her small soft hands. Let her trace my ribcage and my collarbone, let her touch heal me. Let her body, stripped naked, cover me like a bandage.

And as I slid into her warm heat, her willing needy body, her arms wrapping around my back, her hot breath at my ear, I realised she was the only thing holding all my broken pieces together.

The only thing holding me together.

EITHNE

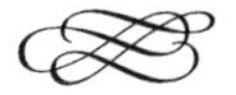

In another life I might have stayed at Rian's apartment, in his bed with him all day. Talking, laughing, fucking.

But I had responsibilities. I had class. And I had Stewart.

I'd already been away all night already.

I'd waited until Rian was asleep before I'd snuck out of his apartment. I knew it was a shitty thing to do. But I doubted he'd let me go if I told him I had to leave. I didn't have enough energy in me to fight.

Stewart had been asleep when I'd returned home the next morning. I moved quietly around my apartment, packing my bag for school.

It wasn't the first sleepless night I'd had before school and I was certain it wouldn't be the last. The IDs were in a tidy pile on the little makeshift nightstand: two textbooks, a box of Kleenex, and an old painting palette balanced atop. I'd written Stewart a note, hoping that I might slip out before he awoke. I didn't want to have to make him tea. Scrounge up some breakfast I didn't even bother with for myself. Check his bandages. Press the back of my hand against his forehead to check for signs of infections. But most of all I just didn't want to see him. Or have him see me.

"Eithne," Stewart mumbled with a thick voice.

For a moment I considered pretending I hadn't heard him. Slipping out the door without glancing in his direction.

But my guilt won out, familial duty heavy on my shoulders.

With gritted teeth, I slipped my bag from my shoulder.

"Stewart," I said, turning to him with a smile I wondered if he could see through, "hey, how are you feeling?"

I watched and tried to draw up sympathy as my older brother swallowed painfully and grimaced with every shift of his prone body. But the well, it seemed, was empty. I just wanted to get out of there. Go to class. Be gone.

"I, um, I left the IDs there," I said when he sank back against the limp pillow with a groan and nothing more. "It's everything Nick asked for. That should end things. I, um, I need to get to class, so—"

A sob broke from my big brother's chapped lips. I was at Stewart's side like a faithful dog before I knew what I was doing. But I was worse than a dog. Because it was guilt that drove me. Shame that made me take my brother's hand. I wondered if he felt how limply I held it.

"Shh," I whispered as Stewart cried. "Shh, it's okay, it's okay."

Tears streaked the spots of dried blood I'd missed cleaning off his cheeks last night. They stained the corners of the bandages I'd applied with care. They pooled in his throat which trembled as he snivelled.

I glanced just once at the clock. And swallowed a sigh. I scooted farther onto the bed and said, "Hey, hey, we're alright."

Stewart's arms knocked the air out of me as he wrapped them around me, drew me tight to him, squeezed me so hard I could barely breathe. His breath was hot against my neck as he whispered in a near panic, "Eithne, I'm sorry. I'm sorry. I'm so, so sorry."

The words kept coming so quickly that I couldn't interrupt. Couldn't say anything in response. I just had to lie there, getting crushed, getting waterboarded by apologies, gagging on each "I'm sorry."

A flare of anger rose up in me. When was it my turn? When was it my fucking turn to break down? To break everything? To have someone else pick up the pieces? Pick up me? Put me back together?

Stewart held open the door for a violent drug dealer. My father held my mother's death over my head. But they didn't hold me. They crushed me. Choked the life out of me. That's not what I needed. That's not being held. That's being held hostage.

And yet empty words came spilling out from between my lips, "Stewart, you don't need to apologise. I'll always be here for you. No, please, it's *me* who should be apologising. Stewart..."

I wanted to scream his name. I wanted to shove him away. I wanted him out of my fucking life.

Instead, I stayed there in the bone-crushing embrace of my big brother, till he cried himself back to sleep. He had my forgiveness. Or rather, he had my assurances that he didn't need my forgiveness. He had the comfort of my body, a pillow that shaped itself perfectly to *his* body. He had Nick's IDs. He had a morning to sleep. To rest. To heal.

I, on the other hand, had boulders on my eyelids. Hammers against my temples. I had no air in my lungs. I had work later. I had yet another missed class. More notes to hunt down. More assignments to make up. More grades to improve. I had a fucked-up professor who fucked me. Who hurt me. Who liked it. Who liked that I liked it.

But I had no one.

RIAN

It wasn't hard finding Stewart. When you know a man's vice and you know the man who supplies that man's vice, it's never very hard. It was almost silly, checking at Eithne's new place across from campus first. In that apartment there was nothing but unconditional love, a fridge full of fresh fruits and vegetables, and a computer to apply for any job in the goddamn world. Of what use was any of that for a junkie?

Still, more for Eithne's sake than for mine, I went there first. Maybe if I'd found Stewart there, writing a heartfelt apology to his little sister or munching on some, I don't know, fecking kale, or researching how to write a cover letter, I might have reconsidered what I was about to do. But of course Stewart wasn't there. And of course there was no bleedin' way I was going to change my mind.

Not after what I'd experienced in that lecture hall. Not when I could still taste her sweet nectar on my tongue. Not when I had the chance, and compulsive, irresistible, probably a little destructive need, to love what needed loving, what *deserved* loving, the chance to finally do some good in this world.

I left the stately brick buildings of Dublin Art School. And entered the part of town where decent, unbroken, *normal* folk didn't go.

I knew these barred windows and chain-link fences like the back of my hand. It wasn't that I felt comfortable there. Just like you weren't comfortable in your recurring nightmare. But I knew it. Knew it all too well.

In abandoned alleyways and low-ceiled living rooms long without lightbulbs, I didn't ask for Stewart. I asked for Nick. It briefly crossed my mind how this would look, should it get back to Mason or Conor. Hell, even Aurnia through her juvenile eejit friends who considered themselves thugs because they bought a pair of jeans one size too big.

I wore a baseball cap low. An unremarkable jacket, too thin for the weather, but ideal for its vague shape and faded black material. I kept my head down, my voice low, and my conversations short. But it wasn't all that long ago that I'd been a resident of a place like the ones I dared to cross the threshold of. No one acknowledged me, but that didn't mean I wasn't registered. Stored away. People that do drugs will sell anything for a fix, least of all petty gossip about a fancy art school professor who was snooping around.

Still, the risk to Eithne's well-being, peace of mind, and future were greater than the risk that my overprotective friends might hear that I was trying to find a dangerous drug dealer we'd already had our run-ins with. So I asked around, not getting as lucky as I might have hoped with my first few glassy-eyed, dirty, barely coherently speaking addicts. But luck didn't have all that much to do with it, in the end. There was no way I wouldn't find Stewart eventually, if I just kept asking. Which I did, regardless of the risk. Or rather, because of it.

I found him in a deserted intersection. Tearing at his hair. Bent over. Growling in frustration. A car was just pulling away. A low, black, smashed-in taillight piece of shite. Stewart, as he looked up wild-eyed, seemed as if he might just run after it. And maybe he would have, had he not seen me first.

He ran up to me, standing there on the corner in front of a liquor store with cardboard taped to its windows, hands in my pocket. It was obvious from the start that he didn't recognise me. Didn't have a fucking clue who I was.

"Boyo, hey boyo," he said quickly, too quickly. "You got a couple bucks? I'm like—

damn, I'm like three or so shy. You gotta have three, hell, five to give a buddy."

I recognised that panic. That need for a fix. The desperation of it being just out of reach.

"They'll circle back around," he said as if to comfort himself. "They'll circle back around and I'll have enough this time. It's alright. It's alright."

I wondered how high he already was. Not that I cared about his well-being. I just wanted him to be able to remember what I was about to tell him. I was studying him when he jerked his head back at the sight of me, startled that I was there.

"Boyo, hey," he said, and I stifled a growl of irritation. "You got—"

"A couple bucks?" I interrupted.

Stewart was high enough that his surprise face contorted cartoonishly.

"Yeah, I'm—"

"Three or so shy?"

Again the theatrics. Stewart clasped his dirty, greasy hair that had shared nothing with Eithne's. He laughed a shrill, unsettling laugh.

"Mate, you would be such a fucking lifesaver."

I considered warning Stewart not to speak too soon. I decided against it. After checking for cops or little thug lords that might snitch to a higher up about someone encroaching on their territory, I swung my backpack around and unzipped just enough for Stewart to see inside. He smelled like shite, but his eyes lit up like gold.

"Think that might be enough?" I asked.

I gave Stewart long enough to stammer stupidly before nodding toward the alley. He followed like a puppy. When we were safely hidden behind dumpsters circled with enough flies to keep even the most curious of junkies away, Stewart scratched at his bare arms and I swallowed my disgust for him.

"So am I goin' to hafta suck you or what?" he asked impatiently.

I sighed. "Or what?"

"What?" Stewart asked, eyes searching the road for the car that he knew, even if it was all he knew, would circle back around and give him his chance for a fix.

I dragged a tired hand over my face and swatted Stewart away when he palmed the front of my pants.

"I don't want you to suck my cock, Stewart," I told him.

He at least had the presence of mind to look slightly concerned, on the verge of fear. That was a good sign. Something going right, it seemed. Though he didn't seem to register that I knew his name.

"You're not one of those organ harvesters, are ye?"

"I am not," I answered, sounding and feeling bored.

"Then?" Stewart asked, letting the question linger as he circled his hand impatiently, eyes twitching between the bag and the road.

"I want you to leave town," I said.

This drew Stewart's attention. His brows tugged together in a frown, his eyes struggled to focus.

I continued in a threatening monotone, "This right here, Stewart Brady, is your fresh new start. Congratulations. You have the once-in-a-lifetime chance to be a giant fuck-up in a whole new city. To find a brand-new host, sweet and kind and too generous, to leech off of like the parasite that you are. I am your angel of salvation. And if not salvation, damnation somewhere else. Consider this backpack of cash your down payment on a condo on the Lake of Fire, *boyo*. You're being upgraded. Bumped. First class to anywhere but here. Isn't that exciting?"

Stewart blinked stupidly. I wasn't sure that even sober he had enough brain cells to comprehend what I was saying. Lord knows, he was far from sober. Catching him by surprise was simple enough. Grabbing him by the throat resulted in little resistance but a few dirty-nailed scratches. He'd been on a diet of cocaine, meth, and heroin for so long that I had no trouble walking him back till his scrawny shoulder blades collided roughly with the brick wall on the opposite side of the alley. I squeezed till Stewart started to gasp. I wanted to keep going for Eithne, to right this fucker's wrongs. But a disappeared brother was a gift; a dead one, a tragedy.

Slightly lightening my grip so that Stewart didn't pass out, I hissed, "Listen here, you human piece of shite. Let me put it in terms you understand. One, get out of Dublin. Two, never, ever come back. Three, break off all contact with Eithne. Forever. No birthday cards. No Christmas letters. No calls out of the blue for money or repentance or reconciliation. Four, tell not a goddamn soul where you are going. There will be no trace of you. I'd buy you a fucking magic carpet if I could, but seeing as life isn't a fairy tale, you're going to have to do without. And five—"

I wasn't sure whether there was a five. Stewart clawed weakly at me as I pondered, head turned away to focus. His toes scraped noisily on the pavement where they could just barely reach.

Jamming Stewart's head back against the brick once more, I said, "And five, you won't ever, ever get your life together. You won't join AA. You won't try to get clean. You won't get a job or find a hobby or ever fall in love. You'll live out your life in the gutters and die in the gutters. Because you don't deserve to turn things around. You don't deserve to be a better man. *That's* five."

I only realised I'd started squeezing too tight again when Stewart began to choke.

"Do you understand?" I asked in an angry growl.

Stewart nodded his head. With gritted teeth, I released him. He fell to the filthy alleyway ground and gasped for air. I threw the backpack of cash, everything I'd had in my savings, down on him. It hit his ribs like it was filled with bricks. It should have frightened me how much the sound thrilled me. It should have been a warning that it was the reason I didn't leave right away, despite the fact that my job was done. What I'd set out to do for Eithne, finished. But I was too busy trying to repeat that sound in my head, grasping at it like a receding tide.

I don't know if I ever really made a decision to kick Stewart. Or if it was just instinct. If something stirred inside of me and I had no choice. My toe collided with his side. He fell into a moaning ball, curled around the backpack. I knew the distinction wouldn't matter to Eithne. But I wasn't thinking of Eithne in that moment in that grey, desolate alley with Stewart moaning at my feet. I was thinking of me.

And it felt good.

"How silly of me," I said with a snarl, spittle at my lips like a wild dog, "I almost forgot all about the stick."

I circled Stewart. Toed the backpack clutched in his arms like a shield. "You've got your carrot, there, Stewart, buddy," I said, leaning over him. "Do you remember what your carrot felt like? Huh?"

I bent down and pressed my knee down on the backpack so it constricted his lungs. His fists felt like gnats against my leg. I almost laughed.

"I want you to remember what the carrot felt like, so you can have a good idea what the stick will look like," I told him, pushing more of weight onto his most likely bruised rib.

He cried out in pain and I lapped up the sound like a wolf over a rabbit's torn throat. Expect Stewart was no rabbit: he was a beast himself, preying on his sister, consuming her, destroying the very life of her. I wanted to hear that cry of pain again and again. But I didn't. I held back. As much as I wanted to hurt him for what he'd done to Eithne, I wanted to scare him away more.

"The stick," I hissed, circling again, "is that if you ever return, ever contact Eithne, ever even *think* that you are worthy of more than exactly what you're feeling right now, I will come for you."

Stewart was nodding, repeating again and again that he understood, clutching the bag of cash to his chest like a safety vest. It was clear he'd gotten the message. I could stop. I should stop. But I hadn't yet gotten my fill.

"I will come for you and that little kick will feel like a love tap. I will make you feel such unimaginable pain that your death —and have no doubt, I will kill you—your death will be the greatest bliss of your fucked-up life," I said. "Better than any hit of cocaine. Better than any high of meth. Better than all the heroin you can shove in your veins."

I stopped. I hadn't felt that in years. Sure I smoked enough weed for a dorm room of freshman, but I'd sworn off the really hard stuff. Learned my lesson and all that bullshite. I never fought cravings for it because I never craved it; life had filled me up, so to speak. But there it was again, that sneaky bastard. The little twitch in my pinkie. The tiny burning of my veins. The whispered temptation, "Isn't forgetting, just for an hour or two, just so nice?"

"Eithne is going to be a great artist, do you hear me?" I screamed at him. "She's going to be with me and nothing will get in the way of it. I'm going to love her. I'm going to be good for her. You won't stop me. Do you fecking hear me, you piece of shite? You won't goddamn stop us!"

I gave Stewart one more final shove and stormed off, tugging at my hair. I punched a brick wall; didn't even feel the pain in my knuckles, the blood on my skin. It was me who felt panicked as I left the alleyway, eyes glancing around like a startled, frightened horse.

Because what was I going to do when Stewart was gone? When there was no one left to hate but me? No one left to blame for ruining Eithne's life, but *me*?

EITHNE

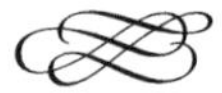

I was studying with Aurnia when I got the call from the dean's office.

My father might have called it justice, retribution, my well-deserved punishment. He might have seen what happened next as his hand reaching out of the grave to make things right, to set me back in my place. I could hear him saying, in my darkest moment still yet out of sight, "That's what you get, Eithne, you whore, that's *exactly* what you get."

I'd pushed things too far, my luck or karma or good fortune or whatever the feck you want to call it. Daring to spend an afternoon with a friendly face. Hoping to nurture a budding friendship. Sharing the workload with someone else of studying, homework, the stress of school. I should have stopped at Rian. At the pleasure of his tongue. Maybe Aurnia was a cherry on top I should have refrained from with my greedy, sticky fingers.

"Is everything okay?" she asked as I hung up the phone.

It's perhaps not very convincing to say "yes, no bother" when your face is white as chalk. But what could I tell her? My world might be falling apart and it was all because I couldn't stay away from Rian Merrick.

"Do you need me to come with you?" she asked as I gathered my things. "I can come with you."

It was too much. I could see it now. Clear as day. Aurnia too kind. Too generous. Too willing to be my friend. That wasn't my life. That was never my lot. I'd been foolish to think it could be. I could add it to the list: slutty, shameful, avaricious.

I smiled sadly and told her no. She couldn't come. I had to do this alone. She didn't realise what I meant when I said goodbye. She couldn't know that this was the end to our friendship, because we barely had a beginning.

In the dean's office, neither of the two men inside were speaking.

"Ms Brady, please sit down."

The dean indicated a high-backed chair in front of the desk. In the one next to it was both my heaven and hell. I wasn't sure if I should look at him or not as I moved timidly forward. Would everything be revealed if I did? Would the dean see it all, the nakedness, the writhing, the mud and paint and cum-smeared tits, if I met his eyes for even half a second?

"Professor Merrick," I muttered in a sort of last-ditch effort to appear polite as I sunk into the chair next to him.

When I dared a glance at him, his gaze was fixed on me, his eyes warm and hungry. There was none of the spine-straightening anxiety I was experiencing. If anything, I expected him to reach out to brush the hair behind my ears, to call me his Raglan Road girl. Did he have nothing to lose? I thought as I tried desperately to maintain my composure. Was the risk always all on me? Could I have been so foolish?

The dean sighed behind his bridged fingertips and he seemed to draw out the moment. Or maybe it was just that my racing heart was counting the seconds in double, triple time. Either way it gave me more than enough time to imagine the repercussions should what I feared might happen actually happen: a permanent black spot on my record, a forfeiting of my scholarship, an expulsion, a stack of rejection letters from every other art school in the nation, an eviction notice on the door, Stewart glassy-eyed in the morgue, my cheek sadistically free of tears, my world an empty room, empty in every way. There was just enough time to convince myself it was something else, that Rian and I were there for something, anything else. There was just enough time to smile and believe that everything would be fine before the dean at last spoke.

"There's been an accusation of impropriety."

I felt faint. This was my worst nightmare come to life. Sexual shame. A ruined career. Destitution and failure and misery, all because of who I was. All because of who I could never stop myself from becoming.

I looked over at Rian in the silence. Because of the silence. He hadn't denied the charges, hadn't said in his commanding, easy way that it was bullshite. No, he sat silent. Looking just a bit as relaxed and at ease as when I walked through the door. Was he high? Did I throw my life away for just another junkie? Was my life crumbling while Rian stared at imaginary fucking rainbows?

I thought I might hate him. I thought, too, that I might have always. Because I hated myself.

The dean continued since there was no reply, "This institution has a reputation to maintain, as I'm sure you are both aware. Ms Brady, I dare say that reputation might have been a reason why you selected Dublin Art School in the first place. Which makes it all the more shocking that you would sully it."

The dean's focus was on me. His beady eyes, swollen and puffy from too many cigarettes and too little moving, assessed me. I didn't give the outward signs of a slut, the superficial items of clothing or makeup people ignorantly point to. My sweatshirt was baggy. My jeans loose. If I pulled my hair back it was always in a low, simple ponytail. Style and fashion had been the first thing, the easiest thing to give up after that night my father turned on me.

Because of this, the dean was trying to look through my clothes. To judge my body. To weigh by tits and deem them the tits of a whore. To measure my thighs, to feel the tightness of my pussy, to check my skin for teeth marks. The worst of it wasn't even the dean himself. The worst was when I looked to Rian for help and found none. A dreamy sigh. Hands folded loosely in his lap. Nothing more.

"Occasionally we hear rumours," the dean said, leaning back victoriously in his chair; apparently he'd found what he was looking for, "but rarely do we have a witness. Nor is the report so…explicit."

I wanted to scream. Not at the dean. But at Rian. I wanted to yell in his face, "Help me! Help me, you fucker! You did this to me! You ruined my life! *Do* something!" I wanted to pound my fists against his chest and shove him out of his chair, out of his pretty little daydream.

"Now, the fact this was," the dean continued, "as it would appear, consensual, does not change the fact that this debauched behaviour was conducted on school grounds, nor does it alter the punishment that I see more than fit given how widespread the knowledge of this scandal and given how terribly it could impact the generous donations our alumnae may bestow upon our institution come tax season." The dean rocked back and forth in his big chair as he raised the guillotine above my head.

In those horrible few seconds where the dean drew a big, lumbering breath, I imagined the blade falling. There was nothing I could do to stop it.

In those horrible few seconds before he sentenced us both, I regretted everything: ever knowing Rian's name, ever drawing him, ever letting him touch me.

Before the dean spoke, Rian did.

"You're quite an accomplished artist yourself, are you not, Dean?" he said, slowly drawing his attention from the window.

This out-of-the-blue question seemed to throw the dean off.

The rocking slowed, stilled. He blustered out a non-committal answer.

"Well, I—I mean I studied at one time, but that's been years and I—well, I'm devoted more to nurturing artists than, um, becoming one myself."

The click of Rian's tongue reminded me too much of a rattlesnake's warning. I turned to him in confusion.

"Such modesty, Dean. Such modesty."

I looked between the dean and Rian; the dean seemed to have no clue what the fuck Rian was talking about. Neither did I. What was this? Both the dean and I watched as Rian pulled a piece of paper from his satchel and slid it face down across the desk.

"From what I've seen, you have some real talent."

Trepidation grew in the pit of my stomach as the dean frowned warily at Rian and then proceeded to peel up just the edge. His laugh felt like the nail in a coffin. I didn't even need to know what was on it as he threw it away from him, snorting in derision.

I covered my mouth in horror when the page tumbled end over end and landed at my feet, facing up. There I was, naked, drawn with a finger in my mouth, a finger in my vagina. I concealed it quickly with my shoe.

"I don't know what you think you're up to, Professor Merrick," the dean said, cheeks red as he leaned forward, belly pressing against his desk. He pointed a shaking finger at Rian. "You and I both know that I did not draw that. Nor would I ever. And if you think anyone else would believe—"

"But Dean," Rian interrupted, calm as ever, voice almost kindly, "they found several more in your car. And not all of Eithne here. Other girls, too. All, it would seem, scholarship girls. And boys, maybe."

The dean was stunned into silence for a moment. He looked to me, but I, too, was staring in shock at Rian.

"They did no such thing," the dean said, a little less assuredly than before.

Rian smiled, a cruel, taunting smile. It made him look like a stranger.

"But they will," he said, placing his fingertips on the edge of the desk. "In a black Mercedes. 2019. License plate…"

Rian rattled off a series of numbers and letters like it was his own birth date. No pausing. No stammering. No hesitation. Before the dean could respond, Rian continued.

"They'll find more of your quite beautiful, quite impressive drawings in your lovely home," he said. "At 3948 Hastings Drive. In the study you have upstairs. In the locked drawer in the bottom of your oak desk. An antique, is it not?"

"There's something wrong with you," the dean whispered, fury and fear twisting the features of his red face. "Something terribly wrong."

Rian shrugged.

"I'm not the one who accidentally mixed-up notebooks with my little seven-year-old daughter, Lily," he said. "Do you think they'll believe you didn't draw them when she goes to draw a unicorn at Rathmines Prep, in Mrs Oliver's class, and sees things of the female anatomy she won't even know about for years?"

"Get out." The dean's voice trembled.

Rian smiled. Gave a little bow of his head. He stood without looking at me. He didn't even seem to know I was there as he reached between my feet and picked up the drawing of me and slid it back across the desk.

Laughing easily, he said, "Oops, wouldn't want to forget about this one of yours, Dean. It's so easy to mix up the envelopes with your letter to your mother in Cork, now isn't it? Happens all the time, I'm afraid."

Rian tapped his forefinger between my expertly drawn tits as the dean's face went purple. Then he left. I stayed where I sat, dumbfounded. I'd never felt like a stay of execution would feel so shitty, so…*wrong*. I wondered whether I wanted to cry or throw up. As I stumbled out of the office, I mumbled an apology, though for what I was sorry I couldn't exactly say.

I found Rian walking down the long hallway lined with windows. I had to run to catch him. He still didn't even glance at me. Every lashing of a tree branch against the heavy glass panes made me flinch; for some reason I kept expecting to get hit. Rian turned a corner into complete shadows, an arched doorway of stone, and without warning, clutched me by the back of the neck, and drew me roughly into a violent kiss.

For one long moment, the world stilled. My body reacted the same way it always did with him, with raging heat like an angry sun, my hands already coming up to fist in his hair before I knew what I was doing.

Then my mind caught up with me. The realisation of where the hell we were slammed into me, as did the memory of what he just did. I pushed Rian away. Shoved at him when he didn't let me go.

"Let go."

"Never."

"Rian, let go!"

He pressed me against the brick archway behind me. "Calm down, Eithne. Everything's okay."

"Okay?" I dragged my fingers through my hair. I felt like I was going insane. "What the hell did you just do?"

"He was going to expel you," was Rian's unemotional answer.

"You, you," I shook my head, trying to wrap my head around everything. "Rian, you *blackmailed* him. And, and you used my naked body to do it."

"I had to scare him."

I rubbed at my eyes on the off chance that I was dreaming.

"We could have—I mean, there had to be another way."

"There wasn't."

I was exasperated as I struggled to get out from his hold. "Let go!"

"No."

"Can't you see that what you did was wrong?"

Rian startled me into pausing when he gripped my chin and pulled it so I faced him, so I couldn't escape the intensity of his gaze.

"I would do *anything* for you, Eithne," he said. "Whatever it takes."

I laughed bitterly. "Like make me an accomplice to a crime?"

"That and anything else," Rian said in a flat tone.

I sucked in a breath. "What does that mean?"

"Exactly what I said," he answered. "If something is in your way, I'll take care of it. You have a problem, I'll fix it. I'm going to be there for you, no matter what…or who."

Again that pit in my stomach. Again that fear that something wasn't quite right.

"What does that mean, Rian?" I repeated, almost too afraid to.

"I have an art studio booked," he said instead of answering. "I'd like to teach you a few things. *Real* art. Not that bullshite you're learning on a computer."

"I can't," I said, measuring each word. "I have to get back for Stewart. His AA meeting ends soon. I need to be there."

I pressed my palms flat against his chest and pushed. This time he stepped back.

Rian's face seemed to disappear into the shadows. "I told you that if there was problem, I'd solve it."

This time I really was too frightened to ask what he meant. And I didn't know if I wanted the answer to the most obvious question: what did you do?

"I need you to leave me alone," I whispered. "We can't keep doing this."

"You don't mean that. You're just scared again. Crawling back into your shell again."

I shook my head.

"I never should have stopped."

"Stopped what?"

"Being scared," I told him.

I moved to leave, to go find Stewart to make sure he was alright. Rian grabbed ahold of my wrist and I wrenched it free. Looking over my shoulder, I hissed, "Don't fucking touch me. Don't ever fucking touch me again. I—"

I was shocked by the state Rian was in. Maybe he'd been getting worse gradually over the months, so gradually that I hadn't noticed. He was still so beautiful. But in that moment, all I could see was his pale skin and shadows around his hollowed eyes.

"Leave me alone, Rian," I told him, pulling away.

What I meant was I didn't want to see him like that. A stranger. An addict. A broken man with a sick obsession. I wanted to see him as I'd seen him just the day before. But I couldn't tell him that. Because I wasn't so sure anymore that that man existed. That he ever had. That I hadn't just conjured him out of some unresolved fucking daddy issues. That I'd made an imaginary man out of a real one.

Maybe there was no other way to see him than as he was then. As I left him in the shadowed archway. As I walked away.

EITHNE

I waited at home for Stewart till dark. Till the rain that had all day been threatening in the swollen bellies of the clouds began to fall. I was bathed in long shadows where I sat on the sunken edge of the bed, hands limp in my lap. I'd replaced all my exhaustion with anger enough to get up, to go out, to find my brother.

The patter of the rain against my thin hood was welcome. It helped to block out all the swirling ideas of what exactly Rian did to Stewart. All the possibilities of how he "fixed" that problem. My mind, without the incessant drone of cold, bitter rain, was prone to imagine the worst: used needles in arms and dirty rags across lips and twitching fingers in quickly flooding ditches. It was all too easy after what I'd experienced, what I'd seen in the dean's office, to paint Rian not as the gentle lover between my legs, but the twisted stalker a little too obsessed with his prey. Too willing to do whatever it took to have her.

I shivered and I was certain it wasn't because of the water soaking through my flimsy jacket. I rested my cheek against the condensation-covered window of the bus and closed my eyes.

Rian wouldn't hurt Stewart, I repeated once more in my

mind. It was a mantra that was keeping me at least half sane. Rian knew how much my older brother meant to me and because he loved me, he wouldn't hurt him. He wouldn't.

The doors rattled open and I was back in the rain. Another homeless shelter without a Stewart Brady. Another soup kitchen that hadn't served the man in the picture I held up with blue-tipped fingers. Another police station that hadn't booked any John Doe junkies that night. The doors of the bus rattled shut and I was soaked through to the bone.

There was one place left to look. It should have been the first place I went. But I guess a tiny part of me still held out hope. A tiny part of me was still a foolish little girl.

Even the city buses didn't go all the way. I rode in the dirtiest one I'd ever been on: brown paper bags littered the dusty corners, graffiti covered every available inch of the windows, the fluorescent bulbs twitched nervously on and off, on and off. Hooded faces huddled against slashed seats. Manic muttering came from the very back row. And eyes shifted threateningly at the smallest movement. It was a disgrace to even pay for such a bus and yet it still stopped more than ten blocks from my final destination.

It was probably my imagination, but I thought the door seemed to close a little hastily on me as I climbed down the sticky stairs, the wheels screeched a little impatiently as the driver shifted into gear, the bus lurched forward, ignoring a stop sign, a little too recklessly. If a massive hunk of steel and aluminium feared the neighbourhood I found myself in, alone and unarmed save a long-ago broken umbrella, what chance in hell did *I* stand?

As the rain dripped from the flopped over lip of my hood, I cursed Rian. Was *this* his idea of being there for me? Keeping me safe? Watching over me? *He* was the reason I was there, staring out at a mile of unlit street, potholes the size of canyons in the dark. Dogs snarling at chain-link fences. Babies wailing. Glass shattering. Professor Fucking Merrick was the reason, not Stewart.

I wouldn't be anywhere near this place if it wasn't for him. And where was he now? My protector. My defender. My lover. I was alone. More alone than ever, it seemed. Before Rian I was at least dry and warm. There was always a pillow to cry into at night. But here I was catching my death on a deserted sidewalk where my tears would be indistinguishable from the rain that cascaded down my cheeks.

Steeling my nerves, I began to walk. I kept my head down. I ignored any shouts from sunken porches with overflowing drainpipes. I checked constantly behind me. I turned down an emaciated little boy who offered an eighth of God knows what; it was no consolation that I wasn't the only defenceless thing out there in the unlit night.

Finding the numbers on the houses proved to be the hardest part. I moved aside overgrown weeds on tilted mailboxes. I squinted in the dim light of flickering television sets past broken blinds at doors. I retraced my steps in the pouring rain more times than I could count. It was the group of unspeaking men huddled in the dark that clued me in that I was in the right place. I couldn't make out their eyes as I stood at the rickety front gate, but I knew they were staring at me. If there were guards, there must be something worth guarding.

My fingers shook as I unclasped the little metal latch. Finding my voice was difficult as the men rose as one, towering over me where I stood at the base of several eroding wooden stairs.

"I'm looking for Nick," I called out to them over the rain, drops splattering on my frozen lips. "Does he live here?"

They were mute. Unmoving.

"I, um, I did some work for him," I tried. "I, um, I did some IDs."

A flicker of movement. A pair of lips against an ear. A nod. A man slipped inside. The light illuminated crumpled up beer cans, a bottle of whiskey half filled with rainwater, and a length of rusted chain like a snake; I followed the end to one man's balled fist.

Licking my lips I tasted the acidity of the rain, the saltiness of my fear. A moment or two later, the door opened. And remained open. The men parted. Not enough for me to feel comfortable, but just enough for me to slip through. I shuddered as callused knuckles brushed against my ass, as a foul-smelling mouth laughed and said, "Come back soon, love."

The light in the low-ceiled living room wasn't more than a bulb on a floor lamp with no shade, but coming from the dark I shielded my eyes as I stepped across the carpet which squelched like a bog underfoot.

"Your boyfriend's not here," came a ragged voice.

I blinked in a sight that startled me more than I could say: Nick, pale-faced and wincing, as he adjusted a broken leg on the couch. I sucked in a breath. He was little of the man I remembered from that night when he attacked Stewart in my apartment. The dangerous flash had sunk from his black eyes. No smile curled his thin lips. Amongst the sagging cushions he looked small and weak. The only thing I recognised was the roughly tattooed white knuckles, except now they gripped the edge of the couch frame instead of the handle of a spiked baseball bat.

"Why don't you draw me?" Nick mumbled irritably. "It'll last longer."

He laughed weakly at his own joke, but soon grimaced as he coughed and curled over his clutched ribs. A deep laceration had bled through the butterfly bandages on his cheek; I didn't think it was the sole reason for his lack of smile. All I could do was stare, my mind whirling as I stood there in the entryway to the living room.

"I'd kill him myself, you know," Nick said in a low, tight voice, "if I didn't know he'd do it himself soon enough."

Again an attempt at laughter. Again quick regret as it disturbed his surely broken ribs.

"Who?" I asked in a hollow whisper, though I feared I already knew the answer.

Nick leaned his head back on the armrest, turned his face toward me, brow glistening in the harsh light of the exposed bulb.

"Your little professor, love."

I shook my head. "I— I came here for my brother."

Nick frowned. "Your brother?"

"Stewart," I said. "Stewart Brady."

"I didn't do anything to your brother," Nick answered with a sigh. "And Rian said nothing about him."

I remained numb where I stood, rainwater dripping to the damp carpet. I glanced over my shoulder at the door. Had they locked it behind me? If I went to leave, would they let me?

"Are you going to hurt me?" I asked, looking back at Nick. "Is that why you let me inside to see you?"

I saw a trace of the dangerous man I remembered from my apartment as he looked me down from head to toe. He grinned.

"It seems you don't know your dog is off his leash," he said. It wasn't an answer, and this frightened me.

I remained silent.

"He's out of control," he continued in an almost solemnly silent voice. "Do you know that?"

He laughed when I said nothing. It seemed he found it answer enough.

"To attack me in the middle of the night with my own baseball bat," he whispered as the rain fell heavily outside. I couldn't look away from his burning gaze. "To cut my face, to break my ribs, to snap my fucking leg in two."

Nick stopped to get control of his breathing. I thought I'd never been colder in my life than right then, waiting for him to speak as he exhaled shakily from his flared nostrils still flaked with blood.

"To provoke me, to call for war with me," he said so softly I almost had to lean forward to hear. "And to be so foolish as to mention your sweet little name. To say it was for you. That it was *all* for you."

Nick clicked his tongue as my blood ran even colder. I was paralysed by fear.

"I just came for my brother," I repeated, voice small, weak, afraid. "Have you seen him?"

"He was high off his mind, you know," Nick continued, penetrating me with his black eyes. "That wagon, if there ever was one, is so far gone I doubt he'll ever find it again. Do you know why?"

I shook my head, my wet hair lashing my pale cheek.

"Because I could see it, see clear as day, that he *liked* it, your little professor. The high, the being out of control, the violence."

"Are you going to hurt me?" I asked.

It didn't seem worth it to tell Nick that I'd tried to stop Rian. That I thought I had stopped him. That I'd given him a reason to stop: me. My body. My devotion. My love, even. What good would it do to tell this drug dealer that I was just as surprised as he was, there with his broken body? That I, too, had seen a different man that day? A man who was needlessly cruel, disturbingly driven, shockingly violent. A man who slipped in behind those pale blue eyes like a Trojan horse. Would it save my life? To tell Nick that part of me never wanted anything to do with Rian, ever again? That I feared he hurt my brother? Or worse. That I wanted to be done with him? Prayed that I would find a way to break the hold he had over me.

"Am I going to hurt you?" Nick questioned, drumming his fingers against the couch. The chance to torture someone after himself being tortured seemed to have raised his spirits, a sort of natural pain killer. "Am I going to hurt my sweet little artist, Eithne Brady?"

I wondered if I would even fight. Or whether I would just take Nick's revenge as the punishment I escaped that afternoon in the dean's office. Maybe it was just better to let him have me. I was, after all, so fucking tired.

Did I start crying? Was that the wetness on my cheeks? Or was it still the rain?

Nick extended his bottom lip as he watched me. It was impressive really, given that he was smiling, too. He made a sympathetic "aww" sound which a lion about to eat me could have done more convincingly.

"Baby doll," he whispered, cooed really. "I'm not going to hurt you."

I sobbed. A sense of relief swept through me. My body ached from the tension. I started to shake.

"I'm not going to hurt you for the same reason I'm not going to hurt your little professor," he said, pouting again as the corners of his mouth curled up even higher. In a baby voice he said, "Because he's going to do it himself."

I ran. Nick laughed, half falling onto the floor as if he made to crawl after me, drag his leg across the wet carpet to grab my ankles and trip me. I yanked at the door handle. It didn't budge.

"Do you hear me?" he shouted. "He'll drown himself and take you down with him."

I tried again and dark faces loomed above me. I pushed through them like branches in a dense forest.

Nick's laughing voice followed me as I ran.

"Rian's going to destroy you."

RIAN

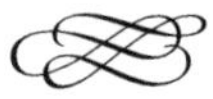

I only answered my phone because I needed someone to yell at.

My head was aching, my body both freezing and burning, my fingers twitching for a lighter, a spoon, a needle. The best solution for coming down was shooting up again. Instead I'd flushed the shite I stole from Nick down the toilet. Eithne scared me enough that afternoon to not go out seeking more. I'd crossed a line, I saw that. Or at least, I told myself I saw that. For me it was all shades of grey, but for her I'd live in the black and white.

But I just needed to get rid of this itch. This drive. This madness I wanted so terribly to give in to. Beating up Stewart had helped. Beating up Nick even more. Verbal abuse wouldn't be the same, but hell, it would be something.

"What sad story do you have about that fucker now, Liam?" I said without even so much as a "hello". "Is he coughing up blood? Is he sweating through his bedsheets? Are his eyes swollen shut? Is karma a bitch yet?"

My toe tapped against the floor, the rain falling so heavily against the windows, my heart thudding in my chest so loud that at first I didn't hear what my brother said.

"What?"

He repeated himself.

I laughed, because what I thought I heard sounded funny. So fucking funny.

"Did you hear me?" Liam asked, voice strained. "Rian, hey, did you hear?"

For some reason I couldn't stop fucking chuckling. In the darkness of my bedroom, laid out and staring at the bars of shadow along the ceiling, my chest rose and fell with uncontrollable stutters. I tried clasping my hand over my mouth. It didn't help.

"Rian?" Liam prodded.

"I obviously didn't," I finally said, snorting. "Because what I heard you say is that our dear father is dead."

There was sigh. Or something else vaguely puritan. Disapproving. Holier than fucking thou. This made me laugh all the harder, because it was priceless coming from him: the older brother who rode in to save the day after the dragons had already burned down the whole goddamn village.

"Wait, wait," I said, gasping for air. "Okay. Okay, I'm ready for it."

There was a pause. Maybe a sad one. Let's say a sad one. It'd be funnier.

"Ready for what?" Liam finally asked sadly, oh, so fucking sadly.

"I'm ready for you to tell me all about how he asked for me on his death bed," I said. "Give me all the details of how he asked for forgiveness with his dying breath. What did he say about what a piece of shite he'd been? What a monster? What a barbarian he'd been to his youngest who dared not be as strong and as cold as him? Please, Liam, I can handle it. Tell me how I missed out on the chance of reconciliation as he called my name into the abyss."

Liam exhaled slowly. He shouldn't have been disappointed in me. He'd been too late all his life. I was just learning from my big brother's example, now wasn't I?

"Listen, Rian," he said, sounding tired, as if he had a fucking right, "I just called to let you know about the funeral. And before you say you're not coming, I know. Alright? God, I know already. I get it. Believe me, I get it."

His words managed to kill off what was left of the bubbling giggles in my chest. I was left feeling empty, hollow. Drained.

"But I need to do this for me, alright?" he said. "I need to know I gave you all you needed to do the right thing. That I gave you every goddamn chance."

"Fuck you," I told him in a snarl, rage flooding in and feeling fucking good.

"Yeah, I've heard that one before," Liam said, a little resentment of his own slipping in. The Golden Boy going Red. "The funeral is going to be—"

"Fuck—"

"Two days from now."

"—you."

"At the farm."

I was up off the bed. Pacing like a lunatic. Shouting into the phone.

"Fuck you, Liam!"

"Everyone's getting here the day before," came Liam's measured, even response. "There's a room for you, if you decide to come."

"Fuck you!" I screamed at the top of my lungs. "I'd rather slit my throat than ever step foot on that godforsaken piece of shite land ever again. I'd rather leap off a bridge than hear that old porch swing moan in the night just one more time. I'd rather burn down the whole fucking country than ever see that rusted windvane spin atop that cursed house!"

Grey fog rolled in at the corners of my vision, the kind that chilled the thin burlap sacks I had to sleep under during those nights locked in the barn. I caught myself with a palm against the wall. I was gasping for air, but nothing was reaching my lungs. I continued to shout nonetheless.

"I hope to God that the worms feast on that piece of shite's body," I screamed. "I hope maggots crawl through his eye sockets and snakes open their jaws wide for those big hands he was so fucking proud of. I hope the bastard's not really dead and he wakes up in that plywood coffin and screams himself hoarse trying to claw his way out and chokes on his own fucking tongue."

My knees gave out and I collapsed into a heap. My lungs burned and I couldn't even make out the edge of the bed. Everything was grey and black shapes with increasingly distorted lines.

My constricted throat barely allowed me to speak as I coughed. "Nothing will grow on whatever land you put him under. Know that. Nothing green will ever fucking find its way there. You might as well pour salt over it. You've condemned something beautiful, something lovely, something that could actually grow. Flourish. *Be* something!"

My forehead dropped against my shaking knees. I sobbed as my back heaved. I struggled for air that wouldn't come.

"Liam?"

I needed help. I needed my brother. I needed his warm washcloth against my bloody lip, even if it was too late. I wanted his voice, dripping warm like honey, even if it was never raised against Alan or my father. I wanted his arms around me even though I imagined a million ways he could have used that strength to protect me all those times that he didn't. I wanted, most of all, to no longer be alone.

"Liam?" I asked again.

I pressed the cell phone tighter to my ear in case it was just the bad connection. I strained to hear his voice.

"Liam?" I cried desperately.

I slammed my forehead against the hard bone of my knees several times. I shouted my brother's name more times than I could count. But he'd hung up long before. He'd been gone for quite some time.

I was alone.

Again.

Liam gone. Eithne gone. How could I turn to Conor or Mason or even Aurnia after how I'd treated them?

There was only one solution: my demons would always be there to keep me company. I just had to find them is all.

And I knew just how to find mine.

EITHNE

When I saw Rian the next day on campus my first instinct was to hit him. I'd never felt such a drive, such a high for violence. The wind was wicked that morning, but I would be wickeder.

I knew Rian had done something to my brother, done something terrible. Stewart hadn't returned at any point during the night while I shivered beneath all the blankets I owned. He hadn't answered any of my calls; his voicemail was filled with my increasingly desperate pleas to just come home. I'd make everything right. I'd fix things. I'd love him all the harder. My love —*my love alone*—could save him. But dawn broke bleak and grey and I stared at the empty apartment in dusky shadows with red-rimmed eyes and I knew he wasn't coming back.

And I knew the reason.

So I wanted to hit Rian. I wanted him to feel a tiny fraction of the pain that throbbed in my aching heart. I wanted to get Rian on those cobblestones slick with deteriorating leaves and drive my toe into his ribs. I wanted to keep going when he cried out for me to stop.

I moved toward him with this intention. Pushed through the

raised umbrellas along the path. My body buzzed with exhaustion and adrenaline, a deadly mix. Rian was in the large square where students moved quickly from class to class in the drizzling rain. I had no umbrella. Neither did he.

I was close enough now that I could see where I wanted my first blow to land. Close enough that I could decide just where I'd need to grab at his collar to yank him backwards, throw him off balance, kick in the back of his knees so that I could launch myself onto him. I'd straddled his hips before, but there would be no pleasure for him this time. I was close enough that my heart thudded wildly in hatred. And in sick longing.

Slipping on the wet stones and blinking rain from my eyelashes, I launched myself at him. Rian stumbled into a student. It was just enough of a display of weakness to make me pause. I wanted Rian at his highest, to bring him to his knees. I needed the Rian from yesterday, in the dean's office, in the archway where he grabbed me. I needed the haughtiness, the god complex, the eyes devoid of anything resembling kindness, gentleness, humanity.

Standing just behind him, I stood and watched as Rian grappled at the lapels of the student's raincoat. Was he still falling? Still stumbling? He clawed at the thick plastic like it was his only lifeline before the depths swallowed him. The rain fell over me and I was transfixed as I stood there, a mere foot behind him. All he had to do was turn around, glance over his shoulder to see me. The steady drops were loud on the frozen stones, the hurried steps of students shouldering past me even louder, but neither were enough to drown out what I heard Rian say, neither were enough to prevent my blood from running cold.

"I know you've got a hook-up," I heard Rian say, his voice hoarse as a man's twice his age. "Don't shake your head, you little shite, I know you do."

Rian was no longer catching himself on the student, but rather shaking him. I saw the difference. His fingers weren't reaching for anything, straining, yearning; they already had their grip on handfuls of the plastic.

I couldn't move as the student fought off Rian. Shoved him aside more easily than I would have expected given the height difference, given the muscles I knew rippled beneath Rian's tattered hoodie. I didn't move when Rian fell hard to his knees. Nor when he turned to snarl at the fleeing student, not noticing me right there beside him. Nor when he shoved himself roughly to his feet, nearly fell again, and stumbled away.

I watched, rain seeping through to my very bones, feet getting wet and then tingly and then numb, heart petrifying into stone with every passing minute, as Rian circled the square around me. He was the frantic needle of a compass desperately trying to find true north and I was its centre. Fixed. Unmoving. Rigid. I watched as Rian grabbed at other students. Demanded and threatened and begged for drugs. I watched his desperation grow. His legs move less steadily. His rantings and ravings when he was turned down again and again became wilder, viler, more caustic.

Rian accosted a girl who screamed and I just watched. He fell and grabbed for passing ankles and I just watched. He gripped the edge of a trash can with shaking arms like he was going to throw up and instead just turned to sink to the mud against it and still I watched. I was horrified. Terrified. And I knew it didn't matter. I knew I wouldn't be able to stop myself from doing what I was going to do.

Maybe I could have tried. I could have tried to take a step back and see things clearly: this was a man who was beyond my help. He was clearly out of his mind. Possibly, no, likely violent. He was someone to run from, not walk closer to through the rain. Look at how he was kicking at the trash can. Look at how he was screaming at students. Look at how hollow his gaze seemed as he slipped again.

Who in their right mind would approach? Who, with any

remaining sanity, would lower herself to her knees and place a hand on his burning shoulder? Who, with any regard for herself, would whisper his name with the gentleness of a mother waking her child from a terrible nightmare?

No, there was no trying. I was doomed. I had been from the very start.

Cold claimed my knees like a prize, Rian's body emanated heat like a furnace, and I hardly recognised my own voice as I whispered, hardly loud enough to hear over the rain, "Professor Merrick."

Recognition came slowly to Rian's swivelling eyes. I wasn't surprised. He wasn't looking for me. He was in search of a hook-up, a fix, and so that painted his world black and white: drugs, or no drugs. Maybe I'd been a sort of drug to him before, but I was no longer. That was clear.

When he finally realised who I was, he laughed. He turned his face up toward the sky and raindrops hit his feverish skin and he laughed. I tried to grab for him, but he fell back in the puddled grass and situated his arms under the back of his head as if to cloud gaze. I glanced nervously around me. Passing students clearly noticed the professor giggling and clearly out of his mind as they passed, slowing as if for a car crash on the interstate.

"Professor Merrick," I said, turning back to him, nudging at his leg. "You need to get up."

"So I'm Professor Merrick now," he said before breaking once more into uncontrollable laughter.

"You were always Professor Merrick," I told him.

Rian replied, "I thought you capable of an anything, Ms Brady, but I never thought you capable of cruelty."

He said this and laughed. Laughed like it wasn't a dagger that he'd stabbed through my heart. I welcomed the chill spreading through my thighs like penance from a priest. It only got worse when Rian stopped laughing long enough to speak once more.

"My father's dead," he told me, giggling between each word as rainwater filled his mouth. "Croaked last night, the bastard."

I flinched when he threw his fists at the churning grey clouds and screamed, "Rot in hell, you piece of shite!"

I heard murmurs behind me. Heard them spread. Heard them multiply like scurrying rats. I laid my hand against Rian's thigh. He batted it away.

"I don't need your goddamn pity, Ms Brady."

"Rian," I said softly.

Rian propped himself up suddenly onto his elbows. When he crooked his head at me, he looked like an owl, hair astray in the rain, eyes wide, pupils blown open. I hardly recognised him.

"Hey, do *you* have any drugs?" he asked. "Ms Straight-Laced, Tight Pussy, would you happen to have any illegal substances I could smoke, inject, or snort on your person?"

I tried again with a hand on Rian's leg. He was too busy staring unseeingly past my shoulder to notice.

"Let me help you," I said. "When is the funeral?"

His laugh sounded like that of a hyena: high-pitched, cruel, revelling in a rotting thing.

"There's no way in hell I'm going to that," he answered before attempting to push himself up. "If you would excuse me, Ms Brady, I must be off."

He would have fallen had I not caught him. My knees nearly buckled under his weight. I could feel the sticky heat of his sweat through his hoodie. He was feverish, either from the drugs or the cold of his soaked clothes. It was frightening that I was stronger than him in his condition as he tried to push away from me. It was as easy as holding onto a sick child.

"We'll go together," I found myself saying without even thinking. "Rian, you and me. We'll go."

Rian laughed again and we lurched sideways together. He was going to drag the two of us down, completely unable to put one foot in front of the other anymore.

I started rambling, half afraid, half heartbroken. "Rian, please. Let me help you. I didn't mean what I said before. About being done. I couldn't be done. I can't. Rian, we'll go together. To your father's funeral. We'll be strong together. Rian, I want to try. Try at you and me. Rian. Rian, please, you have to try and stand up."

His clammy arm round my shoulders had caught my hair; it tugged painfully as he sagged away from me. My back was strained, the muscles of my arms shook. I was struggling to keep him up, to keep us both up. But Rian was gone. I could see in the vacant expression of his eyes that whatever drug he'd taken last had taken him away, far, far away. I knew that look from Stewart. I was alone now.

As I gritted my teeth and struggled to get Rian's body to instinctually move one foot and then the other, I noticed the looks of passing students. It was no longer disdain I saw in their passing glances. The rain fell between us and it was no longer jealousy that divided us. Nobody felt any longer that I was getting an unfair leg up by opening my legs to a college professor. No, it was a simpler, sadder emotion now. It was pity. Plain and simple. Unadulterated, unmasked, uncomplicated *pity*. Maybe it was the rain, cruel and unrelenting and cold. Maybe it was the strain in my face, trying so hard and getting nowhere fast. Maybe it was just that there was class to get to, homework to do after, friends to meet for drinks later that night; a normal life to live. Whatever the reason no one even seemed to have it in them to even appear haughty. This wasn't a punishment. A well-deserved consequence. Karma at work.

It was just *sad*.

I found myself still speaking to Rian even though I knew he wasn't there.

"Where is the funeral going to be? Did you get an address? No bother. We'll figure it out. Check your phone. Check your apartment. I'm sure you have the key. It's going to be alright. I'm here, I'm here."

I knew I couldn't let Rian fall. If he fell, I'd never get him back up. So I groaned and forced myself, no matter what, to keep my feet underneath me.

My voice was cheery as I helped Rian toward the wrought-iron gates where we could hail a cab to his place. Where I could set him down for a second or two. Where I could breathe.

"I didn't mean what I said. I want to be with you. I want us to be together. We can make it work, you know? We can make it work if we just try."

Every step was excruciating. Every step Rian seemed to get heavier. Every step I wondered what it would be like to just let my burden go.

But I kept walking and I kept talking as if there was anyone but the rain to hear me.

"I'm going to help you. I'm going to be there for you. I'm here… I'll always be here…"

RIAN

When I took that first hit, with the full intention of taking many, many more after that, I expected to end up in a hospital like before. Days missing like lost puzzle pieces. Weeks just disappeared. My body thin and weak like it was when I was a child. Tubes snaking into my arms. A machine keeping time with my faintly beating heart. I expected to hit rock bottom. To blink awake to an unknown, empty future. To begin the slow crawl back up the well with bloodied nails and gritted teeth. I expected to be alone once more.

But if I was in a hospital bed, it was moving. Jolting occasionally. Shifting right or left at certain intervals. Pushing me back against the cushions like gravity itself. And if I was in a hospital room, someone was playing music. Soft enough not to make out the words, loud enough for it to enter my fuzzy mind like steadily drifting fog. And if there was a needle slipped into the vein of the underside of my wrist, it was a soft needle. A gentle needle. A needle that for some reason drew up and down my skin like a paintbrush, delicate and careful.

I blinked slowly, groggily, and windshield wipers swept aside a splattering of raindrops to reveal a sight I never could have gotten from the window of a city hospital: rolling green hills, low wooden fences crawling across the landscape like stitches interspersed with sections of yellow gorse bushes, dark clouds on a vast horizon. One thing was certain though: I definitely felt shitty enough to be in a hospital.

A groan slipped from my parched lips as I stirred. A seatbelt cut into my throat; or at least my too sensitive skin made it feel that way and I struggled to breathe. Late autumn wind rattled against the windows, but the air inside the car felt brutally hot to me: unmoving, stale, humid. It reminded me of the drug dens I was fully prepared to end up in—those filthy, boarded-up torture chambers, except without the saving grace of the actual drugs. Claustrophobia came for me with a vengeance as I pressed my fingertips weakly against the fogged-up windows.

I didn't want to be there. I wanted to be unconscious. Out of my mind. Blissed out. I wanted to be killing myself slowly, or not so slowly, I didn't fucking care. If I couldn't have a hospital, with its morphine and crisp white sheets, I wanted a dark hole and a dirty needle. I didn't want in between. I didn't want a second chance. It hurt too fucking bad.

Just when I was about to give in to panic, a pill was slipped into my clammy palm, a water bottle eased between my shaking thighs, and blissful, ice-cold air was sent cascading over me from a rolled-down window. I fumbled with the pill, not even questioning whether it intended me ill or good. My throat stung as the water went down my throat, but I swallowed more and more of it till I was gasping. I collapsed back into the seat and squeezed my eyes shut to breathe shakily through my nose.

"Just give it a minute or two," came Eithne's voice. "You'll feel better soon."

I fought back the urge to throw up, to claw at my skin, to unhook my seatbelt, open the door, and leap out of the moving car into oblivion. A soft, gentle touch was back at my vein, the one on the sensitive underside of my wrist, and it was just enough to distract me, its running back and forth like a paintbrush.

When I cracked open my eyes once more, I saw a signpost flash by on the side of the winding road. We were going to a place I swore I'd never go again. I wasn't in hell after all, just purgatory. Merely on the way to those fiery lakes.

"You're taking me to the funeral," I said in a hollow voice.

Eithne kept her gaze on the road, one hand on the steering wheel of my car, one hand on me. The windshield wipers counted the silent minutes. We both stared out over the landscape, tall grasses thrashed in the wind, swept up and laid low like waves.

"Are you feeling better?" Eithne asked after a while. "That always helps Stewart when he's... that always helps Stewart."

Eithne's eyes finally darted over to mine. I wasn't sure what to expect in them. The last thing I remembered of her was her leaving the administrative building at the Dublin Art School. Her telling me she never wanted to see me again. How she'd come back to me, I didn't know. Nor how she'd learned about my father. His funeral. The ranch out on that godforsaken piece of land. She must have found my car keys and convinced me to get in the car. I wouldn't have complied if I'd known where she was taking me. She must have lied. Told me she was taking me home. Or to hospital. To do the nearest drug den.

She should be angry. She knew I'd done something with her brother. She should be angry, too, because I'd fallen into the same trap that I'd sent away her brother for falling into one too many times. She should be frustrated or annoyed or depressed or frightened. I must have been in a bad state; I know, because I'd meant to be. She should be, most of all, through with me.

But what I saw in Eithne's darting gaze was none of that. I saw instead that she was my student again. I, her professor. She was eager to please. Looking for approval from me. Seeking something that I alone could give her. She'd just turned in an assignment and I was to grade her. Ms Brady and Professor Merrick.

"Eithne," I tried to say, shaking my head till the knives against my temple convinced me to stop. "Eithne—"

"I've got your things in the trunk," she interrupted, as if knowing what I was going to say and not wanting to hear it. "I was going to pack you a bag, but there was already one packed in your closet. I added a black suit. I have my things as well. We're alright. Completely alright. Nothing to bother yourself about."

Her finger against my wrist had started to move faster, a little too fast. Could she sense the wheels coming loose? Could she feel that if she let me speak I would tell her to turn around? To take us back to Dublin? To leave me on the side of the road with my bag and what was secretly hidden amongst the toothpaste and aftershave?

"This is the right thing to do, Rian," she hurriedly said as she flicked a switch to make the windshield wipers move faster, the rain having increased as we drove deeper into the late afternoon storm. "I don't know everything about you and your father. But I know enough to know that it'll be difficult for you, for whatever reason. But I know that this is still the right thing to do. It'll be good for you. It'll, it'll help you. I'm sure of it."

Eithne was nodding to herself as she kept her focus on the road, the twisting black asphalt slick because of the rain, scarred with cracks because of disuse. I saw again the stressed, anxious student. Ill-prepared for her test. Uncertain of the answer. I saw her chin tremble. Her eyes pricked with the threat of tears. Her hand moved to increase the speed of the windshield wipers even though there was no need at all.

Without saying anything, I rested my hand across hers, the one that she used to stroke my skin. I pressed my hand against hers to still her. To let her feel the pulse of that vein, the blood pumped steadily, if a little quickly, to my wrist, to her fingertips. To let her know the best I could that it was okay. It was all okay.

Eithne relaxed slightly. She sucked in a deep, shuddering breath. She reduced the speed of the windshield wipers. She eased the car round the wide bend of the grassy knoll with control. When she nodded once more, it was because she had a sense of being back in control: the test studied for, the quiz known of well in advance, her answers right there in front of her.

"Family is the most important thing in life," she continued, more self-assured than before, voice less trembling. "Nothing comes before family."

"Eithne," I whispered once more.

She rolled down her own window as she shook her head. She was suffering, too. Something was burning her from inside, just like me. The wind tore at her hair, not gently like that first day, but roughly. As if it meant to hurt her. Long, dark strands lashed at her fair cheeks as she gulped in the whipping, freezing cold air. Rain battered her soft skin like stones, but she didn't roll the window back up.

"Eithne," I tried again, pressing my hand tighter over hers.

"Family is blood, you know," she said, losing control again as her voice quivered. "*Blood*. And what do we have if not blood?"

Eithne's hand was shaking on the wheel. The direction of the car no longer steady on those sharply winding country roads. I now felt her pulse through her fingertips. It alighted like the ravens from the old fence post we raced past. Flew high. Swept low.

"We have to be there for our family, even if it hurts," she said, and I could hear the tears in her eyes more than see them. Her eyes were bound with black silk. "Even if it takes everything out of us and we're not sure we can go on. We have to be there. We have to endure. We can't just give up. We can't."

Eithne was shaking. Tears were indistinguishable from droplets of heavy rain, but I was sure there were tears.

"Eithne," I said, breathing deeply, hesitating, "your brother is fine."

Eithne sobbed.

"He's fine, okay?"

She nodded.

"He's alright."

Eithne's chin collapsed to her chest and I feared she might send us right off the road.

"Eithne," I said, eyes darting between her and the faded white line. "Do you believe me?"

Eithne looked up, righted the car as it had slipped out of the lane, and, sniffling, rolled up both windows. Her messied hair she pushed back from her pale face. I watched in concern as she drew the back of her palm under her nose. She pulled her hand slowly from mine, took up position on the steering wheel at ten and two. Her back straightened as if tugged up by a marionette's string. I was watching her still when she glanced over at me and smiled. It was meant to comfort me, but it proved to do just the opposite.

Had she not heard me? Had the wind swallowed my question? Had her hair lashed out over her ears to block my words from reaching them? Or had she heard me just fine? And decided not to answer?

I was too fearful, in the end, to ask which it was. I positioned myself as comfortably as I could in the seat. Closed my eyes briefly to wait for the painkillers to kick in. Sipped timidly again at the water bottle. Sweat through the back of my shirt, which was thankfully hidden from Eithne's view. Clasped my fingers together to hide the trembling.

I'd try for Eithne's sake. I'd try to forgive my brothers, to reconcile, to give things another go. I'd try to make it through the funeral. I'd try to find some kind word for a father who had none for me. I'd try to love him to love her. For Eithne. I'd do it for her.

This could be a new start. Eithne had somehow plucked me from the jaws of destruction. She'd found me. Saved me. Set me on the right path. I would get clean for her. I would let go of anger toward my dead father for her. I would even go find Stewart, help him, help him like his sister had helped me.

We'd get our little life together, my little Raglan Road girl and me. A quiet studio to paint together. A little apartment above it to cook and read and make love. Trees outside that turned the colours I first saw her in, a little reminder of what I had. And how easily it could have been lost.

I could have ended up in the hospital after last night. I could have ended up dead. But I ended up back with Eithne.

And I wouldn't mess it up.

"Thank you," I told Eithne in the silence of the car as the windshield wipers moved slowly.

I held out my open hand and Eithne slipped her fingers into mine. My love for her would be enough.

It had to be enough.

I closed my eyes with the comfort of her skin against mine and tried not to think about what I knew was waiting for me in my bag in the trunk.

EITHNE

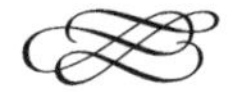

Rian told me very little about his family on our drive into Cork County in the west of Ireland; I asked even less.

I knew there was something unresolved between him and his father, some dark past to justify Rian's state on campus. I feared what I was taking him into, what I was taking myself into, as Rian pointed mutely to the turn onto his family's farm. Every sign seemed to point to something terrible just around the bend: the gravel path littered with potholes left long unfilled, the broken fences, the equipment left to rust in fields given to weeds and wild grasses.

The road to the house was long and several times I glanced over at Rian to see if this was indeed the way as mile stretched after silent mile. Every time I found Rian staring straight ahead. A part of me hoped that I would find his head swivelling from side to side, a forefinger at his chin, mumbling something like, "Well, maybe it was a little way still down the highway…"

We came to halt in front of a dilapidated monstrosity that stuck out on the land like a last rotten tooth in an otherwise empty mouth. I hesitated to turn off the engine as I leaned forward to study the house through the rain-streaked windshield. A wrap-around porch should have conveyed a homey, welcoming presence, but it buckled and warped and sagged from water damage, speckles of mould, and termite-rotted planks of old wood. Clearly unused, it collared the house like a strip of bad leather. Big windows were made small from thick, heavy drapes. All drawn tight. The roof moulted like a flea-ridden dog and the smoke from the chimney coughed up at the low-hanging sky like a deadly black lung. I tried not to grip the steering wheel tighter; I didn't want to show my nervousness in front of Rian. I knew full well he didn't want to be there. If he'd been more conscious, I knew we probably *wouldn't* be there.

The feeling of unease persisted in my stomach as the motor idled, sputtering and popping in the rain. Something terrible was going to happen here. Something completely outside my control. It was too dark a place, too haunted a place for it to go down any other way.

My dread did not lighten when the front door creaked open, a screen door slapped against the weatherboards like a shotgun, and two towering men, careful of their step across the porch, lumbered toward us. In the grey light, shadows made their eyes dark; heads bent against the steady rain made those shadows long, gouging into their coarse, leathery skin. They had shoulders as wide as Conor's with Mason's height. They wore coats made for farm life, durable and thick and unrelenting. They had their hands stuffed into their pockets, but that didn't change the fact that I feared these men capable of violence. It rippled across their tense postures like electricity across power lines; I was sure if I was brave enough to reach out and touch them that I'd jump back with a shock. They were the kind of men you didn't want to encounter alone in a dark alley. And knowing that Rian didn't like them confirmed all of this in my mind, tired by a long journey: be wary, be careful, be on your guard, lock your doors, stay safe.

All of this combined made it all the more startling when Rian, without a word or even a glance in advance toward me beside him, hauled himself with a stifled groan from the car and met his brothers halfway. I expected balled fists or angry words, but Rian held out his hand, awkwardly, and shook first one brother's hand and then the next.

I was numb as Rian came to open my door. Numb as he introduced me first to Liam, handsome in a sturdy, rugged way; he had the same pale blue eyes as his little brother. And then to Alan, who shared nothing at all, who really was the polar opposite of Rian physically, unidentifiable as kin. Where Rian's broody smouldering features were perfectly proportioned as if from a sculptor's loving hand, his eldest brother was gruff and weathered, a harsh chin and hooked nose set upon his face.

I shook their hands, feeling swallowed almost whole by the roughness and size of their calloused palms. Simple but pleasant enough small talk about the trip from the city, the weather, and the food cooking for tonight's dinner was shared between us. We ignored the falling rain just like we apparently ignored the cause of the estrangement in the family, as we ignored the reason we were even all there: a dead man who Rian loathed so much that he'd drown himself in drugs.

"Come on then," Alan finally said when the conversation lulled. "Let's all get inside."

I walked beside Rian as we followed the brothers, who made our hoisted luggage look like handbags. I glanced over at him, raised an eyebrow to express my confusion. He just smiled as an answer, which was really no answer at all. In fact, it raised a million others. I took his hand when offered because the rain was cold and his fingers warm and I wanted to believe everything would be okay.

Inside, the ceilings were low, the air thick and musty, the furniture fading like an old Polaroid picture, but the flames that licked at the blackened stone of the fireplace gave it warmth. I kept waiting for something to cross Rian's face as we were introduced to Alan's wife, Anna, and their children. Something like I had expected: anger, resentment, bitterness. Hatred even. But he shook hands with what I thought was a genuine smile for the small, rather timid woman. He even drew one of Alan's five children up into his arms, a little boy named, I learned later, not just after his father, but his father's father, the now deceased. Little Alan tugged at Rian's wet hair with chubby fingers and I laughed, because Rian did first.

It felt nice. Right. This little world I'd never thought I'd have for myself, this little world of a family. I was invited to cut vegetables for the roast with Anna and it was a simple pleasure to be there in the dingy kitchen with its peeling cabinets and stained linoleum. Anna threw a carrot top at Alan when he teased her about the way she chopped everything to pieces.

"It's all going in the same place, love," he told her. "Stop torturing yourself."

Rian excused himself to the restroom, but came back quickly and with a smile; all was, it seemed, well.

Beers were popped and a quiet little chatter filled the kitchen as we worked and the men leaned heavily against the counters, watching. How backwards, but how little I cared. I liked it. The easy passing of the minutes and then the hours. Children running in, children running out. I smacked at Rian's hand when he tried to dip a pinkie into whipped cream meant for that night's dessert; he grinned at me playfully and it was nice.

From what I could tell there was no tension. No strain. Little Amelia's favourite doll getting stolen by one of the older boys was the most drama I witnessed. I kept checking on Rian as the smell of the roast filled the house and imbued it with a homeliness the bones clearly lacked, and I saw nothing but a brother amongst brothers, family with family. He was relaxed. He smiled easily and often. He joked with his brothers like we were gathered for a reunion or a wedding or baptism and not a funeral. There was life there, in that desolate house. Not death.

I'd always imagined a big dinner like the one we shared together. A big table that left just enough space in the dining room to squeeze in your chair. It laden with so much food that it threatened to buckle the legs should one more side dish of mashed potatoes be placed on top (as if there was even room). It was a silly but sweet dream to lock hands and say grace. To hear the murmur of a dozen people echo "amen". This followed by the screech of chairs pulled in, napkins snapped open, and forks and knives busy at work. I'd always wondered what it would be like, to have the noise of a dinner table rise to the ceiling like a hot air balloon, to hang up there happily, to feel the roar of its flame.

Dinners with my father before that night that ended everything were quiet, fast, and dark, giving Stewart and me the best chance of not setting him off, not incurring his rage, not being forced to huddle against the wall as the little Formica table was flipped with a roar.

It felt like a second chance, there at the dinner table, to get the big family dinner I'd always dreamed of. I almost forgot to eat. I was so enraptured with watching everyone, Alan with Anna, the little kids all up and down the table with smeared and glistening chins and pea-stuffed smiles. A nudge at my elbow reminded me I had my fork and knife suspended above my untouched plate.

"It's good," he said in a soft voice.

He said it like a secret and I suspected he meant more than just the food. I smiled and rested a hand on his knee beneath the frayed white tablecloth, which had been dragged from some dusty closet. He briefly kissed my shoulder.

"It's good," I repeated, before I'd even taken a bite.

During dessert, Alan and Liam shared stories of Rian as a child. They told of a quiet, shy little boy, all elbows and knees. I found myself leaning forward as I heard about Rian nurturing a tiny kitten back to health, a runt much like himself. He caught fireflies while Alan and Liam wrestled, he learned about wildflowers while his two older brothers kicked over anthills, and he spent hours in the attic of the barn staring up at the dust suspended in the golden afternoon sunlight while they wondered what the fuck he was doing.

"Daydreaming," Rian said with a soft smile and a distant gaze.

"About being a cowboy or something?" Alan asked, ruffling the hair of his little boy who he bounced on his knee.

"Or something," Rian replied, gazing down at his lap.

"About being an artist, I'm sure," I piped in, speaking for what felt like the first time. I smiled at Rian, squeezed his hand beneath the tablecloth. "I can't imagine him having any other dream than that."

Rian kissed my cheek.

"Having a good woman like you in his life ain't such a bad dream either," Alan said, nodding politely to me.

"We're taking things slow," Rian corrected.

Alan shrugged, adjusting his little boy. "Ain't nothing slow about the way she looks at you."

"Or him, her," Anna added, leaning over to wipe a smear of chocolate pudding from her littlest's chin.

"Or him, her," Alan relented with a wink. "You know, we just wish Liam could find something like that. Love, support, all that malarkey."

This earned him a jab in the elbows from Anna. We all laughed like we were on a '70s sitcom. I glanced at Rian, but his smile seemed genuine enough. Maybe I was just mistrustful, I thought. Mistrustful that a family could actually be happy.

"I just need a bigger pond," Liam muttered, mostly under his breath.

This drew a sharp eye from Alan.

"No, what you *need* is to want what's best for you: a simple woman. A traditional woman. A woman who will keep you on the straight and narrow," he said. "Ye keep chasing after something too big for you and what do ye t'ink yer going to find?"

I shifted awkwardly in my chair as Liam stared down at the crumbs on his dessert plate.

Alan continued, "Those Jackeens in Dublin are going to chew you up and spit ye out. The women there, especially. They don't want nuthin' from you but what they can get. You think you want sparks, well, don't blame me when your whole life goes up in flames. And not even yer family will be around to watch it burn with ya."

A terse silence descended over the dinner table. Even the young children seemed to sense it, going mute, stopping their tired fidgeting. Anna cleared her throat. I noticed her jerk her chin toward Rian.

Alan scratched at the back of his neck, laughter back in his voice as he said, "I mean, not all city folk are all that bad, of course. And, well, what am I saying, Rian is family. You've got Rian there."

I expected to find Rian stung, hurt. But instead he laughed back, leaning back in his chair to stretch his arms overhead.

"For what it's worth, I think Liam should stay, too," he said teasingly. "I mean, not even the finest restaurants in Dublin hold a candle to your cooking, Anna."

We all laughed again. I expected it all to fall apart. Again it didn't. I kept an eye on Rian as conversation drifted again, wandering here and there, nowhere controversial, nowhere significant. He seemed content. At peace. I imagined many nights like these: easy, slow, good. And I thought, maybe. Maybe everything can be alright.

The dinner was cleared and the children were falling asleep, the night growing long. And there was tomorrow morning, the unspoken event that had brought us all together. It made us all rise in our chairs without needing to say anything. I washed dishes, passed them to Rian to dry. There was the noise of the refrigerator opening, leftovers being stacked, stored, comments about how well everything would reheat. I sensed that the funeral was looming higher, darker. I sensed that this would be the shift, the turn, us adults standing in the darkness at the top of the stairs.

Rian was the first to speak. "Thank you all for the wonderful dinner. I'm glad I came. We'll see you all in the morning for the funeral, then?"

It was natural, calm. He spoke like we were all going grocery shopping. There was discussion about breakfast, what time to leave for the church, cars and carpooling, parking and gas stations. We parted with whispered goodnights. I turned around to look at Rian as he closed the bedroom door behind him, hands behind his back, facing me. I waited. Apprehensively, I guess. Was this when it happened? The falling apart.

Rian smiled at me and turned his gaze to the room, taking it in slowly as I watched him.

"This was my bedroom, you know," he said.

I didn't turn around to look, but instead kept focused on him. I searched his face for any hint of distress. Of pain. Of that claustrophobia I knew from my own childhood. It would kill me to be back in my own little bedroom and I waited for that in Rian: death.

"Liam and Alan crashed into my desk and broke one of the legs," he said, slipping past me as I remained where I stood. "They fixed it with duct tape when I cried and, look, it's still standing."

I heard Rian knock his knuckles against the cheap wood.

"Rian," I said, turning around. I found him spinning a little globe, it creaking on its plastic axis. "Rian..."

I wasn't sure what else to say. Rian came up to me and took my hands. In the darkness, I looked up at him.

"Eithne," he said. "It's good."

He smiled knowingly and I knew it was my job to do the same. Teeth brushed. Clothes slipped off. With the drapes already drawn there was nothing left to do but climb into bed.

Rian cuddled close behind me. His body warm. His fingers tracing circles across my palm. I thought, for the first time in a long time, for the first time ever maybe, that we could make this work. I could help Rian. I *had* helped Rian. I could save him the way I'd failed to save my father. Failed to save Stewart. I could love him enough. I could give him enough.

Look at tonight. I'd brought him back from the brink. My love. My patience. My endurance. I'd dragged him to shore from those black waters. I'd returned him to his family. He was happy. I was happy. We were together. I did that. And I could do it again and again and again.

I could love Rian. I could love Rian enough.

Without a word, I guided Rian's hand to the hem of my panties. I helped him slip them down my thighs, wriggling against the cool sheets till they were off. Rian was already hard when I tugged his pants off. His breathing grew rough as I pushed him back and wrapped my mouth around him.

Did he know that we were making a pact? Deciding on our future? Did he realise what I was offering as I guided his cock to my pussy?

He could have me. He could have all of me. To have. To hold. To claw himself up from the depth with. To cling to. To use. To abuse, if necessary. To rest upon. To rail against. To scream into. To fuck over, to fuck with, to fuck. To love, if he could. One day.

I would be enough. My body, my heart, my love. It would be enough.

It had to be enough.

RIAN

I plunged my cock into Eithne till there was none of me left outside of her and I told myself it was enough.

I felt myself swallowed by her, by her pulsing heat, by her throbbing pressure, by her wetness that quivered around me like ripples from a now sinking stone. I couldn't have been more complete, me fully seated in her. I couldn't have been more drowned in physical pleasure, that brilliant white light that flashes behind closed eyelids. I couldn't have had more of what I wanted, what I'd told myself, assured myself again and again that I wanted.

It *had* to be enough.

But I buried my nose in the soft fragrance of Eithne's dark locks and wanted, needed to bury myself deeper. I pressed in closer till I inhaled the scent of her neck and I still felt like I was exposed. I wanted to be hidden by her, concealed by her. I needed more. More of those dark tangles, her thornless rose stems.

Her little moans reached my ears and I strained to hear more of them. And louder. And more often. I thought maybe if I couldn't hear anything else, I would be alright, I could be alright.

I thought if all I heard was Eithne, I wouldn't hear me. She could drown me out: the growing need, the building desire, the more and more horrifying conviction that I would give in. If I could just get more of those sweet noises from her even sweeter lips, it would be enough.

The pleasure grew in my lower stomach. A sweat broke out across my brow. It was bliss, her against me, my cock driving into her at a steady pace. What more could a man want? This was it, I told myself. This was all.

But that didn't stop my fingers from clutching at her anywhere I could. I grabbed at her hip. I filled my palm with her velvety flesh. I was a thirsty man who held out cupped hands and had them filled with pure, cool water. And it wasn't enough. I drank her thighs, digging my fingers into her pale skin till she whined, not quite in pleasure.

This was a knife to my heart and I squeezed my eyes shut against the hollow of Eithne's throat. My fingers opened and closed, opened and closed at my side. I tried to focus on the sensation of my cock against her buttery soft heat. I tried to focus on her moans, those perfect, fucking perfect little moans. I tried to feel her heart against my chest and tell myself it was enough. I didn't need more. I didn't need anything else.

I bit back a groan of misery as the itch refused to go away. That goddamn *need* for it. My curse. Like a man reaching out for a rope to save him from his fall, I grabbed at Eithne's hair. My fingers wound round it, like I needed not some of it, but all of it. Eithne's head came back, her throat exposed. She clenched around my cock when I sucked at her exposed throat, milky white in the moonlight through the clouds. I saw the pleasure turn to pain as I again tried for more: more of her hair, more of her warm flesh, more of her body around me.

I saw what I did to her. I saw what I would always do to her. The eyebrows, dark and soft, drawn together, knitted in discomfort. I saw her teeth sink into her lower lip, stifling a cry I knew was there in the back of her tensed throat. I saw her eyes close, the lids squeezed a little too tightly. This was me. This was what I did to her. I wanted too much, I needed too much.

I released Eithne's hair, pulled my mouth from her throat, when I drove back inside of her, I didn't claim all of her, but stopped short. Fighting back tears of panic, I wrapped my arms around her. I held her against me, but was careful not to hurt her.

It felt like a goodbye, fucking Eithne softly, gently there in my childhood bed. I feared I knew the future, feared I could read it as if in a glass ball. This would be my last chance to leave her with something good, something worth remembering, something she didn't pray to forget.

It felt like a goodbye, because I was going to give in to my addiction. I knew I would. I knew everything I needed was in the bag Eithne had inadvertently delivered right into my hands. I knew I had a store of bad memories and hateful thoughts and self-destructive tendencies dammed up inside my heart, just ready to burst free with the tiniest prick of a needle. I knew I'd barely made it through those handshakes with my brothers in the rain, barely survived that nerve-grating small talk, that oppressive kitchen with all those ghosts, that dinner where every bite of food I had to force down was like a mouthful of nails. And I knew I could no longer take from Eithne. Suck her dry. Tear her apart. Wrench her in two so that I didn't fall to pieces. I couldn't do it. I just couldn't do it. There just wasn't enough of her to hold onto, not enough for both of us.

I fell away from her after I felt her shudder, heard her muffle her screams in her pillow. I tugged my cock till I came, spasming alone with a hauntingly familiar ceiling collapsing on me. Eithne was reaching for me, drawing me back toward her. But she didn't know I was already gone. It was an emptied husk wrapping his arms back around her, shrivelled lips softly kissing her shoulder, a stranger's voice whispering into her ear, "Go to sleep, my little Raglan Road girl."

My cum was sticky between our sweat-glistened skin. Eithne thought it was glue, something to hold us together, our secret love affair on my childhood bed. But I knew it for what it was: a division between us. And hadn't it always been. Our bodies acting as a barrier for our souls. We'd fucked because we'd needed to fuck. We'd licked and sucked and caressed each other because it felt good and it was enough, for then. We'd lavished physical pleasure upon physical pleasure, stacking them up like a house of cards. But here it was, the end of the line. I couldn't do it. I couldn't give Eithne more than a fuck in the night. I'd failed. I would fail. I would always fail.

I waited till she fell asleep. Self-loathing and excitement pulsed inside of me on the same frequency. I was going to hate what I was about to do; I was going to fucking love it. I was going to feel worse; I was going to feel so much better. I was going down; I was going up.

I waited till Eithne fell asleep and then slipped out of the bed. My father's ghost followed me. I saw him in the shadows. Heard his voice in the creak of the bathroom door as I sat on the edge of the cracked bathtub and pulled out my secret stash from my toiletries bag. He knew where the vein was.

He'd taught me where to find it.

And how to pierce it.

EITHNE

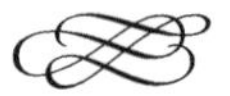

Would it have been better if I'd stayed asleep?

Would things have been alright if something, something I couldn't even pinpoint or describe, hadn't woken me from what was, I thought, a perfectly contented, peaceful, comfortable sleep? Could I have remained blissfully unaware had I just stayed blissfully unconscious? Would I have even known, had I not seen it…watched it…felt it stab through my skin just as it did his?

The yellow light wasn't right. Had the door been closed a little tighter, or had its hinges been located on the other side, I might not have even noticed. The beam of light could have fallen across the thin and worn-down carpet, as harmless as a garment tossed off after a long day onto the floor. But that yellow glare stabbed at my eyes like a knife. I felt it crawl over me like the slick underbelly of a snake. I blinked against its harshness and sat up in bed. I might have yanked the covers over my head, fallen back asleep, if I hadn't heard his groan; something half-like pain, half-like pleasure.

I crept out of bed and tiptoed toward the gap in the bathroom door, pushing away the guilt that I was sneaking up on Rian.

Hating that I felt like I had a reason to. Blaming both of us for my lack of trust in this place, in this, in *him*.

I sucked back a gasp when I saw him, bent over the vein in his elbow. A sick feeling washed over me as my eyes shifted to the suitcase I'd lugged from Rian's apartment. There it was: opened, rifled through, a zipper, unzipped. *I'd* brought it. Rian's bag wasn't for a last-minute vacation or an impromptu business trip for Dublin Ink. It was a getaway bag. A getaway from real life bag. A getaway from your problems bag. A getaway from everything that hurt in this godforsaken world bag.

A getaway from *me* bag.

Was that why he'd been so docile, so friendly, so seemingly unaffected by his reunion with his estranged family? Because he had his escape plan? His way out? His secret weapon? Had he fucked me knowing he was going to do it? Had I been an obstacle along the way? My orgasm like passing Go to collect $200?

I knew if I kept watching I would be sick and I knew I was sick, because I couldn't stop. It made me paralysed the ease with which Rian worked. The familiarity with the rubber strap round his bicep pulled tight but not too tight with his teeth. The dexterity of his fingers over the needle. The exactitude with which he flicked the vein in the crook of his arm. I thought I'd feel better if he trembled. If he hesitated. If he dropped the needle and considered for at least a moment or two whether it was right, whether it was good to pick it up. To continue. To do this to himself. To do this to *me*. I thought I'd forgive him if he at least glanced over toward me, out there in the dark, alone. If I at least saw something like remorse. Or sadness. Or regret.

But Rian worked on himself like he worked on his paintings, on his tattoos, on me: confident, quick, determined, practised, *well*-practised. I didn't have to wait long for him to be ready. For the needle to slip effortlessly into the vein. For the plunger to send whatever poison was loaded into Rian's body.

I should have closed my eyes then. I should have spared myself the rest. But I needed to be punished. So I watched. I watched as Rian's face, pinched with pain and anger, contorted with years of heartache, softened, smoothed. I watched as the tension that made stone of his shoulders and back eased away as he sank against the edge of the old claw-foot tub. And I watched as pleasure drew a smile to his lips, a real smile, a true smile, a smile dissimilar in every way, I was sure, to the ones he was giving me all night long in front of his family, in front of my naked body.

Perhaps I should have been happy for him. He'd clearly found peace when he'd had none, relief when there hadn't been any to find. Perhaps I should have been happy for him, because it was really me I should have been loathsome of.

I'd been the fool who once again believed she could save someone with love. I'd been the idiot who fell into the trap again of thinking, "If I just gave more…if I just gave a little more…" I'd been the stupid little girl who convinced herself she'd healed her drug addicted, broken, obsessive professor. And I'd been the one who fell in love with the idea of being needed, of being necessary, of being worthy.

I watched Rian's eyes close, his body go limp. The needle rolled from his open palm. It clattered gently on the tiled floor. He moaned slightly from the bathroom and the sound drew fresh tears. He hadn't moaned like that in my ear, our bodies rocking as one. He hadn't moaned with such abandon. There was always something held back. Something hidden from me. An armour I couldn't cut through. Rian moaned and I thought I could die.

And he was oblivious to it. The hurt he'd inflicted on me with his escape.

He didn't even know that he'd left me behind.

I should have cried for myself. Hot, fast, unstoppable tears. I should have cried for the little girl who got disowned by her father when she stood up for her brother. For the little girl who'd been trying and trying and trying again just to make things right. I should have cried for that little Raglan Road girl, in the wrong place at the wrong time.

But I cried for Rian. For Professor Merrick. For the man I hated. For the man I so desperately loved.

How stupid of me to think he had ever been there with me. That I'd been anything other than alone. When he wrapped his arms around me, it was the drugs in the bloodstream that held me. When he looked into my eyes, it was only ever my own reflection that I saw in those wide, artificially dilated pupils.

When he told me he loved me, was it really anything he could say sober?

RIAN

The trees were swaying. The rain slanted across the rolling hills that rippled with lashed wild grasses. Eithne's dress trembled about her as she hugged her goose-bumped forearms across her stomach. Her hair whipped across her pale cheeks, veiled her eyes that seemed to look everywhere but at me. As the words of the priest droned on into oblivion hands clutched at black umbrellas that thrashed to escape, to be carried far, far away. The wind and rain were ice. I was sure of it. But I felt none of it.

My face was hot, burning. My clothes seemed to grate against my inflamed skin, prickled and irritated like my father had risen from the grave to drag me across the carpet one last time. Even the air I inhaled in panicked sips scorched the back of my throat while all around me the mourners' fingertips turned purple. The cemetery was wide, vast even. There was more than enough room for the dead in this godforsaken land. And yet I felt an oppressive claustrophobia. I swore as the priest began to pray and heads bowed all around me that they all shifted closer, tighter around me. Even Eithne herself. Just the tiniest brush of her arm against mine felt like a mound of dirt dropped atop me, a coffin lid nailed shut as I pounded against it.

The drugs coursed through my veins and each pulse of my heart felt like a betrayal against her. I thought maybe she could hear it, the poison killing me. I'd been weak the night before. The mask weighed too heavily. The promise of a healed family felt too far out of reach and I'd fallen short, because I was always going to fall short. I wanted to tear at my wrists as the casket bearing my father was lowered into the ground. I wanted to drain it out of me. I wanted to tell Eithne what I'd done, that I was sorry, that I wanted to go back, to let the press of her body, the warmth of her embrace, the strength of her love for me be enough.

But it all felt too late. I was a rotted floor waiting to cave in, taking everyone down with me.

I'm not sure exactly what started it. Probably nothing at all. It was fated, so if it wasn't a glancing shoulder or an innocent glance, it was going to be a benign comment or a passing remark. I was going to fight with Alan. I was going to self-destruct in a way that no one else had ever self-destructed before. What the fuck does it matter how it started?

"Jaysus fuck, let's not do this here," Alan whispered harshly, his eyes scanning the gathered people who were ignorant to the true nature of the man they were there to cry over. My brother obviously wanted it to stay that way.

Alan tried to guide me toward the line of black cars stretching along the cemetery. He wanted to "do this" where no one could see us, where it wouldn't embarrass the family, where he could show his true colours, his rage, his violence. He wanted to "do this" just as much as I wanted to. It was as inevitable for him as it was for me. He just wanted to bloody my lip one last time in private.

I wrenched my arm away and hands curled into fists. This

time, I would fight back. Show him all the things I learned in all those boxing sessions with Conor.

In an instant Liam was there.

"Come on," he said in that calming voice that shocked me like electricity. "Easy, easy."

My muscles tensed, constricted, went so taut I thought they might snap. My jaw locked, trembled. It was an unbearable pain. An unimaginable pain. And I just had to stand there. Take it.

"Let's keep it together for Pa," Liam said, hand at the small of my back.

I shoved him away, hard, and I was free. The current of electricity his soft, calming words had sent through me was gone. I could move again. I felt my blood pumping fast. My hands curling and uncurling. Adrenaline shooting through my veins, the most intoxicating drug there was.

"You never could stand up for me, could you?" I said, not bothering in the slightest to keep my voice low.

Alan eased his wife back behind him. He nodded at the mourners hesitating on their way to the cars, on their way out of the rain. "Everything's fine," he said even as his biceps bulged beneath his ranch-tattered coat. I felt a hand against mine.

"Rian," Eithne said softly. "Rian, don't do this."

She sounded so far away. Maybe it was the wind, the wind that carried her words out of earshot. I could barely hear her. And what was more, I didn't want to. I pointed a shaking finger at Liam.

"You're worse than the two of them," I said loudly, quickly losing control. "They're just animals. Beasts. Brutes. They can't help themselves. They don't know any better. Fists and blood and dominance is their world. But you. You, Liam. You know. You *knew*. And you did nothing."

Alan advanced on me, gripping me by the collar of my rain-soaked jacket and shook me like a ragdoll. I wasn't the lanky runt I was all those years ago, but Alan was still a mammoth.

"You need to shut your mouth if you know what's good for you," he growled, low and threatening. "I won't let you speak ill of the dead in my presence."

But I had eyes for Liam only. Venom and fury and pent-up hurt for him alone. It was to him that I spoke, voice cracking as I yelled.

"You defended them like they were human. You stayed back like they were men, real men. You acted like they were doing nothing wrong, beating me night after night, locking me in the barn, terrorizing me, day after day. You treated them like they weren't rabid dogs that needed to be taken out back and shot!"

The first crack of knuckles across my cheek was pure bliss. I'd longed for it. Practically begged for it. Alan broke my skin and I laughed like a fucking hyena.

"Well, Liam," I shouted from the mud, wiping away a smear of red blood that the pouring rain couldn't seem to wash away, "I'm giving you another chance, because I love you, brother. I'm giving you another chance to step in. To protect me. To be on my side. To be a fucking brother."

"We're done," Alan said. When he turned to leave with his wife I kicked out at his knee.

He howled in pain and returned the favour with a swift fist to my ribs. I cradled my side.

"Come on now, Liam," I said. "It's now or never. You're not going to come to me later with a warm towel. I'll spit in your face. Now or never."

I turned to Alan, whose chest was heaving as he struggled to restrain himself. I grinned.

"You're a fucking animal, Alan," I told him and added, pointing to the grave not yet even filled in with dirt, "You and him, both. This whole 'self-control' thing really isn't in your nature, is it?"

Alan lunged at me as I knew he would. I let him take me to

the ground. With half my face shoved into the mud, I looked at Liam, who stood paralysed in the rain.

"Me or him," I said through gritted teeth. "The beast or your brother, Liam! Choose! Fucking choose!"

When he did nothing, I drove my forearm against Alan's throat. He gasped and I took the moment to get on top of him. I vaguely heard someone call my name as I let loose years of built-up anger on Alan's face. If there hadn't been the wind, I might have heard "That's enough!" If there hadn't been the battering, whipping rain, I might have heard footsteps splashing in the growing puddles. If there hadn't been blood pounding in my ears, I might have heard it was her voice and not Liam's. I might not have pushed back so hard. I might have still saved things. Saved us.

I knew it was her from the second my fingertips brushed against her wet dress. But by then it was too late. As it always was. As it always was bound to be. I shoved Eithne away and didn't even have a chance to watch her fall as Alan's fist connected with my temple. The world shifted and I didn't know if it was because of the massive blow to the head or because Eithne was on the ground and it was my fault.

Alan held onto me as I struggled to get free. Added a few more punches as Eithne pushed herself up, pushed herself away from Alan's wife, from Liam. Alan growled like a beast just like me as I watched her run, the curious crowd parting for her like a black sea.

"Let me the fuck go!"

I slipped in the mud. Couldn't find my footing. She was getting farther and farther away between the gravestones and I was slipping on my own blood. I called her name as I ran after her, but she didn't stop. She didn't turn back.

When I finally caught up to her, it'd felt like we'd run to the end of the earth. The vast wilderness spread out like an eternity in front of me as I gripped her narrow, shaking shoulders.

"I'm sorry, I'm sorry," I muttered stupidly, out of my mind, out of control, desperation taking over. "Eithne, I never meant to hurt you. I didn't know it was you. If I'd known it was you..."

Mud ran down Eithne's chest, dripping from the tips of her hair. She avoided looking at me like she'd done all morning.

"Rian," she said at last. "I can't talk to you right now."

"Right," I said, nodding furiously. "Right. You're right. It's raining. You're freezing. It's freezing out here. Let's get back to the car. We'll find a hotel. We'll get warm. We'll talk then. Everything will be alright then."

I saw the red and blue lights in her eyes when she looked up and gazed distantly over my shoulder. I turned to see the police car pulling into the cemetery. I knew they were here for me. I knew it wouldn't be long before they came. Already people from the funeral were pointing in my direction. I reached for Eithne's hands, but she pulled them gently away. My heart lurched.

"We'll talk," I insisted, trying and failing to catch her eye. "Eithne, we'll talk."

Checking over my shoulder again I saw the officers making their way between the gravestones, rain falling from the brims of their black caps, their eyes shadowed. Desperation made me sweat as I turned back to Eithne.

"Just tell me you won't leave me," I said, stumbling over my words because I was aware that with each thud of my heart the officers were getting closer. "Till we talk. Just tell me you won't leave me till we talk."

The rain fell between us and Eithne remained silent. Her eyes again lifted, but only when the officers called my name. And only to then step back. To step away.

"Eithne," I said, voice suddenly ragged as I felt hands on my shoulders. "Tell me you won't leave me."

When I resisted, the officers grew more forceful.

"Let's go," they said, but I couldn't go. Not yet.

"Eithne!" I called out over the pounding of the rain. "Just tell me you won't leave me."

The officers began to drag me backwards and Eithne just stood there, eyes on her muddy boots, wet hair shadowing her pale face.

"Everything's going to be alright," I shouted, but I wasn't sure if I was convincing her or me. "Just tell me you won't leave me and everything will be alright!"

The officers twisted me around, shoved me forward. I tried to look back, but a black coat streaked with rain blocked my view. When I tried to move to see her, a pair of cuffs closed painfully around my wrists. I caught only one last glimpse of her as I wrenched my neck around. She'd begun walking, too.

Just not in my direction.

EITHNE

It was all the same. Me shivering in the torrential downpour. Me shaking from something deeper than the cold. Rian's plea in my ears, over and over and over again: don't leave me, please, don't leave me.

I'd waited inside the groundskeeper's building till he'd glanced for the last time at his wristwatch and told me he was sorry, he had a family to get home to. I went out into the rain, running for the tiny bus shelter near the graveyard entrance. There I checked the fogged-up plastic cover over the bus times, despairing that nothing, absolutely nothing was coming that night.

Finally realising my last resort was to ask for help.

"Aurnia," I said, struggling to keep my phone in place against my wet cheek with my numb fingertips, "please, just…please don't tell Mason or Conor. Okay?"

There was a hesitation on the line. For a moment all I heard was the rain against the gravestones.

"Aurnia," I said when the silence continued, "I called you because I thought I could trust you. I need you to keep this to yourself."

I rubbed at my arms to try to bring some warmth. None came.

"I'll make something up to tell Conor," Aurnia said at last. "I'm on my way."

I mumbled a "thank you" and hung up. The bench inside the bus stop was half rotted and I feared I would just keep falling and falling and falling if it gave way beneath me. So I stood, shifting from foot to foot as I waited. Just like before. All those years ago.

I'd stood up to my father when he kicked Stewart out of the house. It was the night he unleashed his rage on me. Calling me the words I'd not so easily forget: whore, bitch, slut. I gathered my things as he broke everything he could inside the house. His parting gift to me had been a shattered plate just inches from my head as I walked out the door. I could still hear it falling on the old wood floors.

Stewart and I had waited at a bus stop not unlike the one I waited under now. He made me all those promises. Everything was going to be alright. He was going to take care of us. He was going to be the big brother. The protector. The defender. He'd get a job. Get us a place. We'd be better gone. Safer. Happier. Everything was going to be alright. I don't think he intended to break them, the promises he gave me as he hugged me in the rain that night. I think he believed them as I did, as I hugged him tighter, held on stronger. But those promises were washed away as easily as the mud from the road just inches away from my frozen toes.

Aurnia's headlights were the first headlights I'd seen for hours. I waved my arm out from under the dilapidated bus stop outside the cemetery and she pulled up alongside it. The passenger door was flung open before I even reached for it. Rachel was climbing from the passenger seat into the back as Aurnia leaned over and shouted at me, "Get in."

I ducked out of the rain and slumped into the seat, the rain outside numbing as I closed the door. Finally some peace. Except I frowned at the music coming out the radio. Was that The Dubliners? It was music Pa listened to. Jesus, it'd been an age since I'd heard them, not since I'd left home. I reached out for the dials.

"Don't touch the radio," Aurnia snapped as she pulled back onto the road.

Rachel laughed from the backseat. "Seriously, don't. She'll cut your fingers off."

I was so far removed from that world—girlfriends and joking and the intimacy of fighting over music in a car—that it took me a second to process.

"That's, er, interesting taste in music you have there, Aurnia," I said, taking back my hand.

Rachel let out a snort. "Just cause you're dating an old guy—"

"Shut up, lads. The Dubliners are class," Aurnia said with a sniff even as a smile toyed on her lips.

They'd come with normalcy. With goofiness and stupid, silly, meaningless arguments. They'd come with school and work gossip. They'd come with hot whiskey toddies and a fresh pair of sweatpants and enough blankets to keep a small village warm. They'd come without judgement. Without questions. Without prying eyes or awkward silence. They'd come as simply friends.

When I started crying halfway back to Dublin, Rachel wrapped her arms around my chest from the backseat and Aurnia took one hand off the wheel to interlace her warm, petite fingers with mine. The tears came fast and heavy and hot, a dam finally broken after weeks upon weeks of the cracks widening, splintering, stressing. I didn't bother wiping at them and neither Rachel nor Aurnia offered anything with which to dab them away, anything with which to soak them up. The tears fell from my cheeks, from the tip of my chin, from my lips and soaked the sweatshirt they'd brought me.

Without a word, Aurnia turned up the heat in the car to keep me from getting cold, but said nothing as I cried. When I leaned my head against the condensation-streaked window, the glass cool against my cheek, Rachel just squeezed me tighter. A few of my tears were for them, these two girls who I hardly knew, who I'd hardly allowed myself to get to know. Their kindness was something I wasn't used to, their understanding something I didn't think anyone else could have for me. But me.

But they knew. They knew as I knew. That when something was over, dead and gone, finished, there was nothing to say. No words could fix it. There were no answers to be brought forth with the right question. When you came to the realisation that you couldn't love someone, there was nothing but a hole, a hole that no kind sentiment could fill. It was a wound to the heart and the pressure of Rachel's arms and Aurnia's fingers was all that could staunch the bleeding.

I cried for a long time. The blackness of the rolling hills slowly became dotted with more and more lights and still I cried. The two of them coming for me had been what had finally made it click for me: I needed to move on from Stewart. I needed to leave Rian. Once that decision was made, I didn't know what else to do but cry.

I still loved him. And I was fairly certain I always would. Maybe Aurnia and Rachel understood that, too. Understood that doing what was right sometimes hurt. Understood that making the best choice was sometimes hard. Understood that breaking your own heart was sometimes the only way to heal it.

At some point, I rested my cheek against Aurnia instead of the window. I don't remember deciding to do it. I just remember wanting something softer, something warmer and her hand there, guiding me toward her. Rachel stroked my hair and nestled a blanket tighter against me. I thought it might be something my mother might have done. Not the whore my father called her, but my mother. Gentle. Loving. Kind. Maybe I cried for her, too. The mother I never knew. The love I missed out on. The woman I'd let myself become without her there to tell me I was worth more.

We arrived back in the city and pulled up outside Dublin Ink.

"I guess we should go inside," I said, sniffling.

The glow of the neon, though a soft, diffused pink, burned my already stinging eyes. It was like a dawn I wasn't ready for. A new day I was afraid to face alone.

What would my life look like without someone to take care of? I'd made that my whole reason for existing: Stewart, Rian, uncurable men. What else was there for me except someone else? Who was I without that weight? Would I still be able to breathe when the boulder was removed from my chest?

"I don't know," Aurnia said, nestling deeper into her seat instead of reaching for the door handle, "it's pretty comfy in here."

Rachel held up the thermos in the backseat. "And we still haven't finished our whiskey."

Without saying anything further, Aurnia reached over and turned up the radio.

I guess nothing further needed to be said.

RIAN

Alan wasn't going to press charges.

Liam met me in the lobby of the local police station and acted like this was some great kindness that they'd bestowed upon me. A mercy. An olive branch extended toward familial reconciliation. Liam smiled at me as if to say, "Well, now, he took the first step toward being the bigger man. Are you?" He tried to hug me as if the past was in the past and not right there between us like a fucking brick wall, electrified, topped with barbed wire.

"Rian," he called after me as I shoved open the rickety old door into the frigid night. "Come on! Alan just wants to make things right!"

But I knew better. I knew goddamn better. Alan had declined to press charges because he knew I couldn't self-destruct in a jail cell. He wanted me to fall apart, to break, to shatter into a million pieces, and that wasn't possible under the watchful eye of a guard. No, for Alan to get his revenge I had to be out. On my own. With access to my phone. With access to drugs. With the full weaponry of my self-hatred.

If I'd been stuck in that tiny cell there was no way I could have dialled Eithne's number more than just the one time I was allowed a phone call. If he'd pressed charges and I'd been stuck inside, I could have convinced myself that she just missed the call, the one chance I got at reaching her. I could have come up with a dozen different excuses for why she hadn't picked up: her battery died, she was taking a shower, she just stepped out of the room, whatever room she was in, wherever she was.

But since Alan had declined to press charges and since I'd been released, I was free to dial her number as many times as I wanted as I stumbled down that dark country road, swaying like a drunk, weaving back and forth like a car skidding on ice. The excuses dwindled with each redial.

Between calling, I texted, but these were ignored as well. They stacked up in the messaging app like bricks, the tower growing higher and higher. They were laid out across the screen like railroad ties, each one taking me farther and farther away from her. They kept going till one more seemed like a drop in the ocean.

I wandered along that road, not knowing in which direction I was going, till dawn crept up on the distant hills. The rain kept falling and the cold burrowed deeper into my bones. And Eithne still did not answer.

I pleaded with her over voicemail. Begged her over text. I just needed to talk to her. Just needed to explain. If only I could explain…

But…explain what? My thoughts were hazy. My mind unclear. That was Alan's retribution at work, too. I was certain of it.

If I'd been left in jail, forced to await the judge at the county courthouse on Monday morning, I would have been dry, warm, fed. The cot was hard, but it was something still to lie on. I could have stared up at the grey ceiling and thought through what I was going to tell Eithne: why I was sorry, how I was going to make up for it, how I was going to make everything better, why we had to stay together.

As I snuck onto my family farm and crept into my car, exhausted and feverish, ignoring the way the curtains moved aside then fell back, I could come up with only one reason why Eithne should call me back, why she should give me a chance to explain. One selfish reason: I loved her. Desperately.

But as I drove myself back to Dublin, all I could think about was how I'd hurt her. How all I'd ever done was hurt her. How she was better off without me.

I squeezed my eyes shut in a mad fury. So Alan knew how to fight with more than his fists. I'd underestimated him. He wasn't an animal: pure instinct and violence. He was a human like me: cruel and cunning, wicked and selfish.

He knew when he dropped all the charges against me that I'd be right where I was: watching the countryside slip past through my throbbing black eye, alone. He knew damn well that I'd run like I always ran, right into the only arms that never failed to embrace me. To find love where I could, because wasn't that what we all wanted in the end? Just some fucking love.

Back in Dublin, I stood outside a house, shattered glass on the grass, windows boarded, roof littered with a decade of rotting leaves. Chained dogs barking down the street. Low black cars with tinted windows rolling slowly past.

I waited at the door, its screen hanging off only one hinge. I didn't knock because only police knocked. Only people who weren't supposed to be there knocked. Only people who hadn't been there before made any noise at all.

The door inched open. A suspicious eye blinked out at me. I stared back. Hands in my pocket. Shoulders hunched forward. I looked the part thanks to Alan: bruised face, bloodied lip, a lack of light, of life behind the eyes. A man at the end of his rope. A pitiful thing at the lowest of his lows. And ready, eager, even, to sink lower still.

I didn't have to say a goddamn thing for the stranger behind the door to recede into the murky darkness. To leave the entry unguarded. To invite me in in the simplest way possible: by getting out of the goddamn way. That's all I would have needed, I thought as I stepped inside. Just someone in the way. Mason or Conor. Alan or Liam. Or…Eithne.

Eithne.

Eithne.

But I was alone. And steps away, there was a way to not feel alone. I hardly heard the door click shut behind me. I was too busy adjusting my vision to the dark. Too busy spying vacant, bleary eyes blinking slowly in distant corners. I was too busy remembering my past.

These kinds of places were all the same. Same horrible smell, enough to make you wretch. Same smoke lingering across the water-damaged ceiling like a fire was smouldering somewhere. Like everyone should evacuate even though no one ever would. Same push and pull in your chest: revulsion and desire, disgust and longing.

This place, or a place very much like it, had nearly ruined my life. Taken my life even. It'd taken years to come back from. Years to recover. It had me by the throat and it had been so tempting to just not fight it. To just let go. For a moment, there just inside, with the door handle within reach, I tried to cling to the life I'd climbed out of that hole for: my friends, Dublin Ink, my art, my city. But they all dimmed, my reasons, when it came, as it always would, to her.

Eithne,

Eithne,

Eithne.

My little Ragland Road girl.

And she was gone. I'd driven her away. I'd spoiled what was good and pure and lovely. I'd taken what was art and slashed it with a knife. She would never look at me the same after I'd pushed her to the mud. After I'd treated her just as her brother had. After I'd become just like all the rest of them.

The sunlight from that first autumn afternoon when I spotted her across the street was gone. I'd never get it back. Not in this life. But there was a place where I could close my eyes and still feel it.

I sank into an unoccupied corner in the dingy living room. I worked fast with the needle, the spoon, the lighter. Any hesitation was gone now. Any desire to be better was gone. Any will to be good was gone.

I wanted my sunlight.

I wanted my little Raglan Road girl.

I wanted it however I could get it, even if it would kill me…

RIAN

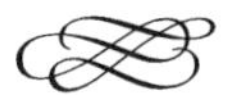

Light stung at my eyes, sharp as a knife. It swallowed me whole, from my bare feet all the way up to my brow slicked with sweat. I couldn't breathe in it as it refused to leave. I struggled against it like it was water, like if I just thrashed enough, I might be able to reach the surface. To gasp. To draw air into my burning, aching lungs. To live; to not feel like I was fucking dying.

But as I kicked my arms and legs, it was clear that the force was too much. I was too weak. The flood had hold of my wrists. My waist. My ankles. I moaned as the brutal light, the drowning water lifted me.

"No," I cried, voice hoarse from disuse.

I wanted the light to go away. I wanted to stop drowning. I wanted the peace of non-existence. The calm of not knowing who the fuck I was, or where or when I was. Everything hurt as I fought with everything I had to escape. To return. To get away from the light.

But it only got brighter. I whipped my head back and forth, but soon a pressure came against my cheek. My face was pressed against something solid, something warm, something beating. I struggled again, but the pressure remained the same. I felt like if I had any air left in my lungs, I would have screamed when I was carried against my will into an even brighter light. But all I could do was gasp and choke. Squeeze my eyes shut against the stabbing pain. Struggle with increasing weakness.

There was a horrible sound of contorted metal. I moaned like a frightened child. I'd never heard anything so loud in my life. I was placed against a fabric that seemed to tear at my skin. The light dimmed enough for me to peel an eye agonisingly open. The vague shape of a car. The blurry motion of arms, of bodies. A boulder was placed across my chest. I swore I wasn't ever going to be able to take another breath again. I heard a voice as nausea swept over me at the sudden motion beneath me.

"Breathe, Rian," it said, too loud, too loud. "Breathe."

But I couldn't. I couldn't.

With the last of my air, I whispered, "Let me go back. Please."

"Breathe, Rian. Just breathe."

Every time I woke up was worse than the time before. Because with each new awakening there was a little less ache in my bones, a little less fever in my mind, a little less acid on my skin. Because every time I jerked awake, lurching like I was falling off a cliff, I was a little more present, a little more lucid. And that was worse than the physical pain.

Knowing was worse. Being unable to escape the truth of what I'd done was worse. Facing myself was so much goddamn worse.

This time when I woke up, I heard voices in the hallway. Seeing Eithne's face there in the doorway was a sun brighter than any that could have shined the day Conor and Mason dragged me from that wretched place. If I'd been stronger I would have shielded my eyes. If I'd been braver I would have let a pained moan escaped from my still parched lips. As it was I simply closed my eyes: a man defeated. The tears that pricked at the corners of my eyelids stung as if made of acid.

I was aware of Eithne moving toward me only by the soft creak of the old wood floors beneath her gentle step. I never would have believed she would have gotten that close had it not been the light indentation as she sat beside me on the sweat-soaked mattress. When her fingers reached for mine, I squeezed my eyes shut more tightly. My heart fluttered erratically, my skin burned, the craving, the need washed over me like pounding waves.

"Eithne," I whispered, hating myself more and more with each word. "I…"

I…what?

Want you?

Need you?

Love you?

She squeezed my fingers. I fought back nausea that twisted my stomach like a dirty rag. I'd put the woman I loved through hell and there I was, thinking I could beg her to stay? I should have told her from the second I heard her voice to run, to leave, to get away from me. With what little strength I'd recovered, I should have pushed her away. I should have said terrible things to get her to turn her back on me, to never want to see me again. I could have done any of these things for *her* own good. But hadn't I? Hadn't I?

I was going to beg her to stay.

To say I hated myself, my weakness, my cowardice, my cruelty, was an understatement. The self-loathing made me gag.

Eithne brushed her fingertips across my cheek and my skin felt like brittle parchment; I wasn't sure how I hadn't shattered into dust. I wanted to moan in misery as I leaned into her soft touch. I was a terrible human, accepting love I did not deserve.

Eithne's voice was low when she spoke. Barely louder than

the pitter patter of rain that had just started on the drape-drawn windows. Her words seemed to take a long time to travel to me. Like they were fallen leaves, meandering to the earth on a late autumn day, a day not unlike the first I ever laid eyes on her. When her words brushed against my skin they were as light as a feather. It wasn't until they sank into the depths of my soul that I knew they were heavier, weightier. It wasn't until I could feel them pressing down against my chest that I knew they would drown me.

"I love you, Rian…but…"

I opened my eyes. *But.*

Eithne's beauty was haunting. Her skin had paled since I'd last seen her. The hollows of her cheeks more defined. Her hair was damp, as if she'd just taken a shower. As if that's what she'd been doing all this time I'd been gone, trying to get clean. I thought she looked cold, her lips a shade of winter berries, her lips trembling slightly. There was a clarity in her eyes despite the shimmer of tears on the surface, like she'd passed beyond a veil and could see more than I could see. She was already a ghost, there at the edge of my bed. Slipping away. Unreachable.

"I'm sorry," she said and as she shook her head, tears streamed down her cheeks.

For a moment, all I felt was numb. They say that, don't they? That when you drown there's pain at first. Panic and fear and pain. But then it passes, right at the end. They say there's even peace. I watched Eithne as if from the bottom of a lake. It was only when her lovely face shimmered that I realised I was crying, too.

"My whole life," Eithne continued, wiping already at her nose with the back of her hand, "I've lived for other people. I thought I had to. I thought there was something inside of me that I had to make up for, to cleanse myself of, to rid myself of like a poison. I always saw myself as less than, undeserving, and it wasn't that I wanted to feel that way. I wanted—I wanted nothing more than to feel the way you made me feel, Rian."

I squeezed her hand. Eithne choked on a sob and she clutched at her stomach like she was detoxing, too. Like she knew, as I did, the brutality of unmet need, a pain worse than hunger, worse than starvation.

Sucking in a trembling breath, Eithne spoke, her voice shuddering, "I thought if I could just earn love, work hard enough, sacrifice enough, one day I'd *be* enough. I tried so hard for my father and so, so fucking hard with Stewart and it was never, *never* enough. And…and…"

Eithne cried and she sounded like a wounded animal. Harsh and raw and real. She looked away toward the window, to the drapes heavy in the dim light. Though I didn't think she saw anything. It was like gasping for air after being under the water for too long; she didn't notice the shoreline, the trees, the sun. There was only relief. That's what looking away from me did for her, for my little Raglan Road girl: it gave her relief.

I squeezed her hand once more, this time because I needed strength. Strength for what I knew she was about to say. Strength for what I had to hear.

When Eithne looked back I thought I saw hesitation. A little flicker of doubt. Maybe she saw for one last time the good in me. Or the good that could be in me. Maybe she saw what I could do with another chance. Maybe she tried to convince herself just one last time that she could help me, fix me, love me just a little harder. Old habits die hard.

"Say it," I whispered.

Eithne's face crumbled and her tears stained my own cheeks as she leaned down to kiss me. Between the desperation of her lips against mine, she said, "I can't do *us* anymore."

It was a loss of everything, all at once. The heat of her lips gone. The presence of her fingers interwoven between mine gone. The weight of her beside me on the bed gone. A trap door opening beneath me. Me falling. All of me. All at once.

The echo of her footsteps, hurried away, then finally they too were gone.

RIAN

My bags were packed at the door. There was a finality to them being there that I'd been avoiding for a long time. It was right. It was good. Still, I avoided looking at them as I scratched at the back of my neck.

"Well, I guess that's it," I said, nudging my tattoo gun a bit to the left.

Ryleigh bumped me with her hip.

"You know explaining all of that was completely unnecessary," she said. "I'm kind of a pro."

She had a wink ready for me when I looked down at her. I smiled weakly and sighed, dragging my fingers through my hair.

"Actually," she added, tapping her chin in contemplation, "I'm kind of the best."

She held her hands out like she was sorry. Her palms were dotted with tiny doodle tattoos; she'd always been impatient. As long as I knew her. When she got the idea for a new design in her head, there was no waiting around for someone to practice on. She'd tattoo herself. And if she'd run out of practical places to add one, she'd use the impractical ones. It gave her palms a perpetual dirty look, like she was a naughty child always getting into the finger paints.

"*Actually*," Ryleigh said, eyeing me with those mischievously flashing green eyes of hers that had gotten her into a world of trouble throughout the years, "I'm kind of way better than you. Really, your clients are going to beg you not to come back. Are you ready for that?"

I rolled my eyes and shoved the little spitfire away, but in truth I appreciated Ryleigh's signature bravado. She was treating me no differently than she ever had. Even all the way back at art school she was a pain in my ass. It was a little taste of normalcy. And I was grateful for it. For her. She was one of my best friends despite her leaving suddenly from Ireland years ago and spending the last few years galivanting across Europe like a gypsy. She was one of my longest friends.

Mason and Conor emerged from the kitchen, thermos of coffee ready to go.

"Just wanted to say thanks," I said quickly to Ryleigh. "Coming here from Berlin and covering my chair, it—"

"Shut up," Ryleigh said before drawing me into a hug. It was fiercer and stronger than you'd give a woman of her size credit for. I squeezed her back even harder.

"Really it's you who's helping me out," she added so quickly and almost so softly that I couldn't hear her. But before I could ask her what she meant by that, she tugged me close again and whispered louder this time, "Get better."

"Shut up," it was my turn to say.

She stuck her tongue out at me when I pulled away. I hesitated, searching for any hint that something wasn't right with one of my best friends. She just gave me the finger. I returned the favour; everything was as it should be it seemed.

I sucked in a shuddering breath as I laid my hand one last time on my tattooing chair. By the time I exhaled, I was already out the door. Into the rain.

~

It was silent inside the car as we sat, engine idling outside the facility. Rain fell in windswept torrents against the windshield. The blades had stopped swiping the slashing streams of water away long ago. The headlights only penetrated a few feet ahead through the low rolling morning fog.

I sat in the passenger side seat, Conor in the back, Mason in the driver's seat. All three of us stared forward, not wanting to say goodbye yet.

We'd had a long, hard three weeks. A few days in, when it was clear enough that I wasn't going to die, Conor had stopped coming up to my room, the spare room upstairs at Dublin Ink. A few days after that, I'd heard him as he destroyed half the parlour downstairs: holes in the walls, chairs bent and broken, the neon light that said "ublin nk" shattered into a million pieces.

I'd listened as he screamed his lungs out at me, taken his rage like a pile of sandbags against a tsunami. I'd held him when he finally broke down and cried. He'd been scared. I'd scared him.

Mason, surprisingly, was the rock. The one with consistent meals and pamphlets for getting help and clean washcloths across my brow. But he was also as distant as a rock. He hid himself behind the business of getting me better. It was only just the night before that he finally said, pausing by my suitcases packed at the door, "Just...get better, yeah? If anything happens to you..."

It was as close as we'd get to saying *I love you.*

"That's it?" I asked. "You don't want to scream? Break things? Hit me?"

He smiled weakly. "I'm afraid if I do any of that I'll break myself."

Mason was barely holding himself together. Conor wasn't much better. Rachel and Aurnia were doing their best to help, but it was me. It was me who had to make things right.

"I, um, I—I tried calling her," Mason said, glancing at me out of the corner of his eye in the car.

I kept my gaze fixed forward. Even when Conor's big paw came to rest on my shoulder. I patted his hand.

"It's alright."

Mason cleared his throat. "I just thought, I don't know, that—that she'd want to be here."

I smiled at my friend, but there was no joy in it. "I hurt her," I said. "Maybe more than anyone. I need to prove to her I'm... worth it before I deserve any more of her time."

"Rian—" Mason started, but I was already opening the door. If he said anything after that it was swallowed by the pouring rain.

They helped bring my suitcases into the in-patient addiction facility. The fluorescent lights were harsh. The art on the walls of the lobby drab, smears of beige and brown in thin wooden frames. I'd given up so much colour, so much life. The attendants spoke to me in low tones. Everything seemed so damn sterile.

I hugged Mason. I hugged Conor. I couldn't yet bring myself to thank them. To utter the words out loud. I hoped they could feel it, though. In the way I wasn't quite ready to let go when I did. When I had to. I didn't look back at them, standing side by side, as I was guided down a carpeted hallway. Maybe it was embarrassment. Maybe I thought I'd call it off if I did. Because there it was, help, aid, love. Right there! Conor, Mason, Dublin Ink!

But I needed help that they couldn't give me. It was time to learn to help myself. So I didn't look back. The door swung closed without a sound. And then there was no going back.

I was shown my room. A simple single bed. A tiny desk without drawers, just a notebook and a pen atop it. A generic lamp. A window overlooking an oak tree in the garden. The rest would stay the same, day in and day out, but it gave me hope, that oak tree. It was bare now, the limbs. They rattled against the windowpane in the wind. There was winter yet to survive.

But spring would come. For the oak tree. For me, maybe. Buds of growth. The speckle of dancing sunlight through a sea of leaves. Blissful shade in unrelenting summer. And then, once more, colour. Green shoots like emeralds. I closed my eyes as I imagined their leaves drifting through my open window.

The words of "Raglan Road" came as if from far away as I began to tack up some drawings I'd brought along.

A knock at the door interrupted my soft singing. Brought me back to where I was.

A middle-aged man with an ill-fitting tweed blazer and wrinkles too soon at the corner of his gentle brown eyes introduced himself as my new therapist. He congratulated me on the bravery it took to make this decision. He somehow managed not to make such trite bullshite sound too much like trite bullshite. As we shook hands, he narrowed his eyes at me.

"You're still hesitant," he said.

I sank onto the bed. He gestured to ask if he could join me and I made a place for him.

"You obviously must have had a reason for coming here," the therapist said.

I stared at the drawings of Eithne. She called to me, stirred my blood. Made my throat tight and my brow sweat. I leaned forward, elbows on my knees.

"It's just—what if my reason is my drug?" I asked. "What if the thing keeping me alive is the thing killing me? What if I can't get better because the only thing I want to get better for is more of *her?*"

My therapist was quiet for a moment as he studied the drawings on the wall across from us.

"Love can feel that way," he finally said, speaking slowly as if he were picking every word carefully. "Love is tricky like that actually. We can call a lot of things love that aren't love. Mean things, selfish things, possessive things, we can all call love. Addictive things, we can mistakenly call love."

I glanced over at the therapist.

"You take drugs because you want them, is that correct?" he asked. "You want to use them? Drain the needle? Empty the pipe? Burn down the joint to nothing?"

It seemed obvious, but he seemed amused when I snorted derisively.

"Is that what you want this woman for?" he asked.

I looked up again at Eithne, there in charcoal and parchment. There as surely as she'd been in flesh and blood. Heart beating. Heart pounding.

"There's your reason for being here, *really* being here," my therapist said, tapping me on the knee as he stood. "Your reason is to become a version of yourself who is capable of truly loving her. You don't love drugs, you *need* them. I'm going to help you not *need* this woman but *love* her. To really *love* her, Rian."

I cried. The tears were unstoppable as the rain against the windowpanes. I cried because it fucking hurt. I cried because I knew the months ahead were going to be some of the hardest of my life. But I cried most of all because I knew now it would be worth it.

I had my reason.

From the very day I saw her, I'd had my reason.

EITHNE

My new apartment sat atop a burger joint that grilled late into the night for all the college kids craving something extra greasy after a night of carefree drinking. It was impossible to fully block out the flashing neon sign situated outside my bedroom window advertising an erotic toy store in the basement below. I had the top floor, a peaked roof attic with ceilings so low you couldn't stand up straight and ceilings so high there was no chance at swatting down a wafting Happy Birthday balloon from the last tenant. But my downstairs neighbours somehow managed to make enough noise to make up for the fact that no one was above me. Despite its bad location, its smell, its logistical quirks, as I unlocked the door that stuck in the late winter humidity, one thing could not be taken away from it: it was mine.

I kicked off my heels and stood for a moment in the entryway. The one-room space with its vaulted ceiling was filled with an orange glow from the early sunset. The light seemed to pour in through the slanted windows, dirty, but large.

It hurt a little, every time I came back home when there was still some light left. A part of me feared the coming of spring, the return of longer days, of stretched hours of light. As it was now, I could leave for class or studying before dawn. And with my new job at the advertising agency, I could work till my eyes stung and the sun was long gone from the horizon. I didn't have to face how perfect the light in this little attic room would be for painting. For real painting. For creating art. For opening my soul and bleeding it onto a simple canvas on a pinewood easel.

With a tired and somewhat sad sigh, I switched on the lamps, an odd array of whatever the last ten or so residents had found at local flea markets and erased the natural glow from the sunset. Erased those memories of the sky above Rian and me as the concrete of the roof burrowed into our skin and our love did the painting for us. Erased from my mind all the art I'd done with my professor, so wrong and yet so damn right. Erased from my future the promise he'd whispered like a serpent into my ear, *"You'll be a great artist. You're special."*

Most days it was easy enough to lose myself in the routine. School. Work. Laundry, cooking, tea at night with three of the same biscuits: the extra buttery ones with a thin layer of chocolate on top. None of it required all that much of me. With Rian out of my life there was no one to push me, to punish me. I earned solid grades. Received good praise from my boss. Kept my apartment tidy and functional.

As the kettle warmed up on the small ancient stove, I clicked through a few more emails from work. It was a job Conor had found for me, a connection through one of his tattoo clients. After everything that had happened, walking into The Jar just felt wrong. Too many faces I knew. Too many questions. Too much guilt. It was something I still struggled with, my decision to walk away from Rian. Everything inside of me told me I was wrong, every life experience, too. Every word my father, Stewart, my own conscience had told me told me I was wrong. I had to cling to it like a weak limb in a rushing river: the truth that I was right.

I hadn't expected anything from Rian's friends. When Conor called, I immediately thought it was to berate me. When I dodged his calls enough and he showed up on campus, I thought for a second about running from the bear of a man. But then he wrapped his arms around me. Held me with a tenderness I didn't think was capable of someone with such big muscles and told me in a gruff, slightly uncomfortable voice, "Everything will be alright."

I'd resisted the urge to break down right then and there in his arms; it didn't seem fair. To put that burden on someone. A stranger. But when he mentioned a job interview he could set up for me I barely made it through by biting my lower lip and pinching my skin through the pocket of my jeans. I planned to wait till I got home to sob like a little child, but I only made it as far as the bus. People moved away from me like I had the plague, but I'd never felt less alone, as strange as it sounds.

The whistle of the tea kettle drew my attention away from the seemingly endless stream of emails on my phone. I'd landed the job, a blessing, though a dull one: designing marketing graphics for a large packaging company. It was the kind of meaningless, rather creatively deficient work that Rian had railed against. But it was stable. My co-workers were kind, if distant. And it paid the bills, a reality Rian had never quite detailed an escape from as far as I could remember.

Mindlessly, I steeped my tea, dipping the bag in and out. It was almost hasty, almost rash, my decision to pull the application Aurnia had given me earlier that day from my purse. I felt naughty. I felt that, despite being alone, I was bound to be caught any second. I felt rebellious even, like the silly teenager I never had the luxury of becoming.

It was for a new exhibition. A call for new artists. A chance to have your work shown. Displayed. *Seen.* At the prestigious Hugh Lane Gallery in Dublin's Parnell Square, no less. I ran my thumb over the glossy pamphlet with a shiver as if it was porn. Tantalizing. Alluring. Wrong. The idea of submitting something, anything, called to me like a siren. The temptation to throw myself against the cliff face I'd walked away from once before nearly knocked me over. I could feel my heart start to race, a sensation close to arousal sending heat through my body.

I jumped when a knock on the door echoed through the airy space. Just as hastily as I'd pulled out the application, I shoved it back out of sight beneath a stack of bills. I took a second to reassure myself that it wasn't some manifestation of karma standing outside my door. It was Aurnia. Or Conor. Or Mason and Rachel even, come with fluffy pink boas and white cat-eye sunglasses to try to convince me once more to join them for karaoke.

I opened the door with that easy confidence, the kind that comes when you expect to see a welcomed face. I gasped when I saw Stewart, his skin bathed a strange green from the neon light flashing.

"Eithne!" my brother said cheerily, holding up a bottle of wine. "Little sis!"

Stewart mistook my stumbling back as an invitation inside. Though I think he would have insisted either way. He made himself at home on the low couch, really more of a pile of cushions at this point than anything with a discernible structure.

"You're—you're…Stewart, you're *okay*?"

Stewart laughed as if he hadn't disappeared without a word.

"I'm better than okay," he said, cosying in like this was *his* place, "I heard that you finally got Rian out of your life."

I turned and closed the door, just so I didn't have to face him. Everyone had been so careful not to say his name in front of me. To hear it thrown around the room so casually made my lungs seize.

"He threatened me, you know?" Stewart went on as I pressed my forehead against the cool wood, back turned to my brother in the lamplight. "Pretty much said he'd kill me if I came back, ever saw you again, yada, yada. Can you believe that?"

Speaking to the shadows between my feet, I said, "Stewart, I looked for you. I searched for you. I—I thought the worst."

"Thank that asshole boyfriend of yours."

I turned around, leaned against the door for support.

"You're my brother," I said, the shock of seeing him there, tapping his fingers against his knees in my apartment making me numb, "you could have tried to let me know you were alright. A letter. A phone call. Something."

"I couldn't," he said. "I'm sure you know how...*convincing* that maniac could be."

Stewart raised his shirt to show me a scar along his ribs.

"Did you even try?" I asked, my voice sounding distant in my cotton-stuffed ears.

Stewart hopped up from the couch with a childlike exuberance and shook me by the shoulders, wine bottle clanging against my elbow.

"Eithne, don't you get it?" he said, smiling widely. "This is a new start. A new start for both of us! You, a new job, me, a new lease on life!"

I stared at him warily.

"Look, look, let's just—where's your corkscrew?"

I remained fixed in place as Stewart bounded toward the little kitchenette just around the corner. I couldn't move as I heard him rooting around the handful of drawers, forks and knives, measuring cups and whisks clattering. I wasn't even sure I'd blinked once as he returned with the bottle opened and two wine glasses wedged between his fingers. He nudged me forward with his foot and I stumbled into the living space. I only accepted a glass because I really did need a fucking drink. Stewart looked hurt when I didn't raise my glass for a cheers, but instead downed the thing in one go.

Shaking off my rudeness, Stewart smiled again and said, raising his own glass, "That's the spirit!"

I took the bottle from Stewart as he rambled on about the

program he'd joined. How it was changing him. How he was a better man now, after being away. How he saw what was important in his life now. How he was ready to make amends, make things better, be the big brother he hadn't been for me for so long.

It wasn't a surprise when he said, "I'll need a little bit of money to get on my feet, of course. But no, I won't ask you. No, no, I'm done with that. I won't ask you, Eithne."

I snorted into my freshly poured glass of wine. "You won't, will ye now?"

Stewart didn't even have the decency to look sheepish as he said, "Well, I mean, if you're offering?"

I laughed, chugged the rest of my wine, and looked my brother straight in the face. "Did Rian offer you money?"

Stewart hesitated. "What?"

"When he threatened you? When he told you to skip town? When he warned you never to see me again? Never interfere with my life again? Was there a carrot to go along with the stick?"

"Eithne," Stewart tried. "I swear, if I thought I could safely—safely for you, of course—get in contact with you, I would have. Really."

My fingernails dug into my palms.

"I left the only home I'd ever known for you, Stewart," I said. "When our father demanded you leave, I stood up to him. I took the insults he hurled at me, the fury he took out on me. I took it and I've carried all that ever since. I gave up a life to stick with you, to be there for you. Because I loved you. And I thought you loved me, too. All these years I sacrificed friends and money and sleep and normalcy and *art,* the thing I love most in the world, Stewart. All for you! And you...you didn't even try to call? You didn't even call. Because you didn't need me. You had all that I could have given you, all that you stuck around me for: money."

"Little sis—"

"Don't call me that," I said, voice trembling. "I want you out."

I pointed toward the door. I stood when Stewart remained in place.

"Out!" I shouted.

Stewart's kind, brotherly demeanour shattered fairly quickly after that. He flipped me off. He called me a whore. He said good fucking riddance before tripping on a box left outside my front door.

"You're a piece of shite, Eithne," he shouted as he stormed down the stairs. "Always have been, always will be! Sucking for the highest bidder!"

I dragged the box inside and slammed the door. For a long time, I ignored it. I paced back and forth, angry but exhilarated. I'd set myself free. I'd finally seen my brother for who he was: a man who did not love me. *Could* not love me, no matter what I did or didn't do. I finished the bottle myself with my heart racing and a strange hope rising in my chest.

I would have left the box for the morning. There were early classes. There were dishes in the sink. There were duties, responsibilities, a good night's sleep calling. But I was too excited for sleep.

I opened the box. Didn't bother checking who it was from. I just tore at the cardboard, yanked out the contents, and fell back on my ass like I'd been struck with lightning as I stared at the pieces of paper that drifted to the floor around me like snow.

I laughed, covering my mouth with my hand like a nervous schoolgirl, because they were the drawings of my vagina, the ones Rian had done. I almost felt embarrassed, but then I stopped myself. There was no one to embarrassed for anymore. My father was dead. Stewart out of my life. I was living for myself now. I had no one but myself to decide who I would be.

The woman who had been brave enough to open herself up to such intimacy had no chains around her. No expectations. No rules or customs. No boundaries. The woman who lay there on the floor of that lecture hall with the hasty scratch of the pencil mixing with her quickened breath took pleasure for herself, had the *courage* to take pleasure for herself. The woman who trusted someone enough to do nothing but receive, not give, not sacrifice, not earn, but simply receive, was free.

I wanted to be that woman.

I'd made a lot of mistakes with Rian. But not letting myself become her, if only for a day or two. That was no mistake. And it never would be. It was only a mistake to let her go. To not cling to her once I'd found her.

I would find her once more.

With conviction in my heart, I pushed myself from the floor and darted into the little kitchenette. The bills scattered on the floor as I yanked free the art exhibition application. I had a lot of work to do and fast.

Morning light was coming. It was going to fill every inch of this place, every darkened corner. I would be ready for it, with nothing but my paint, a canvas…

And *me*.

EITHNE

Months later...

I watched the blossoms on the trees get tugged loose by the late spring breeze as name after name was called over the crackling microphone. Delicate little petals swept across the graduation stage decorated with green, orange and white balloons. Cheers rose and fell like the tides crashing over me, but I was less aware of the noise than swept away by its rhythm.

I was having a hard time deciding whether I was at the end or the beginning. I was finished with school, at last earning my degree. An ending, then. Or was it rather the start of my undecided career?

I clapped along with the rest of my class even though I hadn't heard whose name was called to walk up and receive their diploma from the dean. Did she see this all as a beginning or an end, the girl waving to her family and friends gathered in the chairs spread out across the dewy green grass? Was she sad today? Or happy?

Another name was called and I pre-emptively winced in anticipation for mine. There would not be anything more than a polite spattering: strangers clapping because it was simply expected of them. Aurnia had insisted on coming, but I told her not to bother. When she laughed and said I was being ridiculous, of course she was coming, I said, "No, really." When she shook her head and promised there was nothing that could keep her from being there to celebrate my achievement, I snapped.

"Aurnia!" I'd shouted. "Take a hint: I don't *want* you there!"

I'd apologised later over text. Gave some lame excuse about being stressed about a few of my last finals. Dismissed it all by saying I wasn't even sure I'd go myself; there was always the option to just pick my certificate up from the dean's office a few days after the ceremony.

The truth was something that even I wasn't sure I understood. I felt lost. I'd kept myself so isolated over my last semester, focusing solely on my art, that I wasn't even sure how to act around people anymore. I'd given all of myself, all of what I was sure was my true self, and it had all amounted to nothing. So how could graduation be an ending if I hadn't learned anything? How could it be a start if I wasn't ready? Ready for whatever was out there for me. Ready for whoever I was still clearly becoming.

The dreaded moment came at last. With the start of my name I was already regretting even showing up. As my last name called over the speakers. For a split second, I considered just sinking down into my chair and pretending I wasn't there. It wasn't like many of my classmates could point me out anyway; if they knew me at all, they knew me simply as the girl who'd fucked Professor Merrick.

But from the crowd came the loudest roar so far. I whipped around in confusion. I stood from my chair, in the end, merely to see who could possibly be back there, making absolute fools of themselves over me.

A sudden swift breeze drew a strand of hair across my eyes. I tugged it away. There, up on Conor's shoulders, was Aurnia. She held one end of a banner and Rachel, up on her chair, the other. The letters, "We love you, Eithne", were upside down, but that just made it all the more perfect. Mason was whistling, the crew from The Jar—Noah, Aubrey and Candace—stomping on the grass like they were at a football match. And there, at the very end of the row, waiting for my eyes to fall upon his, was Rian.

His gaze ensnared mine and I heard my name repeated as if I were underwater. It was a small mercy, a small mercy when Rian turned, smiling gently, to take a noisemaker from Rachel, breaking our gaze and releasing me from his hold. I hurried along the row with bright cheeks, glancing back occasionally to see if he was still there, to see if it was all still real.

I basically snatched my diploma out of the dean's hand. I'm not even sure whether I gave him my hand to shake. My heart was racing and all I could think about was *him*.

Time stood still or raced, I wasn't entirely sure. All I knew was that I blinked and the rest of the ceremony was over: graduation caps streaked across the sky instead of petals now. I gripped mine to my chest like a blanket.

The crowds thinned and then they found me where I'd been the whole time, there at my chair. I wondered if Aurnia could feel how I trembled as she embraced me. One after the other I thanked them all for coming, told them, honestly and earnestly, how much it meant to me. I'd found a family I'd not been looking for. Dublin Ink was my home, no matter what. No matter what was about to happen next.

Then I found myself face-to-face with Rian.

The excuses were flimsy for all the others leaving: need to feed the parking meter, find a bathroom, see a rather interesting flower just over there. Rian scratched at the back of his neck as we watched them all leave, giving us space. I gripped my cap tighter in front of me; it felt like it was the only thing I had to hold onto as the world started spinning for the first time in nearly half a year.

"I, um, thank you for coming, Professor Merrick," I said, returned somehow once more to a nervous first year student.

"I'm not your professor anymore," Rian said, his smile tight.

I nodded. Toed at the budding blades of grass at my feet.

"Aurnia says you've been painting," Rian said.

I really was going to have to kill that girl. I loved her, but she most certainly had to die.

"I don't know," I said, blushing with embarrassment. "I'm just —I guess I'm still trying to find…um…trying to find…"

"What you want to say?" Rian asked.

I looked up at him. His eyes were clearer. The purple bags beneath his eyes lighter. But there was a weariness about him that wasn't there before. I feared he might carry it for the rest of his life: knowing always that he was one step away from the edge, knowing how easy it was to fall. He smiled like he'd read my thoughts, like he knew, too, how long the road of life would be for him.

"Yeah," I said, nodding. "Something like that."

Rian studied me. "It's difficult," he said slowly, "trying to find what you want to say."

Petals fluttered on the wind between us. One caught in Rian's hair. It made him look younger. I wondered if there was a time when it was easier for him, a time before his addiction, a time when he was, in fact, younger. The sudden ache for him in my chest nearly stole my breath.

I spoke before there wasn't any air in my lungs, "Rian, please—"

"Just—just let me try."

"Try what?"

"Try to find what I want to say."

Our goodbyes before had been rushed. Outside the dean's office, at the edge of the cemetery, on the corner of his sweat-soaked bed. I could endure one more. I owed him at least that, a proper goodbye.

Still I hesitated. How many times had I let myself fall back into Stewart's manipulation just because of a few kindly spoken words? How long had the road been to finally finding worth in myself? How hard had it been just tearing my eyes away from Rian? Again the confusion swept over me, that unsettled feeling in my stomach: was this all a beginning? Or an end?

"Eithne," Rian said and my name on his tongue sounded like bodies beneath silk sheets in the night. It was a flutter, a gasp, a moan of the mattress. In my name from his mouth, I heard all of our time together condensed: pain and pleasure, misery and pure bliss. I longed for him. With just my name alone, I longed for him.

I'd been Rian's drug. But maybe he'd been mine, too.

"I've been unwell for a long time," he continued. "And that's hard to admit. It's hard enough to admit to myself about those last few weeks we spent together. It's even harder to admit how long it's been since I've been well, long before I ever met you."

Rian swallowed heavily and shifted from foot to foot. Sunlight caught half his face. He turned toward it instead of away from it, taking a moment to close his eyes and breathe in deeply the sweet aroma of the blooming trees. With a sigh, he turned back to me.

"It probably doesn't mean much. And I'm not by any stretch asking for your forgiveness," he said, "but I just want you to know that I always thought what I was giving you was love. That's what I did call it. My possessiveness, my obsession. My demanding more and more of you. My insistence, my pushing. My overwhelming need to have you experience pleasure. I—I loved you, Eithne. I was driven by this thing I called love."

I was going to give in to him. I knew I was. Rian was going to ask me to take him back and I was going to open my arms to him. I wasn't strong enough. Not yet. I hadn't had enough time. Panic filled my chest. It warred with what pooled in my stomach: longing. Missing. Aching for the thing I'd been stripped of and so terribly, terribly wanted back.

"I'm still not...better yet," Rian said, again glancing away. "But I've come to see, at least, that what I was calling 'love' was never love. Not for my friends. Not for myself. Not, most of all, for you. I don't mean for this to sound cruel, please believe me, I don't, and, really, it's maybe been the most painful part of all this healing so far, but Eithne, I never truly *loved* you. I never—"

Rian's voice broke. He looked down at his hands. I felt a strange sensation. Something like chains breaking. A snapping. A freeing. A flying. I watched the wind carry away the blossoms.

"But I want to," Rian said. "I want to love you. I want to ask nothing of you, demand nothing of you, take nothing from you. I just want to give. I want to—to be there with you. Beside you. Just be there. Just *be* with you. I..."

Again Rian's words trailed off. He laughed a little awkwardly and cleared his throat.

"Really this is just a long-winded way of asking if you want to, someday, get coffee together," he said at last.

I saw the apprehension in his eyes as he looked down at me. He squinted against the sun.

I blinked stupidly. "You want to—"

"Coffee," Rian said hastily. He nodded and then added, "Or tea."

I frowned slightly. This wasn't exactly what I was expecting. Stewart read through his lines perfectly, so why had Rian suddenly gone off script? In the silence of my confusion, Rian began again.

"I'm not saying we erase the past. I mean, fuck, I wish we could. God, I stay awake at night praying and crying and screaming to be able to just—but we can't. And we shouldn't. I hurt you. And that can't just—what I mean is, I don't want to pretend that we're strangers. That we've never met. That there isn't this mess of shite between us. That we don't need attending to just like my addiction does. I just...I just mean that we go get coffee and we drink it and we talk, or maybe we don't talk, maybe we don't talk at all at first. I just walk you home and I give you my jacket when it gets cold and—"

"A beginning and an end," I interrupted.

"What?"

I looked around me. At the empty stage. The deserted chairs. The balloons quivering in the wind. At the trees losing their delicate blossoms, gaining their hearty leaves. At the stone buildings of Dublin Art School.

At Rian.

"It's both," I said, smiling.

"Both?"

"If it were just a beginning, I wouldn't be who I am today. I wouldn't have discovered the strength you showed me, the strength to find my own worth, to take my own pleasure, to believe I'm *deserving* of that. If it were just a beginning, I wouldn't be so fucking confused about what I'm doing in life because I'd be headed for some corporate job."

I laughed and Rian smiled.

"And if it were just an end," I said, "we wouldn't have hope. We wouldn't have another chance. We wouldn't have...we wouldn't have coffee."

Rian bit at his lip. "What kind of life would that be? One without...coffee."

I grinned. "A shite one really."

He nodded.

I breathed in deeply. "And really if it's both, it's neither."

"Neither a beginning, nor an end?" Rian said.

I looked back at him. He had petals in his hair. I smiled.

"Just a moment," I said. "Just a moment in life."

"Like when I see a girl from across the street," Rian said.

"Like when I say 'coffee sounds nice'," I replied.

I extended my hand. Rian's hand was warm in mine. We held on for a moment and then we let go.

An end.

A beginning.

RIAN

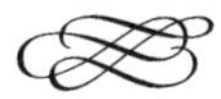

My hands shook as I did my tie.

One of the few moments of kindness I could remember of my father was his rough, callused hands looping the cheap black fabric of a child's tie through, wiggling the knot gently toward my throat, patting the length against my chest as he lowered his eyes.

The last time I wore a tie, it was for my mother's funeral. A memory so distant it felt like a dream.

Now it was for my first coffee date with Eithne, but I felt that same twisting in the stomach. Something had died. Something had passed on. Something would, in time, be forgotten.

I was, in a way, saying goodbye to the man I had been as I straightened the knot in the small bathroom mirror. My father was gone and it was my own gentleness I had to rely on. My own tender hands. My own palm pressed against my beating chest. I would be a better man than he was after the dead was laid into the soft earth. I would not turn to cruelty, to anger, to violence. I was happy to put to rest who I had been. I was happy to let the past fade in the sun of the future.

Still, my hands shook.

On my way out of the apartment I passed Ryleigh's room. She was a force of nature, but she was also a slob. It was a welcomed distraction to nudge back into her bedroom a Limerick Art School sweatshirt, a couple of charcoal pencils, and a notebook haphazardly opened to a drawing of a vaguely familiar man's profile. If I'd paused to look more closely, if I wasn't more consumed with my anxiety of meeting Eithne, I might have recognised the man. It might have softened the blow that was to come in a mere few fateful seconds.

Instead I closed Ryleigh's door and continued on. She'd been a godsend covering for me at Dublin Ink. Even still she worked most of my shifts as I recovered. I wasn't going to repay her by nosing into her business. Besides, I had my own to mind.

There was nothing left to do as I stood at the entryway. My jacket was thrown over my hand. Keys in hand. Wallet tucked into my back pocket. I brushed my fingertips one last time across my tie. Eithne would joke that I looked more like her professor than ever: knit tie, old tweed blazer with leather pads on the elbows, Oxfords. I'd never quite look like a professor with my dark ink peeking out over my collar and across the backs of my hands. But I wanted her to see that I was trying. That I would spend my whole life trying if necessary. Working endlessly to be a better man. For her.

A loud knock came at the door.

I frowned. Had Ry left her keys behind? I opened it, only to freeze in the doorway at my brother standing there.

"Rian," Liam said, "hey, I'm—"

"What the fuck do you want, Liam?" I said, hands gripping the doorframe, holding myself back from lunging at my older brother. I grasped for everything my therapist had taught me. I squeezed my eyes shut and tried to remember all the tools we'd practised for those gruelling months. Liam had visited every week for the whole time I'd been in rehab but I'd refused to see him. It was a shock to see him again. And it pissed me off that it wasn't on *my* terms.

"You look great. Well, I mean better than—"

"Fuck off. I don't need your platitudes."

My chest heaved as I sucked in air, trying to calm myself down. Failing miserably: nothing was ever going to change. My past hounded me at every turn. I could never escape. Not my home. Not my family. Not myself.

He moved towards me as if I'd just step aside and let him in. "I thought I could come in—"

The fucking nerve. I blocked his path. "No."

"Rian," Liam said, his usually calm voice now hurried, desperate, his eyes darting over my shoulder like he could focus on me. "I know things aren't great between us right now and that kills me and I hope it can change—"

"I don't have time for this. I'm going to be late. So kindly fuck off."

I slammed the door shut behind me and crossed my arms as we stood almost toe to toe.

He'd been glancing past my shoulder, through the door before I'd slammed it.

"What are you looking at?" I demanded.

His eyes snapped back to mine. "I'm, um, no one..."

I frowned. *No one?*

The image on Ryleigh's art book floated into my vision, overlaying across Liam's face.

Liam's fucking face.

My Liam. Was *her* Liam.

Rage, red and blinding, overtook me and I stepped right up into Liam's face. My finger was shaking for entirely different reasons now as I pointed it at my brother.

"You go near Ryleigh again and I'll kill you," I said, voice trembling. "Do you hear me? I'll fucking *kill* you. You will not ruin her life! Like you ruined *my* life."

Liam stumbled back. I shook like I was in the throes of a deadly fever. My fists balled so tightly my nails pierced my skin. I wanted to hurt him, to rail on him until he bled out. But Eithne's face in my mind stopped me. She was waiting for me. I wouldn't be late for her. I wouldn't let her down. I wouldn't trade an afternoon drinking coffee with her for an evening in a cell.

So I packed up my rage and satisfied myself with shouldering past the brother I hated so much.

I'm not sure if he called after me or not. The blood rushing in my ears was so all-encompassing that I couldn't even hear the blare of the car horn as I pulled my car out into the intersection. The short drive to the cafe where Eithne was waiting was torturous. I chewed at my lower lip, wiping sweat off my brow with my sleeve, driving erratically. It was a wonder I wasn't pulled over.

I needed to get to Eithne. I needed to drag her into my arms. I needed to throw whatever drink she'd ordered across the room and take her right there on the table. I needed the softness of her skin, the warmth between her legs. I needed her heavy pants in my ears. I needed to see in her face as she came that there was still pleasure in this world, still beauty, still hope. I needed Eithne. I needed, needed, needed my little Raglan Road girl.

I stumbled out of my parked car, tripping and nearly falling like a drunk. I'd scraped my palm and I didn't even care that I swiped it mindlessly across my tweed jacket. The throng of people at the intersection was the only thing that kept me from running across it straight into traffic, straight into her.

I saw her, saw her like I was always destined to see her, there across the road. She sat in a sunny window nook inside the cafe, a small, cosy place I picked because of its view of the park, of the trees, of the colours from the very first day I saw her...

The pedestrian signal turned green and I was jostled side to side as the crowd surged forward. People passed this way and that, but I remained where I was. The red man flashed once more and cars passed, Eithne moving in and out of view. I kept my eyes on her as I leaned against the street pole. It was one of my favourite things, to watch her without her knowing. And I needed a few minutes alone, a few minutes of just enjoying the sight of her *being* to let the last of my rage bleed out.

Leaves of ruby and amber and gold twisted and pirouetted on the breeze. They seemed to dance for her, there in the window, sipping sweetly from a sky-blue mug. I smiled as I remembered her from that first day. She had more colour in her cheeks now. Her hair didn't whip across her face, changing direction with every whim of the wind, but hung in a thick braid down her back. When she looked out the window, there was a peace, I thought, in the steadiness of her gaze as she watched the spinning leaves fall. A strength. No longer a little girl. But a woman.

I felt a great weight lift as I watched her. Like I was returning to a place I'd never realised till then was my true home, my one home.

I studied her hands as she brushed a wayward strand of hair from in front of her face. I imagined the art she'd create in her lifetime. I could practically see it ready to burst from her, beauty, wonderful, lovely things. I imagined her talent, raw and wild, something fierce and magnificent to behold. I saw her as a flower, ready to bloom, to unfold, to brush this cruel, sinister world with colour, with fragrance. I could not wait to see it, every last piece. Even if she never gave me another chance, even if coffee just stayed coffee, I'd be her greatest fan. Always. Forever.

With steady hands, I undid my tie. I tucked it into my back pocket. I folded the tweed jacket and set it beside me on the bench. Someone would find a use for it. I joined the crowd waiting for the crossing signal across the busy intersection.

This wasn't a funeral. I would not wear a jacket. I would not wear a tie. As much as I wanted to bury who I'd been, he was alive and well, as Liam's visit had shown me. A beginning and an end, Eithne had said. Both. This wasn't a funeral. This wasn't a birth. It was life. It was difficult, it was mean and unfair and brutal. But it was a little easier with love.

There would be no magic healing for me. Each day would be hard. But I loved a girl I'd spotted amongst falling leaves and there she was, waiting for me a year later behind a curtain of them. That would be my reason. That would be enough. She would be my beginning. She would be my end. She would be my life.

I entered the café, and Eithne smiled when she spotted me. The radiance of her filled my chest with warmth. I gave her a kiss on the cheek, then sat across from her.

"Are you okay?" she asked, frowning as she studied my face. I could never hide anything from her. And from now on, I never would.

"I am now," I told her, taking her hand across the table.

I squeezed it, she squeezed back. I liked that I couldn't tell where her fingers ended and mine began.

"Well, my little Raglan Road girl," I said, breathing deeply and letting go of Liam…for now, "tell me what you've been painting."

EPILOGUE

It had been weeks of fingertips brushing across warm wood tables. Weeks of hushed conversation over espresso machines and low murmurs and soft indie music. Weeks of blushed cheeks and averted gazes and thighs squeezing beneath the table. Weeks of an elbow offered, a walk home provided, a gentlemanly kiss on the cheek given.

I'd lingered for more under cotton-candy skies, under rain-pattered umbrellas, under fog that gathered in my hair like dew-strung spiderwebs. I'd fumbled with my keys, rooted around in my purse for them, dropped them by accident more times than I could count. I'd cleared my throat, paused in the doorway, glanced back as he walked with stooped shoulders and hands stuffed into his pockets down the sidewalk.

It had been weeks and I'd done everything I could think of to hint at wanting more and I'd gotten nothing. Absolutely nothing.

At first I told myself to be patient, Rachel and Aurnia told me to be patient. He was recovering. We'd agreed to take it slow. It was nice, after all, having my chair pulled out for me, doors held for me, a hand guiding me at the small of my back through coffee shop after coffee shop after coffee shop. But as the weather grew colder, I yearned for warmth. For his warmth. And as my patience thinned like the crisp air, a new fear crept in like the frost on my loft's attic windows: what if things would never be the same? Couldn't ever be the same? What if it wasn't him? But *me*?

What if, without the drugs, he no longer wanted me?

Cupping my hands over yet another chai latte in yet another quaint Dublin coffee shop, I wondered if maybe Rian had lost his fire for me. I could feel the heat of the flames behind me, crackling, sparking as the logs shifted, but his gaze remained steady, cool, embers burned so low reigniting them might be a fool's errand. When he walked me home this time, when he smiled at me outside my door, I interrupted him as he suggested, as always, that we meet again next week.

"I'd like to pick the place," I said, blurting the words out so fast that I couldn't possibly stop myself; even if it was for the best, which it probably was.

I saw a hint of a wry grin on Rian's lips. I kicked at my shoes before glancing back up at him.

"Is that alright?" I asked before shaking my head. "I mean, I don't care if that's alright with you, that's what we're doing. Fuck, that was rude."

I covered my face with my hands. Rian's fingers were ice cold when he gripped my wrists to gently pull them away, but they sent bolts of electricity through me all the same. His face was kind as he looked down at me in the lamplight.

"What I mean to say," I said, smiling weakly, feeling like a silly girl, "is that I know of a good place. That you might like. That I think you might like. If you…I mean, if you want…I mean—"

Rian pressed his lips to my cheek as always, but this time added in a whisper, "It's a date."

The week passed and there he was again at my door. Again he offered his elbow. Again I took it with hesitant fingertips. Again we walked in an all-too-comfortable silence that was beginning to frighten me.

"It's just up here," I said, nodding toward the end of the city block.

Dusk came early for Dublin those days. Streetlamps switched on one by one as we walked along as if to guide our way. The bustle from the coffee shop at the end of the street could be heard from where we were. The light from the condensation-covered windows spilled out onto the grey sidewalk like yellow paint. Rian's eyes were fixed on it.

I could still bail out, I thought, biting my lip nervously. I could pretend that was the destination all along. We could just go have another cup of good coffee with good conversation before a goodnight kiss on the cheek.

Rian let out a startled gasp as I suddenly dragged him up a set of three small stairs. This time there was no fumbling with the key. Rian asked what I was doing, but I ignored him and instead dragged him roughly inside behind me. I fell against the door to close it and breathed heavily in the dark.

"Eithne?" Rian asked.

I could just make out his form in front of me. He was searching for me in the dim light. He was reaching out for me. I could just see the tips of his fingers. My chest heaved. I couldn't do it. I couldn't do it. I couldn't do it. This was a mistake. This was all a big mistake. It was so warm in the coffee shop. So safe.

"Eithne?" Rian asked again.

I was just about to turn the door handle, to let us out, to run, but Rian's fingers brushed my chest. I was sure that an EMT couldn't shock my heart like he did. I inhaled sharply.

"Eithne," Rian said. It was not a question this time, for he'd found me. "Eithne."

Rian laid his hand across my chest in the dark and for a second I didn't breathe. My skin was wet clay and I didn't want to lose the shape of his long artistic fingers, his scared palm. With my eyes closed, I switched on the lights.

I kept my eyes closed as Rian froze. Kept them closed as his hand slowly fell away from my body. As I heard his footsteps echo up to the high ceilings in the spacious room, as silence fell back in, heavy as a final curtain. I kept my eyes closed till I could stand it no longer.

I winced against the light. Blocked my eyes like I was standing in high noon sun. Rian came into my vision, the outline of his shoulders were blurred like a mirage. I blinked and he grew clearer and clearer. He stood across the room. Turned away from me. Elbow held in one hand. Feet shoulder distance apart. Head tilted just slightly to the side.

I walked toward him, resisting the urge to tiptoe like a small child. I told myself to keep my chin held high as I came to stand next to him. As I reminded myself to breathe. As I took in what he was taken in by: a painting of a flower, a painting of a vagina. Not one, not the other. But both. A beginning and an end.

I couldn't get myself to glance up at Rian. I was afraid to read his reaction. To see the critique etched in the harsh lines of his face. To see disapproval in his downturned lips. Or worst of all, to see no reaction at all. Fire gone. Embers burned out. The nothingness of a dead hearth. A cold, empty house.

"I, um, I—my work was accepted," I said, voice sounding small in the big gallery space. "One day I just started painting and I couldn't stop."

There was only silence. That stretched. And stretched.

"I don't know why I didn't want to tell you earlier..." I said, letting the words again fade into this agonising nothingness.

Rian's voice was ragged, pained, when he said, "We need to get out of here."

I barely had time to process what he'd said before he turned on his heel. I wasn't even sure what was going on, but every echo of his retreating footsteps sounded like a gunshot, straight to the heart. I glanced between him and the painting, me at my most vulnerable, me at my most powerful, me. All me. I…of all the things he could have said or not said…this?

"Rian?" I called as I ran after him.

I'd just locked up the art gallery before Rian pulled up in his car along the sidewalk. I'd barely managed to shut the door before he floored it. I placed a hand on Rian's bouncing knee.

"Rian," I said, shaking my head as the city whipped by. "I'm sorry. I—I didn't mean to upset you. If that was too fast, I—"

"Please," Rian said, voice even more strained. "Just—don't. I —just…"

It wasn't till Rian pulled to a stop and dragged me out of the car that I realised this wasn't my place. The front door of Rian's apartment rattled on its hinges as he shoved it open and pulled me inside. He slammed the door shut behind us and pushed me up against the door.

He kissed me, his hands encompassed my face, palms hot against my cheeks. His hard body crushing me against the door. His lips seared mine, marked me as his as I gasped for air. When Rian pulled away there was an intensity in his gaze that I'd almost forgotten, that I'd missed.

"I've been treating you like glass, haven't I?" Rian asked, holding my face up toward his.

I nodded, chest heaving, breaths coming in little stutters.

"But you're not glass are you, Ms Brady?" he said in a low, dangerous whisper.

I shook my head.

"You're strong."

"Yes," I whispered.

"You won't break."

"No."

"Even if things get a little...rough," he said, searching my eyes. His burning, mine burning right back.

I gulped. "No."

His lips crashed into mine, his hips rolled against mine. My arms slipped around his neck, my fingers carded through his hair, squeezed, tore. Rian nipped at my throat and ran his hands along my hips. I whined a pitiful sound when his touch left mine. He fumbled with something at the small of my back and a second later the door swung open. We stumbled together into the darkened room; Rian's arms around me were the only thing that kept me from falling.

I tore at my jacket as I moved toward the bed. I kicked off my shoes and had my blouse halfway unbuttoned when I realised that Rian hadn't followed. I glanced over my shoulder to find him back by the door, a mirror to how I'd been at the art gallery. I felt his gaze on me, steady, searching. In the faint light from the streetlamps through the blinds, I could just make out the shape of him.

"I'm not glass," I said in a low, soft voice. When Rian did not respond, I turned around and walked back toward him, saying, "I'm strong."

I felt his eyes on me more than saw them.

"I won't break," I said, trying to keep my breathing even.

I slipped my fingers in between his.

"I know you, Rian Merrick," I said and then repeated almost breathlessly, "I *know* you."

Rian switch on the lamp. Soft golden light filled his bedroom. I turned toward the bed, but it wasn't the bed that I saw. Covering the walls were paintings. Lined across the floorboards were paintings. Drying on his small work desk were paintings. I was in all of them. I was in all of them, but I was not alone.

Standing with Rian, there at the open door, fingers intertwined, I let my eye travel from one to the next. They showed a future, a future together. There was one of Rian proposing, down on one knee in a whirlwind of leaves the colour of jewels. I saw in such vivid detail that I thought I could hear the lace rustling at our wedding. In Florence, Italy, at a tiny little cafe overlooking a quaint town square, our hands were locked together much like they were now. The colours were so rich I could feel the heat of the sun on my skin even as the bitter Dublin winter wind rattled the windows. I swore Mason and Conor, Aurnia and Rachel were there with us in the room as I gazed at a painting of a big family dinner at Dublin Ink. I couldn't help but tear up when I saw paintings of the two of us smiling over a small stick in a cramped bathroom, the two of us painting a room pink, the two of us holding our child for the first time. There were paintings of more children, more love, more life. As my eyes travelled round the room, Rian and I grew old together, fell more madly in love together, made a life together. There was happiness. There was joy. There was healing.

"I, um, I painted them in rehab," Rian said, sounding as hesitant and nervous as I had at the art gallery when I'd shown him my work. "Well, most of them. I continued after I left. It's…well, I'm still working on getting better, you know."

I nodded numbly.

"They tell you it's important to have a reason," Rian explained further as I ran through this acrylic life before me, over and over and over again. "And…and these paintings, well, they gave me strength. Through withdrawals. Through sleepless nights. Through those weakest moments where all I wanted to do is give up, sign out, find the nearest high and obliterate myself. Through all those times I returned to the canvas, to the paint, to *you*."

I felt Rian's knuckles against mine. The warmth of his skin between mine. I looked up at him.

"I know why you didn't show me these," I said. "I know why you wanted to go slow. I know. But Rian…"

His eyes were on mine, soft in the warm glow of the lamp beside us.

"I don't want to go slow anymore," I said. "I want all of this. I want all of *us*." He didn't move. Didn't speak.

So I lifted up the hem of my skirt and showed him I was serious.

"No panties," he choked out.

I grinned. "Fuck me like your dirty little whore, Professor."

BOOKS BY SIENNA BLAKE

DUBLIN INK

Dublin Ink

Dirty Ink

Dark Ink

TBA (Liam's Story) ~ *coming mid 2023*

IRISH KISS

Irish Kiss

Professor's Kiss

Fighter's Kiss

The Irish Lottery

My Brother's Girl

Player's Kiss

My Secret Irish Baby

IRISH BILLIONAIRES

The Bet

The Fiancé

The Promise

BILLIONAIRES DOWN UNDER

(with Sarah Willows)

To Have & To Hoax

The Paw-fect Mix-up

Riding His Longboard

Maid For You

I Do (Hate You)

Man Toy (Newsletter Exclusive)

ALL HER MEN

Three Irish Brothers

My Irish Kings

Royally Screwed

Cassidy Brothers

DARK ROMEO TRILOGY

Love Sprung From Hate (#1)

The Scent of Roses (#2)

Hanging in the Stars (#3)

BOUND DUET

Bound by Lies (#1)

Bound Forever (#2)

A GOOD WIFE

Beautiful Revenge

Mr. Blackwell's Bride

Paper Dolls

ABOUT SIENNA

Sienna Blake is a dirty girl, a wordspinner of smexy love stories, and an Amazon Top 20 & USA Today Bestselling Author.

She's an Australian living in Dublin, Ireland, where she enjoys reading, exploring this gorgeous country and adding to her personal harem of Irish hotties ;)

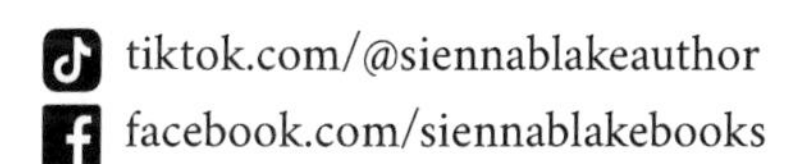

Made in the USA
Middletown, DE
05 April 2023

28284201R00203